Praise for The Steel Beneath the Silk

"*The Steel Beneath the Silk* is a power anthem tribute to history's women-behind-the-scenes. Intelligent, observant Queen Emma might have very little authority as the ignored wife of England's failing king, but she takes her role as peace-weaver seriously as Danish warlords threaten everything she has helped build. Without her hand on the tiller guiding the machinations of rebellious princes, ambitious concubines, and Viking suitors, it might have been a very different Britain--and a very different world. Patricia Bracewell's impeccable research and steely heroine make this a perfect read for fans of Bernard Cornwell's Last Kingdom series!"

Kate Quinn, author of The Rose Code, The Huntress, The Alice Network, The Empress of Rome Saga *and* The Borgia Chronicles

"A magnificent book! This masterful culmination of Patricia Bracewell's epic Emma of Normandy trilogy could rival any Norse saga immortalizing the drama-laden events at the time of the Viking invasions of Anglo-Saxon England. I loved it!"

Anne Easter Smith, author of A Rose for the Crown *and* This Son of York

"*The Steel Beneath the Silk* is a triumph. As her husband King Æthelred and his sons confront the invading Danes on the battlefield, we watch Queen Emma wield power behind the scenes, forging alliances with cunning and diplomacy. Romantic, thrilling, richly embroidered with historical detail, this epic saga will satisfy fans of *The Last Kingdom, Vikings,* and *Outlander.* Highly recommended!

Candace Robb, bestselling author of the Owen Archer mysteries

"The hard-hitting history of the Anglo-Saxon Chronicle comes to life in this sweeping, cinematic saga of Emma of Normandy. In a violent, turbulent world full of treachery and the threat of Viking invasion, one strong woman rises to seize her power with a warrior's valor and a peace-weaver's foresight. In Patricia Bracewell's stunning new novel, Queen Emma makes an unforgettable impression."

Mary Sharratt, author of Revelations *and* Illuminations

"Plotting, deceit and familial divisions keep the reader guessing what fate has in store for eleventh century Queen Emma and her sons. *The Steel Beneath the Silk* is a gripping and fabulous, vividly written story. The detailed scents, sounds and visual period detail pull the reader right into an English eleventh century court threatened with intrigue. This excellently recreated world provides an authentic background to a thrilling story. What a wonderful and dangerous life Queen Emma lived. England, 1013--Strife, Danish conquest, a handsome, clever Viking prince, betrayal; what a thrilling tale this is, one inhabited by vivid, unforgettable characters."

Carol McGrath, author of The Handfasted Wife

"A queen's courage in the face of war, lost love, and betrayal takes center stage in this novel about Emma of Normandy, a woman whose critical role in English history is not as well known as it should be. I felt like I was plunged into the 11th century, thanks to the action-fueled pacing and sharply conveyed atmosphere. Anyone who enjoys Vikings and The Last Kingdom and is eager to read about the lives of women in such a tumultuous era should seize this book and prepare for an unforgettable saga."

Nancy Bilyeau, author of The Blue *and the Joanna Stafford trilogy*

The
Steel
Beneath
The Silk

Books 1 and 11 of the Emma of Normandy Trilogy

Shadow on the Crown

The Price of Blood

The Steel Beneath the Silk

Patricia Bracewell

Bellastoria Press

ISBN: 978-1942209812
THE STEEL BENEATH THE SILK

Cover design by Jenny Quinlan, Historical Fiction Book Covers

Cover photograph by Jeremy Guy

Maps designed by Matt Brown

Bellastoria Press
P.O. Box 60341
Longmeadow, MA 01116

For Joan, Joanne, and Mary

Dramatis Personae

ANGLO-SAXON ENGLAND, 1012-1016

Royal Family

Æthelred II, King of England

Emma, Queen of England

Children of the English King, in birth order
By his first wife

Athelstan

Edmund

Edrid

Edwig

Edyth, wife of Eadric

Ælfgifu (Ælfa), wife of Uhtred

Wulfhilde (Wulfa), wife of Ulfkytel

Mathilda

By Queen Emma

Edward

Godiva (Goda)

Alfred

The English

Ælfhun, Bishop of London

Ælfric, Ealdorman of Hampshire

Ælfsige, Bishop of Winchester

Ælfsy, Abbot of Peterborough

Æthelmaer, Ealdorman of the Western Shires

Aldyth, Siferth's wife

*Alric, Cnut's English hearth man

Eadnoth, Bishop of Crediton

Eadric, Ealdorman of Mercia, husband of Edyth,
the king's daughter

Elgiva, Cnut's English concubine

*Father Martin, the queen's priest

Godwin Wulfnothson, companion of Athelstan

Godwine, Bishop of Rochester

*Hubert, the king's steward

Lyfing, Archbishop of Canterbury

Morcar of the Five Boroughs

Robert, son of Wymarc and companion of Edward Ætheling

Siferth of the Five Boroughs

Thurbrand of Holderness

Uhtred, Ealdorman of Northumbria, husband of Ælfgifu,
the king's daughter

Ulfkytel of East Anglia, husband of Wulfhilde, the king's daughter

Wulfstan, Archbishop of Jorvik

Wymarc, the queen's companion, mother of Robert

NORMANDY

Duke Richard II, Emma's brother

Duchess Judith, Richard's wife

Dowager Duchess Gunnora, Emma's mother

Robert, Archbishop of Rouen, Emma's brother

DENMARK

Royal Family

Swein Forkbeard, King of Denmark

Gytha, Swein's daughter, wife of Eirik

Harald, Swein's son

Cnut, Swein's son

Estrith, Swein's daughter

Gunnhild, mother of Harald, Cnut and Estrith

*Arnor, a shipmaster

Eirik, a Norse warlord, husband of Gytha

*Halfdan, a shipmaster

Olaf, a Norse warlord

*Sihtric, Elgiva's hearth man

Thorkell, a Danish warlord

*Tyra, Elgiva's Sami slave woman

Ulf, a Danish warlord

Glossary

Ægir: in Norse mythology, the god of the ocean

Ætheling: prince; literally, *throne-worthy*. Legitimate sons of the Anglo-Saxon kings were referred to as æthelings

Blot: blood sacrifice

Breecs: Anglo-Saxon term for trousers

Burh: an Anglo-Saxon fort or walled town

Ceap: a trading or market area

Drekar: dragon ship, viking warship

Five Boroughs: a region in Mercia made up of Leicester, Nottingham, Derby, Stamford, and Lincoln; it exercised significant political influence in late Anglo-Saxon England

Fyrd: an armed force that was raised at the command of the king or an ealdorman, usually in response to a viking threat

Geld: tribute paid to a foreign invader to encourage him to depart

Haga: a fenced enclosure; a dwelling in town

Here: an enemy army; a large band of marauders

Holderness: a wedge-shaped territory lying north of the Humber along the southeast coast of Northumbria

Hundreds: local administrative units, and a measure of land, as well as the area served by a hundred-court

Hunns: from the game of tafl, the name for attackers and defenders, i.e. game pieces other than the king.

Huscarles: retainers; house guards

Hythe: Old English term for a wharf or a pier; landing place.

Jomsvikings: a legendary force of highly disciplined warriors, based in the Baltic, associated with Thorkell the Tall

Knarr: large cargo ship, relying almost solely on its rectangular sail for propulsion

Lammas: the first of August; a harvest festival

Lindsey: the district of eastern England between the River Witham and the Humber

Michaelmas: the feast of St. Michael the Archangel, September 29

Morgengifu: literally *morning gift*; the gift given by the husband to the wife on the morning after the consummation of the marriage

Nithing: a pejorative term in Norse and Old English meaning "abject wretch"

Norns: female spirits in Norse mythology associated with fate

Quarter Day: one of the four days marking the quarters of the year, when food rents were due

Sami: a culture indigenous to Norway, believed to have prophetic skills

Scop: storyteller; harper

Seax: A type of knife or dagger

Skald: poet or storyteller

Tafl: a popular board game in early medieval England and Scandinavia with some similarities to modern-day chess

Thegn: literally *one who serves another*; a title that marks a personal relationship—the leading thegns served the king himself; a member of the highest rank in Anglo-Saxon society; a landholder with specified obligations to his lord

Waylisc: Welsh

Wergild: literally *man payment*; the value set on a person's life

Witan: wise men; the king's council

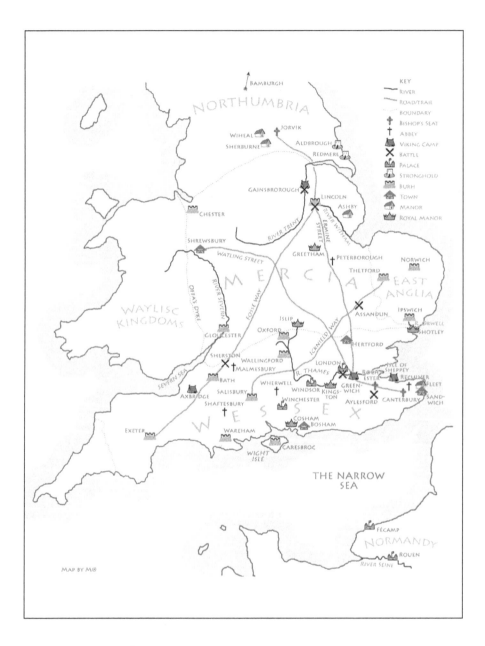

11ᵗʰ Century England

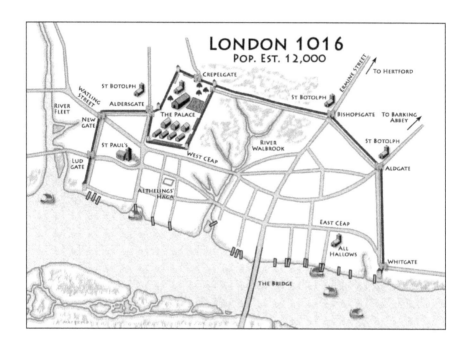

London

Anglo-Saxon England
A.D. 1001 – A.D. 1012

A.D. 1001 This year there was great commotion in England in consequence of an invasion by the Danes, who spread terror and devastation wheresoever they went...**1003** This year was Exeter demolished...**1004** Swein came with his fleet to Norwich, plundering and burning...**1006** Then came the Danish fleet to Sandwich, and they burned and slew as they went...**1009** Thorkell's army came, and everywhere in Sussex, in Hampshire, in Berkshire they plundered and burned...**1011** They beset Canterbury, and seized Archbishop Ælfheah...

A.D. 1012 Then took they the Archbishop Ælfheah, and on the eve of the Sunday after Easter they overwhelmed him with bones and horns of oxen; and one of them smote him with an axe-iron on the head, and his holy blood fell on the earth. The corpse in the morning was carried to London.

The Anglo-Saxon Chronicle

Prologue

*I*t was well past dawn when the corpse arrived in the city. It was carried aboard a viking longship that should have been riding the Thames to the sea. Like the rest of the Danish fleet, its hold was bursting with treasure extorted from the English in return for its swift departure from their kingdom. But while more than a hundred of the dragon ships were already sailing into the sunrise, forty-five of them remained moored at Greenwich, their sails furled. The largest of them, Thorkell's ship, its oars manned by sixty war Danes, had turned its prow west, toward the great walled city; and it was Thorkell himself who watched over the grisly cargo lying on its deck.

The lookout on London's bridge spotted the ship approaching and, nerves on edge, shouted a warning. By the time the drekar's oars were shipped and the vessel bumped to a halt against the hythe, it was greeted by a line of mail-clad English warriors whose threatening swords flashed in the morning light. Curses and questions flew between ship and shore, but eventually a messenger was sent to the palace with a request for parley.

Within the hour a large company from the royal garrison arrived at Thames side to escort the warlord and five of his men, stripped of their weapons, to All Hallows Church, hard by the harbor, where the parley was to take place. The Danes carried the corpse with them on a pallet, shielded from curious eyes by a gold-embroidered cloth.

News of the parley had already spread from the riverside like embers on the wind, and Londoners had crowded into the square in front of the church voicing outrage that enemies had been allowed inside the city walls.

"Why are the bastards coming here? They should be haring back to whatever hell spawned them!"

"*Jesu!* Did not the king give them silver enough to leave us in peace? Must he give them yet more?"

"Nay, it will not be the king who treats with this lot. He is cowering at Windsor until this Danish scum is gone. Likely it will be the high and mighty Lord Eadric who will do the bargaining. And who better to deal with murdering, thieving Danish bastards, I ask you, than a murdering, thieving English one?"

Lord Eadric, ealdorman of Mercia, was a familiar figure to the Londoners for he rarely left King Æthelred's side. Ambitious, smooth-tongued and shrewd, his ruthlessness in serving the king, including murder when it was called for, had earned him the highest royal trust. It had brought him lands, titles, and the hand of Æthelred's eldest daughter in marriage, so that from relatively humble beginnings Eadric had risen to become the wealthiest and most powerful magnate in the kingdom. Indeed, it was a commonly held belief that although King Æthelred ruled England, Lord Eadric ruled the king.

Now, as the crowd milling outside the church watched the Danes enter the square with their burden in their midst, the shouts of protest faded, for the shape of a body was plainly visible beneath that glittering shroud. Men and women crossed themselves when their enemies lumbered past to disappear into the church, leaving behind a buzz of nervous speculation about whose corpse lay on that pallet and what devilry the Danes might be plotting.

Some of the citizens, fearing bloodshed, slipped away to barricade themselves inside their homes. Most, though, were more curious than afraid. Reassured by the heavily armed men from the garrison who stood guard around the church, they waited to see what would happen next. They were soon rewarded by the appearance of a royal company led, as expected, by Ealdorman Eadric. And riding on a white mare at his side was King Æthelred's Norman queen, Emma.

She had arrived in England ten years before to wed the much older, widowed king, and she had been welcomed with celebrations in London and beyond. The king had believed that their union would persuade her brother the duke to cease his hostile practice of allowing viking fleets to launch vicious raids against England from Norman harbors. Yet despite the queen's crown and the bountiful dower that Æthelred had grudgingly bestowed upon his young bride, it soon became apparent that Duke Richard feared the wrath of the Northmen far more than he did that of his new brother-in-law. Norman harbors continued to welcome viking ships; Norman markets kept up their trade in ill-gotten English goods, and as wave after wave of viking raiders descended on his kingdom, the English king bitterly regretted his Norman marriage.

Convinced that he had been ill-used, Æthelred—a suspicious, vengeful man—vented his displeasure on his new bride. The queen found little joy in her marriage, forced as she was by church law and by the king's sheer physical strength to submit to her husband's casual brutalities. Nevertheless, despite his cruelty and his unceasing efforts to minimize her role as queen, Emma had fulfilled her primary duty and had given Æthelred two sons and a daughter. At the same time she had forged alliances with bishops, abbots, and certain members of the king's council to create her own sphere of royal influence at court—adding fuel to the king's already burning resentment.

What was even worse in Æthelred's eyes—the English loved her.

Now, as she neared her twenty-fifth summer, the bloom of Emma's youth had ripened into stately beauty. She had a high forehead, a long, slender nose, and a generous mouth. On this day her pale hair was braided and bound beneath a white linen headrail that was held in place by a thin fillet of gold. Beneath the dark cloak that fell from her shoulders she wore a gown as green as summer grass, its hem and long, draping sleeves lavishly embroidered in scarlet and blue.

But as the queen gazed at the restive Londoners gathered in the square, she was unsettled by their muted watchfulness. Something had disturbed them, something more daunting than the sight of a handful of unarmed Danes in their midst. A shiver of apprehension grazed the back of her neck and she fixed wary green eyes upon the church where she was to meet with England's enemies. She had, much against her will, brought her most precious possession to this parley, and she had a very great deal to lose if there should be some Danish treachery at play here. Honeyed words could mask a dark purpose, and she knew how cunning the Northmen could be—for she was herself descended from viking warlords.

Few in England were aware of her northern lineage—of her family's blood ties to England's foes. Fewer still knew that she could speak the Danish tongue, for she had chosen to reveal it only to those whom she could trust completely. That intimate circle did not include either the king or the whip-thin, richly robed ealdorman who rode at her side and who now tried once again to dissuade her from taking part in the coming parley.

"It is unwise, my lady, for you to meet with this Thorkell," Ealdorman Eadric said, continuing the argument he had begun with her in the palace yard. "He is a liar who knows just enough English to make his lies appear truth. I urge you again to remain outside the church and let me deal with him. The man is dangerous."

The queen gave Eadric a hard look. He was a comely man, dark of hair and beard, with a pleasing face that could inspire trust in anyone who did not know him well. But she knew him; knew that he was subtle and avaricious; knew that her presence in that church was the only thing that would keep him from acting in his interests alone.

She gave him a chilly smile. "All men are dangerous, my lord," she said. "And however dangerous this Thorkell might be, he has asked to parley with England's queen, not its Mercian ealdorman."

They were nearing the church, and Eadric, his expression now surly, gave the queen a curt nod. Dismounting, he barked questions to the guards stationed at the church door and was assured that the Danes were inside and that they had no weapons.

No one, however, told him about the corpse.

Emma, meanwhile, glanced meaningfully at the woman who was today her only attendant. They had been close companions ever since their girlhood in Normandy, and Wymarc understood immediately the queen's unspoken command. She strode toward a brace of Eadric's men who were helping a lad of about seven from his horse. The boy, as dear to Wymarc as her own young son, was dressed in breecs and a brown tunic belted with silver, over which he wore a green mantle that hung to his heels. With a reassuring smile, she guided him toward where his mother, the queen, was following in Eadric's wake.

The boy, Edward, had his mother's blond hair and his father's pale blue eyes, attributes from parents that he saw only rarely, for he was seldom at court. At the age of four, over his mother's objections, the king had ordered him placed in Eadric's care, to be fostered in Mercia.

Of his life before that Edward could recall little. Even his memories of his mother from that earlier time were hazy—more dreamlike than real, and she was little more to him than a regal stranger.

His royal brothers were strangers to him, as well. The youngest, Alfred, was newly born and so young that, certainly in Edward's mind, he hardly counted. His four living half-brothers, the grown sons of the king by his first wife, meant little to him as they swept in and out of his circumscribed world. Like him they were æthelings, heirs to their father's throne. But as their mother had never been consecrated Æthelred's queen, they were less throne-worthy than Edward, or so he had been assured by Ealdorman Eadric. It was Eadric who, despite the existence of those four elder half-brothers, was grooming his royal charge to one day claim the English throne; for Edward was young enough to be molded to Eadric's ambitious purposes while his bothers were not. And it was Eadric who had insisted that the boy be witness to this parley.

As Edward approached the wide door of the little church, he saw Eadric surrender his sword to a guard before stepping inside, and he felt a tremor of misgiving. The darkness that he could see hovering within that gaping doorway seemed to him alive with menace, and he thought it foolhardy to venture unarmed into a meeting with untrustworthy Danes. He did not know why the vikings had come or what they wanted, but he knew that they were evil and bloodthirsty—men to be feared. And because he was very much afraid, he stealthily shifted his cloak to conceal the seax he carried at his belt. It was a breach of parley, he knew, and he masked both his offense and his terror with feigned boldness as he walked briskly past the guards. Once inside, he gripped the hilt of his hidden knife like a talisman as he heard the church door slam shut.

The Danes were waiting near the altar, clustered together in a shaft of light that speared down from a high window. They were big men, rough looking and grim, with hard, weathered faces—fearless warriors who reveled in the thrill of battle. Now, though, stripped of their weapons, they shifted uneasily as the royal party approached. One of them, noticing the bright-haired boy who appeared to be clutching something hidden in the folds of his cloak, watched the lad with narrowed eyes.

Although they had no weapons, the shipmen were dressed in leather and mail, all except their leader, Thorkell. He was a Danish jarl, and he had come to London to parley with a queen. He wore a tunic of fine red wool belted with a colorfully embroidered silken sash. His dark blue cloak was trimmed with fur, and from a chain around his neck hung a slender silver cross. He was a big man who towered over his companions, and he stood with his arms folded across his wide chest, chin jutting forward and jaw clenched. His head was shaved bare except for a long, black tail of hair that hung down his back, and above his thick beard a livid scar seamed his cheek.

Thorkell had seen nearly fifty summers, and had spent a good many of them leading armies that burned and pillaged their way across England. His sword and his savagery had brought him wealth and fame, so that his very name struck fear into English hearts. But his success and reputation, like that of any viking warlord, depended on his skill at asserting authority over violent men who were often drunk on bloodshed; and in his camp the night before, Thorkell had failed at that one thing. A hostage that Thorkell had befriended and had endeavored to protect—an archbishop of England and a trusted counselor to this queen—had been viciously slain; and Thorkell had been helpless to prevent it. So as he watched the queen approach the altar and bend low over the body that lay before it, his every sinew was taut with tension.

Emma lifted the golden shroud, and when she saw the grisly visage beneath she pressed her hand to her mouth to stifle a cry. One side of the dead man's face was little more than a vast, open wound studded with bits of shattered bone; there was not even the suggestion of an eye. The other side of the face was purple with bruises, and the cheek was badly sunken; but there was no mistaking who this was or that he had suffered a cruel death.

Eadric took one look at the corpse and shouted to the guards at the door to allow no one inside, while the queen straightened and strode swiftly to Thorkell.

"I have honored your request for parley," she said in a voice icy with contempt and outrage, "but I did not think to meet with treachery such as this."

Thorkell raised his hands palms outward as if to fend off the accusation. His response in tortured English was defiant.

"My lady, this was not my work! I swear! I tried to save him!"

"Save him?" she cried. "Do you deny that it was your men who killed him?"

"Nay, not mine! They were Norse! Pagans! Mad with drink! I offered silver for his life!" It was an anguished cry, and his scarred face creased with outrage. "But they wanted *blot*," he spat the Danish word as if it fouled his mouth, "a sacrifice to Ægir. I could not stop their..."

"Where are they now," Emma's voice scythed across his, "these heathen Norsemen?"

"At sea," he said bitterly. "Gone at daybreak."

"Yet you are here," Eadric observed, and there was eager speculation in the narrow gaze he focused on the big Dane. "What is it that you want?"

Thorkell paid him no heed. His business was with this queen.

"I gave Ælfheah my oath to seek you out," he said gruffly, "to offer my service to you and to your king."

The queen stared at him in disbelief.

"Why?" she asked. "Why would the archbishop ask for such a pledge? Why send you to *me?*"

Thorkell's eyes held hers, steady and unblinking, and they were dark with warning. "He feared for you; for your bairns. Feared what Swein Forkbeard has sworn to do."

Eadric hissed, "My lady, this is a trick. Do not listen to him! Thorkell is Swein's ally!"

"No!" Thorkell glowered at Eadric, then looked again to the queen. "No more! There is bad blood between us now. Ælfheah knew this and pleaded with me to aid you!"

He made a sudden move toward the queen, and Eadric reached reflexively for a sword that was not at his side. But Thorkell grasped Emma's hand and wrapped it with his own around his silver cross.

"I swear to you, my lady," his voice was hushed and solemn, "that I speak truth."

Bending close to her, he whispered something for her ears alone, and as she listened to him, she stiffened. She was gazing up at him in shock when, with a mighty crash, the church door banged open.

At the sound young Edward spun around, terrified, and pulled his knife from beneath his cloak. Eadric bellowed toward the back of the church that no one must enter. The queen, too, dragging her gaze reluctantly from Thorkell, turned to face the now open church door as armed men poured into the nave.

The king's eldest son, Athelstan, led them. He was a young man, and he was everything that his father was not: bold instead of craven, tolerant instead of vicious, forgiving instead of vengeful. He was not without sin, though, and the one sin that he had never confessed and that still blackened his soul was his desire for his father's queen. His passion did not go unrequited, but it remained a banked, forbidden fire between them, far too dangerous to be allowed to flame.

Now, his cloak dirt-spattered and his fair hair damp with sweat, Athelstan paused to look at the abomination that lay on the altar step, and seeing who it was his face contorted with rage. Striding to where Thorkell stood clutching the queen's hand, Athelstan swept Emma aside, drew his sword and pressed it to the big Dane's chest. Behind him his retainers, too, unsheathed their blades, and instantly the six unarmed Danes were facing a dozen men bristling with weapons.

Emma gave a cry and reached for Athelstan's sword arm at the same time that the Dane whose eyes had never strayed from Edward grabbed the boy, twisted the seax cruelly from his hand and held it against his throat. Edward, numb with terror, bewildered, looked to Eadric, who stared helplessly back at him, frozen with indecision.

"Stop this!" Emma cried. "Athelstan! Put away your sword!"

But Athelstan, at twenty-seven summers old, was a warrior hardened in battle, and this was not the first time that he had faced Danish treachery. He knew them to be tricksters and liars, and that the only way to beat a liar was to tell a bigger lie. Eying Thorkell coldly, he jerked his head toward the helpless Edward and gave a careless shrug.

"Kill the boy or not. It makes no matter to me so long as you and your men die with him."

Edward's eyes widened with terror as the blade at his throat trembled.

"This is madness!" Eadric roared. "These men came here unarmed!"

"These men are murderers and liars!" Athelstan roared back at him. "Are you blind? Can you not see what they did to the archbishop? Whatever they have told you, you cannot believe them! There are more than forty dragon ships still anchored at Greenwich! I have seen them! That means almost three thousand men to bring against us! This is the same kind of treachery they used when they captured Exeter and again when they took Canterbury. Now they want London, and I will not let them have it, whatever the cost!"

While he spoke the queen's eyes flicked to the man holding the seax at her son's throat, and she saw the blade quiver against Edward's all too vulnerable neck. Desperate, driven by fear for her son, she grasped the naked blade of Athelstan's sword, clenching her teeth as pain seared through her hand.

Athelstan's shocked eyes snapped to hers and he swore at her, but she pushed the blade relentlessly down and he dared not resist for blood was already oozing between her fingers. Still gripping the sword she placed herself between the furious Athelstan and the unarmed Thorkell.

"These men are under my protection!" she shouted, her voice echoing through the nave. "Anyone who wishes to do them harm must kill me first!" Fixing her cold gaze on Athelstan, she repeated her cry, this time in her mother's tongue, and the Danish words that fell from the mouth of Æthelred's queen drew astonished looks from English and Danes alike.

For several heartbeats there was not a sound in the little church until Athelstan's voice echoed through the silence.

"*Jesu!* Emma!" he cried. "What lies has he told you, that you would defend him with your life?"

Before she could answer him Thorkell barked a command, and the Dane who held Edward threw the seax to the floor and thrust the boy aside.

Athelstan, though, continued to stare, disbelieving, at the queen. "This man is a monster!" he shouted at her. "You cannot trust him!"

"You have not witnessed all that Thorkell has said here, my lord!" Emma rebuked him, her voice sharp as steel. "And it must be the king, not you, who will determine if he has spoken the truth! Now, put away your sword!" She looked past him to his men. "All of you! Put your swords down!"

For a long moment the very air between the queen and the ætheling crackled with tension, broken at last by a clamor at the back of the church. Moments later the bishop of London was forcing his way to Emma's side and, shouting reproaches at Athelstan, he gently removed the queen's bleeding hand from the threatening blade.

Athelstan, though, kept his eyes fixed on Emma as she stonily repeated her command and, finally accepting that he could not sway her from what he knew was the greatest folly, he sheathed his weapon and signaled to his men to do the same.

"You will regret this, my queen," he said darkly. "The Danes have spilled blood all across England, and they will do so again. Mark me! They will give us all reason to regret what you have done here today." He cast a final, black glance at Thorkell then snarled at his men, "Stay here, and keep a close watch on these Danish bastards!"

Emma watched him stalk away from her and out of the church. Shaken by his hostile words, furious at his recklessness, and still trembling from what could have been a deadly confrontation, she made no attempt to stop him.

The bishop moved swiftly to inspect the body that lay before the altar and to pelt furious questions at the men that Athelstan had left behind. Thorkell remained at the queen's side, using his fine, embroidered belt to staunch the blood welling from the hand that had likely saved his life. They spoke together in Danish as he tended to her wounds.

Eadric had picked up the discarded seax and now he presented it to Edward, who was glaring fixedly at his mother and Thorkell.

"What are they saying?" Edward demanded, his tone surly.

"I do not know, lad, for unlike the queen I cannot speak our enemy's tongue," Eadric replied. "And that," he breathed to himself as he shot a suspicious glance at Emma, "is something that she has kept cleverly hidden until now." He dropped his gaze to the boy, and his expression grew shrewd and calculating. "I agree with Athelstan," he confided quietly to Edward, "that we cannot trust Thorkell and his men. They will always be our enemies. Your mother, though," he feigned a regretful sigh, "well, it seems she has befriended them."

"She cannot," Edward protested, his eyes filling with tears. "They are evil men."

"Ah, but she cares little for that; nor does she care whose blood they shed, for today she put even you in jeopardy." Eadric bent toward Edward, and as he placed a hand on the boy's shoulder his eyes glinted with malice that Edward was too young to discern. "Never forget that she has welcomed our enemies as her friends," he whispered. "Take heed, Edward, and be wary of the queen. From this day forward, you must not trust your mother."

Eadric straightened as Wymarc approached them, and he nodded genially to her.

"Come, Edward," she said. "There are men waiting to escort you to the palace."

But when she attempted to usher him toward the door Edward shrugged out of her reach. He went instead to the altar and gazed down at the archbishop who had always treated him with kindness and whose broken, desecrated body lay on the stone floor, forgotten.

Silently Edward vowed that he would never forget Ælfheah or what horrors had been done to him. And never, ever would he forget that his mother had been willing to shed her blood and his to defend a pack of foul, wicked, murdering Danes.

Part One

Desperate Alliances

A.D. 1012 Then submitted to the king five and forty of the ships of the enemy; and promised him, that they would defend this land, and he should feed and clothe them.

The Anglo-Saxon Chronicle

Chapter One

June 1012
Rochester, Kent

A late afternoon breeze caught the hem of Queen Emma's silken headrail, and the thin fabric fluttered and danced above the long, golden braid of her hair. She was standing on a high bank within Rochester's burh looking down on a wide strip of beach. On the sands below, two boys, one fair-haired and one dark, faced each other, practice swords in hand. The air rang with their shouts and the thwack of wood on wood while their sword master paced beside his charges, his voice rising above theirs in a steady string of alternating commands and curses.

The smaller combatant, his thick brown hair a thatch of curls, was Robert, son of the queen's long-time friend and companion, Wymarc. The other boy, younger than his opponent by mere months, was Edward, the eldest child of the queen. The boys had been raised together since birth, and now that they were nearly eight winters old, their military training was as compulsory as the Latin they had studied earlier in the day.

It seemed to the watching Emma that her son's taller frame gave him no advantage over his shorter but sturdier adversary, and she was not surprised when Wymarc's son drove Edward backward until he tripped and landed with a cry on one elbow. Robert reached down to help his friend scramble to his feet, but Edward could not avoid the smack that his instructor delivered to his backside with the flat of his weapon.

Reluctantly, Emma stepped away from the cliff edge. Edward would not welcome a witness to even this mild reproof, especially not his mother. She recalled how, when he was a babe, she had been the center of his world. That had ended, though, when the king had removed him from her household and placed him well out of her reach. Their meetings since then had been rare and always painfully formal. She suspected that Edward had been fed countless lies about her, for he regarded her now with either indifference or resentment, and every time she saw him, he seemed to have grown yet more distant from her.

Her only daughter, too, was no longer at her side. She may as well, Emma thought, be at the ends of the earth; but it could not be helped. Goda was far safer at Duke Richard's court across the Narrow Sea than she could be in this battle-ravaged kingdom, at least for now. She prayed daily that in the coming months that would change, but until she could be assured that England was truly at peace, the child must remain in Normandy. Yet, how she missed her daughter! Their parting had broken both their hearts, and hers had not mended even when another babe had taken Goda's place—another child who might well be wrenched from her far sooner than she wished, for the king regarded all of his offspring as mere tools to be used however he saw fit, and even a newborn had a purpose.

Æthelred had given their infant son the name of a warrior king, Alfred, making the boy a symbol of England's determination to defeat their Danish enemies. It seemed to her a heavy burden to place upon a babe, but a mother's wishes, even those of a queen, carried little weight in Æthelred's realm.

Lost in such bitter reflections Emma followed a path that led behind a small chapel to a grove perched atop a promontory overlooking the River Medway. Here she could be alone with her thoughts for a time, and she was grateful for the solitude. She had a great many things to think about.

The king would be attending to business in the city, meeting privately with a chosen few—meetings from which she was excluded. She had observed him closely, though, at the larger gatherings that she attended along with the churchmen and nobles summoned from all over England to this week-long witan, now in its fourth day. Æthelred was still a commanding presence among them despite his forty-five winters and the limp that plagued him now, a nagging reminder of a fall he had suffered before Easter when his mount had thrown him—or so he had claimed. There had been whispers that the aging king had merely slipped senseless from the saddle.

She was inclined to believe the whispers. Times without number she had seen him distracted, lost in some vision that struck him with terror and blinded him to all else. In such a state, his senses might well desert him.

The king, she suspected, was haunted by his own sins and by foul deeds that had been committed in his name—and of those there were many. As a mere child he had witnessed the cruel slaying of his half-brother, a royal murder that had brought Æthelred to the throne but had cast a shadow on his reign. Her husband, it seemed to her, feared that God would punish him for claiming a crown that should never have been his. And because of this, he clung fiercely to power, mistrusted even his sons, and saw enemies everywhere. Such guilt, suspicion, and fear, it seemed to her, were hardly the qualities that led to good governance, or even to a peaceful mind.

These were thoughts she kept to herself, though, for her husband would not thank her for them. He had ever seen her as more enemy than friend, and he had little regard for her or her opinions, though just now he was willing to tolerate her presence at his councils. And for that she had to thank his newest ally, the Danish warlord Thorkell. At yesterday's formal oath-taking, the fierce viking had knelt before the king and solemnly sworn allegiance in his Danish tongue while, at Thorkell's request and with the king's grudging acquiescence, she stood beside him to repeat his words in English.

Not many of those watching, she suspected, truly believed that the big Dane would keep the oath he had given. The great men of England would surely question the king's wisdom in taking Thorkell into his service, just as they must harbor doubts about her own motives in befriending him. Even as the oath was pledged she had read suspicion in the faces of those watching.

But they had not been in London, as she had been, when Thorkell bore Archbishop Ælfheah's body to All Hallows Church. They had not seen his anger as he recounted the mindless, drunken cruelty that had led to Ælfheah's death, nor witnessed his anguish at failing to save the man who had, improbably, earned his respect. All they knew was that they had been battered by the blood-stained swords of Thorkell's army, had been beaten to their knees. What else did they have to cling to but their fury?

She could not blame them for their hatred of the Danes, but if it continued there would be trouble in the months to come. Even today she had felt it like an itching on her skin, could see it lurking in the corners where knots of men gathered to whisper and cast furtive glances at their one-time enemies.

Something must be done to appease the rancor in the king's hall, and as queen and peaceweaver, that task must be hers. She must find a way to reconcile the English with their new allies so that, united, they could defend this kingdom.

As she weighed the problem and the difficulties it presented, she heard the faint rasp of footsteps on gravel, and she turned around, expecting to see someone from her household come in search of her. But it was a man who approached, one whose image had been graven on her heart years before. And as she watched him stride purposefully toward her, she felt torn between elation and despair.

She had steeled herself for this meeting three days before, when the king's council had first gathered. But of all the king's sons, Athelstan alone had not answered the summons nor sent any explanation for his absence. Now he had arrived at last, and she was unprepared. She guessed that he must have been traveling for days, for his boots and cloak were caked with mud, his fair hair disheveled, and his face bronzed from long hours in the sun.

He had looked much the same when last she had seen him, on the day that he had stormed into All Hallows Church to find her standing with Thorkell near the body of the murdered archbishop. For several heartbeats she was inside the little church again, caught between Athelstan's drawn sword and a handful of Danes who were weaponless except for one grim-faced shipman who stood well beyond her reach, holding a knife to her son's throat.

She shivered at the memory and at the alarm triggered now by the fierce light in Athelstan's blue eyes as he drew closer.

"What has happened?" she demanded, certain that he brought news of some new calamity.

"We have unfinished business, you and I," he snapped, seizing her wrist and turning her hand palm up to reveal the scars that slashed red and raw across her fingers and thumb. She wanted to pull her hand away, but she did not try. She knew that she could not match his swordsman's strength.

"I took no lasting hurt from your blade, my lord," she said stiffly, "if that is what concerns you." She had grasped his sword to prevent a slaughter and the murder of her son, but the only thing that had perished that day had been the trust between them. There had not been a single day in the three months since that she had not grieved its loss.

He glared at her, and she felt the force of his anger like a blow.

"You believed that I would let Edward die that day," he said. "Why?"

She glared back at him, her own anger swelling now to equal his.

"Do you not remember your own words? *Kill the boy or not*, you said; *it makes no matter!*"

"It was a ruse, Emma!" He was still clutching her wrist, and now he shook it as if she were a disobedient child. "The Danes had to think that any threat they offered to Edward would give them no advantage. How could you not see that?"

"Because I am his mother," she cried, "and there was a knife at his throat!"

"And I was trying to protect him!" he shouted back. "*Jesu!* I was trying to protect you both!" He drew a long breath. "You are too trusting, Emma," he said, his voice stern. "Thorkell could have dragged you to his ship; used you as his shield and no one would have been able to stop him." His blue eyes pierced her with reproach. "It happened once before. Surely you have not forgotten!"

Stricken by his words she closed her eyes. He need not remind her that the Danish King Swein and his son had once held her captive. Every detail of that terrible day was burned into her memory—the narrow lane where her party had been ambushed; the ravaged bodies of her hearthguards who died defending her; the helpless rage she felt when Swein Forkbeard's son thwarted her wild attempt to flee. She remembered her first glimpse of the dragon-ship that would deliver her into captivity, how it had strained against the falling tide to reach the shore; how she had tried again to run, but the young Cnut would not let her go.

Lost in that past, she was aware again of Cnut's dark, fathomless eyes pinning her and of his vise-like grip on her wrist, the memory so real that her breath caught in her throat and her eyes flew open.

But it was not Swein's son who held her wrist, it was Athelstan.

He had been there that night, too, drawn by the same beacon fire that had beckoned Swein's ship to the beach. He had freed her and led her to safety; and she remembered only too well how, alone together for the first time, they had surrendered to temptation that had long been held in check.

But she was Æthelred's queen, and he the king's son. They had known even then that what had happened between them must never be spoken of, and must never happen again. For a decade now, the events of that day and night had been their shared secret.

"After all that has passed between us," Athelstan whispered, "did you think that you could not trust me? At All Hallows I tried to protect Edward with a warrior's trick. But Emma, I would have died to protect you and your son. If you do not know that, if I have lost all your trust, then you must say it now, to my face. Else I will not believe it. I cannot."

She looked into his eyes, and it was not just that terrible night on the beach and the sweetness of what they had shared afterward that she remembered, but all the many times that he had been her protector, her counselor, and her friend. His heart had been as true as tempered steel, and she had loved him for it. If he was not still the man that she had trusted for so long, then there was nothing good or honest in this world, and she had no wish to remain in it.

"I was so afraid for Edward," she said softly, reaching up to touch his cheek, "and you would not listen to me."

He brought her scarred fingers to his lips, kissed them and, reluctantly, gently, released them. Then he ran a hand through his hair, a gesture so familiar it made her weak with yearning, for she loved him still. But she could not succumb to her desire; she dare not submit them both to that temptation. To know that he was not her son's enemy—that was gift enough. She would be content with it.

"I will listen to you now," he said. "You must tell me why you trust Thorkell, because there are many like me who do not."

This, then, was where her peace weaving must begin. If she could persuade Athelstan that Thorkell would keep his pledge, others would follow his lead.

"Thorkell told me that day, in Danish, that Archbishop Ælfheah had revealed to him that I could speak his tongue, and that he could trust me." The archbishop, like Athelstan, had been among the few who had known that secret, and he had pledged never to reveal it except in dire need. "Ælfheah made Thorkell swear that he would seek me out and offer to help us against an even greater enemy."

Athelstan shook his head, his face eloquent with disbelief.

"How could you be certain that he was not lying?"

"I was not certain; but he had come into London unarmed with only a handful of men. He was risking his life, Athelstan, and I was persuaded that he could be trusted. It was a risk, I know, but I do not regret it. And there is more."

As the shadows lengthened around them she strolled with him through the little grove and recounted information that Thorkell had shared with her in the intervening months—of his break with the Danish King Swein and his sons over the murder of Thorkell's brother, a jarl named Hemming; of Swein's determination to drive Æthelred from his throne; of Thorkell's promise to defend her and her children.

Athelstan listened, attentive, his face grave. When she was finished, he halted and drew her around to face him.

"Because of you, Emma, Thorkell is now the king's sworn ally. But have a care where you place your trust because alliances can change without any warning. And it is not just Thorkell who must concern you. Ealdorman Eadric all but owns your son, and he will use Edward—and you, if he can—to maintain his stranglehold on power. I think he will push Edward toward the throne when my father dies no matter who stands in the way." He searched her face, his eyes narrowing. "Is that what you want? To see your son upon the throne, whatever the cost?"

She met his gaze, for he must understand this one thing about her, even if no one else did. "Not at the cost of his soul or mine," she said firmly. "Athelstan, you are the king's heir no matter what Eadric may be planning for my son. But I cannot hope to oppose such a powerful ealdorman without a powerful ally of my own."

And she saw the understanding dawn in his eyes.

"Thorkell," he said. Drawing in a long breath he shook his head and frowned. "Thorkell is the king's man, though, and no one can say how my father will use him—pit him against our own people, perhaps, if he feels threatened." He looked past her suddenly and said, "Wymarc is coming, and I must go to the king. I have kept you too long. But Emma, no matter what pledges Thorkell has made—to you or to my father—do not forget that he is a Dane. One day he may balk at turning against his own people! It would be folly to give him all your trust."

He left her with that warning, and when he was gone the wretched words echoed in her head until she wanted to scream. If he was right and Thorkell proved false, then yes, she had brought a wolf into England's fold.

Yet what was one more wolf, she asked herself, among so very many?

Chapter Two

June 1012
Rochester, Kent

Athelstan retraced his steps through the now-deserted burh and into the city. As he cut through the encampment sheltering the men attending the witan, he considered all that Emma had said, and it worried him. It was true that in placing her trust in the huge Dane, Thorkell, she was doing no more nor less than any of the other magnates in the kingdom—forging a link to someone who had something of value to offer. But such alliances must work in both directions. Even if Thorkell should keep the oaths he made to Emma and the king, he would do so only in return for silver and provisions for his men. One day, though, the king would die, and as a widow—even a royal widow—Emma would have to relinquish many of the lands and resources that she now possessed. She would likely have little to offer a Danish warlord.

Except, perhaps, her body.

The thought seared through him, and his mind recoiled from it even as he forced himself to consider it a likely consequence of the king's death. His father was far from young, while Emma had not yet seen thirty winters. And because an alliance with her meant an alliance with her ducal brother, she would be a valuable political asset. Certainly she would marry again. The Norman duke, anticipating the death of the English king, might already be entertaining offers for his sister's hand, perhaps even from the Danes and the Norse. Was it possible that Thorkell or even King Swein had at some time met with Richard and had already broached a marriage with Emma, once she was widowed?

The words of a prophecy uttered years ago came back to him, as sharp and clear as on the day he had first heard them.

Whoso would hold the scepter of England must first hold the hand of England's queen.

The words had been spoken by one of the old ones—a pagan seeress who had been draped in darkness and surrounded by a circle of ancient stones. He had sinned in merely listening to those words, yet he could not dismiss them. For long years now, the queen and the crown had been linked in his mind—both golden, both a temptation. True prophecy or not, sin or not, his desire for his father's wife had never lessened. If anything, it grew stronger with each passing year. How much longer would his father stand in the way of his desire?

How much longer must he wait to gain a kingdom—and with it the hand of a widowed queen?

Scowling at his unhallowed thoughts, he strode through the gateway of the royal lodging, passing men-at-arms, thegns, priests, and servants as he made his way to the great hall. He could hear raised voices from within, two of which he recognized, and he peered inquiringly at the king's rat-faced little steward who was acting as door ward.

"Is my brother Edmund with the king?"

"He is, lord," Hubert replied.

"Anyone else?"

"The lords Uhtred and Ulfkytel."

His sisters' husbands. So this was a family council, and from the sound of it, as heated as hell. His appearance now would merely add fuel to the fire.

"What of my younger brothers?" he asked.

"Edrid and Edwig have gone with Ealdorman Eadric into the west country on a mission for the king," Hubert pursed his snout-like mouth into an obsequious smile. "Your father will be pleased, my lord, that you have arrived at last. He always values your advice."

That was a lie, and they both knew it. His father wanted him at the council, not because he valued his advice, but because he was suspicious of what his eldest son might be doing behind his royal back.

Athelstan entered the hall, a long, narrow chamber with open shutters on two sides that offered little illumination this late in the day. He could make out his father well enough, though, seated at a trestle table, his face lit by banks of flickering candles. His golden hair and beard had turned to silver in the months since Athelstan had last seen him. And there was a scar marring his right temple that stood out livid against a ruddy flush of anger as the king glared at the three men who faced him.

Athelstan, frowning, remained poised in the shadows, content to watch and listen before wading into the fray.

His brother Edmund was shouting at the king, and Athelstan knew from experience how intimidating Edmund could be. He was a big man, the largest and most formidable of the king's sons. One day, Athelstan thought, Edmund's unwillingness to back down in any kind of a fight, even an argument with the king, was going to bring him to grief.

Just now Edmund was leaning threateningly toward their father, both hands on the table, his dark hair falling forward about his face. Beside him, Uhtred, built like a bear, with long braided hair that gave him the fierce look of a viking, placed a restraining hand on Edmund's arm. But Uhtred's expression, too, was angry, and next to him the tall, lean Ulfkytel, usually so genial, looked thunderous.

"If you continue to ignore the protests of your thegns and ealdormen," Edmund was shouting at their father, "you will lose the trust—"

"Do not threaten me!" Æthelred surged to his feet to glare at Edmund. "The deed is done! I have agreed to Thorkell's terms and I will not go back on my pledge; nor will he! And I do not recall asking for your counsel on this matter, Edmund!"

"My lord king," Ulfkytel's tone was urgent, "your thegns do not trust that Thorkell will keep his pledge. We are here at their behest because they fear him, and they would beg you to—"

"Then you may go back to them and tell them that their fears are groundless!" And now the king's gaze took in all three men. "Thorkell is the answer to our prayers. He was sent to me by God through the intercession of our martyred archbishop. The men you speak for would do well to thank me, not send my sons to offer me counsel that they are too cowardly to give themselves." Edmund seemed about to speak again, but the king held up a forbidding hand and his eyes flicked to where Athelstan stood. "You took your time getting here!" he growled. "Did you lose your way?"

Athelstan crossed the chamber and entered the ring of candlelight.

"I was in Devon, my lord, responding to news of viking raids there, and to a report that they appeared to be making for the Severn."

Beside him, Edmund cursed.

The king grimaced, sat down, and fingered the scar at his brow. "We have heard nothing of this," he snarled. "How many ships?"

"Ten, perhaps twelve."

"Raiders from Ireland?" Æthelred hazarded.

"No, my lord. They were Danes, and led, it appears, by Swein himself."

His father's face paled, and Uhtred joined Edmund in another round of curses.

"I hope you confronted them," Ulfkytel said, "and slaughtered them to a man."

Athelstan drew in a long breath. "That was my intent," he replied, "but a gale blew up, and we watched as two of the vessels were dashed to pieces in the Severn Sea. The rest were swept toward the Waylisc shore." He winced, recalling the terrible sight of those ships going down.

"This is God's hand at work, then," the king breathed. "If Swein is drowned—"

"We must not depend upon that," Edmund warned.

"I agree with Edmund," Athelstan said soberly. "We cannot presume that Swein is dead and no longer a threat."

"Let us presume, then," Ulfkytel mused, "that Swein made it safely to shore. What would he do next? Take his ten ships back to Denmark, or sail up the Severn?"

"If Swein's fleet enters the River Severn," Æthelred said slowly, "it will meet resistance from our garrison at Gloucester. And by now, Eadric should be there, as well, with another two hundred men. The Danes will be outnumbered." His eyes grew distant and he murmured, "That is another sign that God favors us."

Athelstan was about to ask what Eadric's mission was at Gloucester when his father spoke again.

"Tomorrow at the council meeting we shall weigh the matter of Swein and what his death—or his continued presence among the living—may portend." He leaned back in his chair and scowled again at Athelstan. "Now," he said, "I would speak alone with my eldest son."

Athelstan saw Edmund flick a warning glance at him before stalking from the chamber, and he steeled himself to face the king's ire.

"You are pardoned for your late arrival," the king said. "Now that you are here, though, I want it clear that I will brook no challenges from you at the witan session. You have defied me at past councils, and I will not have my decisions questioned again, either by you or by Edmund. I warn you, if you speak against me I will confiscate your lands and fine you both until you bleed."

Angered by his father's insistence on blind obedience, Athelstan replied with bitter irony, "Forgive my ignorance, my lord, but is the king's council chamber not the place to proffer advice and guidance?"

"When my councilors are nearly witless with their own fears it is I who must counsel *them!* Any dissension within my family merely adds confusion to their terror. You know this, Athelstan! You are not a fool. So as the eldest ætheling, your voice will echo mine or you will be silent."

"But if I—"

"Those are your choices! Now get out!"

When Edmund saw his brother emerge from the hall, he fell into step beside him.

"You were not in there long," Edmund observed as he led the way to his lodging.

"Just long enough for him to warn me that we must both keep our mouths shut at the council or risk ruin," Athelstan told him.

Edmund studied his brother's face. It was lined with exhaustion, and his blue eyes were heavy with weariness. He must have ridden like the very devil to get here, only to receive nothing more for his pains than undeserved abuse from the king. Well, *Christ!* There was plenty of that to go around. Ever since their father had wed his Norman bride he had set himself against his sons.

They should have rebelled against him long ago, before the Danes plundered East Anglia and burned their way through the middle shires; before they sacked Canterbury and murdered Archbishop Ælfheah; before the queen convinced the king to accept that bastard Thorkell and his forty-five ships into his service.

Athelstan, though, had always argued against rebellion, had cautioned that it was not yet time to take so irrevocable a step. Now it was too late. In accepting Thorkell's service, the king had acquired a viking army that was nearly three thousand strong, and it would be madness to attempt to move against him.

Once inside his pavilion Edmund filled two cups with ale while Athelstan washed his face and hands.

"Shall we drink to the king's health?" Edmund suggested bitterly, handing Athelstan a cup.

His brother barked a mirthless laugh. "Let us drink instead to the absent Eadric," he said, "in the fervent hope that he remains so." He took a long swallow and wiped his mouth with the back of his hand. "Dare I hope that Eadric's mission to Gloucester is a sign that the king no longer loves him and wants rid of him?"

Edmund shook his head. "Eadric is still golden, I'm afraid. He was sent west to gather tribute that for three years has gone unpaid by our Waylisc neighbors. The king wants a reckoning, and Eadric has taken a force large enough to persuade speedy compliance with his demands for payment."

Athelstan snorted. "No doubt Eadric will keep a healthy portion of whatever he collects."

"More than is due him, I'll warrant; which is why I suggested that Edrid go as well. He will take note of how much silver goes into Eadric's coffers and how much finds its way to the king. If our brother learns that Eadric has played us false, we might be able to loosen his grip on power."

"And if Eadric runs into Swein Forkbeard's raiders, he may return with nothing," Athelstan observed, "or he may not return at all." He peered into his cup and pondered what the sudden death of Eadric might lead to; then, shrugging because it seemed too improbable, he said, "I heard you arguing with the king about Thorkell. Wasting your breath, it seems."

Edmund tossed back his ale; then, acknowledging that this might take a while, he reached for the flagon and filled both their cups again.

"The men of the council, Athelstan, despise Thorkell and his shipmen; and you know why as well as I do. Some of them have seen their wives or daughters raped by Danes; many of them have watched their homes and crops burned by them! Now they will be taxed to pay Thorkell and his men to aid in the kingdom's defense, yet no one believes that they will actually defend us!" He slanted a glance at his brother. "The Danes have set up their camp near the western gates, within easy reach of their ships, and there are rumors flying that they have some dark purpose in mind."

"What purpose?" Athelstan asked. "That they plan to sack Rochester and then flee?"

"Something like that."

Athelstan looked thoughtful. "It's possible," he mused. "Or it may be that the Danes stay close to their ships simply because they trust us no more than we trust them. They must know that they are hated. Has Thorkell spoken in the council?"

"In his own tongue," Edmund said bitterly, "with the queen beside him to interpret for him."

He did not share his black thoughts about the queen's friendship with Thorkell. Athelstan would merely defend her, for he was blind to Emma's ambition. It maddened him that his brother ignored her patient acquisition of allies, influence and power, all for the purpose of one day seeing her son upon the throne. Thorkell was merely another step along that road.

"Make no mistake, though," he observed, "that Danish bastard knows English well enough that he doesn't need Emma to translate for him. *Christ!* He has lived among us long enough to learn our tongue and anything else that might help him betray us. His only counsel so far is that Swein will attack, and soon." He paused a moment as a new idea occurred to him. "If Swein drowned in that shipwreck, though, it must upset whatever the Danes are planning. We might be able to convince the king that he has no need of Thorkell's ships and we can be rid of them."

But Athelstan shook his head. "Even if Swein is dead, his sons are not likely to give us any peace. One of them will merely step into his father's place. Whether we like it or not, we need Thorkell."

"If he keeps his word," Edmund said darkly.

The next day at the council session Edmund was among those who, having listened to Athelstan's report of the foundering of Swein's ships, pounded the table to express satisfaction at their enemy's ill fortune. But in the midst of it, Thorkell rose to his feet and surveyed them all with a grim expression until the men had quieted.

The big Dane spoke into the silence while Emma, seated beside him, translated.

"Even if Swein is dead, feasting now in Ægir's hall, you men of England cannot count yourselves safe. The sons of Swein covet this land, and they have sworn to take it. They will come when you do not look for them and strike where you are most vulnerable."

Thorkell paused, Emma grew quiet, and in the silence the hall was filled with the rustling of nervous men. Edmund studied their faces and saw expressions either too blank or too guarded to read, although he was willing to wager that they were as fearful and suspicious of Thorkell as he was.

After a long moment Thorkell pointed to the king and spoke again. Emma's face paled as she listened to him, and her translation was so long in coming that Edmund wanted to shout at her to speak, for the love of God.

When at last she did speak, he wished that she had not.

"Slacken your vigilance even for a moment," she proclaimed, "and you are lost."

Edmund cursed under his breath while the queen's words echoed through the hall, ringing with portent and prophecy.

Chapter Three

June 1012
Rochester, Kent

King Æthelred sat at the high table in the bishop's great hall and surveyed the men and women gathered there for the witan's closing feast. The midsummer evening was so warm that, although the shutters had been flung wide to catch the breeze, the king was sweating beneath his heavy, gold-embroidered gown and cloak. Torches in brackets throughout the hall warded off the growing dark, and in their light the halos of apostles painted larger than life upon the plastered walls glowed golden, and it seemed to Æthelred that the saints' wide eyes stared fixedly on the company gathered below them.

On either side of him Archbishop Wulfstan of Jorvik and Rochester's Bishop Godwine discussed ecclesiastical matters to which Æthelred paid little heed. Instead, ever and again, his gaze was drawn to his queen.

Emma was gowned in the palest silk, and the gold at her throat and wrists shimmered like the halos of the saints upon the walls. Throughout the meal she had been moving among the guests, offering each in turn the brimming welcome cup.

What private words, he wondered, did she murmur to each man as she placed the vessel in his hands? She had been lingering now for some time at the table where Thorkell sat with his Danish shipmen, speaking to them in their own tongue and beguiling them with her smile.

He muttered, half to himself, "Emma lavishes her attention too freely upon the Danes."

Bishop Godwine, interrupted in mid-sentence, followed his gaze and considered the queen.

"Surely, my lord, she merely performs the office of peaceweaver," he observed, "as any queen must. Her knowledge of the Northmen's tongue is a boon to us, is it not?"

Æthelred grunted. It was a boon that Emma had kept hidden even from him these ten years, until it suited her to reveal it. What other, more damning secrets had she concealed from him? Yet his churchmen, like this bishop, were ever her staunchest defenders.

"What is it that you fear?" Archbishop Wulfstan's harsh voice grated against Æthelred's ear. "That the queen is inserting herself between you and your Danish ally?

"She seeks to augment her influence at my court," he grumbled. "It is unseemly."

Wulfstan was silent for a moment before he observed, "I agree that your queen reaches for power of a kind. But it is a woman's power that she would have, and no threat to your own. She is readying herself for the struggle she will face one day when you and I have gone to our heavenly reward." The archbishop leaned even closer and whispered, "That future is not yours to dictate, lord king. It belongs to those who will survive you. There are other, far more pressing concerns in your realm that demand your attention."

Æthelred, glancing at the archbishop, saw that Wulfstan's penetrating gaze was focused on Thorkell.

"My only concern with Thorkell, archbishop," he replied, "is to keep him well paid and his men fed and happy."

"Nay, my lord. Your concern must be to divine his desires and designs—to come to know his very soul."

Æthelred considered the Dane as he pondered the archbishop's words. Wulfstan, he guessed, had little love for Thorkell. He was not alone in that. Most of the men in this hall would as soon drown their new Danish allies as drink with them. The shipmen sitting at their tables were set apart not just by their foreign tongue, but by ancient enmities. Too many in England had suffered at their hands. Yet he needed these men—trained warriors who would fight for him as long as he paid them well. Wulfstan was probably right, though, that their leader had greater ambitions than a purse full of silver. Thorkell may be a mere tool, but like any good tool, the man who would wield it must know how it worked.

"You would have me learn what I can of Thorkell," he murmured to the archbishop, "the better to make use of him as my ally?"

"No, my lord." Wulfstan fixed him with eyes that burned in the candlelight. "The better to oppose him should he become your foe."

Æthelred frowned. So Wulfstan, too, believed that Thorkell would break his pledges. But Wulfstan was wrong. All the fools who doubted were wrong. Thorkell had been sent to him as a sign of God's forgiveness, a guarantee that his own past sins would no longer haunt him.

"Thorkell will not betray the oaths he made to me," he said confidently. "You will see."

"I will grant you that Thorkell may prove true," the archbishop conceded. "I will grant, too, that Swein Forkbeard may be drowned in the Severn Sea as some claim. But you are a king, my lord. You must be prepared for whatever may come to pass, even those things that you perceive as unlikely. Would you wager your kingdom on nothing but hope and rumor?"

Æthelred scowled at Wulfstan who gazed darkly back at him. The archbishop looked like an Old Testament prophet, large and forbidding in his black garments, his long white beard flowing like a river beneath his chin. And he loved nothing more than to prophesy doom. But doom lay behind them now, and Æthelred would not allow even Wulfstan to cast his shadow on the future.

"God has lately given me signs of His favor," the king insisted, "and I will place my trust in Him. Is that not what you preach, archbishop?"

"Trust in the Lord, yes. But the forces of evil are all around us. It is a foolish man who, because of false pride, will not protect himself from injury. I beg you, do not be a fool. I have spoken to you before of unrest in your northern shires, and I am still uneasy in my mind about the actions there of ungodly—"

"I have heard your fears! Because of them I have bound the most powerful northerners to me by every means that I can. Eadric of Mercia, Uhtred of Northumbria, and the East Anglian leader Ulfkytel are wed to my daughters. The brothers Morcar and Siferth of the Five Boroughs are beholden to me for gifts of lands and rights enough to satisfy the greediest of men. The north is secure!"

"Nay, lord king, there is something still amiss there!" He peered at Æthelred from beneath his heavy white eyebrows. "Your daughters

Ælfgifu and Wulfhilde did not accompany their husbands to this council? Why not? What do Uhtred and Ulfkytel fear that they leave their wives secured behind their fortress walls?"

"Best you put that question to them, archbishop," he said testily, "and leave me in peace."

His remark was met with ponderous silence from Wulfstan while Bishop Godwine addressed himself assiduously to the food on his plate. After a long moment, though, Wulfstan rose from his seat.

"As you wish, lord king," he said.

Æthelred watched him approach the table where Uhtred and Ulfkytel were seated. He already knew what Wulfstan would learn there; his daughters' husbands had already confessed to him their fear that Thorkell and his Danes would commit some savagery here at the council gathering. What they had not confessed, but what he suspected, was that they feared him as well, and that his daughters had remained behind as hostages to ensure their husbands' safe return from his court.

Well, that was all to the good. Men should fear their king for it was fear that kept men's treachery in check.

Yet the archbishop's dire words lingered in his mind, ominous and disturbing, and he felt a sudden familiar heaviness, like a weight pressing against his chest. Alarmed, he searched the chamber for something darker than the shadows cast by the torchlight, looking for the wraith of his murdered brother, whose crown now rested on his brow. Had the thing that had haunted him for years returned to torment him again?

But he could see no baleful presence lurking in the dusky corners of the hall, no ghost glowering at him from the shadows. His brother's vengeful spirit, he was convinced, had finally been laid to rest.

Relieved, he took a long draught of wine and, considering again the gathering below him, he noticed Lady Aldyth, Siferth's wife, staring up at him with wide, glittering eyes. He had not seen her in years, not since he had ordered the deaths of her kin—his old enemy Ælfhelm and his two sons. He nodded, acknowledging her, but she quickly looked away.

She was frightened of him still, no doubt, because he had punished her uncle and cousins for their traitorous alliance with an ambitious viking warlord. He had never discovered which Danish bastard had made that bargain, only that Ælfhelm's daughter had been pledged to him in marriage to seal it.

That had been a fatal mistake, for the girl had wanted no part of such a marriage. And because she was as treacherous as her father, she had betrayed him; and so her father and brothers had died.

The image of the alluring, dark-haired Elgiva came back to him as vividly as if she were standing before him. She had bewitched him for a time, before her father had begun consorting with Danes. He had even taken her for his mistress until he wearied of her. After her father's death, though, Elgiva had disappeared. That beautiful, seductive heiress, a prize for any man who might use her wealth and her father's oath men to challenge him for his crown, simply vanished. The men he sent in search of her could never discover where she had gone, although he suspected that she had taken refuge with the only kin she had left—her cousin Aldyth.

That was all in the past, now; over and done with. Aldyth's husband Siferth and his brother Morcar had brought him word that Elgiva had died of a pestilence, and he had rewarded them handsomely. They were bound to him now with gifts and oaths and—he glanced again at Aldyth—and yes, with fear. The north, as he had assured Wulfstan, was secure.

The traitors were all dead now, all of Aldyth's treacherous kin—her uncle, his sons and, thanks be to God, even the beautiful, cunning Elgiva.

July 1012
Redmere, Holderness, Northumbria

Elgiva stood as near as she dared to the edge of a cliff that reared high above the sea, and from the depths of her hooded cloak she gazed eastward across a vast expanse of slate-colored water and sullen sky. Somewhere out there lay the kingdom of the Danes—her husband's land. But as she searched for a ship that would bring her word of him, the empty horizon and the restless, churning waves of that northern sea seemed to mock her.

"There is nothing out there," she said to her companion.

"We'll see no fleet from Denmark, my lady, until the wind changes," he replied. "We must wait."

Elgiva huffed a frustrated sigh. Through all the twenty-seven summers of her life, men had been telling her that she must wait, and every time she heard those words she wanted to scream. Sihtric, though, who was so young that his beard was no more than dark fuzz on his chin, was a canny shipman, and he knew the sea. She had to believe him.

She felt the babe in her womb give a kick, and she rested her hand upon her belly to quiet the little wretch. Her back ached, and today the walk from her steading had tired her more than usual, even with Sihtric's brawny arm to support her.

She was beyond ready to be rid of this burden, but her Sami wise woman claimed that the child would not be born until Michaelmas, still many weeks away. And Tyra, who was skilled, as well, at reading the future in her rune-marked shards of bone, had agreed with Sihtric about the fleet. No matter how many times she cast the rune sticks, Tyra could find no sign of it.

Elgiva chafed at the delay.

"Cnut should have sent me some word of his plans by now," she fretted to Sihtric.

Her husband had sailed for Denmark when she was newly pregnant, on a cold March day when the sky had looked much like this. And before he boarded his ship he had made her a promise.

Give me another son, and one day I will give you a kingdom.

She was sick of waiting, though—waiting for this child, waiting for news from her husband, waiting for the Danish fleet that would drive Æthelred from his throne, waiting for escape from Holderness.

It had been six years since Æthelred's henchman had murdered her father and brothers, and she had sought refuge here with her father's ally, Thurbrand. She had known that the lord of Holderness paid only lip service to the English king, and she had believed that under his protection she would be safe from Æthelred's wrath as well as from her father's wretched scheme to marry her off to some filthy Dane. But in Thurbrand's hall she had been forced into a handfast marriage with the very man that her father had chosen for her, and she was only reconciled to her fate when she learned that the tall, thin, coppery-haired youth who bedded her was the son of the Danish king.

She had known since she was a girl that she was destined for queenship and that her children would be kings. It was a prophecy that had been repeated to her over and over, and her marriage to Cnut was the beginning of its fulfillment. She had already given Cnut one son. Soon she would give him another.

And when she did, Cnut would give her a kingdom.

She was sick of waiting, though, and sick of Holderness because it was so isolated from news of what was happening in the world beyond its borders. Cnut had ordered Thurbrand to set a wide net of watchers around her steading, and rarely was anyone allowed through. Only once had she managed to slip past her guards. That had been some years ago, when she had fled to her cousin Aldyth.

She shivered, recalling how that journey to Aldyth's hall had nearly been the death of her. She had fallen ill, and when she recovered, her odious cousin, terrified of what the king would do if she was discovered there, had ordered her to leave, threatening to send him word of her if she did not go. She had been forced to return to Holderness, and Thurbrand had seen to it that she remained imprisoned here ever since.

She scanned the sea again, cursing the relentless wind that was her enemy and tormentor. "You are right, Sihtric," she said wearily. "There will be no Danish invasion until this wind shifts, and probably not until harvestide. It seems to me, though, that a single vessel could hazard the Danish Sea and bring me some word from my husband."

Sihtric shrugged. "A ship may have attempted the crossing, my lady," he said, "and may have foundered. The sea is cruel."

She continued to gaze out to sea, irritated with Sihtric for even suggesting such a thing, although she knew it was perfectly true.

At last, weary of staring into emptiness, she said, "Let us return to the hall," and she turned her back on the wide, indifferent sea.

She took his arm and they retraced their steps, following the muddy track that led back to the steading. She kept her eyes on her feet, clinging to Sihtric lest she slip on the treacherous path as it sloped downward into a gloom cast by wych elms and yews. They went slowly, for she was hampered by the filth that caked her boots and by the bulge of her pregnant belly, and as they reached the bottom of the swale, a man strode out from the trees to block their way.

In an instant Sihtric's knife was in his hand.

"My lady," the newcomer said genially, spreading his hands wide, "would you mind assuring him that I am no threat?"

"Alric!" she cried, hardly able to believe that he was actually standing before her. "Sihtric," she snapped, "put away your knife! This is a friend."

It had been near a year since last she had seen him, and he looked as fine as she remembered, if a bit travel-worn. His boots and cloak were even muddier than hers, his thick brown hair was long and his beard unkempt. That seductive smile, though, was still the same. Her mind was suddenly flooded with memories of him—how he had rescued her from Eadric's hall the day that her father had been murdered there; how he had sworn to protect her and had escorted her half way around England to bring her to Thurbrand; how he had brought her news of the outside world when, as Cnut's wife, she had been forced to hide in Holderness from Æthelred's wrath. She remembered, too, what they had done together on those long nights when Cnut had abandoned her for months and, after years of resisting, she had finally taken Alric to her bed.

"By all the gods," she breathed, "I am glad to see you." She released Sihtric's arm. "Leave us," she ordered, "and go tell Tyra to prepare food and drink."

Reluctantly Sihtric obeyed, scowling at Alric as he lumbered up the path.

"The hearth Danes who greeted me in your hall are a surly lot," Alric observed, "and this guard dog of yours is no better it seems."

"Sihtric is more of an ungainly pup than a guard dog," she said, "but he is trustworthy and he answers only to me. The Danes in my hall, though, are Cnut's men and I am wary of them, as you should be." She grasped the arm he offered her as they started up the path. "There are still some among them who believe that you murdered Thorkell's brother, either at my behest or Cnut's. Even Thurbrand is suspicious; and because he knows that Cnut is innocent, he suspects that I planned it and you executed it. I'm afraid that the subject of Hemming's death will always be a threat to us, until we can gull Thurbrand, Cnut and everyone else who matters into believing that neither you nor I had a hand in it."

She did not regret ridding the world of Hemming. His greed had threatened to disrupt Swein's plan to conquer England, and because Cnut had refused to act, she and Alric had dealt with him.

She halted, removed from her thumb a ring that held a large ruby and held it out to him.

"Here is your reward for ridding my husband of that particular encumbrance. Keep it hidden though, lest someone see it and wonder what you did to earn it. Now," she said eagerly, "what news do you bring. me of Cnut and Swein?"

"I have heard nothing about Cnut," he said, slipping the ring into a pouch at his belt, "but there are rumors concerning Swein. One is that he was shipwrecked off Cornwall in the spring and drowned."

She caught her breath. Was that why there had been no word from Denmark? Because Swein was dead and his sons were quarreling over who would succeed him?

"Do you believe it?" she asked.

"No," he scoffed. "It is but English wishful thinking. There is another rumor, though, that Swein will return with a vast army and sweep Æthelred from his throne." He grimaced. "Æthelred must believe it, and that is what I have come to tell you. The king has made an alliance with Thorkell, and there are now scores of Danish ships harbored, not just at London, but at Sandwich and Wight Isle as well."

She gaped at him, more alarmed by this news than by the rumor of Swein's drowning. This changed everything. The Danish fleet, when it came, would find England defended by dozens of ships manned by Thorkell's fierce jomsvikings.

"You must warn Cnut," she said. "Take this news to Thurbrand, and he will provide you with a ship. But you must sail at once, while the winds are with you!"

Alric raised a skeptical eyebrow. "If Thurbrand suspects that I murdered Hemming, he is as likely to clap me in chains as give me a ship."

"He will not!" she said, striding forward again and dragging him with her. "Thurbrand may be a bastard but he is not an idiot. He knows of your service to Cnut in the past, and whatever he may suspect about Hemming, without Cnut's approval he will not dare to lift a finger against you."

Thurbrand would provide a ship, she was certain of it. And if Alric reached Denmark in time and warned Cnut of Thorkell's alliance with the English king, what then?

She thought she knew. It would mean another delay. There would be no invasion this summer, and it would not be the wind that prevented it. She would have done it.

She heard Cnut's voice in her head urging her to be patient; but she was not patient. She wanted an end to her exile from the halls of power. She was destined to be a queen and the mother of kings—a prophecy that she would see fulfilled before she was a witless crone.

But she had no choice. Cnut and Swein must be warned and a new plan put in place, all because England's spineless king had managed to make the one alliance that could bring all their efforts to ruin.

Chapter Four

The king's mead hall was crowded with men who stood shoulder to shoulder at the benches, their faces solemn in the light of candles and torches. High above their heads smoke from the central fire flattened into a thin haze, its acrid scent mingling with the aroma of roasting meat and the stink of wet wool and sweat. Outside a northerly wind buffeted the eaves, piercing the unnatural silence inside with a high, mournful wail that was, Cnut thought, fitting for what they were about to do here.

He stood on the dais beside his father and elder brother as the king recited in a loud, commanding voice the names of the dead. Swein had known each of them, his huscarles, men as close to him as his own blood. He had been with them on the day that the sea swallowed them, when they had all been waging a desperate battle to survive.

Like every man in this hall Cnut had only to shut his eyes to imagine the waves rising like mountains above the prow, to hear the thunder of their crashing. They had all heard the tale of how two ships had plunged sideways from the crest of a massive swell, crashing together into the trough between waves, helpless when the wall of water collapsed on top of them to shatter mast and yard and decking into fragments. His father had been one of the few pulled from the sea's grasp into one of the other vessels.

Cnut looked at him, grateful that he was here. Alive. Swein's long, thick mane of hair—once a rusty red like his own—had been white for near as long as he could remember. The beard was forked and studded with rings, and two golden chains hung at his breast, one bearing the hammer and the other the cross. Which god had kept him alive that day, had pushed him up and out of the thrashing waves? Odin or the Christ? It was a question that his father could not answer, so he dared not choose between them.

Cnut hoped that what they had gained from that venture had been worth the loss of two ships and forty men. His father certainly thought so, for his objective had been policy, not plunder. A great deal of silver and gold—some of it wrested from English coastal towns on that same voyage—had been distributed among the Waylisc princes. In exchange they had pledged that when Swein began his campaign to win the English throne, any pleas from King Æthelred for men and arms would go unanswered.

As Swein reached the end of his long recital, he lifted his cup and a shout went up from the men in the hall as they drank to the dead. Now the feasting began and Cnut, seated on his father's left hand, listened as Harald answered Swein's queries about events that had taken place while he was away. His brother's responses were clear and precise, delivered with the confidence of a man who was certain of his future as his father's heir.

At twenty-three Harald was the elder by one year, but Cnut was keenly aware that it marked a vast difference between them. True, they were similar in appearance, although Harald's long mane was dark while Cnut's was the color of rust. They were both tall and thin, broad-shouldered and wiry, and their closely trimmed beards were more red than brown. But if Swein had drowned in that shipwreck off the Waylisc coast, Cnut thought, Harald would have claimed their father's throne, leaving him with nothing. Now, as he considered how close his father had come to dying, Cnut was struck as never before by the tenuous nature of his future, compared to his brother's.

Suddenly aware that the din of voices echoing in the rafters had lessened considerably, Cnut looked up and saw a knot of men entering the hall. Swein halted in mid-question to survey the newcomers who hesitated just inside the screens passage, and Cnut raised a questioning brow at his brother who responded with a shrug.

At the lower tables men were exchanging greetings with the new arrivals and making space for them on the benches. Not strangers, then, Cnut surmised; then he recognized a face that he knew well. The lone figure striding forward—past the intricately carved wooden columns, the long rows of curious eyes, the central hearth and the mead bowl with its ring of ladles—was one who had answered to *him* once. Before that he had been Elgiva's man, and before that her father's.

Cnut felt a tremor of misgiving.

Who did Alric answer to now? And why had he come? It could be for no small thing, for Alric's very life was at risk here. There were men in this hall who believed that he had murdered Jarl Hemming, brother of Swein's old ally, Thorkell. Poison, they said, because Hemming had slumped over dead in the midst of a feast, and the Englishman Alric had been seated nearby. They deemed Alric guilty because he fled rather than face his accusers. Of course, had he not run, Alric would have been slaughtered by Hemming's men, guilty or not, so no one could accuse him of being slack-witted. But no one could be certain, either, that he hadn't killed a Danish warlord, and now here he was, standing before three of them.

He searched the Mercian's face for some clue to his purpose, but Alric was giving nothing away. Nevertheless, Cnut raised his mead cup in silent salute. He might not completely trust Alric, but he liked the man. He was a good companion and warrior, and his skill with foreign tongues made him a useful envoy.

It also made him a useful spy, and his allegiance, Cnut suspected, could be acquired for the right price.

Alric reached the dais, bent the knee, and rose when Swein bid him speak.

"I am come, lord king, at the behest of Thurbrand and," he glanced at Cnut, "at the bidding of your lady wife, my lord."

Cnut froze and asked, "My son?"

"He thrives," Alric replied quickly. "My news concerns Jarl Thorkell, who has made a pact with your enemy, the English king."

Cnut slowly lowered his cup to the table. Whatever trouble he had been anticipating, it had not been this. An alliance between Thorkell and the English must throw all their plans, and his future, into disarray.

Beside him, his father began to ask questions, and Alric to answer. Cnut listened, and it seemed to him that this step could very well prove fatal to his father's years of painstaking preparations for the conquest of England, and the very end of all his own hopes for a future as its ruler.

The next day, Cnut sat with the other members of the king's war council, facing his father and brother across the long trestle table as Alric told it all again. The news did not get any better with repetition, and the revelation of Thorkell's betrayal was greeted with howls of outrage.

"Thurbrand urges you to put off the invasion," Alric concluded when the men quieted enough to listen, "and wait until next year."

This was met with loud protests that Cnut heard with growing irritation. These men saw Thorkell's alliance with Æthelred as a betrayal and an affront to their king, as a challenge that must be met immediately. He understood their wrath well enough, but he knew Thorkell—had trained under him and fought beside him. Thorkell and the jomsvikings who followed him could not be beaten with skill and might alone. It would take wit, cunning, and a vast number of men to defeat him.

He leaned forward and rapped the table for attention.

"You want to punish Thorkell and thrash the English king," he cried, "as do I. But it would be madness to strike while Thorkell's ships guard the coasts. We have been preparing our assault for years, but I remind you that our purpose is conquest—to add England's fertile lands and England's wealth to our Danish empire. To attempt that now, I promise you, would end in failure. If we are to defeat the combined powers of Æthelred and Thorkell, we need more ships, more arms, and more men."

His words appeared to cool the fervor of most of the ship masters. One man, though, surged to his feet, his weathered face suffused with rage, his thin brown hair hanging loose past his shoulders, and his long beard, plaited on both sides of his mouth, quivering with fury.

Cnut glowered at him, for he knew what was coming. Arnor was a good warrior, but quarrelsome and bullheaded, and he was one of those who believed that Alric had murdered Thorkell's brother. Now he was pounding the table, demanding to be heard.

"Thorkell has no love for Æthelred!" Arnor bellowed. "He would be here with us now if some bastard had not murdered his brother and driven him into the arms of the English." He aimed a black look at Alric. "I say, send Thorkell the murderer's head and our old ally will abandon the English and join us."

The clamor grew loud again as Arnor continued to glare at Alric who gazed mildly back at him. Alric, Cnut thought, was certainly capable of murdering a jarl, although it was just as likely that Hemming had drunk himself to death. He wondered how the Mercian would respond to Arnor's accusation. A heated denial? Oaths? Curses?

The room quieted as Alric rose from his bench. But instead of addressing Arnor, he slowly rounded the table to kneel before Swein.

"Lord king, I am innocent of Hemming's murder," he declared, his voice ringing. "But if my head is what is needed to draw Thorkell back to your side, then you must take it."

It was hardly the response that anyone expected, and the chamber pulsed with tension as all eyes focused on the king. Cnut, though, regarded Alric with mild amusement. He would have to add fiendish cleverness to the man's list of talents. Heaving a sigh, he stood up.

"Your offer is generous, my friend," he said, "but because Jarl Thorkell is convinced that you were acting on my orders, the only way to truly appease him would be to send him *my* head as well as yours. I fear that I do not have your generosity of spirit. I prefer to keep my head where it belongs and use it to find a way to defeat England despite Thorkell's defection."

His words were greeted with shouts and a few guffaws that broke the tension until the king roared for silence.

"The death of Thorkell's brother and how it came about is of no consequence," Swein said. "It divides us, and nothing we say here will bring Hemming back or bring Thorkell to heel. His presence in England, though, must be taken into account as we lay our plans." He paused, frowning. "Cnut and Thurbrand have the right of it; we must wait another year before we strike. But when we attack, it must be where Æthelred is weakest, and we must use the coming months to do all that is needed to ensure our success." He flicked his gaze to Cnut. "It is time to make whatever promises or threats are necessary to convince your English wife's powerful Mercian kin to turn against Æthelred, once and for ever. They were willing to support us in the past. How difficult will it be to draw them back into an alliance?"

Cnut frowned, considering.

"Morcar and Siferth, who were part of that earlier agreement, have made their peace with the king," he said, "but I believe they neither like nor trust him. Certainly, they despise his henchman Eadric, and they must fear and resent Æthelred's alliance with Thorkell. I think they can be persuaded to join us and so give us a foothold in northeastern Mercia."

Swein nodded slowly. "Then the first significant force to come against us will likely be the men of East Anglia." He gazed narrowly at Alric. "I have faced their leader Ulfkytel in battle before, and I am not eager to meet him thus again. Can he be persuaded to transfer his allegiance from Æthelred to me?"

Alric pursed his mouth, his expression thoughtful. Cnut had an opinion, but he kept silent, curious to hear what Alric would say.

"Ulfkytel is married to one of Æthelred's daughters," Alric observed, "so he will be reluctant to defy the king. But he is a realist, I think. Convince him that the force you will bring against him will be so large that he could not hope to repel it, and I expect that he will see reason."

Cnut caught his father's eye and nodded.

Swein fixed his gaze on the fire that burned in the central hearth and was silent for a time before he addressed the gathering.

"I am of a mind to proceed with this plan—to use the coming months to build ships and to re-establish the alliances we will need in Mercia and East Anglia. Next year will be soon enough to thrust Æthelred from England's throne. But if any man objects to this, I would hear him now."

There was silence around the table, and it lengthened until Harald asked, "Who will you send to negotiate with the Mercian lords?"

Now Cnut felt his father's eyes on him again.

"What is Cnut's counsel?" Swein asked.

"We send Alric," Cnut replied swiftly, "if he is willing, and Thurbrand with him. They are already known and trusted there, and we must build upon that." He speared a glance at Alric. "We shall send enough silver with you to persuade the Mercians that they have much to gain by aiding us."

"I am your man, my lord," Alric replied, "but it is a delicate and dangerous business. It will only succeed if no rumor of it reaches Wessex."

"Agreed," Swein said, and his dark eyes raked the faces of the men around the table. "No one leaves this chamber until he has sworn by whatever gods he honors to keep secret all that has been said here today."

Cnut joined in the acclamation that followed and in the oath-taking that came after. At a gesture from Swein, though, he stayed behind with Harald after the others had gone.

"I have it in mind to journey to Rouen in the spring," Swein told them, "before we take our fleet to England. Harald, you will go with me."

Harald frowned. "To Rouen! Why? The Norman duke will not aid us in our endeavor, not while his sister is England's queen."

Swein smiled. "Aid comes in many forms," he said. "Sometimes it is given unwittingly. If Richard believes that we will strike England's southern coast, he is likely to warn Æthelred to fortify those defenses. The English will be looking south while we strike in the north."

"It is a long journey to make," Harald objected, "just for the purpose of spreading a false rumor."

Swein was already at the chamber door, but he turned and said, "I have a second objective, as well." He looked pointedly at Harald. "I wish to plant a seed in Richard's mind about a possible marriage alliance between Denmark and Normandy, once Æthelred's queen is a widow."

And then he left them.

Cnut, stunned that his father was planning for events so far in the future, stared in astonishment at the empty doorway.

Harald remarked ruefully, "His idea is not a bad one, assuming that we win the war, that Æthelred conveniently succumbs to disease, a mortal wound or old age, and that Richard can be persuaded to agree to a marriage alliance with his not yet widowed sister."

"Do not underestimate Swein," Cnut advised him. "He will do all that he can to bring each one of those unlikely events to pass—even your marriage to Æthelred's queen."

Harald barked a laugh. "You are probably right." Then he gazed speculatively at Cnut. "I know nothing about Richard's sister," he said, "but I think you do. Some of the shipmen claim that Swein took her captive on one of his raids, and that you were there. If that's true, why have you never spoken of it?"

Cnut poured himself a cup of ale and took a long draught as he thought back to the events of that day, when he had been a mere youth.

Their plan had been to hold the queen hostage on one of their ships and demand a huge ransom for her release. They had failed. He didn't like to talk about failure.

"There is nothing else to tell," he said curtly. "The queen was our captive, and she escaped."

"Surely there is more to the story than that," Harald pressed him. "How many of you were there? How did she escape?"

Cnut stared into his ale cup, searching reluctantly for the words to describe what had happened.

"There were three of us riding with her toward the sea to meet our ship," he said, "but we were unaware that the lady had a knife hidden in her boot. She managed to cut the leading rein to her horse and she fled. I gave chase, and when I caught up with her she threatened me with the blade and railed at me in Danish." He shook his head. "She had been our captive for hours, but until that moment she never once betrayed that she could understand every word we said."

He narrowed his eyes, seeing again the wild look on the queen's face as she glared at him. Something had flickered between them as they stood frozen, their eyes locked—something that even now he could not name. They had both felt it, though. Of that he was certain.

"Go on," Harald said.

Cnut shrugged. "I wrestled the knife away from her, we put her back on her horse, and we rode toward the sea again. We thought that was the end of it." He raised an eyebrow at his brother. "That night on the beach, though, with our ship just offshore struggling to reach us, a handful of English warriors fell on us out of the darkness like a lightning bolt. There was a skirmish, but by the time our ship landed the English had disarmed us and were threatening to kill Swein unless we released the queen." He took another swallow of ale, wiped his mouth with the back of his hand, and shrugged again. "We had to let her go."

He spoke idly enough, but his father had been pinned against a cliff face with a sword point at his throat, and it still galled him that he had been helpless to do anything about it. He had been terrified that his father would be killed, or at the very least that the queen would reveal to her rescuers that he was Swein's son. Had they discovered that, they would have taken him hostage and thrown him into some English dungeon, or worse. But they had let Swein live in exchange for the queen, and she had held her tongue about who he was.

Why had she done that? He had never been able to fathom it.

Harald snorted and said, "She will not be eager to wed a member of the Danish royal house after that. Still, if her brother agrees to the match, what the lady wishes will not matter."

His brother was right, Cnut knew. The widowed queen's wishes would be of little consequence, and her marriage to Harald, if it could be arranged, would be a shrewd political move on both sides.

Later, as Cnut made his way to his quarters, other memories of that night came flooding back to him—how the queen had run from him again on that moonlit beach; how he had caught her and forced her down onto the shingle, pinning her beneath him; how she had grabbed a rock and struck him hard upside the head as she struggled to get free.

How he had thought her magnificent, and wasted as the bride of an aging king.

Suddenly the image of that glimmering girl naked in his brother's bed rose unbidden in his mind, and he was disturbed by it—far more, he suspected, than it would be wise or politic for him to reveal to Harald, or to anyone.

Chapter Five

October 1012
Winchester, Hampshire

Emma knelt before the altar inside St. Peter's tiny church and whispered a prayer of thanksgiving for a summer that had been free of viking raids. Her companions—her stepdaughter Edyth and Siferth's wife Aldyth—knelt beside her in a shaft of dull light that spilled through one of the church's high glazed windows. Emma slanted a glance at Edyth, whose veiled head was bent over tightly clasped hands. Her prayers, Emma thought, would be for her husband. News had reached Winchester that Eadric's tribute-gathering in Wales had led to bloody clashes with a resentful populace and numerous English deaths. Edyth must be afraid of what the future would hold for her and for her young daughter should Eadric not return.

There were many in the kingdom, though, Emma reflected, who feared and despised the ealdorman of Mercia. They would not mourn if he should be forever lost in Wales; and God forgive her, she was one of them. Edyth, who worshipped her husband, could not see it, but Eadric's ambitious scheming was divisive and a danger to the kingdom.

Emma slid her gaze past Edyth to the beautiful Aldyth—tall and slender, her skin creamy and her mouth wide and sensuous. Soon she would be returning with her husband to their estates in Lindsey, much to Aldyth's relief, Emma suspected. Siferth's wife was clearly unhappy at court; she rarely smiled and was nothing like the merry young bride that Emma remembered from their first encounter six years before.

Since then Aldyth had lost her uncle and cousins to the king's vengeance, and her only two children to pestilence—a heavy burden of sorrow for any woman to bear. But Emma believed that there was more than lingering grief lurking behind those always carefully guarded brown eyes. There was some unspoken fear there, some dark secret that seemed to eat away at her.

Emma bit her lip, beset by a vague apprehension that she could not put to rest. She had often speculated that Aldyth's cousin—the scheming Elgiva who had long been presumed dead—might instead be alive and hidden somewhere in the north of England. She could not prove it, for her suspicion was based merely on rumors that had reached her from far off Holderness, but she could think of nothing else that would explain Aldyth's disquiet. And she knew from long experience that Elgiva was like a beautiful but dangerous bird with claws that could do far worse than scratch. Her powerful, ambitious family had anticipated that the widowed Æthelred would take her as his bride, and when he had not, Elgiva had nevertheless insinuated herself into his bed. As his mistress she had been a spiteful presence at court even as her father and brothers had plotted in secret against the king. When their treachery had been discovered Æthelred had sent Eadric to murder Elgiva's father and had ordered her brothers blinded and allowed to die untended in prison. So if Elgiva was still alive she might well be at the heart of some sinister, vengeful plot brewing in the north. Archbishop Wulfstan's frequent warnings of trouble in the shires beyond the Humber might prove more accurate than Æthelred was willing to believe.

Looking toward the barren altar, Emma whispered a plea to the Virgin to shield England and its people from enemies both within and without the kingdom, and she prayed, too, that she was wrong about Elgiva.

At last she crossed herself and stood up to begin a slow tour of the little church. It occupied one corner of a large haga recently granted her by the king, and its condition, and that of all the buildings on the property, must now be her concern. Her reeve had already inspected it, but she had wished to see it for herself.

Edyth, her voice laced with resentment, remarked, "I wonder why the king has given you this property, here within Winchester. The income you will receive from it hardly seems necessary, as you already have numerous estates elsewhere—far more than my mother had."

Emma paused in her inspection to consider her stepdaughter. Edyth, all of eighteen summers old, was wrapped in a cloak lined with the finest fur and clasped with a pin of heavy gold. She was the eldest daughter of the king and had been wed for five years to the wealthiest lord in all of England. Yet despite her wealth and her status, she yearned for the even greater role that would have been hers had her father not taken a second wife. Her discontent had created an unbridgeable gulf of bitterness between them.

Swallowing a curt reply Emma explained, "My other estates are royal lands under my administration, but they are subject to the king's pleasure. He can reclaim them, Edyth, if he so wishes. This property, however, is my personal possession, for my lifetime and even beyond. And your father gave it to me because I requested it."

A request that she had made while the newly appointed bishop of Winchester stood beside her to add his voice to hers. In return for his support, she had drawn up a will bequeathing this property to his cathedral priory upon her death. The bishop had gained much at very little trouble to himself, and now she counted him among her friends. Thus did a queen garner allies.

"One day," she told Edyth, "one of your brothers will be England's king, and I shall need a sanctuary of my own. I intend to build a manor house here for just that purpose."

She saw Edyth's frown at the mention of her brothers and, her inspection completed, Emma moved quickly toward the door to prevent any further discussion. She had no wish to get into a debate over which of Æthelred's six remaining sons was most likely to inherit England's throne. The witan would decide that when the time came, although she was well aware that factions were already forming.

Outside, a steady rain was falling in slanting gusts, but Emma stepped into it briskly, accompanied by her hearth guards and with Edyth and Aldyth at her heels. After picking her way down the slippery, cobbled lane and across the wide High Street, they entered the palace grounds where the yard in front of the great hall was a maelstrom of armed and shouting men, lathered and sodden horses, frantic servants, and half a dozen wains burdened with all manner of bundles.

"It is Eadric!" Edyth's cry was all but drowned by the clamor of men and by a great clap of thunder that shook the heavens.

Emma watched her hasten through the rain toward the hall as Athelstan and Edmund appeared in its doorway, stepping aside to let their sister enter. She would have followed Edyth to hear whatever news

Eadric had brought, but Athelstan shot her a warning glance that brought her to an abrupt halt.

"Let Edyth go alone, my lady," he said, and his expression was grave as he ushered her away from the hall. "The king has need of her. And I would speak with you."

She allowed Athelstan to steer her toward her own apartments, swallowing her questions until they were within doors. She entered the dim antechamber where the wet-nurse paced up and down with Alfred, heavy-eyed, on her shoulder. Aldyth offered to take the child for a time, and Emma paused only long enough to dispose of her wet cloak and order that no one was to disturb her before entering an adjoining room that, at this time of day, was deserted.

"Tell me what has happened," she said. She looked back and forth between Athelstan and his brother. Both their faces were grave, and she felt her heart falter. "Dear God, what is it?"

"Edrid is dead," Athelstan's voice was hoarse with emotion, "killed on the return journey from Wales. He tried to break up a tavern brawl and took a blade meant for Edwig."

His words stopped her breath. She sank onto a bench and closed her eyes, remembering her stepson—fair-haired and blue-eyed like Athelstan. Not yet twenty winters old, Edrid had ever been the self-appointed guardian angel of his troublesome younger brother, Edwig. She understood now why the king had need of Edyth. He would look to his daughter for comfort at news of the death of yet another of his sons. Two lost to illness, one to accident, and now Edrid.

"We only have Edwig's word for what happened," she heard Edmund say, and she opened her eyes to find him in front of her, offering her a cup of wine. She waved it away.

"I don't understand," Emma said. "If it was a brawl, there must have been others there who witnessed it."

"Witnesses have a way of disappearing, my lady, when royal blood is shed," Edmund said sourly.

Athelstan was pacing the floor, distracted with grief, she supposed. And with anger.

"Edwig claims that he was so drunk," Athelstan's voice was rough with emotion, "that he has no memory of who attacked him." He threw back his dripping cloak and ran his hands over his wet face and hair, as if trying to wake himself from a nightmare. "He recalls a quarrel, a few blows, and then nothing until he woke up on the floor and found Edrid lying beside him, dead." He gestured helplessly, "It is all too vague, too suspicious. There are too many gaps."

Emma stared at him with dawning horror. "You cannot think that Edwig killed his brother!"

"No, not that! God forbid! But I think that he knows or suspects who did, and that he is too frightened to say anything." He looked at Edmund. "You were there in the hall when Edwig made his confession to the king. What did you make of it?"

Edmund dropped his eyes to his cup, swirled the wine, and was silent for a time.

Emma watched his face, aware that he was carefully considering how to frame his response. The most observant of all the king's sons, Edmund kept his thoughts close, hidden behind dark eyes that saw a great deal, she suspected, but revealed very little. Athelstan trusted him utterly, relying on his judgment. But she was wary of Edmund. From the first he had damned her as an ambitious queen, and he perceived her sons not as his half-brothers, but only as rivals for their father's throne.

At last Edmund said, "I saw that Edwig was nervous, yes, and that it was not the king's wrath that he feared." He lifted his gaze and met Athelstan's eyes. "It was Eadric's."

She looked from brother to brother, saw Athelstan's nod of agreement, and felt a growing sense of dread.

"Are you saying that Eadric murdered your brother?" she gasped. "Murdered his wife's brother?"

"Eadric," Edmund said, "or one of his men. More likely some wretch that he paid to do it, who is probably dead now, as well."

"But this is all conjecture!" she cried. "You cannot know what happened!"

"Edwig must know," Athelstan said. "If we could get him to tell us—"

"It would do no good, Athelstan!" Edmund's words were clipped and harsh, strained with fury. "Eadric has grown too powerful to be touched. He has men, he has arms, he has wealth, and he can bring a dozen witnesses to attest to his innocence. The king has lost a son, yes; but Eadric has delivered a small mountain of Waylisc tribute as recompense. Did you not see all that treasure out there? Surely it is sufficient wergild for a murdered ætheling!"

Emma was aghast at what he was implying—that the king would turn a blind eye to his son's murder in exchange for Waylisc silver. She looked to Athelstan, whose face was dark with grief and anger, and she yearned to go to his side, to grieve with him for his brother's loss. But she dared not go near him, not with Edmund watching. They may as well be two distant stars in a darkling sky with nothing between them but endless night.

"This will not be the end of it, Athelstan," Edmund said ominously. "It is only the beginning. You and I would do well to watch our backs."

He pinned her then with dark, suspicious eyes, and although she met his gaze, she felt her pulse beating in her throat for she knew what was in his mind. He was thinking about her son, and what Eadric was willing to do to place Edward—a boy that the ealdorman could easily manipulate—upon England's throne.

"There are now only three æthelings standing between your son and the crown, my lady," Edmund said. "I congratulate you." He raised his cup to her, drained it, and slammed it on a table as he stalked from the chamber.

Emma looked helplessly at Athelstan.

"What if you are wrong about this? What if Edwig is telling the truth and Eadric had nothing to do with your brother's death at all?"

"How would that make a difference?" he asked bitterly. "Eadric would still be my enemy, as he has been for years. And my brother would still be dead."

His eyes lingered on hers for a moment, and she murmured his name. She wanted to go to him, ached to comfort him, but he merely shook his head, then followed his brother.

When he had gone she sat unmoving, rigid with grief and despair.

Athelstan was wrong. The manner of Edrid's death did make a difference, because the suspicion that it had raised was yet another wedge between the powerful Eadric and the eldest sons of the king. With no way to discover the truth, their enmity would only grow and fester, fed by bitterness and mistrust. It would widen the fractures that already existed within the royal family, fractures that must weaken the entire kingdom. She felt sick just thinking about it, and she was very much afraid that the outcome would be disastrous for all of them.

Chapter Six

March 1013
Ashby, Lindsey, Mercia

Swathed in furs against an icy breeze, Elgiva reined in her horse at the crest of a low hill. Alric did the same, and below them the wolds of Lindsey sprawled in waves of winter brown and green while above them clouds were gathering from the west. There would be a storm before nightfall, and Elgiva shivered inside her furs.

"How long does it take a man to make up his mind?" she murmured.

"You are too impatient, lady," Alric said. "Such decisions take time."

Yes, she was impatient! Siferth, Morcar, Thurbrand, even Alric could not seem to comprehend that time was short; that Swein's plans for the conquest of England could not be set in motion until his alliance with the Mercians was in place.

Their efforts to accomplish that, though, had been delayed for months. By the time that Alric had returned to Holderness with word from Swein and Cnut, an early snow was already carpeting the ground. She had been but three weeks out of childbed, yet she would have departed for Lindsey the next day if Thurbrand had not balked. He had insisted that there was no need for haste and had holed up in his northern fastness like a hibernating bear. Only with the arrival of spring did he rouse himself to make this journey south, and then the bastard would have left her in Holderness with her newborn daughter and young son had Alric not taken her part. Ten days of travel on filthy roads, bedeviled by rain and by numerous misdirections, had brought them here at last, where they had been forced to wait another two days for Siferth's brother to join them.

She had filled the time by listening hungrily to news of Æthered and his Norman queen, of their Danish ally Thorkell, of ship placements, Waylisc tribute, and the death of Edrid ætheling. Yesterday, at last, they had delivered Swein's offer of an alliance to both Siferth and Morcar, but they had yet to receive an answer.

She looked out across the wolds, and all the land that she could see was held by Siferth. Her cousin Aldyth's husband was a man of great wealth now, but not, it appeared, a man of decision.

"When my father was alive, Siferth pledged that he would support Swein's war against Æthelred," she said. "Yet now he hesitates. Why?"

"He is not the same man that he was seven years ago, my lady," Alric replied. He indicated back the way they had come, to the tower of Siferth's new stone church that proclaimed his high standing with God and king. "He has much more to lose now. The king has been openhanded with both brothers of late; his generosity must weigh heavily on their minds." He paused, and then said reluctantly, "Also, there is your cousin."

Elgiva sighed. Her cousin; who was fond of the queen and terrified of the king.

"Yes," she agreed. "I expect that Aldyth has been arguing vehemently against this alliance." Aldyth was a fool. But surely Siferth knew that. Then she frowned because until this moment she had not allowed herself to even admit that Siferth might choose to side with Æthelred. "What will Swein do if Siferth and Morcar refuse him, if they go to Æthelred and tell him everything?"

"Tell Æthelred what?" Alric asked. "Confess that they are friendly with the Danes? That their report that you were dead was a lie? That they helped arrange your marriage to Swein's son and that you have already given him two children?" Alric shook his head slowly. "No, their secret sins against the king are far too many; and the king, as you know, is not a forgiving man."

"So they must ally with Swein," she murmured. Despite Aldyth's fears.

"They have no choice," he agreed, "and they know it. What they are trying to determine, I imagine, is how much support they can provide, and what recompense they will demand for it."

Upon returning to the manor they went directly to the great hall. Large and lavishly furnished, its lime-washed walls were hung with brightly colored embroideries, and its stone-flagged floor was strewn with hides. It was far more lavish than her father's hall had been, Elgiva thought resentfully as she strode toward the central hearth. Clearly Siferth had prospered over the last seven years, while her father and brothers lay buried in some ditch and she had been forced to cower in Northumbria like a hunted deer.

She was surprised that the hall was all but empty, for at mid-morning it should have been filled with family and servants. Thurbrand sat at a trestle table, fierce-looking beneath his wild mane of black hair as he grimaced a greeting at them. Beside him two of the retainers who had traveled with them from Holderness faced each other across a tafl board, intent on their game. Her woman Tyra stepped from the shadows to take Elgiva's cloak.

"Where is the household?" Elgiva asked in the Danish that Tyra had taught her years before.

"In the chapel," Tyra said.

"Everyone?"

"No doubt Siferth is praying for guidance," Thurbrand grunted, "and likely he wants a crowd with him in church to ensure that he has his God's attention. He would do better to have Tyra cast the rune sticks and tell him who will win the coming conflict."

That would have done him no good, Elgiva thought. She had already bid Tyra consult the runes, but the woman could tell her only that Swein would arrive before the harvestide and that Cnut would be with him; that much she already knew.

Alric had joined the group at the table and now Elgiva followed him, placing herself where she could watch the door.

"I hope that while he is in his church he finds enough courage to bite the hand of Æthelred rather than lick it," she snapped, this time in English; and looking up, she saw Siferth enter the hall, flanked by his wife and brother.

"Brave words, my lady," Siferth sneered, "coming from one who for three years has feigned death to avoid the king's wrath."

She watched him approach—this tall, sandy-haired man of middle years who was the most powerful of the king's thegns in the Five Boroughs and whose scornful glare and derisive words made her want to slap him. She was vaguely aware of Thurbrand getting to his feet beside her and gesturing to his men and Tyra to leave, but she had eyes only for Siferth.

"How dare you chide me," she snarled, "for trying to stay alive while you ate from the king's hand like his pet hound. Yes, I hid from the king to avoid his wrath. I hid because my father pledged my hand to Swein's son and thus made me Æthelred's enemy and Eadric's prey. I was no more to my father than one of these." She snatched and held up a handful of game pieces before flinging them to the floor.

"Lady, you go too far," Thurbrand growled, but she ignored him, too furious to stop the bitter words.

"I was sacrificed for my father's ambition, and you knew all about it, Siferth—knew and approved. Yet here you are," she spread her arms, "a great lord, while my father rots in an unmarked grave."

Morcar, standing beside his brother, clapped his hands slowly, mocking her. She glared at him. He was a younger version of Siferth, with the same lean frame and ginger hair, and the same sardonic twist to his mouth that so infuriated her.

"You forget, my lady," Morcar said lightly, "that while we were all but licking the king's boots to earn his trust, we were keeping you safe by assuring him that you were dead." His eyes flicked to the golden chains that she wore around her neck. "Forgive me, but you do not appear to have suffered much hardship as Cnut's bride."

She touched the chains at her breast. She had worn them to impress these men with Swein's largesse. Apparently, she had succeeded. She drew in a long breath to calm herself.

Siferth and Morcar were allies, not enemies. She must not antagonize them, no matter the provocation. She crossed her arms to mimic Morcar's stance.

"You are right, my lord," she said. "King Swein and his son have treated me well, as they do all those who prove themselves worthy of their regard. You have already heard what Swein would ask of you. Have you made up your mind?"

She glanced at Aldyth. Her eyes were red-rimmed from weeping, and that was answer enough. Now it was merely a matter of striking a bargain.

Siferth raised an inquisitive brow. "And if we agree to his requests, what will it bring us?"

Thurbrand barked a laugh. "We have already brought you gold," he protested. "What more do you want?"

Siferth smiled and said, "Mercia, I think, will be in need of an ealdorman when that piece of filth Eadric is gone."

Elgiva glanced from Siferth to Morcar, and back again. "Two ealdormen, I think," she said. "One in the east and one in the west. There will, of course, be lands to go with the titles."

Swein had sent no such promises of lands or titles, and she sensed Thurbrand, beside her, about to burst with outrage at what she had just offered. But it was done, and Thurbrand could hardly rebuke her for it—not here, in any case. The only thing that mattered was to ensure that this agreement was in place and that Swein would get all that he needed.

Siferth turned to his brother, and a look passed between them, a silent message—of agreement, she hoped.

But Aldyth clutched at Siferth's arm.

"Husband!" she hissed. "I beg you—"

"Be quiet," he snapped, shaking her off. He turned to Thurbrand. "We are agreed, then." He pulled up a stool and gestured to Thurbrand and Alric to join him at the table while Morcar took his place at Siferth's side. "When will Swein's fleet land?" Siferth asked. "And where?"

Elgiva recognized dismissal when she saw it. For once, she did not care; her part in this was finished. Aldyth was already striding from the hall, and Elgiva followed her, leaving the men to their battle planning.

Her cousin had not gone far. The rain that had been threatening all morning had arrived, and she stood sheltering from it beneath the porch roof. She was a tall woman, and all her life Elgiva had had to look up at her. How she had always hated that! But just now Aldyth was slumped against a wooden column, and her head was bent. She was, Elgiva thought as she stepped up beside her, the very picture of despair; as fragile as glass. Her cousin would surely break before this was over.

Aldyth said, "I wish that you had died with your father and brothers." She was not looking at Elgiva, but into the distance, through the falling rain. "If you had, my husband would not be in there now plotting new treachery against the king."

Elgiva grasped her arm and turned her so they were facing each other.

"Do not delude yourself, cousin," she said roughly. "Your husband is ambitious, and the Danish king has much to offer him. Even if I were dead this alliance would have been struck, sooner or later. They simply would have chosen some other woman to seal their agreement. Be grateful that you have no daughter to be used as a bargaining chip."

Aldyth's eyes clouded with tears.

"Ah, but I did have a daughter, Elgiva. She was just two winters old when she died last Christmastide. You did not know that, did you? No. And nor do you care because the only children who matter to you are your own. My son did not matter to you all those years ago when you came to my hall along with the pestilence that killed him and left you alive! Death follows in your wake, Elgiva, and now you would drag my husband into war—"

"It is men who start the wars, Aldyth!" Whatever pity she had felt for her cousin soured into aggravation. "And men like Siferth are always eager to fight them!"

"But it is women like you who goad them into it! Do you think that I don't know what you want? You will never be satisfied until your Danish prince has won you a crown, and you do not care what it costs!" Her eyes flashed. "I curse you! You and your children. May they die in your arms as mine did, and may you never know a moment's happiness with your viking lord!"

Elgiva responded by slapping her so hard that Aldyth stumbled sideways. Almost instantly, though, Aldyth returned the blow, and Elgiva fingered her burning cheek as she watched her cousin stalk through the rain to her apartments.

Aldyth, apparently, was not as fragile as she had supposed. And that, combined with her fear of the king, made her cousin dangerous.

She would have to warn Siferth to keep a close watch on his wife, lest her terror drive her to betrayal.

Chapter Seven

May 1013
Greetham, Roteland

Emma sat in the finest chair that the reeve's hall at Greetham afforded, her head bent over a lavishly embroidered pall of purple godwebbe that she would soon present to the abbey at Peterborough. The fading afternoon light, though, had become too dim for the fine needlework that her task demanded, so she straightened and set the fabric aside. The last golden angel would have to wait.

Beside her, Wymarc had gathered into her lap a smoc intended for Alfred and was stitching a length of brightly colored tablet-woven trim to the hem. Alfred himself sat on the floor at their feet, oblivious to both of them. A small coffer—a gift from Greetham's reeve—was open before him, and under the watchful eyes of his nurse he was happily despoiling it of the variously shaped blocks of wood that he had found nestled inside.

Emma relaxed against the back of her chair and glanced appreciatively around the hall—its interior freshly plastered and painted, its roof newly thatched, and the scent of beeswax from every wooden surface filling the room. Until today, though, she had spent very little time within doors. She had been far too busy inspecting villages, barns, bridges, churches, weaving sheds, flocks of sheep, herds of cattle, and a stud farm. From here she would go to the abbey at Peterborough, and shortly after that she would make her way to more of her properties before joining the king's court at Windsor for the Midsummer feast.

She could recall similar journeys that she had made when, as a child, she had accompanied her father on his summer progresses across Normandy. For her they had meant welcome respite from confinement behind the ducal walls of Rouen, but for her father and brothers—in addition to the feasting, hunting, and horse-bartering that went on—they had been far more serious endeavors. She could still remember her father's solemn expression on one occasion when he had been speaking to her brother Richard about his duties as a lord.

You must familiarize yourself with all of your properties and with the men who have charge of them. You must make them believe that they can place their trust in you. And that trust, of course, must work in both directions.

Trust. Here in England it was what bound villein to lord, and lord to king—an invisible web that knotted shires and towns and hundreds into a realm that was no stronger than that slender web of trust.

She frowned. It seemed to her unlikely that she had established any strong bonds of trust with the men that she had met in Roteland, except, perhaps, for the reeve. Her time here had been too brief; they did not know her, nor she them.

The hall around her was filling now with the reeve's household and with her own as preparations for the evening meal began. She saw Father Martin making his way toward her, men and women stepping out of his path in deference to his advanced age and his status as her priest. His grey hair was streaked with white now, and his eyesight, she realized as she saw him peering closely at a bit of parchment in his hand, was weakening. His mind, though, was still sharp. Like Wymarc, he had come with her from Normandy and was still one of her closest advisors. The bond of trust between them, at any rate, was as strong as a queen could wish.

"My lady," he said, "a message has come from Abbot Ælfsy at Peterborough. It concerns your stepdaughter, Wulfhilde," he said. Then he read aloud, "Lord Ulfkytel's wife has arrived at the abbey and requests that you meet with her here. I pray that you will grant this, my lady, for I believe that some misfortune weighs upon her mind."

Emma met the priest's concerned gaze. He knew, just as she did, that this was the abbot's way of alerting her to expect trouble. What kind of trouble, though?

Wulfhilde was the youngest but one of Æthelred's four daughters. Her younger sister, Mathilda, had been pledged to the church and sent to Wherwell Abbey as a babe. The others, though, had been wed to powerful lords to ensure their husbands' allegiance to the king. No one

could fault Æthelred for disposing of his daughters thus; it was how
alliances were forged all over Christendom and even among the pagans.
But the girls had been so young! Wulfhilde had become the bride of a
grown man when she was barely twelve.

Emma recalled her first meeting with her stepdaughters, and how
Wulfhilde, only three winters old then and trusting as a kitten, had
climbed into her lap and into her heart. Had the girl been able to soften
the heart of the man she had wed—a man so fierce in battle that even the
Danes feared him?

It had been more than two years since Ulfkytel had brought his wife
with him to attend the king's council, and the vague excuses offered for
her absence had made Emma uneasy. Had Wulfa chosen to stay
behind in East Anglia, perhaps worried that her sisters—already
mothers—would shame her because she was still childless? Or had she
been kept there against her will? She supposed that she was about to
find out.

Two days later, Emma guided her horse along the Fen Road that
ran beside the River Nene. Wymarc and Father Martin rode on either
side of her, banner men rode in front of her, and behind her trailed a
long procession of her household attendants, along with carts, pack
horses, and an escort of three score mounted hearth guards. In the distance she could just make out a darker smudge against the grey sky and
she thought that it must be the abbey walls that rose solidly above the
wraithlike mists of the fens. Golden Burgh it had once been called,
because of its high walls and the many precious relics enshrined within.

It was after midday when she entered those protective walls and was
welcomed by the entire community, led by Abbot Ælfsy. She and the
abbot were old friends, for he frequently attended the king's councils.
He was a thin, spry little priest, perhaps forty winters old, whose ginger
hair and seemingly boundless energy reminded her of a fox kit. During
the formalities occasioned by her visit Emma searched the gathering for
Wulfhilde but did not find her.

"She will attend you once you are settled," the abbot replied when
she asked him about Wulfa. "She wishes to meet with you in private.
Something is worrying her, poor lady, although she conceals it well. I
asked her to confide in me, but she insisted that she would speak only

to you. It may be," he steepled his fingers, his face thoughtful, "that it is some matter that can only be shared with a woman." He lifted brown eyes to hers. "As you know she is more than three years wed now; and although we pray daily to learn that Ulfkytel will soon have an heir, we have been disappointed."

Not as disappointed, Emma thought, as Wulfhilde's husband must be. And the lack of a child was always considered the fault of the wife.

Late that afternoon, as she and Wymarc strolled through the abbey garden, Wulfhilde came in search of her. She was fifteen winters old now, and as Emma embraced her she recalled how, as a child, Wulfa would come to her for help whenever she was hurt or upset. But the sorrows of a girl were much easier to soothe than those of a woman. There were lines of weariness about Wulfa's eyes, and Emma was only too aware that there were a great many difficulties in a woman's life that even a queen could not unravel. She recognized, as well, what the abbot had not—that her stepdaughter was with child.

Wymarc offered to leave the two of them alone, but Wulfa begged her to stay. She was hungry for news of the royal household, and as they walked about the paths that crisscrossed the abbey garth she listened attentively to the answers to all her questions. Emma noted that Wulfa did not ask about the king, nor did she reveal anything about herself.

The abbot was right, she thought. Her stepdaughter was skilled now at concealing whatever was troubling her. Eventually, though, it had to come out, and she made for a stone bench large enough for the three of them to sit.

"Now, daughter," she said gently, taking Wulfa's hand, "I wish you to tell me what it is that troubles you."

Wulfa's brow creased into a frown, and Emma suspected that she was searching for the proper words. At last, drawing in a heavy breath she said, "I am concerned for my husband."

Emma gazed at her in surprise. This was not what she had thought to hear.

"Is Ulfkytel ill?" she asked.

Wulfa shook her head and smiled sadly. "No, it is nothing like that. But something is wrong and I do not know—" She drew another long breath. "Ulfkytel went to London at Easter to attend the king's witan, but when he returned he did not come alone. He was accompanied by a large force led by Siferth and Morcar of Lindsey. Ulfkytel bade me make them all welcome, but I could see that he was angry about something." She shook her head then and corrected herself. "No, it was more than anger. Emma, he was afraid."

So, Emma thought, this was a political problem, and not some rift between husband and wife.

"Did Ulfkytel tell you what was wrong?"

"I asked him, but he refused to answer me. When I pressed him he grew angry and raged that it was none of my concern. We argued and," her voice broke, but she steadied herself. "My husband had never hit me before; but he was in such a rage that I do not think he even knew what he was doing."

Emma squeezed Wulfa's hands in mute sympathy. A wife—even a queen—had little recourse against a husband's violence.

"The men left the next day," Wulfa went on, her voice strained with emotion, "and Ulfkytel went with them. He refused to tell me where he was going or when he would return, but I could see that something was very wrong."

Yes, Emma thought. Something was wrong, and it had nothing to do with Wulfa although she suffered for it. Ulfkytel was the military leader of East Anglia, a powerful man and a great warrior. What was it that he feared? Or whom?

"I do not wish to return to Thetford," Wulfa said, her voice rough with unshed tears. "I have been an outsider at my own hearth from the moment that I arrived there as a bride. The king is feared there and hated; and when my husband's people look at me they see Æthelred's daughter, not Ulfkytel's wife. Now that my husband is absent, I am afraid." She looked up with pleading eyes. "I do not know where to go."

Emma drew the girl into her arms, her mind busily searching for some practical way to help. She knew from experience how cold such a life among strangers could be and how helpless and frightened Wulfa would feel as she prepared for the coming birth.

"Does Ulfkytel know that you are carrying his child?" she asked, and at Wulfa's look of surprise added, "Did you think I wouldn't see the signs?"

Wulfa smiled sadly. "I could not bring myself to tell him. Not while he was so angry."

"My lady," Wymarc said, "can she not come with us to Windsor?"

Wulfa shook her head. "That is not the answer," she said bitterly. "I have considered it, but my father would only send me back to Thetford."

Emma agreed. Wulfa was a pledge between her husband and the king, and if she returned to her father it might sever the bond that, as far as any of them knew, still existed between king and thegn. Æthelred would not allow it.

But there might be another answer.

"Wulfa must remain in East Anglia," she said, "but she need not go to Thetford." She placed her hands on Wulfa's shoulders. "When I leave here, I shall go toward Ipswich, to my Shotley estate. Come with me! Some of your mother's attendants still dwell there, folk who will remember you from when you were a child and who will care for you while you await the birth of your babe. Wymarc can stay there with you if you wish." She studied her stepdaughter's face and was encouraged by the glimmer of hope she read there.

"But how will I get word to my husband? I do not know where he is."

"Send word to Thetford. Ulfkytel must return there eventually. Explain that you need rest and seclusion just now, and ask him to come to you at Shotley." She cupped Wulfa's cheek. "When you do return to Thetford, it will be with Ulfkytel's babe in your arms, and then the hearts of his people must soften toward you. Children, I promise you, can work miracles."

She hoped that it would be so, although she knew that all too often it was not. A great deal would depend on Ulfkytel's relationship—not with his wife, but with the king.

She knew little of Ulfkytel, except that Athelstan had always counted him among his friends and supporters. But the king's alliance with Thorkell had strained old allegiances, and the news that Wulfa had shared with her today raised burning questions in her mind. Where did Ulfkytel go with the lords Morcar and Thurbrand? And what had occurred on that long journey from London to Thetford that had put him in such a rage?

Chapter Eight

June 1013
Windsor, Berkshire

Æthelred arrived in the palace yard with Ealdorman Eadric at his side and a large hunting party behind him. He grimaced as he eyed half a dozen hard-ridden mounts already hobbled near the great hall. He hoped to God that whoever was lying in wait for him within would make short work of what they had to say. He was tired, he was thirsty, his bad leg ached, and despite the chill of late afternoon, he was sweating with exertion from the hunt and the long ride.

Dismounting, he gestured to Eadric to follow him and they made for the entrance to the royal quarters where his steward was waiting.

"Who is it?" he grunted.

"The bishops of Rochester and London, my lord. They have only just arrived and have demanded an immediate audience."

Insistent churchmen. That boded ill. Either they wanted something from him, or they had come to warn him of some impending disaster.

"Where are they?"

"In your private chamber," Hubert said. Then, hesitantly, he added, "The queen is with them."

Of course she was. Emma never missed an opportunity to meddle in affairs that were none of her concern—like Ulfkytel's dealings with Morcar and his brother that she found so suspicious. That was likely some local dispute and no business of hers. Now she was listening, no doubt, to whatever matter the bishops had brought, and she would not hesitate to offer him advice he did not want.

Scowling, he made his way up the stairs and, as he paused for a moment, unseen, in the doorway, he was surprised by the profound silence in the chamber. Shafts of pale daylight streaming through the narrow window embrasures offered some illumination, and a bracket of candles threw light on the needle and the length of silk clutched, unattended, in Emma's hands. She was seated near the center of the room and Ælfhun of London sat on a chair beside her, his grey head bowed as if in prayer. Godwine of Rochester stood at one of the windows, and might have been counting the ducks on the mill pond for all he knew because there was nothing else out there to see.

Emma, he realized, was casting uneasy glances at her two companions, and he guessed that whatever ill news the bishops had brought, they had not yet shared it with the queen. Or she had not yet found a way to pry it out of them.

He entered the chamber, called for ale and lowered himself into his chair, sighing with relief as the pain in his leg eased. Eadric came to stand at his side and Hubert took his accustomed place at the writing stand in the corner. Bishop Ælfhun stood and offered him a low bow, and Æthelred noticed that there was a man in the shadows along the wall who had dropped to one knee. He wore leather boots and breecs, an embroidered tunic, and a fine woolen cloak. After a moment he was able to place him. Brihtwold, a ship's master and wealthy merchant with close ties to the London bishop.

"Well, my lords," he addressed the bishops brusquely, "What is this about?"

Bishop Godwine—stout, with a fringe of curly hair on his head and a beard the color of iron—left the window to stand beside the tall, silver-haired Ælfhun. Neither man seemed in any hurry to speak, and Godwine was looking down at Emma with an expression on his face of—what was it? Grief? Regret?

Christ! Was Godwine about to denounce the queen? That would be a welcome change. Usually the bishops bobbed and twittered at her side like pet starlings.

He leaned forward a little in his chair, eager now and curious. Finally Bishop Godwine cleared his throat to speak.

"Lord king," he said, "I have had news of King Swein of Denmark. It appears that he did not drown in the Severn."

Æthelred recoiled as if the bishop had raised his hand and struck him. It was a bitter blow, if it was true. God—or the devil—must have some terrible purpose in allowing Swein Forkbeard to remain on this earth. He wished to heaven that he knew what it was

"Are you sure of this?" he asked.

Bishop Godwine's eyes flicked again to Emma as he said, "A courier from the Archbishop of Rouen brought word to me at Rochester several days ago that King Swein is very much alive."

"I see." The damned churchmen knew more about his enemies than he did. "And what makes the Rouen archbishop so certain of this?"

Bishop Godwine pursed his mouth and took a long breath.

"The archbishop and his brother Duke Richard met with Swein in Rouen a sennight ago."

Eadric muttered a curse, and Æthelred speared a glance toward Emma. She was gazing steadily at Bishop Godwine, her face as blank as a cloudless sky. But the needle and silk lay discarded in her lap, and her tightly twined fingers told him what her face did not. She was afraid. Had she known what Godwine was going to say? Known that her brothers had been parleying with Æthelred's enemies? He had wed her to forestall just such an event as this, yet here they were in the midst of it—like a nightmare from which he could not wake.

"My lord," Godwine said, "the purpose of the archbishop's message—"

"Never mind the archbishop's purpose!" Eadric interjected. "What did Forkbeard want with Richard?"

"What do you think he wanted, my lord?" Godwine snapped. "He wanted an alliance! He wanted Norman ships and warriors to bring against us along with his own!"

Eadric spat another curse and Æthelred echoed it. If the Danes and Normans allied against him they would be an unstoppable foe. He felt a dull pain begin to throb at his temple.

"But Duke Richard refused him!" Godwine added quickly. "The archbishop assured me that the Danish king left with nothing more than a pledge of continued peace between Normandy and Denmark."

"And what is that assurance worth, bishop?" Eadric sneered. "Duke Richard is clearly negotiating with our enemies and I cannot believe that

Swein left his court empty-handed! Why should we take the archbishop's word as gospel?"

"Because he sent a warning as well! That the Danish fleet will strike soon, and that it will land at Sandwich."

"*Good Christ!*" Eadric swore, "that is no more than we already knew, or guessed. Lord king," his voice was insistent, "even if Richard has done no more than give Swein a pledge of peace, he has pitted himself against us. The friend of our enemy is no friend to us."

"Lord Eadric!" Emma's outraged cry rang through the chamber. "You wrong my brother! Richard would never—"

"Richard be damned!" Æthelred shouted at her. "When has he ever been a friend to us?" He glared at Godwine. "Swein will strike soon, you say. When is that? Tomorrow? Next week? Next month? Without that knowledge, bishop, your warning is worthless. If I call out the fyrd now and Swein delays until Michaelmas I shall have fed thousands of men for three months, while our fields go unharvested. Swein is coming, yes! But I must know when!"

Bishop Ælfhun, who had been silently listening, now spoke decisively. "It will be at Lammastide." He turned and beckoned to the shipmaster. "Brihtwold here is my eyes and ears in Rouen when I need information that I cannot attain through ecclesiastical channels. He has news that I thought you should hear from him directly."

Æthelred studied the merchant who now dropped to one knee before him. He was fair-haired and stocky, with a full beard and a high, broad forehead that bespoke intelligence. Brihtwold was the bishop's spy, it seemed—the perfect role for a merchant who was likely familiar with every language that could be heard in the markets of Rouen. No doubt he frequented the riverside taverns in Richard's ducal stronghold to listen when tongues had been loosened by Norman wine.

"Well?" Æthelred said.

"A call has gone out all across the northern lands, lord king, for ships and men," Brihtwold said. "The muster is to be on the Danish coast at Ribe in mid-July."

"They will strike us as the harvest begins," Ælfhun added, "when food will be plentiful for a ravaging army."

Æthelred stroked his temple in a vain effort to ease the pain there.

"And when men will be least willing to leave their fields to fight an enemy in some other shire," he mused. How many would answer the

English call to arms? And how large an army would they face? He turned to Brihtwold. "Did you discover anything about the number of ships in Swein's fleet?"

But the merchant shook his head. "No numbers, my lord. There was heated talk, though, about Thorkell and the forty ships he has now pledged to you. That has weakened Swein's hand, they say, although not his resolve. Thorkell's defection may be why Swein is forced to search beyond his borders for men and ships."

"If Duke Richard has in fact turned him down," Eadric said, "Swein's fleet may be far smaller than he would wish. That would be to our advantage. Still," he cautioned, "it would be unwise to depend on that."

Æthelred nodded slowly. "We must be ready with as many men as we can muster." He looked at Bishop Godwine. "We shall need all the food stores that you can supply, bishop, once our forces begin to assemble. Hubert, send word to the Canterbury archbishop that we shall look to him for food and horses and arms. And summon my sons and every minister within a day's ride to meet with me here in three days. At that time we shall appoint a date for the marshalling of the fyrds of Wessex and Mercia."

The pain at his temple surged suddenly and he closed his eyes against it. He was tired, and he could do nothing more today. All had been set in motion.

He dismissed the men, but when his wife, too, would have left he ordered her to stay. "Your brother," he said darkly, "continues to entertain my enemies at his court and that, lady, is a dangerous game."

She stood before him, clutching that length of silk like a shield, her mouth set in a defiant line.

"This would not be the first time, my lord, that the Danish king has arrived in Normandy, uninvited. If he offered no threat and asked for parley, my brother could hardly refuse him food and shelter."

"And if Richard has given him more than that?"

"In that case, my lord, I think you would have heard nothing at all of Swein's appearance at my brother's court! You heard Bishop Godwine! Swein asked for ships and men, and Richard refused."

"You are certain of that, are you?"

"Yes, I am certain. My brother is your ally and I am his bond to you."

He grunted, searching her face for guile and seeing only a bold confidence which he suspected was exactly what she wished him to see. Then a movement behind her drew his gaze to the shadows. He stared, disbelieving, while a cold thrill ran down the back of his neck.

"My lord?" The sound of Emma's voice seemed to come to him as if from a great distance, faint amid the roaring in his ears.

"Leave me," he whispered, and when she placed a hand upon his sleeve he shook her off and shouted, "Leave me!"

Alone, he stared at the long wall where the flickering candlelight did not reach. There, in the grey stillness, the ghost of his murdered half-brother was watching him with baleful eyes.

It had been a twelve month and more since that blood drenched face had last tormented him—so long that he had been convinced that Edward's shade would trouble him no more. It seemed that he had been wrong.

"Why have you come back?" Æthelred's voice was nearly a sob. "I did not steal your crown! That was the work of others!" He had been a mere child, too frightened to shout a warning before the knives fell and he watched his brother die.

He tried to stand, but his limbs had turned to water, and even the hand he tried to raise to ward the thing away would not obey him.

"What do you want?" he whispered.

The shadow grew and shrank and grew again until the flickering movement dizzied him and he forced his eyes to shut. When he opened them again Edward's wraith was gone, and his question hung in the air, unanswered.

Chapter Nine

lgiva allowed one of Thurbrand's men to help her dismount, and pulling her cloak about her, she gazed up at Thurbrand's great hall where Cnut awaited her. She had been summoned here from Redmere to attend her husband, and now she waited while the cart laden with her bundles, coffers, attendants, and two children lumbered to a halt. Had it been up to her, she would have left the children behind, but the message had been clear.

Cnut will see you at Aldbrough now. Bring your children. Be prepared to travel.

He had summoned her. Summoned her! As if she were a household slave and not his wife. He seemed to have forgotten that she was an ealdorman's daughter and the key to the success of this entire venture.

She nearly ground her teeth when she thought of how she had been ill-used these past months. Once she had secured Siferth's pledge of support for King Swein's campaign, she had been ignored. Even Alric had deserted her. He was Cnut's man now, or Swein's, and gone on some mission she knew nothing about.

It was all Thurbrand's doing, she was certain of that. Whatever messages had come from across the Danish Sea had been relayed to him, and that bastard had told her next to nothing. He rarely answered her questions, and when he did it was with hints that he fed to her like table scraps that he might toss to a dog. She had bribed his people for news, but she could never be certain if what they told her was truth or rumor.

Thurbrand had kept her deaf and blind because, as he was ever quick to remind her, he believed that women should not meddle in matters of great import. The brute was wrong about that. It may be that women did not fight in the shield wall, but they had minds and tongues. Their words could sway the actions of their men, and although a fool like Thurbrand would not listen to a woman's counsel, Cnut would. He was no fool, and he was nothing like Thurbrand.

She took quick stock of her children now. Swein, two winters old and the image of Cnut with his coppery hair and dark eyes, had already managed to cover himself in mud up to his knees despite Tyra's efforts to corral him. Nine-month-old Thyri was clutched in the arms of her wet-nurse, invisible beneath layers of swaddling. They looked more like beggars than royal offspring.

She muttered an oath under her breath. They should have been richly garbed and gilded for this meeting so they could be properly acknowledged as Cnut's son and daughter in front of his men. She should be gowned in silk and in silver, but the messengers Cnut had sent for her had been adamant that she must leave without delay. She would have to hide her irritation about it, greet her husband with as loving an expression as she could summon, and play the part of dutiful wife. For now, at least.

Once inside the hall she found it was just what she expected—noisy and filled with rough men, half of them roaring drunk, she guessed, and the rest well on the way. She made sure that her little company was behind her, then followed the door ward as he pushed, elbowed and kicked his way through the groups of shipmen. She searched for Thurbrand's wife as she went, but could not find her among the women who scurried about to fill ale cups. Hardly a surprise. Catla was a mouse, and far too timid to endure the chaos of so many men. She would be cowering in her quarters or busying herself at the kitchens or the brew house. Anywhere but here.

As they neared the far end of the hall, she could see Cnut seated at a table. He looked much as he did when he had left her more than a year ago. His hair, darker than their son's, was the color of rust and he wore it loose so that it fell to his shoulders. His beard was thicker than she remembered and he looked older than his twenty-three winters.

There was gold at his neck and arms, she noted approvingly, marking his status as the son of a king—although to her mind there was not enough of it. Beside him Thurbrand was nodding, his face half hidden behind his ale cup as he listened to Cnut. She could not make out Cnut's words, but as she drew closer Thurbrand slammed his cup to the table and roared with laughter.

"So Swein went to Normandy," he said, "gulled Duke Richard, and he gulled the English king for you."

She halted in front of them and looked at her husband with a raised eyebrow. That King Swein had met with the Norman duke was news indeed. She, of course, had heard not a whisper of it.

"I should like to hear more about your father's Norman journey, husband," she said, shouting to be heard above the noise of the hall.

Cnut rose from his stool and, rounding the table, took her hands and kissed them.

"You shall hear that and more soon enough," he said.

"Do these men understand," she waved a hand at the boisterous Danes, "that they are in England not to feast but to fight?"

"They drink before battle, lady," Thurbrand's voice was surly, "because they may not be alive to do it after."

She ignored him. Cnut had turned away from her to pluck his son from Tyra's arms. He swung the boy on to the table so that father and son gazed at each other eye to eye for a few heartbeats. Elgiva watched, amused, as her little wretch of a son reached out and grasped his father's hair.

Cnut gave a low growl, but that only made little Swein laugh and tug again.

"The lad has courage," Cnut said. Then glancing at her, "He needs a brother."

She would have asked him how they were to accomplish that while he was leading an army across England, but her daughter had begun to bawl.

Cnut had not yet even seen the babe. Like most men, he was only interested in the getting of a child, not the birthing of it. Once her belly had begun to swell he had left her to go to his father in Denmark.

Always, his father came first.

"I named the girl Thyri," Elgiva said, frowning at the nurse who was clutching the screaming child. Could she not quiet the brat?

Cnut peered into his daughter's outraged face but made no move to take the squirming bundle.

"You will like her better when she is older," Elgiva said dryly. At least the boy had impressed his father. The girl was too young to matter in any case.

"Elgiva," Thurbrand thundered, "you and your children have no place here. A chamber has been prepared for you. Best you get to it."

She looked at him coldly. "I am here at my lord's command, Thurbrand, not yours. My place is at his side, wherever he—"

Cnut placed a finger against her lips.

"We sail for Gainsborough with tomorrow's tide," he said. "Take the children to your quarters now and get them settled. And take care," he said with a sly smile, "that they are not in your bed. I will come to you when I can."

She was about to protest, but he gave her a warning look and she thought better of it. This was not the time for arguments. Not here. Not in front of his shipmen.

She nodded and, biting back her questions and complaints, she led her brood back out of the hall. She would play the part of submissive wife for now; but it was not a role that she relished.

Many hours later she lay in Cnut's bed, still awake and still alone. Her children and attendants slept on the other side of the chamber, separated from her by a tall wooden screen. She could hear the quiet rustle of flames in the central hearth and an occasional light snore, but aside from that, all was quiet. Cnut, she decided, was not coming. Likely he had fallen asleep in the hall, drunk like the rest of his men.

She felt feverish, both from ill temper and from the warmth of the chamber. She began to wrestle free of the suffocating bed clothes, but when she heard the snick of the door opening, loud in the silence, all her senses sharpened. A moment later a figure loomed over her, his face barely visible in the firelight.

So, her husband had come at last.

He sat on the bed and removed his boots, and as she watched him strip to his skin her mind was busy. She wanted to know more about the Norman duke and the gulling of Æthelred.

"Tell me about Normandy," she whispered when he had climbed into bed.

"I did not come to talk," he murmured against her ear, and slipping his hand beneath her night-rail, he found her breast.

His agile fingers touched and teased, and when she would have insisted on an answer, he pressed his mouth on hers in a tender yet demanding assault that, knowing Cnut, she should have expected. He tasted of mead and smelled of wood smoke and leather, and his hand moved down her body to explore its secret places, reminding her that he was a man first and a warrior second. It was one of the things about her husband that pleased her.

His stroking fingers demanded all her attention so that her question about Normandy was forgotten. She would be a dutiful wife for a little longer. After all, little Swein needed a brother. So when Cnut covered her body with his, she spread her legs in welcome.

She could not say how much time passed as they pleasured each other, but when their coupling was done, the questions she wanted answered were still there. She turned on her side toward him and, draping her arm across his chest and half covering his body with hers, she toyed absently with his long hair.

"Thurbrand said that your father used the Norman duke to deceive the English king," she said. "What did he mean?"

He grazed her arm with his fingers, and she rested her head on his shoulder, content for the moment.

"While my father was in Rouen courting Duke Richard, he made no secret of his intention to seize the English throne. He also implied that our fleet would land at Sandwich, hoping that Richard would warn Æthelred, and it appears that Richard did. Alric has sent word that the English are mustering near Canterbury, which is just where we want them—looking south while we strike their undefended northern shires."

She imagined Æthelred's reaction to news of Swein's alliance with the Norman duke, and how enraged he would be when Swein's army arrived in the north while the English were mustered in Wessex.

"Æthelred will think that Emma's brother purposely deceived him," she mused. "He will be furious with his queen." Poor Emma, she thought. And smiled.

"I had not considered that," he murmured, "but you are right. Likely he will blame the queen."

There was something in his voice, a hint of concern that she found disquieting.

"No one needs fear for Emma," she said dryly. "The king may have little love for his Norman queen, but she is not without friends at his court. His churchmen think that she walks on water, and one of the æthelings is moon mad for her. What any of them see in such a milk-faced, scheming witch I cannot fathom."

"Can you not?" Cnut asked. He planted a kiss on her forehead. "She is a queen and she is beautiful. Why wouldn't men love her?"

She snorted. "How do you know that she is beautiful? You have never seen her."

He made no reply, and his silence made her suddenly alert and wary. She sat up, curling her legs beneath her as she turned to study his face in the dim light.

"You *have* seen her," she whispered. "When?"

His eyes had gone distant with memory. "It was years ago, on my first voyage to England."

She listened, utterly still and her hands tightly clenched as he spoke of a day that she remembered well, although for years she had tried to banish it from her mind. It had been a day of blood and death, when the city of Exeter had perished in fire, and she had escaped from its hilltop fortress through a steep and narrow tunnel that burrowed down into endless darkness. Even now she shuddered as the horror of that day washed over her once again—of being swallowed alive by the earth, certain that she would never emerge into the light.

But Cnut spoke of events about which she knew nothing, of the capture of a queen outside the city, and of her rescue after a bloody night-time skirmish.

She wanted to know more, but his breathing had become steady and even, and she realized that the mead had done its work and he was heavily asleep. It would be pointless to question him any further, to ask him why he had never before spoken to her of Emma and the day that she had been his prisoner.

She lay back down and closed her eyes, and the image of England's queen stalked her like a pale ghost. Had it not been for Emma, she would be the queen in Winchester right now.

Her father had broached the union to the king, and Æthelred had nearly agreed when Emma got in the way.

The Norman witch had robbed her of a royal marriage and a crown, of father and brothers. Everything that she should have had, Emma had taken.

A shimmer of foreboding, thinner than a knife blade, grazed her spine.

She is beautiful, Cnut had said. *Why wouldn't men love her?*

Because, she thought, Emma was a mother now three times over, no longer young, and likely no longer beautiful.

She turned over on her side, shook off her disquiet, and stared into the glowing embers of the fire.

It would not be long, now, until Swein would thrust Æthelred from his throne. When that happened, Emma would not even be a queen. No one would love her then.

Part Two

Perilous Tides

Chapter Ten

Emma knelt alone before the altar, searching for comfort in the silence of the tiny chapel. When she heard Athelstan softly call her name, though, she abandoned her prayers and rose swiftly. There would be time enough for prayers in the days to come.

She turned to face him and caught her breath. Even in the meager light of the sanctuary candle he seemed to shine, clad as he was in gleaming mail with a sword at his side. He looked like one of the warriors that the scops sang of—men who rode to battle and fought bravely. Men who died, their bright mail all ravaged and bloodied.

And for what?

She gestured helplessly toward the altar.

"I have been praying that God will intervene in some way," she said, "that he will prevent Swein's fleet from making landfall but," she twisted her hands in despair as she fought back tears, "my faith is not strong enough, Athelstan. I do not believe that even God has the power to stop the madness of war-besotted men."

Before she finished speaking he had taken her trembling hands in his. For a long moment she gazed into his face, into the blue eyes that met hers with tenderness.

"The madness will not end, Emma," he said, "until either Swein or my father is dead. There will be no truce offered this time, no tribute demanded, and no peace. If our enemies win, they will show us no mercy, and your sons will be in grave danger."

"It cannot come to that!"

"It may! We are setting a trap for Swein in Kent, but if we fail to stop his army we will not get a second chance. My father will be loath to accept defeat, and likely he will deny even his own danger, but you must not hesitate. If we lose the coming battle, you and your sons must flee. Promise me that you will make preparations now, and have a ship ready."

She drew in a shuddering breath. She wanted to argue with him, to insist that his fear of defeat was unfounded. But she had listened to the king's thegns as they reported the number of men that each could bring to the coming battle—far fewer than in the past because so many had been lost in this endless strife. Nor could she deny that if the worst should occur, her sons would be at great risk.

She nodded, and when he pulled her into his arms she clung to him. She wanted to hold him here beside her, keep him safe from whatever was to come. But Athelstan was not hers to govern or even to love, and she had not the power to protect him.

She drew back and, looking up at him she asked, "What of your sisters? If the worst happens—"

"Their husbands are lords and warriors," he said. "They will be well defended. And Mathilda should be safe enough at the abbey. If the abbess feels they need the protection of city walls she will bring the community into Winchester." He frowned. "The king leaves tomorrow for London. Do you go with him?"

"Not on the morrow, but soon. Edward is there already."

"Good. But Emma, if you hear that Swein has been victorious, do not linger, not even in London. Do whatever you must to live and to thrive. Do not look back!"

She reached up to touch his face.

"I am afraid for you," she murmured.

"I am afraid for all of us." He grasped her hand and kissed it. "Will you grant me your blessing, my lady?"

She kissed his cheek, the chaste kiss of blessing that was his due from a queen of the English. But in the next instant he was pressing his lips to hers, and she responded with all the fierce yearning that she had denied for so long. When she would have drawn away he did not allow it, but sought her mouth again, and for a long moment they clung to each other with a long-suppressed desire that she knew could not be slaked.

"God keep you," he murmured when at last he let her go.

A moment later she was watching him walk away from her, his tall figure receding until he stepped through the outer doorway and vanished from her sight.

Boneless with fear—for him, for her sons, for herself—she sank to her knees and began to weep. Yet even as she gave in to despair, a small voice at the back of her mind demanded that she find a way to master it.

She did not know how long she knelt there, alone in the chapel, seeking solace and finding none. At last, steeling her body against her fear, she pushed herself to her feet and took a long, shuddering breath. Then she straightened her shoulders, wiped her eyes with her fingertips, and forced herself to think.

Once in London she would send word to Thorkell to have a ship standing ready. It would carry her sons to Normandy should the worst happen.

But she would continue to hope that the worst would never happen. For the first time, the English knew where and when the Danish army would strike. For the first time they had powerful allies in the jomsvikings led by Thorkell.

There was hope, and she must cling to it, even as she prepared to face disaster.

Late July 1013
Archbishop's Manor of Fleet, Kent

Athelstan stepped from the dim light of the manor's smoky hall into the turmoil of an army camp. The archbishop's ordered estate was now hectic with men readying for battle. The farms like this one that had once supplied the larders of Canterbury's deacons would now keep the bellies of English warriors filled while they waited for orders to move against the enemy.

In the east, above the forest of oaks that blocked his view to the shore, the rising sun bloodied the sky. He stood for a moment, gazing into the growing light and wondering how many more dawns he would live to see. God willing, enough to drive this latest plague of Danes out of England.

The Normans had been right about where and when Swein's fleet would make landfall, and he supposed that he should be grateful for that, but the sight of dragon ships streaming into the sheltered bay at Sandwich for days on end had sickened him. Now there were nearly two hundred of them. Most of the folk living nearby had already fled with whatever they could carry; but his scouts remained, hidden, keeping watch. If the Danes followed their usual pattern, they would soon abandon their ships and their makeshift camps on the shore to strike west, into the heart of Wessex.

He shifted his gaze that way, to the distant hills where the English forces were gathered, waiting to challenge Swein's army. He hoped to God that the Wessex fyrds had all arrived. They would need the advantage of numbers when the battle began in earnest.

As he eyed the western horizon he saw movement; riders approaching—still some distance away, but clearly visible in the growing light.

"Is it Edmund?" Godwin Wulfnothson emerged from the hall to stand beside him.

"Yes." He could make out his brother's red banner now, streaming above the heads of the dozen or so men who were cutting across the archbishop's meadow toward him. "He will want to know why Swein's army is still lingering on the shore."

It was a good question. He'd like to know the answer himself.

He looked to the southeast where the sky had grown hazy with smoke as the light grew. Swein's massive army lay beneath that haze, thousands of men gathered around cooking fires; and apparently they were in no hurry to move. Meantime, all of Wessex was holding its breath, waiting.

Swein, too, appeared to be waiting. For what?

In front of him, his brother reined in his horse and dismounted.

"Why haven't the bastards left the beach?" Edmund demanded.

His brother was a man of few words and could always be counted on to drive straight to the point. Athelstan did not answer because he had none to give; instead he led Edmund and his companions into the hall where they gathered around one of the trestle tables. Edmund, apparently too restless to sit, stood at one end. Taller than most men, he towered over all of them now as he repeated his question.

"Swein may simply want his hounds well rested before he sets them on us," Godwin suggested.

It was possible, Athelstan supposed. There were several other possibilities, though, that struck him as more likely.

"They may have gotten wind of the welcome we've prepared," he said. "Swein had to be expecting something, in any case. We could not keep our war preparations a secret any more than he could." Then he frowned as another thought struck him. "*Jesu*, is it possible they are waiting for more ships?"

"If there are two hundred ships out there we are already facing an army of six thousand men," Edmund replied, "so you had damn well better hope that there are no more on the way."

"Are all our levies in place?" Athelstan asked. "Can we match their numbers?"

"Nearly," Edmund said. "The men of the western shires came in yesterday, but Eadric's Mercians are still two days' march away." His eyes met Athelstan's. "I don't like this. The Danes should have made some move by now. They are up to some trickery. I can feel it, can't you?" Once again, he cut to the heart of the matter. "Where is Thorkell?"

Thorkell. Emma's Danish protector, and the man that none of them completely trusted.

"On the Thames at London with twenty of his ships," Godwin said. "I saw him there four days ago."

"I cannot believe that Swein would attempt to take London." Ælfric, the greybeard who had been ealdorman for as long as Athelstan could remember, spoke with the authority of age and experience. "Its defenses are too strong. The walls alone—"

"But how many Danes are inside those walls?" Edmund demanded.

"Only a few," Godwin assured him. "The rest of them are either on the ships below the bridge or at their camp at Greenwich. And not all of Thorkell's ships are on the Thames. Some are—"

But Godwin broke off as a scout appeared at the hall entrance. Athelstan beckoned him forward.

"My lord, the Danes are on the move," he announced.

"Marching toward the west?"

"No, lord. They are boarding their ships."

There was a moment's stunned silence before the air filled with curses and the clatter of overturned benches. Once outside, Athelstan shouted an order to light the warning beacons and called for his mount.

Within the hour their small band was within sight of Sandwich's wide bay. The Danish ships were sailing north, riding the tide through the channel that would take them into the Thames estuary.

"*Jesu!*" Athelstan breathed. "What in God's name are they planning?"

"Swein wants conquest," Edmund said, his voice steely with conviction, "and he wants London. Because whoever holds London holds England."

Athelstan looked into his brother's grim face and saw his own despair reflected in Edmund's eyes.

"And you believe that Thorkell will betray us and give him London?"

Edmund said gruffly, "Don't you?"

Athelstan made no answer. He did not know what to believe. Emma trusted Thorkell because Archbishop Ælfheah had trusted him. But Edmund was right. London was the key to control of England, and Swein could not hope to take it unless Thorkell helped him.

They could do nothing more here. The beacons had been lit, and the men of London would know that a Danish fleet was sailing toward them.

"We must get to the king," he said. But even as he urged his horse back toward the camp to collect his men, he knew that it was already too late. Whatever was going to happen in London would have happened long before he could reach the city.

Three days later as he crossed London's bridge with Edmund and a company of mounted warriors he found the city tense, but quiet. The Danish fleet had not entered the Thames, but sailed further north. According to reports that reached the king's council, Swein's fleet had vanished into a wall of fog.

Somewhere in England a massive viking army was making landfall, but no one in London knew where.

Chapter Eleven

August 1013
London

For two weeks, no word reached London of the great Danish fleet that had sailed north and disappeared into the mist. As summer mornings bright with sunshine faded into cool evenings, on the city's streets and on the river's hythes the sense of threat that had loomed so large in July slowly eased. Swein, it was said, had been frightened off and had sailed back to Denmark, or else some of his fleet had foundered in a sudden squall and the East Anglian shore was littered with Danish dead.

Such tales, Emma thought, had the glow of moon dust about them, and the mood in her household and at court was far less sanguine. Like Emma, those closest to the king knew that it was only a matter of time until they would learn of the Danish fleet's landfall somewhere on the eastern coast, and as days passed with no such news, tension and tempers worsened.

Word arrived at last with a messenger sent from Jorvik by Archbishop Wulfstan. Emma was in the hall when the archbishop's man, travel-stained and exhausted after his punishing ten days' ride down the length of England, appeared before the king and his council. Swein's Danish fleet, he reported, had been sighted in the River Humber. And north of the Humber, Ealdorman Uhtred was gathering an army.

Emma was not surprised when the shouting began. Athelstan and Edmund urged their father to go to Uhtred's aid, despite the difficulties of re-assembling the army and taking it over such a vast distance. Thorkell lent his support to the æthelings, suggesting that at the very least the king should summon his levies and prepare for war. Eadric and the nobles of the western shires, though, argued passionately against such a move, with Eadric's voice the loudest. He warned that the men of Wessex and Mercia would be reluctant to abandon their harvests to go to the defense of distant Northumbria.

And so the arguments went, back and forth, while the king prowled the hall, restless as a caged animal, only half listening to the dispute raging among the men at his council table. Emma saw him halt sometimes and stare into the shadows, and when he spoke at all, it was to question the continued silence from his ealdorman in the north.

"If Uhtred has confronted the enemy, why has he sent no word?" he fretted. "Rumors of battle are carried on the wind, yet from Northumbria we hear nothing!"

"There may be nothing yet to tell, my lord," Eadric soothed him. "Soon, I promise you, we shall hear of Uhtred's victory, and of Swein's head grinning from a spike atop Jorvik's walls."

Emma, though, believed that Æthelred was right to be concerned about the deafening silence from the north. She knew, as they all did, how cunning Swein Forkbeard could be. In years past he had captured the walled cities of Exeter and Canterbury, not through overwhelming force, but through trickery. Why should Jorvik be any different? And if Swein took Jorvik, what was to stop him from leading his army toward London?

She had been listening attentively to the arguments around the table, but she could remain silent no longer. Rising from her place beside Thorkell, she approached her pacing husband, blocking his way so that he was forced to stop and listen to her.

"My lord," she said, quietly but urgently, "listen to your sons! Listen to Thorkell who knows Swein better than any man here. Call up your army and lead it against your enemy, lest you find yourself wrong-footed with Swein's sword at your throat!"

Æthelred scowled at her, and she read in his face that he would pay her no heed. Abruptly he thrust her aside, declaring that he wanted no more advice until he had heard from Uhtred. The meeting ended with no decision made, no orders given, and no war preparations begun.

Over the next few days the king kept to his chamber, attended only by a handful of his closest advisors that did not include either Emma or his sons. Meantime, in the great hall a score of anxious thegns and churchmen gathered daily, hungry for news that did not come.

On the fourth day, as Emma made her way from the physic garden to the royal apartments with several attendants about her and a sleepy Alfred in her arms, she saw three horsemen ride swiftly through the palace gates. Messengers from Wulfstan, she guessed as they dismounted, their priestly robes grimed from hard travel.

She entrusted Alfred to his nurse, then hurried after the men who were already climbing the stairs to the king's chamber. She had gone no more than a few paces when four more riders swept through the gates— Athelstan, Edmund, Godwin, and another man she did not recognize. Edmund flung himself from his horse and took the stairs to the king's apartment two at a time, his companions at his heels. Athelstan, seeing her, waited as she hastened toward him.

"Messengers have just arrived," she said quickly, "from Archbishop Wulfstan, I believe."

"Likely they carry the same evil tidings that we have had," he gestured her forward and followed her up the stairs.

"How bad is it?" she asked, a knot of foreboding rising in her throat while her feet felt heavy as lead.

"Worse even than I feared."

Moments later they were in the king's chamber where Edmund and his two companions had halted just inside the doorway. The small room was crowded with nobles, clerics, and hearth guards who were all staring apprehensively at the three priests kneeling before Æthelred. The king had risen from his great chair and was clutching a sealed packet. Eadric and Bishop Ælfhun stood on his right hand and Hubert on his left, while the churchmen on their knees before him bent their heads beneath his forbidding gaze.

"You bring me bitter news, it seems," Æthelred murmured. He scowled at the packet they had delivered as if offended by the very sight of it, then he thrust it toward Hubert. "Answer me this: Has Uhtred's army been defeated by the Danish host?"

There was a pause before one of the men raised his head to reply.

"The archbishop has written to you of Ealdorman Uhtred, lord king." He gestured toward the leather pouch that Hubert was hastening to unseal. "It is all in the letter."

"I would hear it from your lips, priest. Is Ealdorman Uhtred dead?"

"My lord," the man pleaded, "if you would but read—"

"Is Uhtred dead?"

There was another silence, filled with a crackling tension that turned Emma's skin to gooseflesh. She wrapped her arms about her middle, bracing herself—afraid of what she was about to hear and of what the king might do once he heard it.

"He lives, lord king. But..." The priest hesitated again. Then, seeming to find courage, he said, "There was no battle. Ealdorman Uhtred led his army to Gainsborough, and there he submitted to King Swein. There was no battle."

Emma felt her heart plummet.

At first no one said a word, too overwhelmed, she guessed, by such a disaster to utter even a cry of outrage or dismay. Æthelred's face darkened, and because she knew him to be a man not given to governing his rage, she took a step forward. But Athelstan clutched her arm, holding her back and she could only cry out as the king struck the priest a savage blow. The bishop, too, shouted in protest, but Æthelred paid no heed.

"You are a foul liar!" the king raised his arm to strike again, but Athelstan surged forward to shield the priest.

"It is no lie!" he cried. "Uhtred has bent the knee to the Danish king." He drew a long breath, then said, "He was not the only one to do so. Thurbrand in Holderness, Siferth and Morcar in the Five Boroughs, Ulfkytel in East Anglia have all pledged their oaths to Swein."

Emma closed her eyes, stunned by the enormity of the betrayal. When she opened them again the king's face was pale as wax while, beside him, Athelstan's furious gaze encompassed everyone in the chamber.

"We have lost the north, my lords," he said bitterly, "and not a single sword was raised to prevent it."

Æthelred sank into his chair, buffeted by Athelstan's words as if by a chilling wave. It was true, then. His northern lords had willingly bent the knee to the devil.

A familiar throbbing, like a drumbeat, began in his head—a sign that somewhere in the shadows his brother's wraith was watching him with mocking eyes.

Beside him, Bishop Ælfhun observed, "The Northerners may have submitted to Swein, lord king, but there will be many among them who will find it a bitter physick. They will come to regret such a move."

They will indeed regret it, Æthelred thought. He would make certain of it. He flicked a glance at Wulfstan's priests, still on their knees and eyeing him warily.

"Where is the archbishop?" he demanded. "Why did he not come himself?"

One of them found the courage to squeak, "He has retired to his estate in Elmet, my lord. He claims that you will have need of eyes and ears in the north."

Æthelred grunted. Wulfstan had been precious little use to him so far. For years he had bleated about trouble in the north with never a finger pointed at who was behind it. Yet the place had ever been a vipers' nest. *Christ!* Had he not schemed, bribed, bullied, even murdered in his efforts to bring his northern lords to heel? Now they had slipped through his fingers, curse them, as easily as water through a weir.

He glared at Wulfstan's priests. They were Northerners like the treacherous bastards who had betrayed him. They sickened him.

"Get these men out of here!" he ordered. He fingered his forehead, probing for the source of his pain even though he knew that it was hell-spawned, sent by that thing that was lurking somewhere in the shadows. "Hubert, is there anything more to learn from the archbishop's letter?"

"There is news, my lord, of Ælfhelm's daughter, Elgiva."

At the sound of that name the drum beat in his head quickened. Ælfhelm's daughter was dead. Had she, like his brother, come from the grave to haunt him?

"What of her?"

"She is alive, my lord."

Æthelred tensed, already guessing the rest. "Go on," he murmured.

"She is the concubine of Swein's son Cnut. This missive claims that she has given him a son."

So that's where she'd been hiding all this time—she'd crawled into the bed of a Danish prince. Ælfhelm's ambitions for his daughter had been even greater than he had imagined.

He closed his eyes, and random incidents suddenly fell into place like shards of a broken glass made whole. Elgiva's long-ago message that her father would wed her to a Danish lord; Siferth's wife gazing up at him at an Easter feast with wide, terrified eyes; Wulfstan's interminable warnings of trouble in the north; and now the swiftness with which his northern lords had bent the knee to a Danish king.

If Elgiva already had a son by this Cnut, then the Northerners must have been scheming against him in secret for years. How was it that he had not seen it?

"Swein hopes to establish a Danish realm in our northern shires," he murmured, half to himself. Raising his voice he declared, "Swein will fail, as others like him have failed in the past. With God's help we shall drive the Danish cuckoo from our northern nest." Then, catching sight of a worried glance that flashed between Athelstan and Edmund he growled, "If there is more that you wish to share with us, Athelstan, say it now."

But Edmund stepped forward instead, drawing a stranger with him.

"My lord, this man has arrived within the last hour from Lindsey. When he left there five days ago, Lincoln had already submitted, and Swein's army was preparing to move again—their outriders already scouting the road they planned to take. They have set their faces south, my lord, along Ermine Street."

Athelstan moved to his brother's side, and now there were three of them facing him like harbingers of doom.

"Swein will not be satisfied with a kingdom in the north, my lord," Athelstan said urgently. "He wants all of England. He wants your throne. If we do not meet him and stop him, he will be at London's gates in a matter of weeks."

The whispers of frightened men buzzed about the chamber, mingling with the drumbeat in his ears. Æthelred tried to ignore both as he studied the grim faces of his sons. Athelstan had ever been rash, eager for action no matter the provocation. Edmund was more cautious, and he was shrewd. But he would follow his brother into hell if Athelstan led the way.

The two of them were watching him, tense and unblinking, convinced that they had given him the answer to Swein's threat, and that he would follow their advice.

He pushed himself to his feet and snarled, "It would be sheer folly to lead an army northward against the combined forces of Swein and whatever traitors ride at his side! Let them march south! London is the key to this kingdom, and it has never been taken, nor ever will be. Swein's army will break against our walls until it is naught but flotsam—if he even makes it this far and our garrisoned burhs don't defeat him." Out of the corner of his eye he saw a flicker of movement deep in the shadows, but he refused to look at it. "If Swein wants my throne," he bellowed, so loud that even his brother's hell-spawned wraith must hear him, "then let the bastard come to London and try to take it!"

A.D. 1013 Then soon submitted...Earl Uhtred, and all the Northumbrians, and all the people of Lindsey, and afterwards the people of the Five Boroughs, and soon after all the army to the north of Watling-street; and hostages were given Swein from each shire. When he understood that all the people were subject to him, then ordered he that his army should have provision and horses; and he then went southward with his main army, committing his ships and the hostages to his son Cnut...And after Swein came over Watling-street, they wrought the greatest mischief that any army could do. Then Swein went to Oxford; and the population soon submitted, and gave hostages...

The Anglo-Saxon Chronicle

Chapter Twelve

The Danish army that had engulfed Oxford lunged next toward Wallingford and then Reading, and each city, its forces vastly outnumbered, swiftly submitted. With every dawn that followed, the king and his war council expected to see Swein's army approaching London's gates, and frantic preparations for a siege were under way. Instead, the Danes swept farther south toward the royal city of Winchester.

Despite pleas from his elder sons and from Winchester's bishop to go to the city's aid, Æthelred refused.

"We make our stand here, at London," he insisted. "As long as London remains in our hands, England can withstand anything that our enemies will do, just as it always has."

Hearing this Emma looked to Athelstan, and he met her gaze with a surreptitious shake of his head that she understood only too well. Athelstan believed that his father was deluded and that his refusal to act would lead to disaster.

Meantime, a vast tide of England's dispossessed swarmed into London seeking refuge. Every vacant field, every churchyard, every spare bit of unused ground became an encampment for those with nowhere else to go. St. Paul's churchyard was the largest of these, and on a grey September morning Emma, along with the abbess of Barking Abbey, led a covey of nuns and royal attendants into the camp.

While the queen's men set up tents or met with the bishop's cellarer to arrange for the distribution of food and clothing, Emma and the nuns, in dark linen gowns and cloaks, tended to the sick and the injured. There were families clustered together in the open or under canopies or, for those most in need of shelter, inside a scattering of tents. Many of the men bore wounds they had suffered as they tried to protect their families, while the grim faces of their women testified to deeper, invisible wounds. Their children, some nearly naked and with wide, frightened eyes, were too exhausted and hungry even to cry.

Emma and Abbess Ælfwynn entered first a tent that housed a mother and daughter who had walked for days to reach London. The younger woman lay on a cot, curled up on her side, her face dirty, her mouth and cheek split and swollen, her eyes wide, but vacant, and her brown hair loose. She was filthy, for if anyone touched her she began to thrash and scream. While the abbess knelt beside her to pray Emma turned to the older woman who was seated on a pile of bundles, her face blank as a stone.

Her name, Emma had learned, was Edburga. Crouching before her with a cloth and a basin of water, Emma took the woman's hands and inspected them. The palms were badly cut up and encrusted with grit, and Emma gently began to cleanse them.

"Can you tell me what happened?" she asked.

Edburga drew a long, shuddering breath, and she began to rock back and forth, her eyes fixed on nothing.

"They came in the dawn," she murmured. "Devils. With fire and swords. They murdered the men, even my infant grandson. My daughter and granddaughter they raped, I don't know how many times. Eleven summers old, the girl was, and the last thing she knew in this life was the savagery of men. Of beasts." Her voice was hoarse with horror. "They made me watch while they did their filthy business—"

She began to sob, weeping with the abandon of a child, mouth agape, nose and eyes streaming.

"I tried to stop it, but they held me back; and when they were done they just threw me aside. Why?" she wailed. "Why did they let me live? I would rather have died than watch what they did."

Emma met Abbess Ælfwynn's eyes. They both knew why the Danes had let this woman live. They wanted her story and hundreds like it to rob the English of hope, to leave them paralyzed with despair. But God, too, had a purpose, and Emma was as certain of it as she was of anything on this earth.

"It was God who let you live," she whispered to Edburga. "You must believe that. Had you died, your daughter would have died with you. Now you must live for her sake. She needs your courage and your strength. You must be her rock."

Edburga dropped her head into her torn palms, and Emma let her weep, caressing her shoulder as she would a child, painfully aware that there was little else that even a queen could do to ease such anguish.

Over the next few hours she spoke with more families, listened to their stories, wept with them, and prayed with them, until one of the nuns informed her that a messenger from the palace had been asking for her. She found that her escort was already horsed and that young Robert was with them, waiting to help her mount. She could tell from his guarded expression that she was about to hear bitter news. As they left the cathedral grounds, she asked him, heavy-hearted, "Has Winchester fallen, then?"

"The city submitted three days ago," he replied. "It was the same as at Oxford. They surrendered to the Danish king without even a battle, the cowards."

Emma looked at the boy. He was nine winters old now, and she had known him from the moment of his birth. He was her son's closest companion, just as his mother had been hers. And although he and Edward had been trained to fight with sword and shield, they had never witnessed the savagery of war.

But she had seen it, and she did not believe that the men of Oxford were cowards. They had merely wished to save their city and its people from destruction. If London should be attacked, though, its defenders would not submit. The city was preparing for war, and everyone within its walls would be witness to slaughter, or victim to it.

The words of Edburga and the fate of her murdered grandchildren continued to trouble her. Pity gave way first to anger and then to fear. If her own children should fall into Danish hands, they would likely meet a similar fate.

By the time she reached the palace gate, she had made up her mind about what she must do. Hastening to her apartments, she discarded her soiled cloak before scooping Alfred into her arms. Whispering assurances, she settled him on her hip and beckoned his nurse to follow her. Then she went to the king.

A small group of family members, nobles and churchmen were gathered within the royal chamber, and the steady murmur of hushed voices that greeted her was as solemn as a death watch. As usual, she looked first for Athelstan, and she saw him in huddled conversation with Godwin and Edwig. When his eyes met hers they were dark with anger—furious with his father, she guessed, for his inaction in the face of the Danish assault.

Æthelred sat on his great chair, one hand kneading his forehead as if it pained him. Eadric stood next to the king, speaking quietly to him, with Edyth and Edward close at his side. Edmund, too, had placed himself near the king, listening to what Eadric was saying and, judging from the frown on his face, not much liking it. On the far side of the chamber Bishop Ælfhun was bending over a man seated on a stool—the bishop of Winchester, she realized—and he was weeping.

She was not here, though, either to weep for Winchester or to upbraid the king for his failures. She had come to reason with him, to plead with him if she must. She stepped into the chamber and, with Alfred in her arms she dropped to one knee before the king.

"I would ask a boon, my lord," she said, "not for myself, but for my children." Then, correcting herself she said vehemently, "For our children."

The chamber went silent, and the faded blue eyes that Æthelred turned on her were bloodshot, weary, and filled with grief. He had loved Winchester, she knew. For generations it had been the center of royal administration and religious devotion. Now the people of the city that lay at the very heart of Wessex had transferred their allegiance to a Danish king.

In that moment she found some pity for him in her heart, but she would not allow herself to indulge in it. She must use his grief to her advantage. When the king remained silent she said, "I would have you send our sons to my brother in Normandy as soon as a ship can be readied to take them."

The king's expression did not change, but Eadric, beside him, gave a start of alarm.

"My lord," Eadric said, "I would advise against this. Your people will see it as an admission of defeat. If members of your family flee there will be panic in the streets of London."

She had expected just such an argument from Eadric. He hoped one day to rule England through Edward, and he would not wish to see her son sent away for fear that the boy might never return.

"Send our sons as envoys to their uncle in your name, my lord," she said to the king, "No one will interpret an embassy sent to persuade my brother to help us in our time of need as a sign of surrender! Let Edward tell Richard of the misery he has witnessed here in London." She hazarded a glance at Edward, who seemed to stand up a little straighter at this mention of a role for him. "But the ship must sail before winter when travel across the Narrow Sea becomes perilous."

Eadric again was quick to object. "Duke Richard will never help us! He has given Swein a pledge of eternal friendship! Why should we send good men to accompany the æthelings on a hopeless mission? We need every man in London who can wield a sword to stay here and fight!"

Before she could reply Edmund stepped forward.

"The crew of a single ship, Eadric, will hardly be missed! And it is not necessarily a hopeless mission. Such an embassy as the queen suggests, though, is a task for an adult and not a child. If Richard is to be convinced of our need, the queen should accompany her sons to Normandy."

Emma felt a rush of alarm. Of course Edmund wanted her gone. He had always resented her, always regarded her sons as rivals for the throne. This was the perfect opportunity to be rid of them all.

"I am afraid, Edmund," she replied stiffly, "that my brother will be less inclined to aid England if all of his kin are safely in Normandy." She addressed the king again. "Send the children or send me, my lord, but it would do more harm than good, I think, to send all of us."

Æthelred did not speak, but his eyes narrowed on her face, as if searching for the answer to a puzzle. She met his gaze unflinching, although her heart was pounding. She was taking a risk, giving him this option to send her away. Æthelred thought that she was lusting for power that should be his alone, and he might welcome this chance to free himself of what he considered her grasping ambition. She was terrified that he might send her away while her sons remained here and in danger.

Alfred, growing restless, began to squirm and whimper, and as she waited for the king's response, she shifted her son in her arms, trying to hush him.

Finally, Æthelred called to Bishop Ælfhun.

"Your shipmaster Brihtwold is still in London, bishop, is he not?"

"Yes, my lord."

"Command him to prepare his ship to sail in two days' time. He will take my youngest sons to Normandy, and you, bishop, will accompany them. You will carry, too, letters from me and from the queen which you will deliver to the duke." Once more he fixed his eyes on hers. "Eadric is correct that it would be a gesture of defeat to send the queen away, and I will not do so. Her presence here in London will be an added inducement for her brother to grant our request for help."

Emma felt a huge weight lift from her heart.

"Thank you, my lord," she whispered.

Two days later, Emma stood on the hythe as Brihtwold's merchant vessel bore Alfred, Edward, Robert, the bishop and a number of priests and attendants eastward toward the mouth of the Thames. Father Martin accompanied them as well, with messages for her mother that she dared not put in writing and could trust no one else to deliver.

Athelstan watched with her as the ship caught the tide, and although he did not touch her, his mere presence was a solace and a comfort.

"Do you believe that your brother will grant your request and send us aid?" he asked.

Emma drew in a long breath and studied the sky. In the distance she could see a line of grey—a bank of cloud that might dissipate before day's end or might swell into the kind of tempest that drove ships to the bottom of the Narrow Sea.

"I cannot tell what my brother will do," she answered him, "any more than I can tell if I have indeed sent my sons to safety."

Late the next day the news arrived from Hampshire that Swein's army had begun to burn its way toward London.

Chapter Thirteen

September 1013
Gainsborough, Lindsey, Mercia

On a bright, crisp morning Cnut rode with his huscarles north from Gainsborough and up a steep dirt track to the encampment that would shelter Swein's army through the coming winter. It sprawled atop a high, broad ridge that rose abruptly from the River Trent to offer a wide view of the river and the surrounding countryside. Cnut's own headquarters were in the town itself, but Gainsborough was too small to house the thousands of men who would return to winter here after the season's campaigning.

The camp was noisy with activity as men completed the construction of its defenses. Cnut noted with approval that the original earthen rampart thrown up eight weeks earlier was now topped with a wooden palisade. Two watchtowers had been built, and two more were under construction. The surrounding defensive ditch had been widened and deepened since his last visit. Tents stood in neat rows, there were corrals for horses and livestock, a forge had been set up, and waste ditches marked off. In the distance, outside the palisade, storehouses were being constructed inside their own earthen ramparts.

"You've made good progress," he said to Arnor, who had overseen all the work that had been done.

They were standing now atop one of the watchtowers that overlooked the Trent, and Cnut narrowed his eyes to reckon the distance between the fort and the river, where scores of drekar lined the bank.

Squinting up at the sky, Cnut said, "This clear spell is not likely to last much longer. How much food do you have stored?"

"Not enough," Arnor replied, "especially if your father continues to send us hostages for safekeeping. I have three foraging parties out just now. A fourth returned this morning."

Food, Cnut thought, was going to be their biggest problem. The English would resist having their harvests stripped from them; but his father's army needed to be fed through the winter, so the English must go without.

"I see that you have found a use for our hostages," he said, watching a group of youths unload several cartloads of goods under the watchful eyes of six Danish shipmen. "Have they made any trouble?"

Arnor snorted. "They're a sullen bunch, that lot. They think that because their fathers bent the knee to Swein they should be treated as allies." He scowled. "I told them that if we do that, we will find it much harder to kill them if things go sour down south and their kinsmen turn against us." He spat. "They didn't much like that. We keep them fed, we keep them working, and we keep them penned up at night. It's better that way."

Not for the hostages, Cnut reflected, who, if all went as planned, must one day become allies. Arnor was right, though. For now they were hostages, younger sons or younger brothers of English magnates, and the guarantees of their kinsmen's new allegiance to his father.

His inspection of the fortress finished, Cnut and his huscarles returned to Gainsborough, following the path along the river. As they neared the town, he saw a knarr angling toward shore from the south. For nearly three weeks there had been a worrying silence from the army, but it appeared that he was about to get some news at last.

He could see Halfdan at the ship's prow, easily recognizable by his fair hair and beard, and by the snaking lines inked on his cheeks and forehead. Cnut called out to him, and Halfdan, his long, blond plait swinging behind him, vaulted over the gunwale to greet him, grinning widely.

Good news then. Cnut dismounted and tossed his reins to one of his men.

"I've brought you more hostages, my lord," Halfdan called.

Cnut looked past him to where a group of young men were being herded on to the shore.

"You've taken your sweet time getting here," he replied with mock reproof. "We have been without news for weeks."

Halfdan barked a laugh.

"We have come from farther south than you would credit. Some of these lads hale from Oxford and Wallingford, but most from Winchester."

"Winchester!" Cnut stared at him in surprise. "My father has taken Winchester?"

"Aye," Halfdan confirmed. "I've a tale to tell."

"And I will hear it as soon as I have dealt with this cargo you've brought me."

He ordered the hostages lined up in front of him, eyeing them as they were jostled into place. They wore good wool and leather, and the sacks they carried no doubt held clothing to see them through the coming winter. They were the sons of wealthy English thegns, and they were about to learn the brutal realities of war.

He paced along the line, looking into their faces, reading each one in turn. In some he saw dejection and despair. Others glared boldly at him with resentment; they were the ones likely to be troublesome. He trusted that Arnor would spot them and would take precautions. Anyone who provoked Arnor would find himself chained to a stake day and night until he became more compliant.

"You men," he shouted, "will be treated well, but only as long as you do as you are told. Disobey, and you will be punished." He drew his sword and noted with satisfaction the stir of agitation among them. Fear, he thought, might keep the more defiant among them from doing something stupid. He clasped the blade just beneath the hilt so that it formed a cross as he held it up in front of him. "I give you my word that you will not be harmed so long as your kinsmen keep the oaths that they have made to us."

And God help you, he thought, if your kin should break those oaths.

He gestured to the guards to take them up to the camp, and turned back to where Halfdan waited for him beneath the shade of an oak. As they started toward the hall Cnut said, "Tell me how my father took Winchester. Our English allies all swore that it would be a hard-fought battle; that the garrison there would resist to the last man."

"Swein gave them a choice; told them they could surrender and live, or they could fight and die." Halfdan shook his head. "They could see that we had them far outnumbered, and Winchester, it turned out, was not prepared to outlast a siege. It wasn't a difficult decision. They submitted. The same thing happened at Oxford. The English have no fight left in them. I think they're beaten."

"What about our numbers? Have we lost many men?"

"More than your father would like," Halfdan admitted. "We lost sixty men one night when they tried to ford a river and blundered into deep water. They were swept away in the dark before we even realized what was happening."

"Where was this? Near Winchester?"

"No, it was on the Thames, on the way to London. There was a bridge, but—"

"London!" Cnut halted and grasped Halfdan's arm. "My father is marching on London?"

Halfdan cocked a brow.

"Aye, London," he said. "You know Swein. He wants Æthelred. He thought to find him in Winchester, but it seems the king has burrowed himself into London. Your father has sworn to take him. That's what this war is all about, is it not? Ridding England of its king and replacing him with ours?" He grinned.

But striking at London now, Cnut thought, might prove their undoing. It had not been part of their original plan. Why stray from tactics that had so far proved successful beyond their imagining?

"It is too soon to march on London," he worried aloud. "The city walls are too strong, and the river is a barrier to a siege, especially with Thorkell's fleet moored there. The men of London are stubborn bastards and they will fight like feral dogs. They will never surrender."

Halfdan glanced sidelong at him. "They said that about Winchester, too, lord," he said.

Winchester, though, was not London. And if the Londoners scored a victory against his father, it might well kindle a fire in the hearts of the English that could prove fatal to Swein's campaign.

Still, Halfdan had brought good news, and it must be shared.

They had reached the hall and he sent for casks of ale and ordered all his men to assemble. Halfdan stood with him on the dais and told his tale—at great length and making much of Swein's leadership, skill, and courage—while Cnut watched the faces of his English allies as they listened.

Siferth and his men raised their cups and cheered. The Northumbrian leader Uhtred, though, kept his eyes downcast, his forehead creased in a frown. Cnut felt a tremor of unease—not the first misgiving he had had about Uhtred. Alric had warned him that Uhtred and Ulfkytel, married to daughters of the king, had been most reluctant to join their alliance. Both men, Cnut thought, would bear watching.

A flash of gold drew his gaze to where Elgiva stood amid a clutch of Mercian noblewomen. Her dark hair fell in waves to her waist, and she had adorned herself with ropes of golden chains studded with jewels. Beside her beauty and brilliance the other women seemed to pale into insignificance.

He admired his wife. She was as voluptuous and alluring as any man could wish. She had an understanding of royal pageantry, and she knew how to use it as a symbol of power and prestige. He could see her efforts all around him. The lavishly intricate, colorful designs that now covered the walls of this hall, proclaiming to the English that their Danish overlords were here to stay, had been her doing.

Elgiva was also, he reminded himself, clever, cunning, and so willful that he did not quite trust her. Like Uhtred and Ulfkytel, she needed watching.

Just now, his wife was listening with ill-concealed displeasure to Halfdan's account of Swein's intention to march on London. Elgiva knew London well. She must believe, as he did, that such a move was dangerous and foolhardy. Yet there was nothing to be done about it. Halfdan had left Swein's camp six days ago. By now, whatever plan Swein had devised to take London would already be in motion. They could do nothing but wait for news and hope that when it came, it did not stink of disaster.

Hours later, his head buzzing from ale and from the wild celebration that would likely continue until near dawn, Cnut slipped out of the hall. The cooling breeze that greeted him was sobering, and welcome after the oppressive heat and noise he had left behind. He drew in a long breath and raked his hands across his scalp to help clear his head.

The hour was late, but there was still enough light that he could discern the men standing guard at the gates across the yard. When a movement near his own quarters caught his eye, he saw Elgiva emerge from the shadows. As she walked past the fire burning in the center of the yard, the chains that she still wore at her breast glittered golden in its light.

Two nights ago she had come to his bed wearing those golden chains and nothing else, and the memory of it made him smile as she approached him. He welcomed the distraction. It would keep him from worrying about what might be happening at London.

"Tell me something, husband." She stood on her toes to kiss him. "Why are you here?"

There was an edge to her voice that sent a warning chill up his spine despite the kiss. She was up to something. Suddenly he was stone sober, and his smile faded.

"What do you mean?"

"Why have you been left here in charge of a fleet of empty ships, while your father's army is poised to take London?" She wrapped her arms about his waist and looked up at him, her brow furrowed in disapproval.

Their minds were at odds, then. He was afraid that his father's attack on London would be a disastrous failure, while she expected that it would succeed and that he was somehow at fault for not being a part of it.

"You know why I am here," he said patiently. He disliked being baited by his wife, but he placed his hands on her shoulders and explained, "My father needs someone to oversee this newly gained territory, and he assigned it to me."

"But there are others who could do that," she purred. "Halfdan or even Siferth. My lord, you are wasted here. Place someone else in charge and join your father in the south. You should be at Swein's side when he takes the city."

"Why?" He snapped. "Why should I even consider doing that?"

"Because the men of England must see you waging war at your father's right hand! If you remain here they will think you a craven, like Æthelred. It will be Swein that they fear, not you, and when one day you sit upon the English throne men will challenge your authority." She snorted. "First among them will be your old friend Thorkell."

He scowled. "There will always be those who challenge authority, Elgiva. Nothing I do now will prevent that."

"Don't be a fool!" Her voice was laced with contempt. "The reputation that you make now will cling to you in years to come, and you know it! Do you wish to be seen as a warrior? Or are you content to sit here counting sheep? You should be making the English fear you! Go to your father! Join the assault on London!"

He barked a mirthless laugh. He had wanted a respite from thinking about London, but she was worrying at it like a dog with a bone. She saw only that there was no glory in what he was doing here, blind to the fact that it was of far more use to Swein than another sword at his side would be. It was glory that she wanted—that, and a queen's crown.

"Elgiva, you are asking me to break the pledge that I made to my king. I will not do that."

"Pah!" she spat. "Men break pledges all the time. It does not matter."

"It matters to my father," he said through clenched teeth. "It matters to me! Something you would do well to remember."

But there were some things—loyalty, trust, obedience—that Elgiva would never be able to understand. And if his father's decision to go to London ended in catastrophe, nothing they said here tonight would matter anyway.

Too irritated now to sleep, he clasped her wrists and pushed her aside, striding past her toward the gate and the path that led to the river.

"Where are you going?" her peevish cry echoed behind him.

"To count sheep!"

Chapter Fourteen

October 1013
London

Emma quickly adjusted the girdle at her waist while her body servant plaited and pinned her hair. It was just after dawn, and the clanging of alarm bells and the shouting of men announced that palace guards were anticipating another Danish assault upon the city. Six nights before, she had accompanied the king as he walked the walls between the Newgate and the Ludgate to survey the campfires of Swein's army—so many that it seemed to her there could not be enough wood in England to feed them all. The next day, the battle for London had begun.

The city was an armed camp now, under daily attack, and every man, woman and child within the walls willingly saw to the needs of its defenders. Today, she and her household would once again feed men exhausted from long hours of duty, tend the wounded and the sick, calm frightened children, and distribute bread to the wretched homeless who had come to the city for shelter. At day's end they would pray, and then return here to sleep. Tomorrow they would do it all again.

The women of her household were stirring, each one seeing to her appointed task. She glanced at the small alcove near her bed where Alfred had slept until he and Edward had been sent across the Narrow Sea—to safety, she hoped. The anxiety that always hovered at her breast rose into her throat so that she had to swallow hard to keep it at bay. Fourteen days had passed since their ship had sailed, and she had been hoping for news of her sons long before any word could possibly have arrived from her brother's court. Perhaps, she thought, a message would come today. Men, supplies, and messages still got through, for despite their numbers, the Danes had not been able to completely blockade the city.

Her hair plaited and her headrail in place, she crossed the now-deserted outer chamber with her servant following close behind. Before she reached the door, though, it was thrust open, and she was startled by the sight of a man heavily wrapped in a traveling cloak who dropped to one knee at her feet.

"I am sorry to trouble you so early and without warning, my lady," he said, lifting his head so that his hood fell away and she was looking into a familiar, aged face.

She gave a glad cry and reached for the man's hands to raise him to his feet and draw him into her chamber.

"Are they safe?" she asked.

"They are," Father Martin said with a weary smile.

She led him to a bench and urged him to sit, then sent the servant to fetch food and drink. She took his hands again, so thin and cold that it was all she could do not to weep. Gently chafing them, she listened as he described their voyage and their arrival at the ducal court.

"Rough seas and high winds, my lady, and Edward loved every moment of it. Your brother greeted your sons most warmly," he assured her, "and the dowager duchess has taken them into her household. They have been reunited with their sister, and their young Norman cousins were making much of them when I left Rouen."

"And my mother?" she asked, eagerly. "Is she still a force of nature?" Gunnora had been on this earth more than sixty winters, as unchanging and permanent, in Emma's mind, as a mountain.

"She wears her years well," Father Martin said, then pursed his lips as if he might say more but was uncertain how to begin.

"Yet something is amiss, I see," Emma said. "What is it?"

"There has been discord between your mother and the duke ever since the visit of King Swein last spring. It seems that the dowager duchess advised your brother against making any kind of alliance with the Danes, but Richard believed that he could pledge friendship to Swein—for profit—then outwit him by warning King Æthelred about where Swein's war on England would begin. It was only when he learned of Swein's landing in the north that Richard understood that he had been purposely misled. Your mother will not let him forget it, and the mood in your brother's court is more than a little strained because of it."

It was some comfort to be reassured that her brother was not, in fact, England's enemy, although it was distressing to learn how easily Richard had been cozened by the Danish king. It was distressing, too, to see how weary her old friend was after his voyage.

"Father, I am most grateful for your news, but a letter would have sufficed. I sent you to Normandy to spare you having to live through this nightmare that we are facing now."

"There are things that I must tell you that cannot be conveyed in a letter," he said quickly. "My lady, your brother would have you come to him as soon as you may. He wishes you to seek refuge in Normandy now, before it is too late."

His words sent a tremor of anxiety through her. "Then he must believe that Swein's army will defeat us," she whispered. She had never allowed herself to believe that. She could not.

"It is more than that, I fear."

The servant reappeared with a tray of food and drink, and he fell silent. Before he could take up his tale again, Edyth appeared at the chamber door.

"The king is closeted with messengers from Normandy and I have not been able to learn anything about—" Edyth stopped abruptly as she caught sight of the priest. "Ah. I see you have your own envoy. Good. I trust, then, that Edward made it safely to Rouen."

"Edward and Alfred are safe, yes," Emma said. "They are in my mother's care."

Edyth offered her a sour smile.

"You must be relieved, Emma, that your children are out of London when so many others are trapped here in this wretched city."

"If it had been up to me, Edyth, your daughter would have accompanied my sons to Normandy." Eadric, though, had forbidden it, claiming that to send his small daughter away would be a tacit acknowledgement that England was lost. So Æthelflaed remained in the London palace with her mother, and Emma's successful bid to send her own children away had added fuel to Edyth's long-standing resentment toward her.

"What of my father's request for aid against the Danes?" Edyth asked the priest. "Has Duke Richard sent ships? Men?"

Father Martin drew a long breath, hesitating, seeming to carefully consider his response, and Emma had little hope that what he was about to say would bring them any joy.

"No, my lady," he said at last. "Duke Richard could spare neither men nor ships at this time, but he was able to send weapons and wheat."

"Wheat!" Edyth scoffed. "When what we truly need are warriors?"

"You will be grateful for the wheat, Edyth," Emma said, "if our own stores run low in the months to come. In Mercia, the Danes have either burned the fields or confiscated the crops. Abbot Ælfsy has told me that even in East Anglia most of the harvest has been sent to Swein's camp at Gainsborough."

"Is the abbot in London, then?" Father Martin asked.

"He arrived shortly after you sailed for Rouen," Emma replied. "The Danes overran the abbey at Peterborough, but Ælfsy had enough warning that he was able to flee. He stayed for a time with Wulfa at my manor at Shotley before coming here."

"Wulfa should have come with him to London," Edyth said. "She was a fool to stay with that traitorous husband of hers, and she will have cause to regret it."

Emma sometimes wondered if Edyth had a single compassionate bone in her body.

"The journey would have been far too dangerous for her, so late in her pregnancy," she reminded Edyth as patiently as she could. "And I learned from Abbot Ælfsy that Ulfkytel bent the knee to Swein against his will and only because he saw no way to stop what was to come. You cannot possibly know what difficulties he faced in making his—"

"Ulfkytel is a traitor," Edyth insisted, "and so is Uhtred! My father showered them with lands and titles. He gave them his daughters to wed! They should have died rather than bend the knee to a foreign master!" Her face was livid with passion, and Emma could not say if the cause was fury or if it was the same fear that everyone in the city was living with now. "My sisters dishonor us all by remaining loyal to their craven husbands. They are damned in the eyes of God and of men."

Emma's patience snapped. "That is enough! Your sisters do not deserve your censure, Edyth, and I will hear no more of it."

Edyth managed to look both outraged and affronted at the same time.

"As you wish, my lady," she said with exaggerated courtesy before stalking from the chamber.

Emma watched her go, her anger mixed with exasperation. The world that Edyth inhabited was a stark one, drawn in shades of black and white only. She was fiercely loyal to her father, and fiercely hostile to anyone who opposed him in word or deed. In Edyth's eyes the king could do no wrong—except for his one great sin of taking a second wife—and anyone who Edyth judged to be the king's enemy was Edyth's enemy as well.

"It is her fear that causes her to speak thus," Father Martin observed softly." Forgive her, my lady. She will come to her senses eventually, and see how she has wronged her sisters."

Emma sat with him again and sighed.

"I am finding it more and more difficult to forgive Edyth," she said, "and I am weary of trying to talk sense into her. Eadric has molded her into his own image, so that she sees with his eyes and speaks with his voice. Nothing that anyone can do will change that now, I'm afraid." Edyth judged her sisters harshly for staying with their husbands, yet what other choice did they have? And in truth, she reminded herself, Edyth, too, had no other choice. Few royal women did, herself included. "Ælfswith," she said, turning to the servant who had taken a seat in a corner and was quietly spinning, "go to the hall now and break your fast. I will join you there shortly." When the girl was gone she said, "Now, Father, what more have you to tell me?"

"Your mother wishes you to know that Richard does not expect Æthelred to survive this conflict. He believes the king will succumb either to an injury or to some illness brought on by age. The duke, it appears, is already entertaining offers for your widow's hand in marriage."

Emma stared at him, appalled as much by her brother's callous opportunism as by his casual dismissal of a king who Richard now considered irrelevant. If by some twist of fate she should find herself subject to her brother's authority, Richard would be no champion or ally but would use her as he saw fit, without recourse to her needs or desires. It was something she would have to avoid at all costs.

"Did my mother send any advice along with this warning?" she asked wryly.

Father Martin smiled and took her hands. His grip was strong despite his age, and it steeled her just as much as it comforted.

"Only that whatever ordeal you may face in the days and weeks to come—even if your husband should die—you must never show your fear. And you must never forget that you are a queen."

She had heard those words before—all those years ago when she had first learned that she was to wed the king of England and had fallen to her knees, sick, and helpless with despair. Somehow her mother had had some glimmer, then, of what lay ahead of her.

There will be worse than this to come. But you must never show your fear.

She recognized the wisdom of that counsel, although with each trial that she faced it became harder to follow. Far greater trials lay ahead if England should fracture under the Danish assault, but she would do what she must: hide her fear, and remember that before she was a woman, a wife, or even a mother, she was a queen.

October 1013
London

Athelstan and Edmund stood with the sentinels who had gathered on the Newgate tower. The chilly breeze promised a clear, cold day ahead, although above them the sky was still grey with the twilight that comes before the dawn.

The hour of the wolf, Athelstan thought, glancing up at the still darkling sky before peering into the west where he could just make out a dark smudge spreading northward like a black stain upon the land. Swein Forkbeard's wolves, it seemed, were on the move.

"The bastards are leaving," Edmund muttered, "and God curse their every step."

"Tell the king," Athelstan ordered the man-at-arms nearest him.

For fourteen days the Danish army had thrown itself against the walls of London, and if Swein had expected the city to succumb as Winchester and Oxford had done, he had badly misjudged his prey. The city had been battered, its ramparts drenched in the blood and gore of its wounded and dead, but London had not broken. Apparently Swein had concluded that this prize was beyond his reach for now. The stain that had once been an army encampment was retreating northward along Watling Street.

"Where are they going, I wonder," Edmund mused.

"To gather more provisions at the very least," Athelstan said, "and possibly, more men." The Danes, too, had suffered losses.

"Swein will lead his warriors back to Gainsborough." Eadric's voice came from behind them as he stepped up to the fighting platform. "He will wait out the winter there and will not raise his banners again until the spring."

Athelstan turned to look at his brother-in-law, whose face radiated satisfaction as he surveyed the retreating army. Eadric seemed to think this Danish retreat a great victory, despite the fact that Swein now controlled half of England.

"Has God sent you tidings of Swein's intentions?" Athelstan asked, resisting the urge to toss the ealdorman over the parapet.

"Swein's failure to take London is a blow that he was not expecting," Eadric declared, oozing confidence as if he actually knew what he was talking about. "His men will be questioning both his leadership and his luck, and his English allies are no doubt regretting the oaths that they made to him. Swein knows this, and he is not a fool. He will use the advent of winter as an excuse to crawl into some hole he has dug for himself up north, and hope that by plying his allies with mead and ale they will forget what has happened here."

"Winter, real winter, is still more than a month away," Athelstan argued, although he knew it was pointless. "Yes, we have denied Swein London, but that will merely slow his advance, not stop it."

"His advance is already stopped!" Eadric cried. "Look!" He gestured toward the departing army. "That road will take his army back into the shires that have already submitted to him. For now, he will be content with what he has—eastern Mercia and the north. He will winter beside his ships and lick his wounds. Perhaps by winter's end our northern cousins will remember who their true king is. By then their stomachs will be empty and griping because Swein's army will have devoured their harvests."

He broke off as a royal guard approached him with a summons to wait upon the king and with a curt nod he left them.

"You know what counsel he will offer the king," Edmund snarled. "He will advise him to cower here in the city throughout the winter, and the king will do whatever he says. But you are right. Swein will not hare back to Gainsborough until the snow falls, and God alone knows where he will go next."

Athelstan's eyes were still fixed upon the distant stain that was the Danish army. The sun was rising now, and the growing light revealed the scars on the land that they left in their wake.

"As there is nothing and no one to stop him," he said bitterly. "Swein can go wherever he pleases. My fear is that he will strike at the soft underbelly of Wessex." He sighed. "And I hope to God that I am wrong."

A.D. 1013 Then went King Swein thence to Wallingford; and so over Thames westward to Bath, where he abode with his army. Thither came Alderman Æthelmær, and all the western thanes with him, and all submitted to Swein, and gave hostages.

The Anglo-Saxon Chronicle

Chapter Fifteen

November 1013
Gainsborough, Lindsey, Mercia

The steady drumming of rain on the roof thatch nearly drowned out the shrill cries of the child in Elgiva's arms. Her daughter's shrieks made every moment seem an eternity, and Elgiva looked continually toward the doorway, hoping to see the wet-nurse.

What was keeping the woman? How difficult could it be to find a pot of salve?

She paced the floor, carefully stepping around her son and his fleet of tiny wooden ships and imagining herself entombed in this cramped space throughout the coming winter months. That prospect did nothing to improve her mood. While Cnut was in the great hall where he and his men were no doubt drinking ale and regaling each other with stories, her only companions were ill-tempered children and the bitter wives of Swein's English allies.

The women were never referred to as hostages, but they knew exactly what they were. Their presence here ensured that their husbands, most of them somewhere in the south with Swein, would remain loyal to their Danish overlords. And did they blame Swein or Cnut for this? No. They blamed her, and she had to put up with their sour looks, their endless grumbling and their spite.

Her cousin Aldyth was the worst of them, sitting there by herself, looking as though she despised everyone. There was a cold, brittle hatred lurking behind her great cow eyes—eyes that, just now, lingered so long on Thyri that Elgiva, recalling the curse that Aldyth had laid upon her children, clutched her daughter more closely to her, which only made the little imp scream the louder.

She had sometimes thought that Aldyth's heartbreak over the deaths of her own children had driven her to a kind of madness, but she had never been able to convince anyone else of it.

"It is not madness," Tyra had claimed, "but the shadow of grief that hangs about that one. She will never escape it, but she will harm no one, least of all a child."

Nevertheless, Elgiva did not trust Aldyth. And where under heaven was the wet-nurse?

When the woman finally rushed in with the salve that promised to sooth Thyri's pain, Elgiva eagerly thrust the child into her arms.

"There is word come from the harbor, my lady," the nurse said as she took the squirming infant, "of ships arriving from the south."

Elgiva felt her heart give a little thump. This would be either Swein returning or messengers sent by him with news of events in Wessex. Whoever it was, they would go first to the hall.

She threw on a cloak and, not waiting to see if any of the others followed, she ran through the pelting rain and across the wide, muddy yard.

The noise inside the hall was deafening, and it stank of sweat, wet wool, leather and unwashed bodies.

It stank of men.

She made straight for the dais, where Cnut stood with Halfdan at his side, their heads bent together in conversation. As she approached, Cnut reached out to take her hand, drawing her on to the dais beside him.

"Do you know who it is?" she asked.

"No," he replied, "but we shall learn soon enough."

The wait, though, seemed interminable. Her stomach was knotted with anxiety and her hands were damp, while beside her Cnut went on speaking calmly with Halfdan, as if he had little interest in what they were about to hear.

What if Swein had failed? Until this moment she had been utterly confident that he would succeed in thrusting Æilthered from his throne, but suddenly it seemed as if this entire endeavor had been nothing more than a wild dream. Æthelred had ruled for more years even than she had walked this earth; it seemed unthinkable that anyone could wrench the kingdom from his fierce grasp.

Cnut had feared that Swein's decision to march upon London would lead to disaster. Had he been right? What if even now the shipmen were escorting Swein's body up from the harbor? She searched her mind frantically for some other reason for this long delay but could think of nothing.

The massive door at the far end of the hall stood open, and at last she could see figures gathering outside. The rumble of voices around her stilled as a knot of men strode solemnly into their midst. At the procession's head was a standard bearer, and her breath caught in her throat as she saw Swein's banner hanging limply from the staff. But where was Swein? She looked, but could not find him.

She could see Alric walking just behind the standard bearer, and despite her anxiety she felt a jolt of relief that he, at least, had survived whatever trials these men had faced in the south. The hood of Alric's wet cloak was thrown back, and she searched his face for some hint as to what they were about to hear, but she read neither joy nor sorrow there. That he did not even glance toward her was a bad sign, and she was so frightened that she could scarcely breathe.

She watched, her hand at her throat, as he reached the dais and dropped to one knee and bowed his head. The men behind him did the same, and for what seemed like an eternity there was not a sound in the room. She thought that if Alric did not speak soon, she was going to scream.

At last he lifted his face to Cnut.

In a clear, ringing voice he proclaimed, "I bring you greetings, my lord from Swein Haraldsson, King of Denmark and now, King of all England."

She froze, stunned, while the hall erupted with wild cheers. Swein had done it! Æthelred was dead, and the murders of her father and brothers had been avenged.

Beside her Cnut was urging Alric to join him on the dais. Through eyes filling with glad tears she saw Alric murmur something to Cnut and her husband's answering nod. She would have to discover what that was about. A moment later a cup of mead was thrust into her hand, and when Cnut saluted his father, the warriors in the hall roared Swein's name again and again.

The sound of that name repeated over and over by hundreds of thundering voices crashed over her like a series of massive waves, but as she listened her own mood soured. Cnut should have been the one they were cheering. He should have been the one to lead the army that defeated the English king, not his father. Instead, England belonged to Swein, to a fierce warrior whose name struck terror into English hearts. Even now Swein was likely seated on Æthelred's throne, while Cnut languished here in the north.

While she languished here beside him.

Had that been Swein's plan all along—to keep England for himself rather than deliver it to his son as he had promised? Suddenly, that seemed all too likely. What a fool she had been to trust him, to believe that Cnut would rule England and that she would be the queen at his side. As long as Swein lived, she would be nothing more than the wife of a second son who was king of nothing.

While the cheering continued, Cnut and Alric stepped off the dais and into the throng below, and she watched them move slowly through the hall toward the door. Men swarmed about Cnut, clasping his hand or pounding on his shoulder. She could see Halfdan making for the door as well, and the three of them left together.

Cnut, she knew, would wish to question Alric in private about events in the south. Apparently, even without his wife beside him.

Well, she would not let that stand.

She left the dais and made her way out of the hall and into the rain, clutching her cloak about her as the wind tried to rip it from her.

When she reached Cnut's quarters she found the three men gathered around a table where a parchment had been spread, its corners anchored with candles. She marched straight to Cnut's side as if she had been invited to this meeting. Cnut, though, did not even look at her, so intent was he on what Alric was saying.

As she listened to Alric's account of the events of the past month it became all too clear to her that Swein's campaign had not resulted in the kind of conquest that the men in the hall were celebrating. London had not yet submitted. Worse than that, and to her outrage, Æthelred was still alive.

"Why did Swein not tear down the walls of London and take him?" she hissed. "Take his sons as well, and that filthy Eadric—"

"Be silent, Elgiva, or be gone!" Cnut shot her a quelling glance that she knew well, and she snapped her mouth shut.

"My lady," Alric said gently, "I fear that you make far too light of London's walls. Æthelred is alive, yes, but he cannot hold out for much longer. His ministers—the lords who make up his witan and supply his armies—most of them have submitted."

Most of them, Elgiva thought. But not all. Some would remain at the king's side because they had too much to lose by turning against him. She could guess who those men might be; she had known them. Her father had once been the most powerful magnate among them until the king had ordered Eadric to butcher him.

"Only London still clings to the old king," Alric was speaking to Cnut again, "and the city continues to harbor him. Your father, though, has a plan that he believes will change that. It will require your help, my lord."

"Where is my father?"

"By now he should be well on his way here with two thousand of his men, many of them wounded, so it will take them some weeks to make the journey."

Why, she wondered, was he coming back? She dared not ask it aloud, though, for fear that Cnut would send her away.

"And the remaining men?" Cnut asked.

"Some we lost beneath the walls of London. Of the rest," he bent over the parchment that was covered with lines and marks that meant nothing to her, "half of them are garrisoning the major towns—Wallingford, here; Oxford, here." His finger moved around the parchment as he spoke. "Bath, Winchester, Exeter. They are to keep the populace under control throughout the winter. Thurbrand, though, is leading more than two thousand men toward London from the west. You, my lord, are to take as many ships and men as can be spared and approach from the east. The Londoners must know that if they do not surrender, we will lay siege. They cannot win."

Cnut studied the map, then pointed to a circle that she guessed marked London.

"What about Thorkell's ships?" he asked. "If his fleet still lies in the Thames, he will prevent my own ships from getting anywhere near the city. I cannot hope to match his numbers with the men at my disposal."

"You are not to engage Thorkell," Alric said. "Those were your father's exact words, my lord. Instead you are to make landfall at the southern end of East Anglia and link up with Ulfkytel." He rested his finger upon another mark on the parchment. "You will find him there, on the River Orwell, close by Ipswich. Despite the tribute he has sent, his support has been half-hearted. Swein believes that it is time for Ulfkytel to prove his loyalty. You are to press him to gather as many men as he can assemble, and together you will lead your forces to London. There is a good road that will take you all the way to the Aldgate. From Ipswich to London," he dragged his finger along the parchment, "will be a sennight's march, even if the weather turns foul. London cannot hold out, my lord," he said, "not for long. And your father believes that the Londoners will not even attempt to fight. The city stands alone."

The talk then was of ships, food supplies, weapons, and the number of men who could be spared, and of Halfdan's role as camp commander until Swein's arrival. Elgiva paid little heed. She stared at the map and at the mark that designated London, and a thrill of satisfaction coursed through her. In a matter of days, two armies would meet at London. They would engulf the city and it would all be over.

Years of planning and waiting, of aggravation and desperation were about to end.

And what then?

She could not say. She would have to bid Tyra to cast the rune sticks and scry the future for her. And, she had to admit, she had done Swein a disservice. He would not be the one to ride through the streets of London to accept its submission and force its people to deliver Æthelred into Danish hands. It would be Cnut.

When their planning was done and Cnut had sent Alric and Halfdan back to the hall to join the celebration there, she went to her husband. Wrapping her arms around his middle she gazed up at him.

"Take me with you to London," she said.

For a long moment he searched her face, and she knew that he was trying to read what was in her mind. But she endured it because, for once, she had nothing to hide.

"Why do you wish to go to London?" he asked. "Are you weary of Gainsborough? Would you brave a sea voyage and days of hard travel through winter storms just to escape the tedium of your life here?"

It would be a wet, cold, miserable voyage, she did not doubt it. But at the end of it, there would be London.

"I have braved difficult winter journeys before this, and I promise you that I can suffer it without complaint."

"You have not answered my question. Why?"

She placed her palm on his cheek, caressed the rough beard beneath her hand and, gazing into those dark eyes of his she said, "Because I would see my husband, who is destined to be England's king, ride through the streets of this kingdom's greatest city in triumph."

She did not add that she also wished to be witness to Æthelred's humiliation and perhaps even his well-deserved end. Far better to let her husband believe that she thought of no one but him.

Again he was silent, and she held her breath. He rarely granted her requests. Sometimes she had been forced to act in secret to get what she wanted. She hoped just this once that it would not come to that.

Then, to her surprise, he kissed her—a long, lingering kiss that she responded to willingly, although she feared he was merely trying to distract her.

When he lifted his mouth from hers, he whispered, "We leave in two days. Bring your body servant with you and no one else."

His words sent a shiver of delight coursing through her, and she stood on her toes to kiss him again.

To be sure, the journey would be more difficult with only Tyra along to attend her; and in any case, who else would she have chosen to accompany her? Certainly not that mouse Catla, whom she hated, or her witch of a cousin, Aldyth.

"There is something else that you must agree to," Cnut said, his voice stern. "You will obey any order I give you without question. And you will expect no special privileges because you are a woman or because you are my wife. Is that understood?"

She clasped her hands about his neck and said, "As it pleases you, my lord. But I have another request."

He eyed her suspiciously.

"Go on."

"If I am to be denied wifely privileges on the journey ahead, I would very much like to have them now."

And, as she had hoped, he laughed, lifted her in his arms and carried her to his bed.

Chapter Sixteen

November 1013
London

The cluster of six, stout-bellied merchant vessels slipped from their London moorings in the light of a cold winter dawn and turned their prows eastward. Near the steering platform of the largest ship, Athelstan stood with Godwin, peering upward as the great sail bellied. Brihtwold had assured him that if the wind held, the ships would drop anchor for the night near the queen's estate in East Anglia. On the morrow they would set out again for Bruges, and from there sail to the mouth of the Seine and up river to the ducal court of Richard at Rouen.

He lowered his gaze to survey his fellow passengers. There was nothing in the appearance of the fifteen or so men and women who mingled with the crew and the handful of his own hearth guards that would mark them as members of the royal household. Even Emma, clad in a dark grey gown and heavy woolen cloak, looked more like a merchant's wife than a queen.

It was what lay hidden in the ships' holds, he thought uneasily, that would be their undoing should any of Swein's drekar have left their harbor at Gainsborough to prowl the coast for prey. This vessel and three others carried the wealth of a king buried beneath piles of mundane trading goods. The other two had a vast supply of arms stored under their decking, cargo that was not destined for Normandy, although only a trusted few knew it.

Thinking about how he meant to use those weapons, he turned to Godwin.

"Withar and Ulfkytel will be waiting for us when we arrive at Shotley," he said. "They will have as large a force of warriors as they can gather. Do you know what you are to do?"

"Aye, my lord. Get the men and supplies on board two of our ships under cover of darkness and have them ready to sail for Bosham at first light." Godwin cocked a brow at him. "Your father will be furious when he learns that you have defied him and will stay in England."

"He will. Does that worry you?"

In the silence that followed Athelstan considered Godwin, weighing what he knew of him. The man had seen only twenty winters, but he was a born warrior—sturdily built, strong as a bull and quick with a sword. His brown eyes were set in a round, genial face that was framed by light brown hair and a thick beard. But there was a sharp wit behind his ready smile, and a cleverness that Athelstan had learned to respect.

"Your father," Godwin said at last, "has a long reach, my lord. And there are a great many men in England who still fear him."

He was counseling caution, and Athelstan knew what lay behind the warning. It had been—how many years now? It must be eight. Eight years since Godwin's father had been falsely accused of treachery against the king. Afraid for his life, Wulfnoth had fled England, and his lands had been forfeit. Godwin had never seen his father again. Now he was risking the enmity of a king just as his father had done. He was right to be wary.

Athelstan looked toward the shore where the sun cast a golden light on the marsh reeds and grasses—on a kingdom that he could no longer claim, although by right of birth and heritage it should one day be his. The Danes had beaten and cowed the English into submission, and most of the great lords now regarded King Swein as England's ruler. Even in London, the city leaders had met with his father and begged him to seek refuge elsewhere. No one could blame them. Æthelred was now an outlaw in his own realm and should he remain in London he would draw disaster down upon the city.

Athelstan had said as much at his father's council, insisting that despite its walls London was no longer safe; that if the king, his family, and his supporters did not get out of England soon they might never get out at all. Yet it was only with reluctance that his father had agreed to Emma's departure for Normandy and to Athelstan's own suggestion that he accompany her.

The king, though, had refused to leave the city. As long as Thorkell and his fleet guarded the Thames his father was hoping that he could somehow defy Swein. He was hoping for a miracle.

"My father cannot, I think, stay in England much longer," he assured Godwin, "now that nearly every shire has submitted to Swein. The queen will certainly persuade her brother to extend an offer of refuge, and the king will join her in Rouen. When he does, he will no longer rule England, and our vows of loyalty to him will no longer bind us. We need not fear his wrath."

He could not say how soon that would happen, but when it did, he and Edmund intended to rally the men of England to resist the Danes. He would do what many nobles had been urging him to do for so long—forge his own path to the throne. The queen, although she did not yet know it, would have to rely on others to escort her across the sea.

As if she had somehow heard his thought, Emma, standing on the ship's foredeck, turned around to look at him, and their eyes met and held.

God forgive me, he thought, I shall always love her.

After all the years that had passed and all the trouble they had witnessed, his yearning for her still tormented him. Soon he would have to let her go, admit that their destinies must be forever sundered because he could not forsake England and because she, he knew, would not forsake her children.

The moment of silent communication between them lengthened, and the words of the old prophecy came back to him, as haunting and disturbing as on the day he had first heard them.

Whoever would hold the scepter of England must first hold the hand of the queen.

There had been more to the foretelling. It had warned of fire and destruction for England, and a dark road for the sons of Æthelred—calamities that had now come to pass, for the kingdom had been ravaged, and the future of Æthelred's remaining sons was dark indeed.

Would the prophecy about the queen's hand prove true as well? If so, Swein Forkbeard's conquest would be futile. He could never be anointed king of England, for how could he or anyone win the hand of the queen while Emma remained in Normandy, the wife of Æthelred?

Nevertheless, that part of the prophecy continued to seduce him, continued to hold out the promise of possibilities that he could not yet grasp.

And that made him no different from his father. For like his father, he was hoping for a miracle.

Shotley, Suffolk, East Anglia

It was near dark when Brihtwold's six ships entered the estuary of the River Orwell. The business of dropping anchor and sail took far longer than Emma could have wished, for she was anxious to get to shore, to the manor where she had left Wymarc and Wulfa in the spring to await the birth of Wulfa's child. By the time that she was seated at last in the ship's small wherry next to Athelstan, with Brihtwold and Godwin facing them and manning the oars, the first stars glimmered in the night sky.

As the little boat carried them over the broad stretch of river, she wondered what Athelstan was thinking. He was peering into the gloom ahead, his mouth tight and his brow furrowed. Was it anxiety that she read there, or despair? Her own fears and misgivings weighed heavily upon her, and she longed for the reassuring comfort of his arms around her. But that solace was forbidden, and she forced herself to look away from him, to ignore the dark flame of desire sparked by the mere touch of his shoulder against hers.

Instead she peered back at the huge bulk of the *Wind Rider* where the passengers were gathering to partake of their cold meal. She had wanted them all to come ashore, to spend the night at Shotley where they would be warm and dry and well-fed on this, their last night in England. But Brihtwold had refused even to consider it.

"The Orwell is tidal, my lady, and the ships must remain in mid-river. I dare not bring them any closer to shore for fear of grounding them at low tide," he had explained. "We have not the time it will take to ferry everyone ashore tonight and back to the ships at dawn. I am sorry for it, but your people must spend the night on the river."

Now she turned to address him. "Do your captains have their orders for the morning?" she asked.

"Aye," he assured her. "The ships sail at first light, except for the *Wind Rider*. She will wait until you are aboard. But, I beg you, my lady, do not tarry long ashore. It will take us a full day to make the crossing to Bruges, and then only if the winds are kind."

"You have my word," she said, hoping that she could keep that promise. If Wulfa's babe had not yet been born, the journey to Bruges must be delayed, for she would not leave her stepdaughter behind.

She fixed her eyes on the shore and on the single light that glimmered there—a lantern, she guessed. Someone was watching for them. In the gathering darkness beyond that light lay her manor with its hall and outbuildings, its forests and meadows, and its royal household—sadly depleted now, but still clinging to ancient allegiances despite the Danish threat.

"What if Ulfkytel is with Wulfa at the manor?" she murmured to Athelstan. "He has submitted to Swein however unwillingly. Athelstan, you may be in danger here."

"You need have no fear of that," he replied. "I promise you."

She looked at him then, surprised by his certainty, and alarmed as well. He was keeping something from her, but this was not the time to question him. They were nearing the shore now and Athelstan stood up to toss a rope to the man who waited for them on the hythe. In the lantern light she saw with relief that it was Athelstan's retainer, Withar, sent ahead some days before to alert the household of their arrival. Godwin scrambled out of the wherry and reached down to hand her up beside him. Athelstan and Brihtwold quickly followed, and Withar, holding the lantern high to light the way, led them briskly up the narrow path toward the manor buildings.

Inside the hall a fire blazed in the central hearth, and they were met by Wymarc and a small clutch of servants who greeted them with courtly courtesy. Emma embraced her old friend.

"How is it with you?" she asked.

"I am better for the sight of you," Wymarc said, "and grateful that you have made it safely to us."

"And Wulfa?"

"She was delivered of a son this morning. Lord Ulfkytel is with her, and they are both eager to see you," and turning to Athelstan she added, "and you, as well, my lord."

They shed their cloaks, and as Wymarc led them up a wooden staircase she confided to Emma that Wulfa had had a long and difficult labor. At the top of the stairs they passed through a gap between two woven screens that afforded some privacy to the upper chamber. Wulfa lay on the bed, bolstered by pillows, holding her swaddled babe in her arms, and weeping as Ulfkytel bent over her, speaking urgently. Gently he caressed her cheek, and she reached for his hand to kiss it.

So this, Emma thought, was a farewell. For how long? she wondered. She greeted Wulfa and admired the babe, and when she stepped aside to give Athelstan and his sister some moments together, Ulfkytel approached her.

"I am placing my wife and son into your care, my lady," he said with stiff formality. "I trust that you will see them safely away on the morrow. It is imperative that they leave England as soon as may be."

"I will see them safely to Normandy, my lord," she assured him. She looked up into the face of this warrior whom even the Danes feared. He towered over her, comely, fair-haired and beardless with a high brow and deep-set brown eyes. She recalled what Wulfa had said of him at Peterborough in the spring. He had hit her, just the once, she had said. Wulfa's greatest concern, though, had been for him, and Emma recalled her words.

He was not angry. He was afraid. Something was very wrong.

Something, indeed, had been wrong, for when the Danish force landed some months later, the mighty warrior Ulfkytel had bent the knee to Swein without raising his sword. Why? She had assumed he had been persuaded, however reluctantly, with promises he could not bring himself to refuse. Now, though, she wondered if it had been threats that had forced his submission—threats, perhaps, against his wife, the daughter of the English king.

Ulfkytel's gaze strayed to Wulfa, and his expression softened. It was plain to see how very much he cared for her.

"I am grateful, my lady, for your help," he said, his voice gruff with emotion. Then he called to Athelstan, "My lord, we have much to discuss."

Emma watched, uncertain and uneasy, as the two men went down the stairs. They had some scheme in hand, it appeared, and it surely meant that Ulfkytel had already renounced, at least privately, whatever oaths he had given Swein. She wished that Athelstan had told her what he was planning to do, but there had been few chances for them even to speak together.

She sighed, frustrated, and returned to Wulfa's bedside. Wymarc reappeared with a tray of food for Emma and a strengthening brew of warm ale and butter for the new mother. The three of them sat together for a time discussing the babe, and the birth, and the rigors of the journey that lay ahead. Wulfa, looking tired and pale, was dreading the voyage, and Emma did not blame her. Crossing the sea on an open ship would be a misery for a woman barely out of childbed, especially as the birth had been difficult.

When Wulfa at last began to doze, Wymarc rose to replace the guttering candle on the table near the door. Emma bade her get some sleep, and she left the two women curled up on the bed with the child between them.

In the hall she found the few women of the household setting out pallets around the central hearth. She looked for Athelstan, but there was no sign of him. Indeed, there were no men about at all, and she found that unsettling. Once again, she wondered what Athelstan and Ulfkytel were planning.

An elderly woman approached with Emma's cloak in her arms, and Emma recognized her as one of the attendants who had been in the household of Æthelred's first wife.

"Mildreth," she said, as the woman gave a little bob of respect, "Wulfa tells me that you will be accompanying us to Normandy."

Mildreth gestured toward numerous boxes and bundles that were piled near the door.

"Yes, my lady. All is in readiness for the morrow, as you see. And I shall go gladly. My home now is with the Lady Wulfhilde, wherever she may be." She shook her head, her lined face grave. "Our people will have a bad winter here, I fear. Even on these royal lands our food stores have been plundered to feed the foreign armies, and I think there will be even darker days ahead." She drew a long breath, then looked stricken. "But you must be weary after your journey and will be wanting your bed! Your chamber is prepared, and I would be honored to attend you through the night, my lady, if you wish."

"Thank you, but there is no need," Emma replied, stepping into the cloak that Mildreth held up for her. "Tonight I shall sleep dressed as you see me." And as she had a great deal on her mind, she doubted she would sleep much at all. "Please send someone, though, to fetch me at dawn." At the door, she turned back to ask, "Can you tell me where Lord Athelstan has gone?"

"He left some time ago with the other men but, I am sorry, my lady, I cannot say where they went."

Cannot say? Emma thought. Was that because she did not know, or because she had been forbidden to speak? Mildreth's deepest loyalty, she guessed, was to Athelstan and Wulfa, whom she had served since their childhood; and that, she supposed, was as it should be.

She nodded, resigned. She would have to wait until the morning to speak with him. Once outside the hall she stood for a time with her back pressed against the great door. The sky was clear, and a full moon had risen, so bright that shadows dappled the yard. She looked around her, at this royal manor of hers that was but a small fragment of a once mighty kingdom. It was, she feared, the last glimpse of England that she would ever have.

Unlike Mildreth, she had no wish to leave this land that she had grown to love. Home, for her, would always be England, where she had been queen, but where she was queen no longer.

The enormity of what had occurred over the last few months—and of the terrible uncertainty that lay ahead—washed over her with a force and suddenness that all but drove her to her knees. Swein of Denmark was England's conqueror, and she had little hope that he would be gentle with its people. His followers would demand power, wealth, and lands, and they would take what they desired by force of arms.

There will be no mercy, Athelstan had once warned her, and surely that was the truth. In London she had tended men who had been wounded in battle and women who had been raped. She had seen the terrible consequences of power unleashed without mercy.

Æthelred's thegns had abandoned him because he had failed to protect his people from the ravages of the Danes. Who would they turn to now for protection?

She picked her way across the yard toward the familiar, squat building that had long housed the queen's bedchamber, and she forced herself to think at last about the task that lay ahead of her in Normandy. She had been charged with securing a place of refuge for the king, his family, and the retainers who would accompany him. It would not be easy, for she expected to find only recrimination and resentment awaiting her in Rouen. Her brother had gambled that her marriage to the wealthiest monarch in Christendom would bring him status and influence, but instead she would be asking him to support an exiled king.

That burden weighed heavily upon her as she lifted the door latch and stepped into the dimly lit chamber.

She remembered this room from her time here in the spring, and in all but one respect it remained exactly the same as she had known it then. Pallet beds for royal attendants lined two of the walls, and in the far corner, shrouded by thick, embroidered hangings, stood the oaken bed that had, over the course of many years, welcomed the wives of numerous kings. Immediately in front of her a fire burned in the central hearth, casting a warm glow upon the single thing in the chamber that was different.

Beside the hearth, Athelstan stood watching her, his eyes shining in the firelight.

She did not move, rooted to the floor, not daring to take even a step closer to him, frightened as she was by the force of her own desire.

"You should not be here," she whispered.

He shook his head with a rueful smile.

"I have ever been accused of doing what I should not," he replied. "A failing, I confess. I should not love my father's wife, and yet—" he shrugged, but the look in his eyes burned her.

She wrapped her mantle closer about her, as if she could somehow shield herself from his searing gaze. Her need for him was so great, where was she to find the courage to send him away?

"What else have you been doing, Athelstan, that you should not?" she asked, trying to ease the tension that arced between them. "What is it that you and Ulfkytel—"

"I am not going to Normandy, Emma," he said.

She felt as if he had slapped her, and her heart seemed to stop with the shock of it. For a moment she could not speak, and Athelstan filled the silence.

"I will sail at dawn for Bosham, not Bruges. I cannot leave England in Danish hands. Surely that cannot surprise you."

No, she was not surprised. But she had convinced herself that he would do as his father had commanded; he would go into exile because it was what she wanted him to do, because she could not bear to leave him. And now, it seemed, he was to leave her.

"You will take up the fight against the Danes," she sighed. And with a sinking heart, she found the answers to the questions that had puzzled her. "Ulfkytel has already, it seems, broken his oath of allegiance to Swein, and he will fight beside you. That is why he is so insistent that his wife and son must leave England."

"In Normandy they will be safe from Danish vengeance," he said.

"And what of your safety, Athelstan?" she cried. "If you are captured—" She could not say it, nor did she need to. He knew the risks, but he also knew what he might gain. Once his father no longer stood in his way, Athelstan would make his own bid for the throne, she saw that now. And because this ætheling was a warrior proven in battle and, unlike his father, a leader to be trusted, he would inspire the men of England to throw off their new Danish overlord. The crown of England was Athelstan's by right, and if he survived the conflict that lay ahead he would be a good and just king.

But first he must survive.

"Does your father know what you intend?"

"No. He would think me a traitor for challenging Swein under my own banner. You know how his mind works. Despite all that has happened, my father believes that the crown of England should still be his and that somehow God will relent and give it back to him." He took a single step, erasing the distance between them and placing his hands on her shoulders. "Emma, I have no choice. There will be nothing for me in Normandy—nothing there that I could possibly want, except you. Yet you are the one thing on this earth that I can never have."

She looked at him through eyes brimming with tears that she could not stem. On the morrow he would leave her, and the future without him yawned dark and cold and empty. She could not see past this parting, and she did not know how she was to let him go, for her heart told her that he was leaving her for the last time.

"I have always been yours," she whispered, "even though my body belonged to another."

"And now?" he asked, bending to tentatively, questioningly graze his lips against hers.

She could not move away. For too many years she had denied herself—denied them both—what body and soul had craved, and she could do it no longer. She responded hungrily to his gentle kiss and bound herself to him, mouth to mouth and breath to breath.

It was as if she had set a flame to dry tinder. Pressing herself into his embrace, she abandoned the constraint that had kept them so long apart. Despite duty and family and even God, she surrendered to his need and to hers—two lovers joined as one.

There was little joy in their coupling. The tender caresses and whispered endearments that she gave and received were steeped in grief, and their passion was laced with despair.

When, exhausted but not sated, she lay naked in his arms, she wept silent tears for what was not the beginning of their love, but the end of it. She listened to him speak of what he was about to do, of his ships and his men, and of the war he meant to wage against Swein. His was a world that no longer included her, and she was forced to contemplate her life without him in it.

At last the inevitable moment of leave taking came, and bitter as it was, she made no protest. They helped each other don discarded garments, fastening belts and laces with hands that still found opportunities to caress. Standing in front of him, she took from her thumb a ring that had once been her father's. It was a simple, golden circle, with a looping design engraved upon it that had no beginning and no end.

"Let this be your talisman against harm," she said, placing it upon his smallest finger. "Promise me that you will wear it always."

She slipped her arms about his waist for a final, long embrace, as if she could somehow make him a part of her again. He kissed her with a tenderness that fractured her heart into a thousand pieces. Then he stepped into the night and she was alone.

River Orwell, East Anglia

The sun stood three fingers above the horizon and the rest of the little fleet was already gone when the *Wind Rider* began its final preparations for departure. Emma and Wymarc, their cloaks wrapped about them against a chilly breeze, watched from its deck as the wherry, with Wulfa seated on its bench and her babe in her arms, made the last of its four trips ferrying passengers and supplies from the manor.

Wymarc glanced skyward, at clouds scudding toward them on a northerly wind.

"This will be an unpleasant voyage, I think," Wymarc murmured to Emma. "We shall all be sick before we reach Bruges."

"It will be hardest on Wulfa," Emma replied, "but we shall give her what little comfort is to be had."

As she watched Wulfa and her child handed aboard, she thought about the king's other daughters who remained behind—Mathilda in her convent at Wherwell, Ælfa all but a prisoner in her husband's Northumbrian fastness, Edyth still in London with Eadric and the king. She whispered a prayer that the Virgin would keep them safe from harm.

While the crew prepared to sail, Wulfa, Mildreth, and the baby were settled into a tent that had been erected for them on the deck. Emma, emerging from it with Wymarc as the ship began to move, joined Brihtwold at the prow. The few oarsmen were maneuvering the ship toward the river's mouth when Brihtwold shaded his eyes against the sun and muttered a quiet curse. Emma, following his gaze, saw ships coming swiftly toward them from somewhere out at sea, their oars beating the water like wings.

"Those are Danish warships, my lady, and a swarm of them. They will be upon us soon."

"We are the larger ship," Emma said, "and we have men and weapons. Can we not fend them off and get away?"

"This barque is far too slow to outrun them, and they will have three times the warriors that we have. If we try to fight, we will kill some of them but they will slaughter all of us."

As they watched the approaching ships they were joined by Ealdorman Ælfric, two of his retainers and Abbot Ælfsy.

"We must try to beguile them," Ælfric said. "Our men will keep their swords out of sight and you, my lady, must be the wife of this good merchant here."

Emma nodded and looked pointedly at Brihtwold.

"Perhaps, my lord, a bribe is in order?"

He nodded agreement. "It's a rare Dane who will turn down the offer of easy gain," he said. "A coffer heavy with coin may buy us their favor. When they board us, let me speak with them and see if we cannot come to some agreement."

A great deal, she thought, would depend on the temper of the men who led the Danes—whether they were merely avaricious, or whether they were cruel as well. The stories came back to her again of women raped and children slaughtered.

Children were so easy to kill.

She turned to Wymarc and said, "See that Wulfa stays inside the tent with her babe. And stay there with her."

Abbot Ælfsy had dropped to his knees on the foredeck, and her people had gathered around him to pray. Emma, standing at Brihtwold's side, prayed with them but kept her eyes on the approaching ships.

It did not take long. Iron hooks and chains were used to bind the *Wind Rider* to the smaller ships, and a handful of armed men scurried aboard. Some of them, threatening with shouts and drawn swords, surrounded the unresisting passengers and crew. Others began a cursory inspection of the cargo in the hold—like ravens, Emma thought, looking for something shiny.

She searched among them for their leader, for someone with whom Brihtwold might strike a bargain. She knew she had found him when she saw a tall figure come aboard with a retinue in his wake, a man garbed in a fur-trimmed cloak that bespoke wealth and standing. He wore no helmet, but his mail burney and his broad, muscular shoulders marked him as a warrior. His hair was rust-colored like his beard, and he wore it pulled back from his face in a long plait.

When he looked toward their little group, though, any hope she had of deceiving him was shattered. A flash of recognition crossed his face, and as she returned his penetrating gaze her mind was flooded by the memory of watchful black eyes and the painful grip of strong, slender fingers upon her wrists. She had been his captive once, on a day seared into her memory by cruelty and bloodshed. Now, here he was again— Cnut, son of Swein, a wielder of death and destruction just like his father.

And it appeared that she was once again his captive.

Beside her Brihtwold stirred, preparing to meet their captor and initiate a parley, unaware that the figure stalking toward them was the son of the Danish king. She placed a hand upon his arm.

"I will speak to this man," she said. Brihtwold looked at her in surprise and she curled her lips in distaste. "I know him."

She stepped forward, and at a word from Cnut the shipmen allowed her to pass. As she drew close to him she tried to read his intent. His expression seemed a mix of curiosity and speculation. He knew who she was and so he must suspect that there was royal treasure hidden somewhere beneath his feet. As they halted, facing each other, a flurry of movement behind him drew her gaze. There, stepping briskly on to the deck of the *Wind Rider* like some malign shade haunting her from the past, was Elgiva.

Chapter Seventeen

November 1013
River Orwell, East Anglia

Elgiva strode swiftly toward the captives that had been herded together on the foredeck of the huge merchant vessel, and when she saw the tall woman who stepped forward to confront Cnut she laughed aloud. Emma had swaddled herself in a dull grey cloak and hidden her bright hair beneath a woolen veil. Except for her arrogant expression she bore little resemblance to the glittering queen she had once been. Anyone who did not know her might mistake her for an abbess or a merchant's wife.

Cnut knew her though, and he was greeting her with a deep bow. What a foolish, empty gesture, Elgiva thought, to offer this wife of a conquered king. Emma did not even deign to acknowledge his obeisance. Indeed, she looked angrier than Elgiva had ever seen her. Those green eyes were blazing, and the pale face was so rigid with fury that it could have been carved from ice.

Poor Emma. She did not yet understand how very impotent her anger was. She was a hostage now, and helpless in the hands of her captors.

"Well done, my lord," Elgiva said in Danish to Cnut. "You have taken a fine prize indeed." And then, in English, she said to Emma, "Greetings, my lady. I did not think to find you so far from the comforts of your hall at Winchester."

Emma did not even look at her, but continued to glare at Cnut.

"By what right, lord," Emma demanded, "do you board this ship?"

Her words—Danish words—startled Elgiva. When had Emma learned to speak the Northmen's tongue?

Then she remembered that Emma's mother had been born a Dane, and that she must have schooled her daughter in that language. How clever of Emma to hide that from Æthelred and his court. It would have linked her in people's minds to England's Danish enemies and earned her nothing but hostility. What a skilled dissembler she was!

Cnut, though, appeared unsurprised by the Danish that had spilled from Emma's mouth. No doubt he had discovered her secret when she had been his captive all those years ago.

Elgiva peered at her husband through narrowed eyes. What else did he know about Emma that she did not?

"My right," Cnut said, "is one of conquest, my lady. All of England is Danish now, and that includes this ship."

His reply did not appease Emma. She was still glaring at him, her voice icy as she said, "We are not on English soil here, lord, but on the sea. This ship and everything on it is mine, and I am a Norman. You have, I think, no quarrel with Normandy."

Elgiva, impatient with this banter, glared at Cnut. She wanted to slap him into action. He should already have ordered his men to search this vessel. Instead he wore the same bemused expression she had seen on the faces of other men that Emma had turned into helpless idiots as she swayed them to do her bidding.

"Her children are English, my lord," she hissed. She pointed to the tent that had been rigged up in front of the mast. "Have your men look for them in there." If the children were here it would be easy to dispose of them and be rid of claimants to the English throne who may one day prove troublesome. "Your father," she added pointedly, "would have done it already."

As if to confirm her suspicions, the wail of an infant pierced the air and was quickly silenced.

Cnut gestured to one of his warriors who pushed his way roughly through the English captives to peer into the tent.

"There are three women here, my lord," he called, "and a babe. Newborn, by the look of it."

Cnut frowned at Emma. "Is it your child?" he demanded. He was far less genial now, Elgiva thought smugly.

Emma, though, lifted her chin, still defiant as she replied, "My children are not on this ship."

Elgiva laughed. "A mother's lie, I do not doubt. It is simple enough to discover the truth, my lord, if the lady will remove her cloak."

Cnut cocked his head at Emma.

"If you would oblige us, my lady," he said.

Emma's mouth tightened into a thin, angry line, but she unclasped the brooch at her throat and allowed her cloak to slip from her shoulders and into her hands. Elgiva peered at the slender figure in its grey woolen gown with neither the breasts nor the belly of a new mother. She answered Cnut's questioning glance with a shake of her head.

She studied the faces of Emma's companions, disappointed when she found none of the elder æthelings among them. She recognized the king's thegn Ælfric, though, glaring at her as if he'd like to slit her throat. He was one of those who had always been besotted with Emma, the old fool.

"There is an ealdorman there," she told Cnut, "that greybeard standing beside the priest."

"The only greybeard I care about is Æthelred," Cnut muttered, and he again frowned at Emma. "Where is your husband? Does he live still?"

"He lives," she said stiffly. "Where he is at present I do not know, nor would I tell you if I did."

Cnut nodded, his expression thoughtful. "Yet he has sent you away from his side. To what purpose, I wonder. As an emissary, perhaps?"

"She must have a wealth of treasure hidden on this ship," Elgiva hissed. "How many Norman warriors will it buy, I wonder, to help Æthelred attempt to win back his throne come the spring?"

"What say you to that, my lady?" Cnut addressed Emma. "Shall I have my men empty this ship down to the ballast stones to discover what gifts Æthelred is sending to your brother?"

"My brother," she replied, "entertained your father in Rouen not long ago. He treated King Swein with great honor, and I am told that they pledged each other lasting friendship. Surely you must know that Richard will perceive any hostile act against me as a violation of that oath. Are you willing to risk his anger?"

Elgiva did not like that word *oath*. Cnut held oaths in high regard—far too high in her opinion. She folded her arms, impatient, flicking her gaze from Cnut to Emma and back again while the two of them faced each other, their eyes locked in some silent contest in which she played no part.

Surely Cnut was not thinking of letting Emma go! He could not be foolish enough to allow the wealth hidden here to slip through his fingers!

"This is the wife of your enemy," she reminded him, although he should not have needed reminding. "You owe her nothing."

To her surprise, Emma at last fixed her with that icy gaze.

"You are mistaken, Elgiva. This son of Swein is in my debt." She glared again at Cnut. "Or perhaps, lord, you have forgotten?"

Elgiva looked at Cnut, confused. "What does she mean?" she demanded.

But he remained silent and thoughtful, and he never took his eyes off of Emma. Finally, his mouth curled into a half-smile.

"I have forgotten neither the debt that I owe you, my lady," he said, "nor the oaths that my father and your brother pledged to one another." He paused, and his expression grew stern. "Go to Richard, then, as my emissary. Bid him remember his pledge of friendship and, if you love him, warn him of the peril that he will face should he break it."

Elgiva hissed a protest, but he ignored her. He leaned close to Emma and said, "Take care that you do not fall into my hands again, for next time I will not be so generous. My debt to you is paid."

Even before he finished speaking, Elgiva turned away, disgusted. The fool had squandered an opportunity that he would likely never see again, and before this day was over she would know why.

Ipswich, East Anglia

Cnut spent a rainy afternoon seeing that his ships were made secure, that necessary food supplies had been wrung from the resentful townsfolk, and that his nearly two hundred men were sheltered from what promised to be a filthy night. By nightfall he was tired, cold, and hungry.

He ducked into Ulfkytel's hall and, shrugging his dripping cloak into waiting hands, he paused to speak with the shipman guarding the door.

"Have you seen Alric?"

"No, my lord."

"When he gets here send him straight to me."

"Yes, lord."

He made his way past tables crowded with men who had stood when they saw him enter, and when he barked at them to sit and save their feet for the march to London they collapsed, laughing, back to their benches.

Elgiva was sitting at a table on one side of the hall, surrounded by women whom he assumed were residents of the town—every one of them looking either sullen or scared.

He frowned. If his wife had made any effort to befriend them, she had not succeeded. He doubted that she had even tried. Her dislike of other women was one of her failings.

He stepped on to the dais and took the seat at the high table that would normally have been Ulfkytel's. A moment later Elgiva was at his elbow placing a cup of ale and a platter of bread and roasted meat in front of him.

"Has everything been settled to your liking?" she asked, sitting beside him and pouring ale for herself.

"Nearly settled," he replied as he tore a piece off the loaf, "although not to my liking. A group of townsfolk decided they did not wish to follow our orders, and what should have been a negotiation turned into a battle. There are ten dead as a result, four of them my shipmen. I blame Ulfkytel. He was supposed to be here to intercede between his people and mine. I expected to find allies here, not resistance." He gestured toward the table where she had been sitting. "Did you learn anything from the women?"

"Only that they are afraid," she said. "Did you not send messengers to Ulfkytel, to alert him of your arrival? Where is he?"

Cnut scowled. He had no answer to that question yet, and it worried him. Nor had he found any sign of the men that he had sent here with that message.

"I spoke with his steward," he pointed with his knife at the man, who had just entered the hall. "He claims that three days ago Ulfkytel rode south with a large company of men. He did not know where they went, exactly, or why. I have sent Alric and Siferth to look for him, but they have not yet returned." He eyed the steward—a tall, gaunt old man with a prominent nose who had given him a chilly welcome. If he discovered that the man had lied about Ulfkytel's whereabouts, he would order someone to slit that long nose of his.

"And if Ulfkytel cannot be found?" Elgiva asked. "What happens then?"

He glanced at her, irritated by her endless questions; but he answered her.

"Without Ulfkytel to lead them, the men of East Anglia will be unwilling to march on London. Even if we were to force them, they would likely slip away from us in the night. They know this land and the tracks through its marshes, and we do not."

"So you will have far fewer men," she observed. "What a pity, my lord, that you did not seize Emma's treasure. You might have used it to secure the allegiance of the East Anglians even without Ulfkytel. But you were honoring a debt, were you not—from that time when you met Emma before? She was your captive on that occasion, too. Strange, then, that she claimed *you* should be in debt to *her.*"

Her voice was brittle, taunting. Something else to add to the list of things that were irritating him tonight.

"If you wish to know something, Elgiva," he said coldly, "you might consider simply asking me."

"Then I am asking," she snapped.

He took a long draught of his ale before he answered her.

"That night, when the queen was rescued," he said, "she could have revealed to the English that I was Swein's son. Had she done so, I would certainly have been taken hostage, and I might, even now, be languishing in some English prison; or I might be dead. But the queen chose to say nothing, and her silence put me in her debt. Today, I repaid that debt. I hope," he added, "that it will buy me some influence with her brother and keep him from meddling in England, now that it is ours."

Elgiva snorted. "And do you think that is worth a ship filled with treasure and valuable hostages?"

"I think," he said, savagely stabbing a chunk of meat and dropping it to his plate, "that we have conquered a kingdom, and that now we must rule it. To do that, we must make peace with its people and their leaders. It is why I brought you here, and why you and Siferth and Ulfkytel, if we can find him, will ride with me into London—to be the English faces of Danish rule in England. To convince its leaders, especially its bishops, to accept us." He gestured toward her with his knife. "You have told me yourself that the clergy admire and revere Emma. If I had imprisoned the queen, or mistreated her in some way, it would hardly have won me friends among them."

"She is no longer their queen," Elgiva snapped, her tone waspish.

Exasperated, he threw down his knife.

"And now she is gone from England! You should be glad of it! In a matter of weeks we shall be celebrating the Yule feast in Æthelred's London palace. Will that not satisfy you, at least for a time?" He glared at her and, clearly offended, she snatched up her ale cup and left the dais.

He picked up his knife again, relieved that she was gone. He was discovering that the more time he spent with his wife, the more she wearied him.

Before he could turn again to his meat, he spotted Alric and Siferth entering the hall, and as there was no one else with them, he suspected that he was about to receive more unwelcome news.

"Well?" he asked.

"Ulfkytel was at Shotley yester-even, south of here, near where we met the queen's ship this morning," Alric reported. "It seems that her knarr was not the only vessel that anchored in the Orwell last night; there were five more, and those five sailed at dawn. Ulfkytel must have been on one of them, and he did not go alone. We found a camp site near the shore that may have held a hundred men or more. Wherever they went, I'll wager it wasn't Normandy."

"No. Ulfkytel would not go to Normandy," Cnut said, "not with a hundred men." And he did not at all like what that could mean.

"He may have sailed to London," Siferth suggested. "His wife is Æthelred's daughter, and she may have convinced him to seek out the king."

"His hundred men will be of little help to the Londoners," Alric observed. "Jarl Eirik will be at the city gates in a matter of days with an army of more than two thousand."

Cnut steepled his hands and considered the concerned faces of the two men.

"We could sit here all night trying to guess where Ulfkytel has fled," he said, "and it would be a useless endeavor. He is gone. There is no help for it. We will march on London as planned, but without him and without his men. I shall have to leave a larger force here than I had intended to garrison this town and guard our ships, but nothing else has changed. With winter almost upon us, London will, I think, submit quickly. The city cannot hold out long, now that the rest of England has submitted. So, we will set out tomorrow. Get something to eat, and get some rest."

He said nothing to them about what worried him the most about Ulfkytel—that the lord of East Anglia had broken his oath to Swein, and that others might follow his lead.

No longer hungry, he rested his chin on folded hands and considered all of the players who remained in the game: Æthelred, still alive, perhaps still in London and still obstinately refusing to submit; the king's grown sons, no doubt angry, spoiling for a fight and likely with followers of their own; and Thorkell, with his fleet of ships, his army of jomsvikings, and his thirst to avenge his brother's murder.

Which of them had Ulfkytel run to?

As of yesterday he had believed that the English had lost the will to fight, that England had been conquered and the game was all but finished. Now, things did not look quite so simple or so easy. There were still more hunns in play. The game was not over. Not yet.

Chapter Eighteen

December 1013
Normandy

The voyage across the North Sea proved to be as rough and miserable for Emma and her companions as Wymarc had predicted. Under Brihtwold's skillful piloting, however, the ship made harbor in the Low Country more swiftly than Emma had hoped. It was dusk when the *Wind Rider* moored at Bruges beneath stormy skies to join its three companion ships. The tiny fleet rested for a single day before setting out again, sailing along the coast and mooring close to shore every night until, five days out from Bruges, it reached Fécamp. There the company disembarked, settling into the ducal palace to recover from their long days at sea.

During that brief stay Emma often strolled with Wymarc through the winter-bleak gardens of Fécamp's abbey, recalling summer days when they had guided their horses along nearby lanes beside apple orchards, or had raced down the beach beneath high, white cliffs.

There were darker memories, too—of Danish ships entering the harbor, their decks bristling with men and weapons; of her brother's hall crowded with viking warriors whose rapacious eyes seemed to strip her bare. She remembered hiding in Fécamp's stables, listening as Swein Forkbeard broached a marriage alliance between Denmark and Normandy—an alliance that her brother had lightly dismissed, only to agree to an offer from the English a few months later that had sent her to England as Æthelred's queen.

Walking slowly through the abbey gardens with Wymarc on the day before she intended to depart for Rouen, Emma's mind was not on the past, though, but on the task that lay ahead of her.

"I am afraid," she said to Wymarc, "that my brother will balk at granting refuge to Æthelred."

"But he must grant it!" Wymarc cried. "My lady, the duke bound himself to the English king when he agreed to your marriage."

"That agreement was made a dozen years ago," Emma said, frowning, "and with Swein now in control of both Denmark and England, Richard has little to gain by harboring my exiled husband and his court. And Æthelred, I am certain, will want far more than shelter. He will ask for men, arms, and ships to aid him in taking back his throne come spring. Unless Richard sees some advantage to himself," she sighed, "he will not be eager to make Rouen the center of English resistance to Swein's rule. Nor am I at all certain that he could supply the vast numbers of men that will be needed to drive Swein from England."

And if the king did somehow obtain Norman aid and return to England, Emma thought, would Athelstan support him? Or would Athelstan raise his banner against not only Swein but Æthelred as well? If so, there would be three armies and three would-be kings ravaging England, and English allegiance would be divided between Æthelred and his son.

She had tried to warn Athelstan of this when she lay in his arms at Shotley. But he believed that when his father left England he would never return.

She hoped that he was right.

Athelstan hovered in her thoughts now as he had nearly every moment since she had watched him walk away from her, into the night. He had not left her with the seed of a child; her courses had begun on the day that she left Bruges. Nevertheless, she carried him in her heart, and she prayed that if retribution must be paid for the sin of their love, she should be the one to pay it. What punishment God might visit upon her she could not say, except that as Æthelred's queen it would be her duty to support the king in everything he wished to do—even if it meant waging war in England against his own son. That, it seemed to her, would be a terrible punishment for her indeed.

The next day she again boarded the *Wind Rider*, accompanied by Wymarc and two attendants, leaving the rest of her company and a single ship at Fécamp. It took another two days for her tiny fleet of three ships, all of them laden with royal treasure, to reach Rouen's busy port, where they docked in the shadow of the palace wall. Emma's heart fell when, gazing upward, she found no ducal banner fluttering from the ramparts. Despite what she had been told at Fécamp, Richard was not here.

And what of her children, she wondered. Where were they?

News of her coming had run ahead of her, and when she entered the palace she was escorted to the apartments that she had once shared with her sisters. Almost immediately she was summoned to attend her mother, but she took the time necessary to robe herself in a manner befitting the splendor of her brother's palace.

"I may be a supplicant," she said as Wymarc placed a golden circlet over her pale headrail, "but I am no beggar."

Wymarc nodded approvingly at her dark blue gown of heavy silk with its intricate embroidery at cuffs and hem; and Emma went to meet her mother.

She entered Gunnora's brightly lit chamber to find it empty except for a figure gowned in shimmering, russet colored silk. She would have made an obeisance, but her mother rose from her chair and reached for her hands to prevent her.

"Never forget who you are, daughter," Gunnora said. She kissed Emma's forehead. "England's queen is welcome at Richard's court."

So, Emma thought, word of Swein's conquest had not yet made its way here. She looked into her mother's face, reading there the passage of years, for it had been more than a decade since last she had seen her. There were new lines graven around Gunnora's mouth and eyes, and her cheeks had hollowed some with age. Yet despite her more than sixty winters, her mother stood ramrod straight and as tall as Emma remembered. Gunnora's eyes—as green as her own—gazed back at her, though, with a tenderness that Emma did not remember. Her memories of her mother were of a woman more stern than loving.

Was that how her own children would recall her one day, despite the love she bore for them?

"Are my children here in Rouen?" she asked. News of Æthelred and Swein must wait.

"They are here and safe," Gunnora said. "You will see them soon, but," she paused, gripping Emma's hands a little tighter, "you must not expect too much from them, daughter. Godiva will not remember you, although we speak of you often. Alfred is still an infant, and it is not you but his nurse who is the one constant in his young life. And Edward—"

Gunnora frowned, and it seemed that she had no words to describe Edward.

"Edward is his father's son," Emma said evenly, unwilling to reveal, even to her mother, how wounded she was by Edward's growing hostility toward her. "His half-sister Edyth and her husband Eadric had him in their care for many years, and they have no love for me. They persuaded Edward that I have no regard for him or for his welfare. It has placed a barrier between us that I have not been able to surmount, although I continue to try."

"Ah," Gunnora murmured, "that explains a great deal." She gazed past Emma into the middle distance. "I understand now why the boy is so unhappy here, among his mother's people; why his answers, when I have asked him about you, are evasive. Edward speaks the Frankish tongue—as I am sure you intended—but he will not speak of you." She regarded Emma now with eyes filled with sympathy. "You are breaking your heart over the child, I think. But Emma," she shook her head, "it is often so, that mothers lose their sons' affections—many times through no fault of their own. Perhaps, seeing you here, away from the influences that have shaped him, Edward will come to see you differently."

It occurred to Emma then that her mother's relationships with her own four sons must have often been fraught with pain. She could recall her brothers' numerous arguments in the years after their father died, and now she guessed that her mother must have often been caught in the middle, forced to mediate between her sons. Those turbulent tides continued even now, she suspected, for Father Martin had spoken of a quarrel between Gunnora and Richard over his dealings with King Swein.

Her mother sighed and, sitting, she gestured to Emma to sit beside her.

"You are come with ill news," Gunnora began, "or you would not be here at all. You will want to speak with Richard, I presume."

"As soon as may be," Emma said. "I am come as envoy for my husband."

"Richard sailed to Paris two days ago, summoned there by the French king. Duchess Judith accompanied him, as did your brother the archbishop. I cannot say when they will return because Richard must wait upon King Robert's pleasure. Whatever message you would convey from Æthelred must wait, I fear. Helena!" At her call, a girl appeared from an adjoining room. "Bring us hot wine and send for more charcoal for the brazier." She turned back to Emma. "Now," she said, straightening her shoulders as if to steel herself for whatever was to come, "tell me what has happened."

Emma told her the long, harrowing tale of all that had occurred in England over the past months and of the task that she had been given. She said nothing, though, about her meeting with Cnut aboard the *Wind Rider* nor the warning that he had charged her to convey to Richard. She was the peaceweaver between her husband and her brother, not the emissary of a Danish prince. Cnut was her enemy, and she owed him nothing.

Gunnora listened, showing no surprise at what she heard, although her mouth was pursed with concern and dismay. When Emma paused, waiting for her mother's reaction to Æthelred's request for refuge, Gunnora responded swiftly.

"Your brother," she said firmly, "cannot refuse to shelter your family and whatever retainers will accompany the king. He owes Æthelred that much. Nevertheless," she sighed, "it puts Richard in an awkward position. He has, unfortunately, made a pledge of peace with King Swein, and I doubt that he will be willing to break it by aiding Æthelred in reclaiming his throne."

"Æthelred will ask him for that, though." Emma knew her husband. His arrival in Normandy—should he be invited—would not mark the end of his reign in England, merely the beginning of his efforts to return.

"But you, my daughter, must not ask it," Gunnora counseled her. "Leave that to the king. Speak to Richard of refuge only, and he will surely grant it. But ask for too much and you may get nothing at all."

Some time later, when Emma was at last reunited with her children, it was not the joyful meeting that she had envisioned. More than two years had passed since last she had seen her daughter, and at four winters old Godiva had no memory of the mother who had kissed her goodbye on a windswept beach half her lifetime ago. Emma knelt to greet the child, but Godiva was too shy even to speak to her.

Alfred, though, had not yet forgotten her, and when he burrowed into her arms, pressing his face against her neck as she held him, it was a balm to her soul.

Edward greeted her with the politeness of a court official, cold and distant. But as she walked about the chamber with Alfred's head resting against her shoulder, she could see her eldest son—his pale blue eyes so like his father's—watching her, and she wondered what he was thinking. It seemed to her that his stiff formality masked an uneasiness that he did not wish anyone to see, least of all her. Eventually, though, when his brother and sister had been led away, Edward's sullen silence broke. Hungry for news, he was forced to turn to her to get it.

Had his sister Edyth come with her?

Had Lord Eadric or the king sent him any message?

Had the Danish army been beaten?

Where were his elder brothers?

Where was the king?

She drew him to a bench and sat beside him to answer his questions, knowing that each reply would be more disheartening than the last. And as she saw him absorb all that she said, she realized something about her son that she had not understood before.

Each of the nine years of his life had been filled with conflict and turmoil that had matured him beyond his years. Even his role here at her brother's court had initially been one of emissary, tasked with a man's responsibility. Now, though, he was regarded as merely a child and dismissed as irrelevant.

How he must hate that! Little wonder that he was angry about it, but kept his anger locked within, for who would listen to him? Yes, he was safe here, but he was also isolated—as she, too, would be—from events taking place in England that must determine both their futures. And like her, he must be frightened of what was to come—of what he could neither foresee nor control.

She wished that she could console him as she would any other terrified child. But Edward neither needed nor wanted that—not from her. The gulf between them was too vast, and she dared not try to cross it with a touch or an embrace. There had to be some other way forward; and by the time he ran out of questions, she had determined what that might be.

"Edward," she said, careful to keep her tone as formal as he could wish, "whatever I learn of events taking place in England, I shall share with you. You will not be kept ignorant of anything that may affect you. I give you my word on that."

He regarded her with a pinched, sullen expression that did little to assure her that her words had eased the strain between them. Still, he gave her a curt nod, and that, she hoped, was a beginning.

In the days that followed there came no word at all from England. Tempests and high winds prevented ships from venturing across the Narrow Sea in either direction and Emma languished in Rouen in an agony of suspense. The first test of her promise to Edward came when the weather finally calmed and, while there was no word as yet of Richard's return from Paris, a ship flying the banner of the bishop of Winchester sailed up the Seine and into the harbor. Emma sent for her son, and when the bishop entered her chamber, Edward was at her side.

She remembered Bishop Ælfsige as a vigorous man in his forties, tall and solid as an English oak. She remembered him, too, as she had last seen him in the king's hall, weeping over the Danish capture of Winchester. As he approached her now, his comely face was haggard, and his shoulders slumped beneath the weight of whatever news he bore. Concern for him drove her to her feet, and she took his arm to lead him to the chair that had been placed near hers.

"I see that you bring me grievous news, bishop," she said. "But please tell me first—where is the king?"

"He has fled to Wight Isle, my lady, to the burh of Caresbroc." On the last word his voice broke and he drew a long, heavy breath while she held hers, waiting for him to collect himself. "London has yielded," he said heavily. "The Danes now hold all of England."

This was what she had feared, what she had long dreaded to hear, and his words seemed to flay her skin so that she felt hot and cold all at once.

Beside her, Edward brushed his hands across his eyes, swiping at tears, and in a high voice that he struggled to control he said, "I hope that my father took no harm."

"He is safe, my lord, and well protected for now." With another heavy sigh Ælfsige turned to Emma. "The king insists that he will remain at Wight through the winter, and hopes to retake London in the spring. But Lord Eadric fears for the king's very life if he remains within reach of Swein's army, and he is eager for some word of assurance from you that the king will be welcome here at your brother's court."

For a moment she could not speak. Her anguish at the news he brought was matched by her frustration at having not yet fulfilled the task that had been set her.

"The instant that I have an answer, bishop, I will send word to Wight. I have not yet been able even to speak with my brother. He is in Paris at the behest of the Frankish king, and we do not know when he is likely to return." She studied his face, still grey with grief and exhaustion. "You say the king is safe. Is he well?"

"The king is," he paused as if searching for words, "uneasy in his mind."

Uneasy in his mind. Dear God, was he shouting at shadows? She had witnessed that herself, far too often.

"Is Edyth with him?"

"She is," he assured her, "as are a good number of the king's councilors."

"And the ætheling Edmund?"

He hesitated, glancing uncertainly from her to Edward and back again.

"Alas, no," he said. "Soon after our landing at Wight, Edmund and the king quarreled, and despite all our efforts, they could not be reconciled." He shook his head. "Edmund and his brother Edwig left the island, taking many of the king's guard with them. The king, as you may imagine, is furious with his sons for deserting him in his time of need."

Emma was silent for a moment. Edmund and his brother must have left the king in order to join Athelstan. Was the king even aware that his eldest son had remained in England?

"What was the quarrel about?" she asked.

Ælfsige frowned and pursed his lips, clearly reluctant to say any more.

"Bishop," she said sternly, "You do me no favors by keeping silent about events that concern the king and his family."

The bishop glanced down at his folded hands, clearly troubled by whatever had occurred. At last he said, "It had to do with Thorkell, my lady."

His answer did not surprise her. "What about him?"

"Edmund tried to convince the king that Thorkell could not be trusted," he said unhappily. "He insisted that with all of England in Danish hands, Thorkell would transfer his allegiance back to Swein. My lady, forgive me. I know that Thorkell has been a friend to you and to the king, but there are many who agree with Edmund that King Æthelred was wrong to accept Thorkell's allegiance. Some argue that Swein invaded England only because he wished to punish Thorkell for entering King Æthelred's service; others warn that Thorkell long ago made a pact with Swein that they would dispose of the king and his sons and then divide England between them."

Emma frowned, imagining the recriminations and accusations that must now be filling the ears of a king who had never been certain whom he could trust. She remembered, though, the anguish on Thorkell's face at All Hallows Church when he told her of Archbishop Ælfheah's death. Thorkell, she knew, would not break the oaths he had made to the archbishop, to the king, and to her—at least not while Æthelred lived. Her conviction, though, was of little use when the men who advised the king did not share it.

"They are wrong to blame my father," Edward's high voice suddenly rang in the silence, as he stood up to face the bishop, hands clenched into fists at his sides. "It was not my father who welcomed Thorkell into England. It was my lady mother. I was there. I saw it." He turned to her, his face contorted with fury. "You brought the Danes down upon us," he cried, his voice breaking with tears, "and I hate you for it! I will always hate you!"

She stared at him, stunned into speechlessness as he turned and fled from the chamber. She did not call him back or attempt to offer an explanation to the startled bishop. Let him think that it was merely a child's tantrum, spurred by fear.

But she knew the truth, and the pain of it scored her heart. Edward hated her with a passion nurtured by lies that had been fed him by Eadric and Edyth for too many years to be easily disproved now. No. She had lost her son, and she could think of nothing that she could ever say or do that would win him back.

Chapter Nineteen

December 1013
London

"*Hagall. Nied. Othel. Tire.*" Elgiva mouthed the names of the few runes that she could recall and edged forward on her chair to search the markings on the narrow, yellowed shards at her feet. After a few moments, frustrated, she thrust herself back against the cushions.

What did it matter that she knew what they were called? The bits of scored bone scattered on the floor looked to her like nothing more than kitchen refuse. She did not have Tyra's gift and never would.

She watched her Sami slave as, with eyes shut, Tyra stretched her hands above the rune sticks. Her long, dark braid fell over her shoulder and into her lap, and the shadows cast by candlelight played against her skin so that her pale, narrow face seemed to shift from something familiar to something not of this earth. It made Elgiva's flesh creep. Tyra would start chanting soon, the sound of it so familiar now that Elgiva sometimes heard it in her sleep. Mournful and eerie, it turned her dreams to nightmares. She did not like it, did not want to hear it. But the song was part of the ritual. If she wanted an answer to her question, it had to be endured.

"If I leave London tomorrow," she had asked Tyra, "when will I return?"

The question was a simple one, but Tyra's answers were never simple, and scrying the future always took far longer than Elgiva liked.

When the chanting began she gritted her teeth and, eager to distance herself from it, Elgiva pushed herself to her feet and paced to the far end of the chamber, frowning at the barren state of the walls that surrounded her.

This was the queen's apartment, and it should have been draped with lavishly embroidered hangings. Emma, though, had taken everything of value or beauty with her when she fled. Only the large wooden bed had been left behind, and even that had been stripped of its curtains and linens.

These quarters had turned out to be a bitter disappointment, just like London itself and the stiff-necked people who dwelt here. They had thronged the streets when she rode through the gates at Cnut's side, but the silence of the crowd had been so menacing that it had made the hairs rise along her arms. Even now the memory of all those faces glaring at her in silent contempt made her blood run cold.

"London is like a cur," Cnut had said, "savagely beaten into submission by its master. Its people will never love us. Best you learn that."

She did not want to learn it, did not want to be met with that silent loathing every time she ventured outside the palace. The Londoners had been conquered, and if they had not yet accepted their fate they must be seduced into doing so. She had begun making plans to do just that—to throw lavish feasts for the city leaders, flatter them with gifts and attention. She had expected to welcome their wives and daughters into her household.

And then the message from Swein had arrived, ordering Cnut to return to Gainsborough for the winter months.

She looked around the room and felt like weeping at the thought of leaving it. This chamber, barren as it was, at least held a brazier that offered much-needed heat on bitter cold nights. Cnut and Swein would force her to trade it for long, miserable days in a tent on a dragon-ship and put her again at the mercy of winter winds and seas. It was cruel.

At the far end of the chamber Tyra's chanting suddenly stopped. She sat unmoving, her head bent and drooping like a wilted blossom on a thin stalk, and her face was so grey that Elgiva worried that she might faint. She went swiftly to a bench that held a flagon of wine, poured some of the spiced liquid into a cup and, kneeling, placed it in Tyra's hand. She waited while Tyra sipped some of it and a little color returned to her sallow cheeks.

"Well?" Elgiva said. "How long will it be until I can return to London?"

Tyra stared at the cup in her hand. "What you desire," her voice sounded strange and hollow, "may be beyond your reach."

Elgiva frowned at the bones scattered on the floor, then placed a finger beneath Tyra's chin and lifted her head so that she could peer into her face.

"What I desire," she said through clenched teeth, "is to return here as soon as possible. How can that be beyond my reach?"

Tyra's gaze was unfocused and her face blank. It was the face of prophecy, Elgiva realized, and she held her breath, waiting for it.

"The road that lies before you is strewn with difficulties. There are malignant forces at work over which you have no control." The voice—flat, dead, and empty—did not even sound human. Elgiva had to force her hands into her lap to keep from covering her ears. But now Tyra's eyes fixed upon her at last as she whispered, "I cannot promise that you will ever return to London."

A chill crept down Elgiva's spine. Never before had Tyra given her a reading so dire. She pushed herself to her feet and with shaking hands she poured a cup of wine for herself and downed half of it.

"What are these malignant forces?" she asked. Men, most likely. It was always men.

"All I can see, lady, is that trouble lies ahead," Tyra's voice was human again, but cold and sullen, "and that you cannot avoid it."

"I do not believe you," Elgiva snapped. "Trouble can be avoided if you know where it is and what it is."

Tyra barked a grim laugh. "Sometimes perhaps," she said. "Not this time, I think. And never have I lied to you."

It was true that Tyra would not lie, especially about the runes because she believed that her gods would punish her if she did not speak the truth. But there was something wrong here. Never before had Tyra avoided her gaze. Could it be that she was not lying, yet not speaking all the truth?

She crouched above the bones scattered on the floor and picked up the one that lay in the middle of the grouping. She held it in front of Tyra. "What does this mean?"

Tyra blanched and shook her head. "By itself it is meaningless."

"Perhaps," Elgiva said. "But it is not by itself. It is at the heart of everything you have just told me. I want to know what it means!"

Tyra clenched her lips tight, and Elgiva thought she would have to slap her to get her to speak. The silence lengthened between them, but finally Tyra murmured, "It means death."

Elgiva stared at the piece of bone in her hand, then dropped it as if it had burned her.

She straightened, clenching her hands into fists at her sides. She had to find Cnut and persuade him that they must stay in London. Whatever trouble was waiting to overtake them would be somewhere along the whale road or in Gainsborough itself. If they should leave London now, they might never return.

She might never return.

She found him in the king's chamber with Siferth, Thurbrand, and half a dozen of his war leaders. Halting just inside the door, she listened as Cnut admonished them about maintaining London's defenses in his absence. Despite her eagerness to speak with him, she dared not interrupt. He would not thank her for it, and in any case, it was late. Surely this meeting must end soon.

She waited, biting her lip, uncertain as yet how she would persuade him to abandon his plan to go north. It would mean disobeying his father's command, something that, despite her urging, he had never yet been willing to do. This time would be no different unless—an idea blossomed in her mind—unless she could convince him that Tyra's warning was meant for him. Surely, if Cnut believed his life was at stake, he would do as she asked.

When he finally brought the meeting to an end and the men filed out, Cnut sat on one of the benches that lined the walls and beckoned to his body servant.

"I did not think to see you tonight, Elgiva," he said.

The servant knelt before Cnut to remove his shoes and hose, but Elgiva stopped him.

"Leave that," she said. "Wait outside until you are called."

The lad looked to Cnut, who nodded. When he was gone Elgiva took his place, folding her hands on his knee.

"My lord," she said softly, "I come to you because I have discovered something that makes me afraid for you."

He raised a brow, and she could not tell if it signaled curiosity, surprise, or disbelief.

"I presume this has something to do with tomorrow's journey," he said. "I am moved by your concern, Elgiva, but barring a gale that keeps us in port, we shall board ship at dawn despite whatever is worrying you."

This was a bad beginning, but she kept her temper in check. If she allowed her anger to show she would never convince him.

"I beg you," she pleaded, "do not make up your mind until you have heard me out."

"I have already made up my mind," he said, folding his arms and regarding her with those piercing black eyes. "We leave on the morrow for Gainsborough, and from there we go to Jorvik to see my father consecrated king. Thurbrand, Siferth and Eglaf will remain here in charge of the city and the garrison, and in the spring I shall return to act as my father's deputy. For now, though, with Thorkell's fleet gone and Æthelred with it, London is under no threat and my place is in the north. Elgiva, you know all this. We have already—"

"Tyra has seen your death!" she cried. "She has cast the runes and seen malignant forces working against you in the north. If you go there you will—"

"There are forces working against me all over England! I cannot avoid them, not even here in London! I am a Dane, and no Dane is safe in this land while its people despise us."

"My lord, the gods have sent you a warning. Would you defy them?"

"Before I would defy my father? Yes! This is a Christian kingdom, and Tyra's gods have no power here. When my father receives the English crown, and when someday I receive it in my turn, it will be from the hands of a Christian archbishop, not a pagan priestess."

She stood up and glared at him. "Tyra's gods are more powerful than you know, my lord! Defy them if you will, but I will not. If danger awaits you in the north, I want no part of it. Go if you must, but you will go without me!"

She started for the door, but before she had taken a second step Cnut was beside her, pulling her roughly around to look at him. His face was stern and uncompromising.

"You will board that ship with me at dawn, and I will place a guard at your door through the night to make certain of it."

"Why does it matter to you if I go to Gainsborough or remain here?" she cried, frantic now. Nothing about this meeting had gone as she had planned. She would have been better off simply hiding somewhere in the palace so that in the morning he could not find her. Now, that path was closed to her.

"It matters," he said through clenched teeth, "because as my English wife your place, as you have so often reminded me, is at my side. It matters because when you asked to accompany me here to London, you swore that you would do everything I told you to do, without question. And it matters," he shook her as if she were a disobedient child, "because I do not trust you enough to leave you here without me."

Chapter Twenty

January 1014
Rouen, Normandy

The old year had already passed when Æthelred finally abandoned Wight Isle for Normandy, and in January he arrived in Rouen and was greeted by Duke Richard with all courtesy. He was given chambers in the ducal palace that were lavishly furnished—stone walls draped with thick woolen hangings of deep blue, carved wooden chairs festooned with brightly embroidered pillows, branches of candles to provide light, and braziers radiating warmth. Usually the king found his accommodation comfortable enough, but on this chilly winter morning a dull, familiar pain nagged at his temples, and his heart lurched inside his chest as if it sought some means of escape. The sound of agitated voices faded beneath the roaring of blood in his ears, and out of the corner of his eye—just there, in the patch of darkness at the edge of his vision—he could make out his brother's ghost.

What evil purpose, he wondered, had drawn that thing to him here, across the Narrow Sea? Had it come to feast upon his despair? Or did it presage some event yet to come, something even more calamitous than the cascading disasters that had driven him from England?

But those were not the questions that he had meant to voice just a few heartbeats ago. He had wanted to know something else. Wrenching his mind away from the now fading, malignant shadow he considered the faces of those gathered around him.

Emma was there, and his councilors Eadric and Ælfric, and his bishops Ælfhun and Lyfing.

And there was a priest—a messenger who had braved the filthy winter crossing to bring news from Canterbury.

Canterbury. His question had been about Canterbury.

"Where is Ælfheah?" His tongue felt thick in his mouth, but the words he uttered were clear enough. "Where is the Canterbury archbishop?"

No one answered him. They were keeping some secret from him. He could see it in the furtive glances they cast at one another, and he clenched his fists, frustrated and angry with the lot of them. He would throttle it out of them if he had to.

Something touched his shoulder and he flinched, but it was only Emma, leaning toward him to whisper in his ear.

"Ælfheah has gone to God, my lord," she said gently. "You named Bishop Lyfing here to take his place as Archbishop of Canterbury."

He stared at the round face of Lyfing with its full beard and tonsured grey hair, and for the space of a breath it was Ælfheah's thin, ascetic visage that stared back at him and then was gone.

He pressed his fingertips to his aching head in a vain effort to knead away his pain and confusion. How had he forgotten that his friend Ælfheah had been dead these many months, murdered by Northmen?

He could feel the doubt-filled eyes of his advisors raking him, and he grimaced at them, silently daring anyone to question the mind of a king. And then his eyes fell on the messenger.

"You. Priest," he said gruffly, addressing the cleric who had brought him word of his treacherous son. "You say that Athelstan is raising an army?"

"It is but a rumor, lord king," the priest said, his tone measured, "but I heard it whispered again and again as I made my way through Kent and Sussex. The men of the southern shires are looking to the ætheling to drive the Danes from Wessex, if not from all of England."

Æthelred grunted and waved a dismissive hand that trembled despite his efforts to steady it.

"They are fools then," he said. "The southern lords have given Swein hostages—their brothers and sons. If they take up arms against him Swein will murder their kin without a second thought. The nobles know this. Athelstan may persuade some of them to join him, but he cannot hope to raise an army large enough to outnumber Swein's force and defeat him."

He need not fear his son. Athelstan's overweening ambition would earn him more enemies than friends.

"But my lord," the priest said, "Swein led the bulk of his army north some weeks ago, and although men have been left behind to garrison the burhs, they are few in number. The hope is that the aetheling will overwhelm the burhs one by one and retake Wessex before Swein can return in the spring—"

"Stop there!" Eadric clamped a hand on the kneeling priest's shoulder, and bent to peer into his face. "You say Swein went north? He is not in London?"

Æthelred, too, was stricken by the messenger's claim. Was Swein's hold on England so secure that he could turn his back on London?

"Swein was never in London, my lord. The Danish force that threatened the city was led by Swein's son, and it was to him that the Londoners submitted. The greater part of that army, too, has now marched north, taking many hostages with them. It is not a Danish lord who commands the garrison that holds London, but one of Swein's English allies."

Who then? Æthelred wondered. Siferth? Morcar? Perhaps even his daughter's husband, Uhtred? He exchanged a stunned glance with Eadric.

"Swein is wintering near his ships at Gainsborough," Eadric said, his voice oily with satisfaction, "just as I told you he would, my lord. That may prove his undoing."

"Surely this is good news," the archbishop suggested eagerly. "If the aetheling can raise even a small army and harry the Danes from their strongholds in the south, it will prepare the way for the king's return."

"You may well be right, archbishop," Eadric agreed. "But if Athelstan drives the Danes from the south, there is nothing to prevent him from claiming the crown for himself."

His warning echoed the fear that beat with dark wings in Æthelred's mind. Athelstan was still in England, free to command the allegiance of English men eager to throw off their new, Danish overlords.

"Surely the aetheling would not attempt to take the throne," Bishop Ælfhun's protest was little more than a whisper.

Æthelred glared at the old man, prepared to rebuke him for his blind faith in a faithless aetheling, but the harsh words stuck in his throat. Ælfhun, he realized, was wasting away here. His bishop's robes hung on him like grave clothes on a dead man, and his face was little more than a skull. The man would not live long enough to see England again.

Christ! None of them would see England again if he could not find some way through this stinking mire of misfortune and treachery that plagued him.

"My son has long coveted my crown, bishop," he murmured. "If Athelstan should convince the men of Wessex to forsake the hostages and take up arms against Swein, he will be robbing me of their support and their loyalty." He muttered a curse and glowered at the faces around him. "I see now that I erred in following the counsel you gave me at Wight. I should never have left England. I have not only delivered my kingdom to Swein but I have given my son all the opportunity he needs to seize the throne for himself." He slumped in his chair and drew an unsteady hand across his eyes. The pain at his temples had eased, but he was weary and heart sore. "I want no more of your counsel tonight," he said. "Leave me."

He watched through slitted eyes as his advisors, damn them, shuffled out. When Emma moved to follow them, though, he grabbed her arm and held her back.

"I am cut off from England by winter gales and a churning sea," he said when the others were gone. "If I am to have a stake in this game come spring, I will need an army and enough ships to transport it." He shook her arm and snarled through his teeth, "I will need Richard, and you will give him to me!"

He studied her face, certain that there were secrets behind her eyes. Had she known what was in Athelstan's mind when he abandoned her and all her household in East Anglia? Was she privy to the names of men who would throw their support behind his traitorous son? If he were to clasp that beautiful head between his hands and press and press, would she reveal all that she knew or suspected?

No, she would not. She would lie to him in every tongue that she knew.

Well, she could keep her secrets, for she was going to give him her brother instead. It was Richard who would open the door to his return to England, and it was Emma who held the key. Her future was at stake here along with his own. Emma coveted the wealth and lands, the dignity and prestige that came with queenship. More than that, she coveted power. Had she not tried to wrest it from him during all the years of their marriage?

For a long moment she said nothing, gazing fixedly at him with a sober, thoughtful expression. He still clasped her arm, and now he shook it again.

"Did you hear me?" he hissed. "Have you nothing to say?"

"My lord," she replied stiffly, "I shall of course do all that is in my power to promote your welfare and that of my sons. But my brother's forces are massed along his borders to defend them against assaults from his neighbors. It is unlikely that he could spare the vast numbers of warriors that you will need to retake your kingdom. I shall urge Richard to aid you in any way that he can, but if you need an army, you must look elsewhere."

He gaped at her, stunned. Was Richard to be of so little use to him then? No! She was lying! What could a woman know about Norman military resources? For that matter, what could Emma know of her brother and what Richard would or would not do? *Christ!* What a fool he was, to think that she might intercede for him.

"Get out!" he snarled, and thrust her toward the doorway.

He would speak to the duke himself, and with or without Norman ships and men, he would find a way back to England—back to his throne.

And then, let all those who had defied him beware.

Chapter Twenty-One

February 1014
Jorvik, Northumbria

Elgiva rested her arms atop the gunwale of the longship, one of three that sailed in a line up the River Ouse beneath an afternoon sky dark with clouds. As the ships neared Jorvik's southern edge she drew in a breath, then scowled at the stink.

There must be tanneries here somewhere, she thought, and by the gods, their stench was foul. She held her breath, afraid that the ships would make for the shore and that she would be forced to remain in this noisome place throughout the winter.

But it appeared that their destination was further north, for the oarsmen continued rowing at a steady pace, carrying the ships past bustling hythes where all manner of vessels docked. Elgiva could see wooden buildings facing the river—warehouses and workshops, she presumed, for she could hear the distant pounding of hammer upon metal. And somewhere near the city's heart there would be a great market bustling with buyers and sellers. She had never been to Jorvik before, but she knew it to be a traders' paradise.

Did any of the folk who lived here, she wondered, recognize Uhtred's wisdom in being among the first to give his oath to Swein? Because the Danes had been welcomed here in Northumbria, Jorvik had been spared the savagery that Swein's army had inflicted on the towns and villages in the shires of the south.

She squinted as she peered into the fine haze of smoke that rose from what must be thousands of hearths, and she found the distant minster, its shoulders rising from the warren of smaller buildings that spilled down to the river. In four days' time, on the Feast of the Wise

Men which, no doubt, Archbishop Wulfstan fancied to be most appropriate, the witan would gather in that place to proclaim Swein king of all England. The thought of it made her smile, not least because so many of the wise men at that gathering would find the prospect of Danish kingship as welcome as the bitterest of poisons, even as they forced themselves to swallow it. Swein would wear England's crown here in Jorvik, in the city that had once been the heart of a kingdom held by Northmen, and now would be so again.

And, thankfully, in a matter of weeks Cnut would return to London, and she would be at his side.

Tyra's warnings of malignant forces and the threat of death that had so frightened her had proved false. There had been no calamity, no death, no danger even. The journey from London to Gainsborough had been bitterly cold and wet, to be sure; she had hated every miserable hour of it. But it had been uneventful. They had arrived safely at Gainsborough, in good time for the Yule feast. Five weeks had slipped peacefully by since then, and none of the dire events that Tyra had predicted had come to pass.

Had her Sami slave misread the runes? Had the runes themselves lied?

When she posed these questions to Tyra, the wretched woman had merely clenched her mouth shut and grimaced. She had been silent, cold and distant ever since, and Elgiva, sick of her foul mood, had bid her remain in Gainsborough to care for the children rather than attend her to Jorvik. The questions still nagged at her, though. Relieved as she was that the dire foretelling had been false, it meant that she dared no longer place her trust in Tyra's visions.

Up ahead she could see a bridge spanning the river, and from its guard towers men in mail watched their ships approach. Uhtred, standing in the prow of her vessel, shouted a greeting up to them, and one of the warriors above shouted an answer and waved them on. She looked back at the two vessels that followed, their oars shipped to avoid the wooden bridge supports as they slipped under the span. When the first of them emerged she had a clear view of Swein standing with Cnut on the foredeck.

The king's long white beard was plaited into two braids and his mane of pale hair was pulled back and bound. It struck her suddenly how ashen his face was compared to Cnut's sun-bronzed skin. Was it possible that Denmark's mightiest warrior quailed at the prospect of facing a clutch of English bishops and abbots who would bitterly resent having to offer him England's crown? No. Swein feared nothing and no one. Even the fearsome Archbishop Wulfstan was not likely to worry the mighty Swein. So what was disturbing the Danish king?

She saw him say something to Cnut, who nodded as they carried on a conversation that she was too far away to hear.

Yes, husband, she thought. Listen to your father. Agree with him. Do whatever he tells you. Stand by his side and keep your wife so distant that she has no idea what it is that weighs upon your minds.

Annoyed, she turned away from the two men who held her life in their hands, and looked at the city drifting past. When the ramparts that marked its northern boundary were behind them, the ships made for the eastern bank. There, above a broad palisade, she could just glimpse the high roof of what must be Ealdorman Uhtred's great hall and their journey's end. Now, the celebrations could begin.

That evening, clothed in a gown of fine crimson wool, adorned with necklaces and bracelets of gold, and her black curls unbound, she attended Uhtred's lavish feast in honor of the victorious Swein. The ealdorman's vast hall was wreathed in winter darkness despite the fire that blazed in the central hearth and the thick candles that burned on the tables. She took note of the men on the mead benches—half of them Swein's Danish hearth guards and the rest Northumbrians who served Uhtred. Cnut, she thought, would not like those evenly balanced numbers. He had pressed his father to bring more Danes with him to this gathering—a massive show of force to ensure that the meeting with the witan went as planned. Swein, though, had scoffed at what he called his son's too abundant caution.

"The English have sworn oaths to me on their holy relics," Swein said. "Fear of God's punishment will keep them from breaking those pledges. You need not be concerned. All will go as it should."

Just now Cnut was sitting at his father's right hand and gazing thoughtfully at Uhtred, who was seated on Swein's left. Cnut, she suspected, did not completely trust Uhtred. She agreed with Swein, though, that fear of God's wrath would bind the English, even powerful men like Uhtred, to the oaths that they would pledge on the morrow.

As she bore the brimming welcome cup to each of the magnates gathered in the hall, she felt a stab of pity for Uhtred's wife, who should have been the one formally greeting these men. But Ælfgifu was one of Æthelred's daughters, and Uhtred, no fool, likely wanted her nowhere near this gathering. He had sent her to his distant fortress of Bamburgh, far to the north.

What a humiliating fate, to have gone from royal daughter to noble prisoner. She wondered how Ælfgifu could bear it.

At last, her ceremonial duties completed, Elgiva approached the women's table. The wives of Siferth and Morcar waited there for her, their expressions sour. She wished that it was Æthelred's daughter who would sup with her tonight instead of these two. She had told Cnut to leave them behind in Gainsborough, but he had refused.

"Their husbands were our first allies, and they control all of northeastern Mercia. We need their support," he had insisted, "so however much their wives may vex you, you cannot ignore them."

Grinding her teeth at the recollection, she offered a thin smile as she took her seat at the board. Neither woman responded, and their meal began in sullen silence amid the boisterous clamor of the men.

Stupid cows, she thought. What was the matter with them? Now that the battle for England was over they were no longer hostages but her chosen companions; yet there they sat, scowling beneath their grey headrails, as glum as sacks of dirty wool. The very sight of them spoiled her appetite.

Still, Cnut might be watching, so she would have to make some effort to speak with them.

"It is unfortunate," she said, turning to her cousin and infusing her voice with sympathy, "that Siferth's duties in London keep him so far from you and prevent him from joining us tonight."

Aldyth remained stonily silent, her expression hostile. Elgiva toyed with the food on her plate, her eyes fixed on her cousin and her temper rising.

"I once told you, Aldyth," she said silkily, "that Swein would be victorious over the king who ordered the murder of my father, your uncle. What I promised has come to pass, has it not? Æthelred may not be dead, but he is gone."

Her cousin still refused to respond or even to look at her. Those enormous eyes remained downcast and her mouth a thin line.

Elgiva's temper flared. She slammed her hand on the table, so that both women flinched and gaped at her.

Good. Now she had their attention.

"I promised you," she said, biting each word, "that if Siferth and his brother were to give their allegiance to Swein, they would be rewarded with lands and wealth and power. That, too, has come to pass." She drew in a long breath and smiled as she turned her hands toward them, palms up. "So I would know why you two continue to regard me with such ill will, as if I had done you some terrible injury, when I have been the means whereby you have achieved great good fortune. I confess that I do not understand it. So I will give you a choice." She reached for her cup, swallowed a mouthful of the potent mead and continued, "Either you will treat me with the respect and the gratitude that I deserve or you will get out of my sight and stay out of it."

She regarded them, brows arched, waiting.

They were both staring at her now, Aldyth's mouth pursed and Wynflæd's open in astonishment. Finally Aldyth rose slowly to her feet.

"My husband and his brother," Aldyth said, her voice tight with fury, "swore their allegiance to Æthelred upon holy relics and in the sight of God. Now that they have foresworn those oaths, God will punish them, either in this world or the next. And for what, Elgiva? Look at your new king." She gestured to the high table, but Elgiva kept her eyes on Aldyth's face. "No," her cousin scoffed, "you will not look. I do not blame you, for if you did you would see a drunken tyrant who will bleed our kingdom dry to satisfy his greed. I am not grateful to you for anything, cousin, except for your dismissal, which I shall happily obey."

Aldyth turned and strode swiftly from the hall and Wynflæd jumped up to scurry after her. Elgiva watched them go, then looked anxiously toward the high table, fearing that Cnut had seen them leave and would be frowning at her. But her husband was frowning at Swein, whose face was gaunt and grey, and whose black eyes were hidden by lids that drooped as if he were half asleep.

The king was drunk, then; not just on mead, it seemed to her, but with the exaltation that came with victory. That was what Aldyth had seen. But what else had she expected? Swein was a warrior king, and he had arrived in England bent on conquest. He had succeeded and, yes, he had brought havoc and bloodshed, but in doing so he had rid

England of a monster. Now there would be peace. They should all be drunk with his victory, just as he was.

She saw Cnut whisper to his father, and the old man opened his eyes. He staggered to his feet and the men on the benches below cheered him wildly. Acknowledging their shouts with a wave of his hand, he then followed a light bearer from the hall with slow, measured steps.

She looked at Cnut, who stood with his eyes fixed upon his father's retreating figure. She willed him to look at her, not the old man, and when at last he did meet her gaze, he left the dais to join her.

"My father wishes to know more about the members of the witan," he said, "and as you are familiar with many of them, you are to attend him in his chamber. Morcar, Uhtred, and Alric are to join us as well."

"Would it not be more prudent to wait until the morrow?" she suggested. "The king appears," she searched for an acceptable word to describe the besotted Swein, "unwell."

Cnut's brow furrowed. "He claims that he is not ill, only weary. His sleep, it seems, has been troubled of late. The sooner we meet with him, the sooner he can rest."

He did not wait to accompany her, but hastened after his father.

Always, she thought, his father came first. She sighed, then called for her cloak and made her way alone through the muddy yard to the guest house.

Swein was lodged in the finest chamber in Uhtred's burh, but it was cold despite the brazier and the embroidered hangings gracing its walls. A trio of oil lamps hung suspended from the ceiling, and in their dim light she saw Morcar, Uhtred, and Alric already grouped around the great, curtained bed where Swein sat bolstered by pillows. She was given a chair beside the bed, facing Cnut who stood at the king's right hand.

Like her, Swein was wrapped in furs. His face, though, was the color of parchment. It seemed to Elgiva that, whatever Cnut might wish to believe, his father was very much unwell. Nevertheless, when Swein began to speak his voice was as strong as ever.

"The archbishop, this Wulfstan who summoned the witan," Swein began, "is no friend to me, I think." He grimaced, pawed at his chest, cleared his throat and continued, "If I cannot discover some means of making him my ally, I fear that he will be my fiercest enemy among the

English magnates. That is why I have summoned you here. I wish to have your counsel."

She remembered Wulfstan all too well. He was Æthelred's man to his bones, and he was powerful. Swein was right. The archbishop could oppose England's new rulers by castigating them in sermons and letters. There were likely other means that he might use to undermine them, as well, measures that she could not even imagine.

It was Morcar, though, who spoke first.

"Archbishop Wulfstan believes that you are a heathen, my lord," he said. "Convince him that you are a Christian and that you will rule England as a Christian king. That is the surest way to win his support."

That would be no simple task, she thought. Swein made no secret of the fact that he was both Christian and heathen. Indeed, the large silver cross and the golden hammer of Thor that he wore on chains about his neck all but shouted it.

"My lord," she said, "words alone will not convince Wulfstan of your devotion to Christ. He will expect you to renounce all other gods, and he will demand gifts of land and treasure for his precious churches."

"He will want more than that, lord," Uhtred added. "He will attempt to position himself as your senior advisor. He will expect you to listen to his counsel and follow it to the letter."

"No!" Swein barked, pounding the mattress to emphasize his objection. "That, I will never do. I will not be the tool of any Christian bishop, no matter—"

His voice suddenly faltered, mouth quivering as it shaped words that he did not speak.

Cnut touched his father's shoulder. "My lord?"

But the king seemed to be locked in some inner struggle. He was staring straight ahead, a trembling arm outstretched as if reaching for something. Abruptly he lurched forward, and Uhtred, at the foot of the bed, swore and reared away from him. Swein, gasping, threw himself back against his pillows, and with a tremendous roar he slammed his fist against his chest.

Elgiva sprang to her feet and cried, "What is happening to him?"

His face—so pale and gaunt just moments before—had grown hideously swollen and purple. His eyes seemed to bulge from their sockets, and as he drew another gasping, rattling breath his entire body jerked, as if buffeted by some huge, invisible hand. His clenched fist fell atop the gold and silver amulets at his chest, then slipped to his side. His mouth gaped and his eyes were open wide, but Swein did not move again.

In the stunned silence that followed, Elgiva clutched her throat and stared, horrified, at that grotesque face. She had never witnessed death up close before, and her mind recoiled from its suddenness and ferocity. When she could drag her gaze from Swein, she looked at the men who surrounded the bed. They were all of them intimate with death, had often enough been its deliverer, but even they were stunned by what they had just witnessed. Even Cnut stood frozen, his eyes fixed upon his father.

Someone murmured, *Sweet Jesu*, and as if in response, a terrible wail like the baying of a hound from hell filled the chamber. It came from the open mouth of the dead king, and the men around the bed crossed themselves while Elgiva clapped her hands to her ears.

Closing her eyes, she saw in her mind the rune stick that she had held out to Tyra in London, demanding to know what it meant. And once more she heard the Sami woman's reply.

Death. It means death.

Now Death had found them, just as Tyra had foretold. And slithering into Elgiva's memory like a poisonous snake came the other thing that Tyra had said.

There are malignant forces working against you, over which you have no control.

She felt a shimmer of fear. If Tyra had been right about one thing, then she was likely right about the other.

The dead man's wail had died away, and Elgiva opened her eyes. The men were casting nervous glances at Cnut, and surely her husband must realize that they would be looking to him now for direction and leadership. Swein was dead, and if his son did not seize this opportunity, someone else would.

Finally, Cnut seemed to come out of his stupor.

"Guards!" he bellowed.

Two of Swein's hearth guards burst into the room, and Cnut, pointing to Uhtred, ordered, "Bind him. Bjorn, you will stay here and keep him quiet."

Uhtred struggled against the rough hands that pinioned him, his outrage written on his face.

"You cannot think that I had aught to do with your father's death!"

"Oh, but I can, my lord." Cnut grimly assured him. "And I intend to make certain that you will have nothing to do with mine."

Cnut ordered his men to dig a grave beside the tiny wooden church that lay within the walls of Uhtred's burh. The ground, though not frozen, was muddy, and in spite of the bitter cold of the winter night, the men's faces dripped with sweat as they dug. Torches held high above their heads cast yellow light into the black hole that was to house a king.

Cnut watched, along with Elgiva and a score of somber, uneasy Danes, as Swein's hastily fashioned coffin was lowered into its resting place. Nervously clutching the hilt of his sword, he listened for any sound other than the heavy thudding of mud as it was cast into the grave. He could not say what had caused his father's death, but its swiftness and its timing made him suspicious of men that, until tonight, he had considered allies. He eyed Morcar and Alric who stood on either side of Elgiva, but he could not read their faces. He thought they could be trusted, but he could not be certain. Now that his father was dead, he had no way of knowing who among the English would turn against him.

He had done what he could to secure the burh. All of Uhtred's Northumbrians lay bound and gagged in the great hall with the doors barred while his own men were stationed on the palisade. The dawn, though, was likely to bring trouble, and if the English mounted an attack, he did not have enough men to resist it. He would have to act before his enemies did.

He waited until the final shovelful of mud had been tossed and the ground atop the grave tamped down, and then he spoke.

"My father's death puts all of us in danger, even if it is not part of some trap. We will leave Jorvik tonight and bring Uhtred with us as hostage. He is now my enemy. Halfdan, take a dozen of these men and get him aboard my ship. Alric and Morcar, go with them."

As the men moved off, he beckoned to Halfdan. "Keep a close watch on our English friends," he whispered. "I am not certain that we can trust them." Then he turned to Elgiva. "Go and fetch the women.

Tell them nothing, just get them on the ships. You two men, go with her. The rest of you see that all our men get aboard."

To his irritation, though, Elgiva clutched at his arm.

"This is a mistake, Cnut," she hissed. "What are you afraid of? The lords of England have already accepted Swein as their king, and as his son you inherit every pledge he was given. Your father's men hold burhs throughout the kingdom, and when the witan meets they will have no choice but to offer you the crown. Stay here and treat with them or you risk losing everything!"

"I cannot treat with them, Elgiva, without an army at my back, and I have only sixty men here that I can trust. The English lords will have retinues of their own and will most assuredly outnumber us. They will not, I think, be persuaded to favor my claim to the crown."

"You hold their sons and brothers hostage at Gainsborough! You need only remind them of that to bind them to the oaths they made to your father."

Irritated by her blindness, he grasped her arm and turned her to face the newly turned earth.

"The man who brought England to its knees lies in that grave," he snarled at her. "When word of his death gets out, every priest in Jorvik will be howling that it was God who struck him down. They will claim that Christ wants the Danes driven out of England, and the English will take heart from it. Every man in Jorvik will be thirsting for our blood!"

"Because they do not fear you!" She glared at him, her voice filled with scorn. "I warned you that this would—"

"Do what you are told, Elgiva, or we are all likely to die here!" He thrust her toward the cluster of buildings at the center of the burh and, reaching for one of the torches, he gestured to his men to go with her.

Alone, he lifted the torch and looked down at the mound that marked his father's grave. For a moment he could only stare at it, still unable to grasp the enormous reversal of fortune that had blindsided him. He swallowed, and the tide of grief that threatened to engulf him abated somewhat. This was not the time to mourn. That duty must wait.

"Had you lived but a few weeks longer, father," he whispered, "you would have been anointed king of England. Even the Christian church was prepared to accept you. Now..."

Now, the great lords of England would be re-thinking their allegiances. Æthelred had fled, but his sons were out there somewhere.

Their claims, he did not doubt, would find favor with men that they had known all their lives, and those men would disavow the pledges they had made to Swein. He could not even be certain that the army waiting for him now at Gainsborough would accept him as leader. Some of the men pledged to his father might balk at following his younger son. He had to get to Gainsborough to secure their allegiance.

First, though, he had to stay alive.

"I am sorry," he whispered.

One day, he vowed, he would bury his father in Denmark with the honor that he deserved. Men from all over the kingdom would pay tribute to the great warrior king who had conquered the English. Skalds would compose songs of praise. Tonight, though, he was concerned with the living, not the dead.

He left the grave and made for the river. When he reached the hythe where the ships were docked, Halfdan was waiting for him.

"Uhtred has escaped, my lord," Halfdan said. "Bjorn is dead, and Siferth's wife, the Lady Aldyth, is missing."

Cnut swore. "Where is Morcar?"

"On the ship. His wife claims that she does not know where Aldyth is."

"With Uhtred, no doubt," Cnut murmured. "She must have helped him escape; he could not have done it alone." It had been a mistake to bring Aldyth here with them. Elgiva had warned him about her cousin, and he had not listened. But there was no help for it now. "They will carry word of my father's death into Jorvik," he said, "and the English may try to stop us at the bridge. Is everyone else aboard?

"Yes."

"Good. Let us hope that we can make it through the city before Uhtred raises the alarm. Pass the word that there may be archers on the bridge. Have shields at the ready and no one is to make a sound."

As the ships were launched, he peered up at a sky blanketed with clouds. The absence of moonlight would be a help to them if there were bowmen on the bridge ahead.

His steersmen found the Ouse's central channel easily enough, and the current carried them swiftly downstream. Cnut knelt in the bow of the leading ship with Halfdan at his side. After a short time he could make out the towers that faced each other across the river and marked the line of the city walls, their great bulk visible even in the dark. Then the Ouse curved and the bridge appeared before them, lit by fires that the men on watch had kindled for warmth.

The only sound was the murmur of the river. No one challenged them as they approached the bridge, and the three ships glided silently beneath it. Soon, the foul stench from the tanneries signaled that they had reached the city's southern edge, and Cnut's tension eased. High above them a breeze rearranged the clouds, and as a shaft of moonlight turned the river to silver the oarsmen began to row.

"What now?" Halfdan murmured.

"When we reach Gainsborough, we send word of my father's death to our garrisons," Cnut replied. "And we prepare for war."

His father's death—or murder—would embolden the English to take back their kingdom, he was certain of it. The only thing he did not know was who they would choose to lead them.

Chapter Twenty-Two

March 1014
Rouen, Normandy

Over the course of a cold, wet, and dreary February, word of King Swein's death slowly made its way through the heartland of England. The news was carried by men who traveled along frozen, rutted trails and muddy highways; who crossed rain-swollen fords, or who ventured in boats down rivers that churned with the filth of late winter. It took eleven days for the news to reach London. The first of Cnut's commanders there to hear of it was Siferth, and in the bitter cold of a dismal dawn he slipped secretly from the city and rode alone into the west.

It took far longer for news of the passing of the Danish king to arrive in Rouen, conveyed in a letter delivered from Jorvik by the hand of the bishop of Durham. The missive carried, as well, a plea that the king return to England to take up again the reins of power and drive Swein's son from the kingdom.

"For no sovereign is dearer to us than our natural lord," the Durham bishop read, pausing an instant to glance nervously at Æthelred before continuing, "if he would but govern us more justly than in the past."

It seemed clear to Emma, listening with the king and his advisors, that Archbishop Wulfstan must have been the moving force behind this offer. His was the only voice powerful enough to convince the witan to turn for help to a king whom they had forsaken only months before. In the archbishop's eyes, the claim of an anointed, exiled king would carry far more weight than that of a Danish conqueror's son or even that of an ætheling of England. Wulfstan would see Swein's death as a miracle sent by God, and there was no one, either in England or here in Rouen, who would argue otherwise.

Æthelred, more than anyone, would see God's hand in this.

She saw her husband's expression of satisfaction change to determination, and her mind raced across the Narrow Sea to Athelstan. Surely, he would already have learned of Swein's death by now, but did he know of the witan's offer to the king? And would Athelstan place his sword at the king's feet when, eventually, Æthelred landed in England; or would he defy his father? That question tormented her, for she had long feared such a conflict between father and son, and now it might well come to pass.

In the days that followed, the king's councilors in Rouen made plans for his return to his kingdom. Æthelred spent long hours consulting with Emma's brothers and with the combined councils of England and Normandy. Thorkell, too, took part in the discussions, along with the Norse commander of a viking fleet that lay in the harbor at Honfleur, an ally of Richard's who arrived one morning at her brother's invitation.

Emma watched as this Olaf took his place at the council table. He was as tall and fierce-looking as Thorkell, though many years younger. His beard was short, and his fair hair fell loose and thick about his shoulders. When his eyes fixed upon her face and his lip curled in a feral smile, she shuddered. She had heard tales of this Norseman, and none of them good. He was a brutal man, it was said, who loved violence for its own sake, and he led men who, like him, found joy in slaughter.

It was through her brother's efforts that Olaf had arrived to pledge his sword and his men to the cause of England's king, and in doing this Richard had accomplished, it seemed to Emma, two things at once. He assisted Æthelred in taking back his kingdom at little cost to himself, and at the same time he rid his duchy of Olaf's viking army, a dangerous weapon that he had used against his enemies, but now no longer wanted or needed. Meanwhile, in the coming spring, England would be ravaged again by war, overrun by men like Olaf who would once again sweep across the land like a savage tide.

She attended the planning sessions that Æthelred held in the great cathedral of Rouen, but the king also consulted with her brothers in private meetings that were closed to her. It was after one of these, late at night, that her mother sought her out and revealed what her palace spies had learned of the role that Edward was to play in his father's return to England. Distraught, Emma went immediately to Æthelred, determined to persuade him to change his mind.

Despite the lateness of the hour she found him seated in a cushioned chair with his steward hovering beside him. He looked the very picture of old age. His once golden hair had gone white in the weeks since he had arrived in Rouen. It hung to his chin, limp and disheveled, and his face was grey with weariness. She felt no compassion for him, though. She was far too angry.

She approached his chair, made an obeisance, then stood and regarded him warily. She must choose her words with care and master her fury enough to make him listen to her.

"My lord, I beg your leave to speak with you about your plan to send Edward back to England."

Æthelred considered her a moment, his lips pursed in distaste. Then he gestured to Hubert to leave them, and when the steward was gone, he folded his arms and heaved an irritated sigh.

"Well?"

"I think it would be unwise to send Edward as your envoy," she said. "It is a heavy task, and far too difficult for one so young to undertake."

"Edward will not be conducting the negotiations, Emma," he said. "Eadric will go with him, and that task will be his. But the boy will be a pledge to Archbishop Wulfstan and the witan of my good faith. He is old enough for that. When I was little older than he is now, I was given a crown."

"On that occasion, my lord, you did not have to make a dangerous voyage over the sea, nor was your kingdom crawling with Danish enemies."

"On that occasion," he echoed, "my brother had just been murdered. All royal sons have enemies, Emma, all the time. You know that. And as for the journey across the Narrow Sea, Edward must make it sooner or later if he is to return to England. He will find it less treacherous, I expect, than when he left London last winter."

"But why Edward?" she persisted. "Why now? Surely Eadric can—"

"Do not upbraid me, lady," he snarled. "I am merely acquiescing to the demands of your brother! He would see his nephew upon my throne when I am dead, and this role as my emissary affirms that he is my designated heir."

She was not surprised. Her brother seized advantage wherever he could find it, and he would not care that he was toying with the life of her son.

"And if Edward is captured by your enemies? If the Danes should discover that he is your son?"

"Do you imagine that I would send him without protection?" He thrust himself from his chair and limped past her. "He will have an armed escort and will be sent to a safe harbor where the meetings will be held in secret." He turned to face her from across the chamber, and it seemed to her that the distance between them was vast. "No one, Emma, will know of his coming."

Nevertheless, she thought, that large, armed escort would be a signal to anyone who saw it that it was guarding a great treasure. In this case, a royal son. She remembered Cnut's search for her children aboard the *Wind Rider*. She had spoken of that encounter to no one, so she could hardly use it as an argument now. She would have to explain far too much.

Instead she said, "It takes only one man to reveal a secret, my lord." And then the truth of what this was really about struck her. How had she not seen it already? "Edward will be no emissary," she said coldly. "He will be a hostage. He is your pledge that you will not seek vengeance against your thegns who welcomed Swein. And should you fail to drive Cnut from your kingdom, the men holding our son will deliver him to the Danish prince to curry his favor."

And Cnut would have absolutely no reason to keep Edward alive.

"Of course he is a hostage!" he barked. "It is how such alliances are sealed." He began to pace, restless, muttering almost to himself. "My older sons are all plotting against me for their own gain. Edward is the only one that I can trust, and that makes him all the more valuable."

She stared at him, stunned by his callous disregard for the life of his son. She tried to think of some further argument that would dissuade him from his purpose, but she had already raised every objection that might sway a father. Against the resolve of a king, a duke, and no doubt her brother the archbishop as well, she was powerless.

She asked, "Does Edward know that he is to be a hostage?"

"He knows that he is to represent his father and king." He gave her a defiant look. "He welcomes this as an honor, Emma, which it is. What purpose would it serve to tell him the rest of it?"

None at all, she thought miserably. It would only frighten him. And if he should discover that she had argued against the great honor that his father and uncle had bestowed upon him, Edward would merely add it to the list of whatever other sins he held against her.

Two days later, on a morning of fitful rain, Emma stood between Wymarc and her mother at the river's edge as Edward, his companion Robert, Eadric, and their escort prepared to board the ship that would carry them to Canterbury. She watched her son clasp the hands of his cousins as they wished him godspeed, and she smiled when Godiva laughed at something that Edward whispered in her ear. When he approached his grandmother, thanking her for her courtesy during his stay in Rouen, Gunnora caressed his cheek, and Edward took her hand and kissed it. When his gaze fell upon Emma, he nodded stiffly at her before turning to receive the blessings of his uncles and his father.

Feeling the sympathetic touch of her mother's hand as it slipped about her waist, Emma said, "I know that I should not grieve over what I cannot change."

"That is so," Gunnora replied, and Emma saw her own sorrow reflected in her mother's aged face, "but it is a difficult lesson to learn. I, too, once sent a child to an uncertain fate across the sea, not knowing if I would ever see her again. I did not stop grieving, Emma, until the day you returned to Rouen."

When the ships had rounded the Seine's westward bend and disappeared, Emma walked slowly back to the ducal palace that, for as long as she could foresee, must be her home. She carried Alfred in her arms, and Godiva walked beside her, clinging to her skirt with one hand and to Wymarc's fingers with the other. But Emma's thoughts were with Edward, trying to work out when she might hope to see him again.

It would not be soon. When the negotiations were completed—and they would take weeks, if not months—Edward must remain a hostage in England. He would not be freed until Æthelred and his viking army had won back his kingdom. How long that would take even Æthelred was not prepared to say. It might be months. Or years. It may never happen at all.

Her thoughts turned then to Athelstan whose ambitions and schemes so directly opposed those of his royal father and her own son.

She did not see how their desires could ever be reconciled, and her fear for what the future might hold for all of them was a physical pain that, like a cancer, seemed to eat at her from within.

Shaftesbury Abbey, Dorset

The abbey guest hall was lit on this gloomy March afternoon by a blazing fire in its central hearth and half a dozen hanging oil lamps that spilled halos of light. The chamber could easily accommodate twenty pilgrims, and Athelstan hoped that on the morrow there might be twice that number here—lords of England come in answer to his summons. This evening, though, only Edmund, Ulfkytel, Godwin, and Siferth were sharing a meal with him at the hall's trestle table.

Above their heads a storm was battering the tiles of the slate roof—the fifth such deluge in as many days. The clamor of the rain was inescapable, an endless pounding in Athelstan's ears and an ominous warning that tomorrow's gathering might well end in failure. He was hoping to convince the Wessex nobles to support him in an early spring campaign against the Danes. But because this constant rain would likely delay the spring planting for weeks all across the southern shires, the lords of England would be loath to force their men to fight until their crops were in.

Worried, he was picking at the convent's Lenten fare of bread and fish when the hall door slammed open and Withar was blown in on a gust of wind, his face barely visible in the folds of his dripping cloak. Athelstan reached eagerly for the small, rolled parchment that Withar held out to him, gestured to him to join them at table, and read the missive. There was too little information in it, though, to suit him.

"Edwig writes that he did not find Archbishop Wulfstan at Sherburne," Athelstan said to Withar. "Did he discover where the archbishop has gone?"

Withar, helping himself to one of the small, brown loaves, shook his head.

"Wulfstan left Sherburne more than a week before we arrived there, but no one was able to tell us where he went. I promise you, my lord," he waved a chunk of bread for emphasis, "we pressed them, and I am convinced that his people did not know. When your brother and I parted ways, Edwig rode further north to search for the archbishop in Jorvik. We shall have to wait to see if he was successful."

Frustrated, Athelstan muttered an oath. It was imperative that the messages he had sent with Edwig should reach the archbishop, and soon. He would need Wulfstan's support in the weeks to come. He glanced again at the bit of parchment; then he studied Siferth for several long moments as he weighed his next words. Finally he said to Withar, "Tell us about the Lady Aldyth."

Siferth looked up from his plate in surprise. "There is news of my wife?"

"Yes, lord," Withar said. "She is no longer a hostage of the Danes. It seems she was with them in Jorvik when Swein died—or was killed, no one seems to know for certain how he met his end—but somehow she slipped away from them and sought refuge with the archbishop. He brought her to Sherburne for safekeeping."

"Did you speak to her?" Siferth asked eagerly. "Could she tell you anything about my brother?"

But Withar shook his head. "We asked to see her, but she refused; the archbishop's people wouldn't let us near her."

Athelstan wondered what was going through Siferth's mind as he continued to stare, transfixed, at Withar. Relief, he supposed, that Aldyth was safe. Siferth's greatest fear when he had arrived here bearing news of Swein's death was that the Danes would punish his wife when they learned that he had deserted his post in London. That worry was behind him now, although he still had a brother to be concerned about.

Had Morcar, like Siferth, turned his back on the Danes now that Swein was dead? Was Morcar even still alive? And what of Uhtred? Where was he, and where now did his allegiance lie?

Once more Athelstan was frustrated by how much he did not know.

"Were you able to learn anything about my brother-in-law Uhtred, or about Cnut's army at Gainsborough?" he asked Withar.

"The rumor is that Uhtred is in Northumbria, at Bamburgh, but whether he will stay there no one can say. As for Cnut's army, there has been heavy snowfall in the Humber region, and the Danes have all but buried themselves in their camp. That will change, surely, with the spring thaw, but it will be some weeks, I expect, before they take up arms again."

"If Uhtred is at Bamburgh," Ulfkytel mused, "I doubt that he will return south to join Cnut. His submission to Swein was only half-hearted. Once we have cleared the southern burhs of Danes, my lord," he nodded to Athelstan, "the throne may at last be within your reach."

But Athelstan was not so certain. "This silence that surrounds Wulfstan troubles me," he said. "I would give a very great deal to know where the archbishop is and what he is doing."

"Is Wulfstan so important?" Withar asked. "Surely we can rid England of Danes without his blessing."

"It appears that we may have to," Athelstan said. "But it would be a mistake to underestimate Wulfstan's influence. In the absence of both an anointed king and the Canterbury archbishop, the Jorvik archbishop is the highest authority in the kingdom. The witan must decide who is to be offered the crown, but Wulfstan's voice will be the loudest and most persuasive."

"You are the eldest ætheling," Edmund said firmly. "The crown must go to you."

"Swein's son, though, has a Danish army camped not fifty miles from Wulfstan's see at Jorvik," Ulfkytel pointed out. "Surely the archbishop must feel that threat."

"Perhaps Wulfstan is hiding somewhere, looking to God to give him a sign," Godwin suggested.

"Swein is dead," Edmund snarled. "Surely that is sign enough."

"Unfortunately, Swein's death is the only certainty that we have," Athelstan said. It was, he thought, as though England itself was holding its breath, waiting for someone to make a move. "While there is nothing but silence from the north, we cannot know what is in the mind of Wulfstan, or of Uhtred or Morcar for that matter." He looked pointedly at Siferth. "And a few months ago they were all, like you, willing to bend the knee to the Danish king."

"Because we feared Swein," Siferth insisted.

"Because we were weary of war," Ulfkytel added, "and had not the men nor the will to resist."

"And now," Athelstan said, waving aside their excuses, "the Northerners face another viking warlord and another war. What is to prevent them from pledging fealty to Cnut out of fear and despair?"

There was, too, another possibility. His eyes met Edmund's, and he knew that they were both pondering the same bitter prospect that neither one of them was willing yet to say out loud.

What if Wulfstan had reached out to their father the king and urged him to return?

The next day, despite the bitter weather, the leading men from Dorset, Hampshire, Wiltshire, and Devon filled the benches of the abbey's chapter house, and Athelstan laid out his plan for cleaning out the nests of Danes who were garrisoning the surrounding burhs. He was prepared for arguments, and they came thick and fast. The discussion went on throughout the morning as he listened to the concerns of the men who had answered his summons. Their gravest fear was for the safety of the hostages held by the Danes, sons and brothers whose lives would be forfeit should the English turn against their conquerors—which was exactly what he was now asking them to do.

"You fear for the hostages," Athelstan said, "and I understand that. But do you not realize that we are all hostages of the Danes? For are we not all risking injury or death when we raise our swords against our conquerors? Yet we do it," he paused and looked around the chamber, "for our fathers and mothers, our wives and children, and for all those yet unborn who will inherit this soil, this England. God Himself has rid us of the tyrant Swein, and we must seize the opportunity He has granted us! If we do not take it, if we continue to bend our necks beneath the Danish yoke, then we deserve the wretched fate that a Danish king on the throne of England will surely bring!"

He listened with relief to the cheers and shouts of approval that greeted his words. By day's end an agreement had been struck and pledges given. In mid-April—when the crops must be in if there was to be any harvest at all—their forces would muster to begin the series of raids that they hoped would drive the Danes from Wessex.

There were still two burning questions, though, for which Athelstan had no answers.

How soon would the Danish army at Gainsborough move south to reinforce Cnut's claim to the kingdom?

And where, in the name of God, was Archbishop Wulfstan?

Chapter Twenty-Three

Easter Sunday, 25 April 1014
Reculver, Kent

A flock of sea birds wheeled and soared over Herne Bay, and a stiff, afternoon breeze flung itself against the stone walls of St. Mary's Abbey on its high bluff above the sea. Under the wind's relentless assault, the closed shutters of the monks' refectory quivered and rattled, forcing the men gathered within to raise their voices to be heard. They had been breaking bread together for some time now, seated at a trestle table long enough to accommodate all thirty of them. In their midst Æthelred sat wrapped in furs despite the hall's roaring fire, for he was still bedeviled by the bone-deep cold of days and nights at sea.

His archbishops Wulfstan and Lyfing held places of honor on either side of him, across the table were his ealdormen Eadric and Ælfric, and beside them the warlords Thorkell and Olaf. The rest of the company consisted of bishops, abbots, and some of Æthelred's most powerful magnates who had traveled here in secret by ancient pilgrim roads and forest tracks as yet undiscovered by their Danish conquerors.

These men, who had so recently abandoned him and who now feasted with him to celebrate his return, had come here today because they wanted something from him. They wanted him to rid them of the Danish vermin that had seized control of England and had left armed garrisons like rat droppings in towns throughout the kingdom. And he would give his lords what they wanted because, for once, their interests were in accord with his.

It was the men who were not here that worried him. Where were his ministers from Dorset, Devon and Wiltshire; or the lords and clergy from Somerset and Gloucestershire? They had sent no word of either excuse or delay, and that silence from out of the west gnawed at him.

He swept his gaze up and down the table, studying the faces lit by the flickering gleam of fat candles scattered along the board. Nearly every man whose eyes met his wore an expression of either doubt or trepidation. They were just as wary of him as he was of them. Nevertheless, the thing was done. This morning they had witnessed his anointing and the renewal of his royal vows; he had grasped the hands of each man in turn as one by one they had sworn undying allegiance to him.

Undying allegiance, he thought. Well, we shall see.

Now that the feasting was nearly done, he would have them understand what must come next. He pushed his plate away and cast a flinty glance at Eadric.

"Is Swein's son still in the north?" he asked.

His question speared through the rumble of conversation up and down the table, and other voices quieted as men set down their cups or knives or shanks of roast lamb to listen.

Eadric, his wine cup halfway to his lips, froze. Then his mouth creased into a confident smile.

"As of three days ago, my lord, yes. Cnut is at Gainsborough, along with a great part of his army. But he has placed a large garrison at Lincoln, in addition to garrisons at London, Nottingham, Leicester, North—"

"I am aware of the garrisons," Æthelred interrupted him. "We take Lincoln and Gainsborough first. The rest can wait." He scanned their faces again and, certain that he had everyone's attention now, he continued, "My fleet is made up of eighty ships and near two thousand warriors under the command of Thorkell and Olaf. Duke Richard has supplied forty horses and enough food and fodder to last fifteen days. It leaves me little time for courtly niceties, and I have already squandered two days here at Reculver. Thorkell! How many days' sailing will it take to reach Lincoln?"

"Three, lord, if the weather holds," came the reply. "Longer, if the winds are against us. A week at the most, round the rump of East Anglia and up the Witham. We can take Lincoln at night, while its men are still in their beds."

Æthelred nodded. "From Lincoln, we march swiftly to Gainsborough. I want to destroy Cnut's encampment there and leave no Dane left alive."

"But, lord king!" It was the newly consecrated bishop of London, calling to him from the far end of the table. "Should not London be your first objective? It is closer than Lincoln, and its people clung steadfastly to you when the rest of your kingdom turned away. Surely they should be the first to be delivered from the enemy!"

Æthelred considered the bald-pated, broad-faced London bishop whose predecessor, Ælfhun, now lay dead and buried in Rouen. This new man should be rebuked for questioning his king, but today he must be conciliatory, even toward a foolish priest.

"You are correct, bishop, that London is closer," he observed mildly, "but because of that, word of our presence here will even now be making its way to the city. The Danish garrison there will be readying to meet our assault, and the city walls and even the bridge across the Thames will be heavily defended. So instead we shall strike in the north at Lincoln and take our enemy there by surprise. It is a viking tactic, and we must use it to our advantage."

Olaf now leaned across the table, grinning, his eyes bright.

"London is rich, lord king." Like Thorkell, he spoke in a blend of English and Norse that Æthelred had grudgingly learned to construe with only a modicum of misunderstanding. "If you bring your army against its walls, I shall bring my ships to pull down that bridge! For good silver, of course!"

Olaf barked a raucous laugh that set Æthelred's teeth on edge. The over proud young pup could use a good cuffing. But he had the skill—or the blind luck—to have made a name for himself as a fierce warrior, and that was reason enough to tolerate him for now.

"Pull down that bridge, Olaf," Æthelred grunted, "and you can name your reward." It was a safe enough promise. The bastard had never even set eyes on the Thames bridge, so his boast was an empty one. "But London has to wait until we drive Cnut from England and punish all those in the north who harbored him."

Beside him, Archbishop Wulfstan cleared his throat, and Æthelred, certain that he was about to hear yet another sermon about royal compassion for his subjects, stood to take his leave. His bad leg was still a torment, but he forced himself to walk with studied care to conceal the hitch in his stride from men who would surely be alert for any sign of weakness.

Inside his bedchamber the oil lamps had been lit, a fire burned in the hearth, and his body servant waited to attend him; soon he was resting his back against the bank of pillows on the bed. Dismissing his servant to the adjoining room, he closed his eyes and waited for the pain in his aching leg to ease. He knew, though, that he would not sleep. Every sinew in his body was still throbbing with the tension brought on by the day's events.

Christ! He felt old. His exile from England had lasted only months, but in that time he must have aged a full decade. He felt it in his bones, and he had seen it reflected in the eyes of those men in the hall when they knelt before him today to swear their fealty.

He had put a bold face on things in there, but now uncertainty about the fate that awaited him in the north descended like a black cloud. It would be no easy task to wrestle his kingdom back under his control. He had the will to do what was needed, but he could not be certain that in the days to come he would have the vigor that it would take to wreak vengeance on the men who had betrayed him. If he did not, then once again his enemies would defeat him.

And what was God's design in all this? The Almighty had cast Swein into hell's fire, but would the Lord favor his efforts to retake his throne?

He tried to pray, fixing his eyes upon the small crucifix that hung on the wall beyond the foot of the bed. Slowly, though, he became aware of a roaring in his ears, and his prayer caught in his throat as dread seeped into his veins like poison. He sat up, clenching impotent fists as he looked wildly about the chamber for his brother's grim visage.

Had God answered his prayers by sending Edward's vengeful ghost to prey upon him, even here within abbey walls?

"Damn you!" His cry emerged as little more than a whimper. "Where are you?"

But he could see no movement other than the tiniest flicker of lamplight, and he realized that the noise in his ears was no more than the wind that had, for a time, lessened and now had risen again. The shadows lurking in the corners of the chamber were only that—shadows.

He fell back against the pillows and as his terror drained away the pounding of his heart lessened.

Surely, then, this must be a sign! His brother's ghost would have hounded him tonight if the days ahead were to bring him defeat and humiliation—or death. But there had been no ominous visitation, only the sound of the wind and the shimmer of lamp light.

This, then, was God's answer to his prayer.

Sleep still eluded him, though, and when his servant announced that Eadric wished to speak with him, he nodded acquiescence.

"Tell me what my councilors are saying," he snapped when Eadric appeared. "I expect that my departure from the hall has combined with the abbot's wine to loosen some tongues."

"My lord, they are troubled by your viking army. They had assumed that it would be the men of Wessex and Mercia that you would lead against Cnut."

Æthelred barked a bitter laugh.

"I do not trust my English subjects enough for that. Not yet." He frowned, turning over in his mind what he intended to do in the coming weeks, and confident now that he would be victorious. "Once I have dealt with Swein's son, I must teach the men of Lindsey a lesson. They cannot go unpunished, but their English brethren might be reluctant to do what is necessary. My viking allies, though, will be ruthless. It is their nature." He pinned Eadric with a dark look. "Say nothing of that to anyone. I'll not have Wulfstan plaguing me about leaving vengeance to God."

"Of course," Eadric agreed. "You are wise, lord king, to use all the weapons at your disposal. I must warn you, though, that the men out there are already grumbling about what this mercenary army is going to cost them."

"Are they indeed? They will do more than grumble by the time this is finished." He had promised his viking army twenty-one thousand pounds for their swords, and when he taxed his people to pay for it, they would do more than grumble. They would howl.

"There are some," Eadric went on, "who believe that the Northmen will betray you."

Æthelred grunted. "I have heard that argument countless times. Olaf, though, is newly baptized and has sworn on holy relics to defend me to the death. As for Thorkell the Dane, he has been at my side for two years! If he were going to betray me, he could have done it long before this." He slanted a glance at his son-in-law. "I trust them just as much as I trust you, Eadric, and far more than I trust that lot out there. What else are they complaining about? I may as well hear all of it."

"There is a great deal of mewling about the hostages, and what will happen to them when you attack the Danish camp."

"Dear God! We do not even know where the hostages are! What do they think I am, a prophet?" He pointed at Eadric to emphasize his next words. "You will go back to those men in the hall and tell them that they should plead with the Almighty to have mercy upon the hostages because the Danish devils at Gainsborough will show them none." He pulled in a long breath and released it with a huff. "Now, what can you tell me about my treacherous sons? Is Athelstan gathering an army? Must I watch my back while I am in the north?"

"It appears so, my lord. The æthelings are rumored to be somewhere in Hampshire or Wiltshire, and Athelstan is calling for men to join him."

Æthelred scowled. "That explains why so many western lords are missing from this gathering," he murmured.

"No doubt the lords of the west have been beguiled by the promise of future favors," Eadric said. "It means, though, that you cannot trust your elder sons, my lord. Now, even less than before."

Æthelred felt suddenly weary again. He had ever been suspicious of Athelstan's ambition for the throne. Now it seemed that Edmund was disloyal as well. As for Edwig, he hardly mattered. He had ever been a worthless fool.

"Once I have vanquished Cnut in the north I shall deal with my rebellious sons," he said. "What of young Edward? Where is he?"

"He is at St. Augustine's Abbey in Canterbury in the keeping of Wulfgar of Kent. Edward will come to no harm unless..."

Eadric's voice faded into silence, but he did not have to say any more. Emma had been right about what would happen if the campaign against Cnut failed. Edward's captors would barter him to the Danish victors, and the boy would be quietly disposed of.

"Send word to the Norman duke that he is safe," Æthelred let his gaze drift past Eadric, to the crucifix on the wall, and he felt again that surge of confidence. "No harm will come to Edward," he said firmly. "I shall be victorious in the north; God has given me a sign."

Easter Monday, April 1014
Gainsborough, Lindsey, Mercia

Elgiva was shivering with cold, and she pulled the thick bedclothes up to her chin, turning on her side as she did so to face her husband. In the dim light of the hearth fire she could make out the frown lines on his forehead as he tried to resolve whatever problem was eating at him.

Their coupling tonight had been swift and brusque, affording her little pleasure. That was the way of it now. He took her as if by habit or instinct, and then lay long awake, his mind unreadable. She did not like this change in him. She had thought that with his father dead, he would turn to her with renewed trust and passion. But ever since Swein's death, Cnut had paid her little heed, burdened as he was with the cares of kingship.

Or near kingship.

She closed her eyes, and the string of misfortunes that had plagued them over the past few months streamed through her mind. It had begun the night that Swein had died, when they had fled Jorvik, and Cnut could no longer depend upon Uhtred's Northumbrians to swell his army. The winter had been bitter, and spring had brought heavy rains, hunger, and sickness. Some in the camp had died, despite all of Tyra's possets and potions. Morcar's wife had succumbed to a fever, and three days later Morcar had crept out of Gainsborough in the dead of night along with his retainers.

That betrayal had paled, though, beside the loss of the two hundred Danish shipmen who had refused to accept the leadership of Swein's twenty-four-year old son. Content with their plunder and unwilling to follow a man they considered too young and inexperienced to solidify his tenuous hold on England, they had sailed for home. To her disgust, Cnut made no effort to stop them.

"At the rate that you are losing men," she had warned him, "by midsummer you will have no army left."

"What would you have me do?" he had snapped at her. "Chain them here?"

And so her husband was a king with no kingdom to speak of, and a warlord with a dwindling army.

She opened her eyes. Cnut was still staring into the dark. Tomorrow he would lead some of his men across Lindsey to gather horses and supplies. She did not know when she would see him again.

"How long will you be away, collecting your horses?" she asked, since neither of them was sleeping.

"No more than ten days," he replied. "While I am gone, you, the children and the camp will be in Eirik's hands."

She stirred uneasily. She had heard Eirik complaining that Cnut was leaving him with too few men to defend the camp.

"Ten days is a long time," she said. "What if Uhtred decides to attack us from the north while you are gone?"

He snorted. "You needn't worry about Uhtred. I have scouts in Northumbria watching him, and if he were gathering an army, I would have had word of it by now. The English lords in the south, though," he said, thoughtfully, "have likely been chafing all winter long at the prospect of Danish rule. My father erred in thinking that he could control all of England from Jorvik. We should have wintered at London."

She pursed her mouth, swallowing the retort that sprang to her lips. She had urged him to stay in London, and he had refused. It would do little good to throw that in his face now, though. Instead she asked, "What about the garrisons your father placed in towns all across Mercia and Wessex? Will they not keep the south secure?"

"Nothing is secure while there are men in England who will oppose my claim to the throne. I had word today from Thurbrand in London warning that Æthelred's sons are preparing for war. They may not come soon, but when they do, they will come from the south."

"So," she breathed, "they did not go to Normandy with their father."

"It seems that they did not, nor does that surprise me." He turned on his side to face her. "You knew them. What can you tell me about them?"

She closed her eyes tight, drifting in memory to the time eight years before when she had last served in the queen's household. That was the year that Eadric had murdered her father, and the king had ordered her brothers blinded and left to die. She had fled to Holderness to escape Æthelred's wrath, and her world had been turned upside down when, against her will, she had been wed to this son of a Danish king.

She felt his finger graze her cheek, and she opened her eyes.

"I was not asleep," she whispered. "I was remembering."

"And?"

In the darkness, the faces of the three eldest æthelings swam before her—Athelstan, Ecbert, and Edmund. Ecbert was long dead now, but as far as she knew, the other two were still alive.

"The king's eldest son and heir is Athelstan," she said. How she had once lusted after that golden-haired ætheling! "He is well-liked, far more so than his father. I cannot speak to how skilled a warrior he is, but he wields an ancient sword that once belonged to a great Mercian king. Offa's sword, they call it, and it is a symbol of royal authority."

"I don't like the sound of that," Cnut murmured. "Men will be quick to rally behind someone who carries such a talisman. What of Æthelred's other sons?"

"There is Edmund, who always seemed content to live in Athelstan's shadow. If he throws his support behind his elder brother, together they could be formidable. The third ætheling was just a boy when I was at court, so I know nothing about him. And Emma's sons, even if they are in England, are still too young to matter." They would all have to be destroyed, though, before Cnut could force the English to accept his rule. "You must rid yourself of the æthelings, my lord," she urged him. "Do that, and there will be no one to oppose you."

Cnut made no reply, but turned to stare again at the rafters. Brooding about the future, she supposed. She closed her eyes and summoned an image of the future that she wished to have, seated at his side in the great hall in London, fulfilling the destiny that had been foretold her all those years ago. Just as she was drifting into sleep, Tyra's eerie chanting crept into her mind, the unsettling sounds shaping themselves into words.

I cannot promise that you will ever return to London.

And she shivered, this time with foreboding.

Chapter Twenty-Four

May 1014
Gainsborough, Lindsey, Mercia

Elgiva hesitated just inside the door of the squat, timbered shed where Tyra mixed her potions and kept the growing supply of the salves, elixirs, and herbs she used for treating wounds. She considered the array of boxes and bags that lined the walls and sprawled across the floor and, spotting a pile of empty sacks, she grabbed one. Wrestling her armload of neatly folded, narrow lengths of scrap linen into it, she secured it with a bit of string before placing it on the hard-packed, dirt floor between bags of herbs and a stack of sealed pots of salted honey.

In less than a week everything stored here, she thought bitterly, would go south with Cnut and his army, and once again he would leave her behind. Tyra would go with him, because her healing skills would be needed. And Lindsey women who had attached themselves to Danish warriors would go simply because there was no one to stop them. But she had been ordered to remain here.

"It is war, Elgiva," Cnut had told her, "and you have no place in it."

And so Cnut would ride to London and claim his throne without her.

Resentment chafed at her like a blistered heel, and although she was still trying to discover a way to circumvent Cnut's edict that she stay behind, she had not yet found it.

Stepping back outside, she raised her hand to block the late afternoon sun as she cast a nervous glance toward the gate. It had been ten days since Cnut left on his mission to gather supplies and men, and it worried her that he had not yet returned. She had an edgy feeling—a prickling against her skin—that some trouble lurked nearby, just out of sight.

With an effort she shrugged off her disquiet. Nothing was wrong, she told herself. Cnut would surely return today, as he had promised. Dragging her eyes away from the gate she went to where Tyra stood in the shade of an oak tree, straining something viscous into one of several bronze vessels that were arrayed on a trestle table in front of her.

"We have eight sacks of bandages now," Elgiva told her. The lengths of linen would be used to bind broken heads, limbs, and she did not like to think what else. "Should I tell the women to prepare more?"

"If I need any more," Tyra murmured, her eyes focused on her work, "I shall cut strips from the tunics of the dead."

Her reply evoked images of dead men stripped naked, and Elgiva grimaced. She grimaced again when a foul smell reached her, wafting from a nearby trio of cauldrons that hung suspended over cooking fires. It was the salve that Tyra smeared on wounds to aid in healing—radish, wormwood, and cropleek pounded and boiled in butter and celandine.

She was about to ask how much longer the wretched stuff needed to simmer when there was a cry from the gate ward and she saw three horsemen race into the yard, sending up a flurry of mud and gravel. They had barely halted when two of the riders slid to the ground and ran to the third who appeared to be tied to his horse.

Terrified that it was Cnut slumped there in the saddle, Elgiva began to run.

Men had sprinted from every corner of the yard to help, and she shoved her way through them. When she was close enough to get a look at the injured man, she saw his long, chestnut colored hair.

Not Cnut, then. She grasped the sleeve of one of the riders and drew him aside.

"What happened?" she demanded. "Who is it?"

"Name's Eilaf, my lady, from the garrison at Lincoln. We found him clinging to his horse, barely conscious. All we could get out of him was that Lincoln was attacked."

Lincoln! Little more than a day's ride south.

Cnut had warned her that trouble, if it came, would come from the south.

"Go alert Eirik," she said.

Tyra was already kneeling on the ground beside Eilaf, lifting his closed eyelids then placing her ear against his mouth.

"He is breathing," Tyra said. "Get him inside."

By the time they had carried him into Tyra's shed, a girl had appeared with a pail of hot water, and Tyra had set an array of small pots on the floor near him and taken up a pair of shears. Elgiva pulled a length of bandage from the sack she had brought in earlier and, snatching some wool wadding from a bundle, she placed it near Tyra's hand. She watched as the Sami woman reached for the hem of the man's tunic, cut it away from his body and gently pried the fabric from the blood-encrusted gash in his side. The bleeding began anew, seeping through Tyra's fingers as she used the wool to staunch it.

"Will he live?" Elgiva asked.

"For a day," Tyra murmured, "perhaps two. He has lost too much blood. If there is fighting at Lincoln, he'll likely not be the first to die."

Elgiva stood frozen, staring at the ugly, gaping wound, and her mouth went dry. Cnut had planned to take his army south, but now, somehow without their hearing any rumor of it, an English army had marched north. If Lincoln should fall, then the æthelings—for it must be the æthelings who led the attack—would strike here next. Within days, perhaps. She could only guess at the timing, but even if it took longer, Cnut's army was not ready. Their numbers were depleted.

And Cnut was not here.

Her heart thudding, she darted from the hut, and it was a relief to run, to put her trembling limbs to work as she dodged her way across the yard that was now boiling with men. When she found Eirik he was already sheathed in mail and adjusting the saddle girth of his horse.

"Have you sent someone to find Cnut?" she cried.

He heaved himself astride his mount before frowning down at her.

"That would be a fool's errand," he said. "He could be anywhere in all of Lindsey. Rumor of an army from the south must reach him soon, though, and when he returns he will want to know what is happening at Lincoln. I'm going to find out."

She watched him ride through the gate with a handful of men. By tomorrow at this time there would be news, and by then Cnut may have returned. But the dread that had been nagging at her earlier mushroomed into a dark cloud, and now she could not shake it.

Her sleep that night was broken and troubled, and when there was no news the next day she had to endure a second night of restless dreams.

On the morning that followed, Eilaf was laid in his grave and there was still no sign of Cnut or Eirik. The sky was heavy with the threat of rain and by midday it was as dark as twilight. Elgiva, in her chamber with her children and her small household, had just ordered the lamps kindled and the shutters closed against the coming storm when Halfdan surged in, along with two other men who were cloaked for travel.

"My lady," Halfdan said urgently, "you, the children, Thurbrand's wife, and any servants you need are to sail immediately to Holderness. Take whatever you can pack quickly and go down to the river. The ship is being readied now. These men will help you."

She stood up, alarm mingling with irritation that he would presume to tell her what to do. Catla, though, as easily frightened as a hare, was already snatching up blankets and clothing.

"Has Cnut returned?" Elgiva demanded.

"No, but Lincoln has fallen, and we will soon be under attack. Jarl Eirik wants you and the children on a ship to Holderness before the—"

"I will speak with Eirik." She was not going anywhere until Cnut returned. She tried to shove past Halfdan and his men, but it was like trying to break through a wall.

"There is no time, my lady," Halfdan insisted.

She gestured toward the window. "He would put us on a ship with a storm about to break over our heads?"

"The storm may hold off, my lady, but the tide will not wait."

"It will have to wait," she snapped. "I will not leave without—"

"Get them packed," Halfdan barked at his men, "and get them on the ship."

He stalked out of the chamber, and the two men began grabbing at things—anything, she supposed, that looked of value. They would make a mess of it.

"I'll do it!" she cried, pushing them aside. She pointed to the coffers that held the children's clothes. "Take those to the ship." Swiftly she gathered her own clothing, jewels, and a coffer filled with coin, and set them apart. She would be prepared to flee at a moment's notice, but she would not leave Gainsborough until Cnut returned.

More men arrived, sent by Eirik to ensure that her household and all their bundles and boxes made it to the ship. As Elgiva stepped outside with a howling Thyri in her arms, she glanced back to make certain that her treasures were safely tucked out of sight. When she reached the hythe it had not yet begun to rain, but the wind was up and the storm would be on them soon. She was relieved to see that a makeshift tent near the ship's mast would provide some shelter for her children.

"Catla!" she shouted against the wind, "take Thyri!" She thrust her daughter into Catla's arms. "When Cnut returns, and if he orders me to Holderness, I will join you!"

"Nay, lady," a man's voice bawled from behind her. "You are sailing today, and on my ship. Eirik's orders."

She turned, and when she saw Arnor striding up the hythe toward her, his mouth twisted in a scowl, she cursed under her breath. This surly bastard had never made any secret of his contempt for her. Likely he would drown her if he got the chance.

"You are mistaken, Arnor," she corrected him coldly. "I am not going anywhere with you."

She tried to push past him but he blocked her way on the narrow hythe, and when she glared up at him, she saw his face set in the familiar, knowing sneer that she hated.

"My orders are to put you on this ship," he said, "and while you are under my protection you will do what I tell you. Now get on board!"

He grabbed her arm, thrusting her toward the ship, and she stumbled, banging her knees against the boat's hull. With a cry of pain she clutched the top strake to keep from falling then swung around to face him again, almost blind with fury.

"I do not take orders from Eirik or from you, and I will not leave Gainsborough until Cnut returns!" She could hear both of her children screaming now, and silently she cursed Catla for allowing them to see this. "My husband expects me to be here when he—"

"I have no time for this," were the last words she heard before the world went black.

When she opened her eyes, Elgiva found that she was lying on the deck of a moving ship, her head supported by what she presumed was a bundle of clothing or blankets. Pain throbbed behind her eyes, and touching the side of her head she found the tender spot that was its source. The bastard had hit her! How long had she been lying here? And how far were they from Gainsborough?

Catla was kneeling at her side, and she could hear Thyri's muffled sobs although she couldn't see her children.

"My things," she groaned.

"They are here, my lady," Catla said. "Tyra brought them down before we sailed."

"Is Tyra on the ship?"

"No. She stayed behind."

Of course she did. If there was to be a battle, Cnut would need her to tend the wounded.

She clutched Catla's shoulder and pulled herself to a sitting position. She could see Arnor standing near the prow with his back to her, his long hair streaming in the wind, and she wondered if she could find the strength to shove him over the side. Just then he turned around, and as he started toward her, she pulled herself to her feet, planting them wide to steady herself against the throbbing pain in her head and the motion of the ship. Catla stood, too, somehow supporting her at the same time that she shrank behind her.

Arnor drew so close to her that she could smell his rank odor. He was a big man, far taller and wider than she was—as large as a massive block of stone and just as hard. No shoving him overboard, then.

"How dare you strike me!" she snarled at him. But when a wave of dizziness swept over her she had to grasp Catla's arm to steady herself. "If Cnut does not kill you for it, I will!"

"You would be wise to save your venom for our enemies, lady," he said.

"Take me back to Gainsborough, then, and I will spit at them! I do not fear Æthelred's sons."

He shouted a humorless laugh.

"It was not the æthelings who attacked Lincoln," he said. "It was the old king."

She stared at him, stunned. That was impossible! Æthelred was gone!

"How?" She cried. "With what army?"

"With a viking army led by Thorkell. You remember Thorkell," he sneered, "the jomsviking who was once our ally? Who thinks that Cnut murdered his brother and is hungry for vengeance?" He shook his head. "Every man in that army will be after Cnut's blood, so whoever it was that poisoned Hemming did Cnut no favor." He fixed her with cruel, suspicious eyes. "And the whole world knows, my lady, that poison is a woman's weapon."

She felt her stomach lurch as she imagined a thousand swords pointed at Cnut. It did not matter that he was innocent of Hemming's murder, that she and Alric had secretly conspired to bring about his well-deserved death, or that Arnor suspected what they had done. It only mattered that Thorkell held Cnut to blame, and if he should kill Cnut, what would happen to her?

She staggered to the ship's rail, clutched at it with trembling hands, and retched over the side. When her stomach stopped heaving, she wiped her mouth with the back of her hand and drew in a long, shuddering breath.

Tyra had warned of malignant forces threatening her, and she could feel them all around her now, ready to engulf her. Staring at the flat lands sweeping past and with the wind clawing at her face and hair, she felt her throat tighten with fear and despair.

After so many years of waiting and planning, after so much silver squandered and lives lost, King Swein had ruled this kingdom for only two months; Cnut had ruled it not at all. Now Æthelred and Thorkell had returned, and Cnut's claim to England seemed to be crumbling like a tower built of sand.

From somewhere behind her she caught the faint sound of a child's querying voice—her son's voice—and she remembered another of Tyra's prophecies.

You will have two sons, and both will grow to manhood.

She placed a hand against her belly. Was she even now carrying Cnut's second son? She hoped not—not yet. She had to believe that Cnut would survive; that someday she would join him in London and that there he would fill her with the seed of another child.

She turned her face into the wind, steeling herself against whatever lay ahead. She had lived through other perils, and she would not give in to despair now. Not yet. Not while there was still hope and while Cnut, as far as she knew, was still alive.

A.D. 1014 After the death of Swein, sat Cnut with his army in Gainsborough until Easter...But King Æthelred with his full force came to Lindsey before they were ready; and they plundered and burned, and slew all the men that they could reach. Cnut, the son of Swein, went out with his fleet...and proceeded southward until he came to Sandwich. There he landed the hostages that were given to his father, and cut off their hands and ears and their noses.

The Anglo-Saxon Chronicle

Chapter Twenty-Five

June 1014
Rouen, Normandy

Emma stood at the door of her eldest brother's private chamber waiting to be admitted. She could see Richard at the far end of the room, seated alone at a narrow table that was awash in morning light.

Her brother, now in his fifth decade, was still the imposing figure that he had ever been, although his elegant beard had gone grey, and what had once been a shock of thick blond hair was now faded and thin. Age and wealth had burnished him—given him an air of regal grace that she suspected must irritate the Frankish king whenever they met. Nevertheless, Richard was still branded by the Franks as the spawn—and the ally—of vikings.

Just now he was intent upon a document that lay on the table before him, and when Emma saw him raise his hand, forestalling his steward's attempt to announce her, she flung her patience aside.

She strode into the chamber, ignoring the protesting steward and the clerk who stared at her, open-mouthed, from his post beside tall shelves laden with scrolls.

"Richard," she said, waving aside the chair that the steward hastily offered her and standing squarely across the table from her brother. "Is it true that Cnut has been driven from England?"

Her brother looked up and with a flick of his hand dismissed both steward and clerk before answering her.

"It is true," he said, and he handed her the document he had been reading.

She studied it quickly, noting that it was from Archbishop Wulfstan. But she had read only half of it when the words began to swim before her eyes. Horrified, she sank to the chair and looked up at Richard.

"The hostages," she whispered. "Dear God."

He shrugged. "Cnut could have murdered them, Emma, yet he did not." Her brother settled back in his chair and pressed his fingertips together. "You must understand that Swein's son is a dangerous and shrewd adversary. By mutilating the hostages he has sent a message to their noble kin that oath breakers will be punished. But by leaving them alive he has conveyed another, subtler message as well."

Emma stared at him, chilled by what he was implying.

"It is a warning," she whispered. "And a promise. Cnut intends to return."

"Exactly. He covets the English throne just as his father did. I have no doubt that he will raise another army to pursue his claim to it."

"What claim? He has no claim!"

"Of course he does, and you know it as well as I do. He is the son of Swein who, for however brief a time, was accepted as England's king even though he was never crowned. No doubt Cnut believes that he has as much right to the English throne as Æthelred or his sons. And that, my dear sister," he straightened, intent, leaning forward to rest his hands flat upon the table in front of him, "includes your own sons. You had best prepare yourself for what is to come. Cnut may have fled to Denmark for now, but his brother Harald is no fool. He must be worried that Cnut might challenge him for the Danish throne, so he will do whatever he can to support Cnut's aims in England just to be rid of him. Cnut will strike again. The only question is when."

So there would be more battles and more bloodshed, Emma thought. It wasn't over. The English had merely been given a respite.

She turned back to Wulfstan's letter, hoping to find some crumb of comfort there. Instead she was sickened by the archbishop's description of Æthelred's cruel ravaging of Lindsey. The king had returned with vengeance in his heart, not mercy.

"Must the punishment for faithlessness be so savage?" she protested.

"Yes," her brother replied. "Else there would be chaos. The foundation of kingship is fear, Emma, not mercy. Never forget it. And be grateful that your son has now been delivered to the Canterbury archbishop. Lyfing will keep him safe from reprisals by your husband's nobles who might try to repay his vengeance with vengeance of their own."

She wanted to weep at the cruelty of men, but she bit her lip and drew in a deep breath to forestall the tears that would brand her as weak in Richard's eyes. She scanned the letter again, searching for some mention of Athelstan. Finding none, she looked at her brother.

"This letter says nothing about where the king is now," she said, "or about the elder æthelings." Did Athelstan know that his father had ravaged Lindsey? That Cnut had mutilated the hostages and sailed for Denmark?

"I have news of the æthelings, as it happens," Richard replied, "news that Wulfstan either was not aware of or did not see fit to share in that letter. While your husband has been setting northern Mercia aflame, his sons have been in Wessex attacking Danish strongholds. One of my agents sailed from Wareham a sennight ago, and he claims that the Danes there have been driven out and that nearly all the major trading centers along the southern coast are now back in English hands due to raids led by the æthelings. Bath, too, has been re-taken, and it appears that Athelstan and his brother might make for Winchester soon." He frowned. "If the king is leading his force south through Mercia, he may find when he approaches London that he has to face an army led by his eldest sons."

She could envisage what would happen. Edmund would urge Athelstan to challenge his father for the throne, while Eadric would encourage the king to confront and punish the æthelings. There would be no one on either side to counsel caution or patience or forgiveness. That was a queen's task and there was no queen in England to shoulder it.

"I must go back," she said.

"Why? Would you play the peaceweaver between the king and his sons? Must I remind you that any enmity between them is to your own son's advantage?"

She studied her brother's face, trying to read what was in his mind. It was his hope that when Æthelred died, Edward would be offered England's throne. That much she knew. But she could not fathom how Richard believed that such a thing could be brought about while Æthelred's elder sons still lived.

"Richard," she said, "Edward's half-brothers are grown men. They are warriors who have raised their banners against the Danes. Through their family allegiances they have strong ties to powerful men all across England. When Æthelred dies—tomorrow or next year or in five years' time—one of his elder sons will be offered the throne, not Edward. My husband may have promised you that he will promote my son as his heir, but it will be the witan that will decide who will take the throne, without regard to the wishes of a dead king."

Especially a king who had punished his people so brutally that there must be many who now wished that he had remained in exile.

He offered her a sour smile. "All the more reason," he said, "to stand aside now and let the English royals themselves whittle down the choices, I think. Even if you try to play the peaceweaver, how would you find your way to the king's side? And what of your younger children? Would you take them with you back to a kingdom still engulfed in war? Or do you think to leave them on my hands while you wander the byways of England searching for your husband?"

With a trembling hand she placed Wulfstan's letter on the table and, reluctantly, she acknowledged the truth of that last argument. She could not take her children back to England. Not yet. Nor was it only her children that she must consider. It was her entire household. She was responsible for them as well, and for Edyth and Wulfa and their children. She could not abandon them in their Norman exile any more than she could abandon Godiva and Alfred.

She must wait until England was safe and there was a court to return to. Nevertheless, she would begin making plans for the journey that lay ahead. And she would write to the archbishops—to Wulfstan and to Lyfing—urging them to mediate some kind of reconciliation between the king and his sons.

Such a reconciliation, though, would come at a cost. Æthelred had exacted a cruel vengeance on the Lindsey men with fire and sword. What would he do to his sons?

June 1014
Near Winchester, Hampshire

The last hour before dawn, Edmund thought, had to be the longest hour of the night.

He sat astride his mount on the brow of St. Giles Hill, one of nearly a dozen horsemen, all of them as apprehensive, he suspected, as he was. In the dim half-light he could see Athelstan on his left, his body taut and so still that he seemed carved from stone. On his right, Godwin was restlessly fingering his sword hilt, his usually genial face grim and drawn. Neither one of them met his glance. Their eyes were fixed upon the city below as they waited for dawn.

Now he, too, considered Winchester's walls. He could make out five men on the ramparts above the gatehouse, visible only because they were clustered around a glowing brazier for warmth. He envied them their small blaze because the westerly breeze was turning his backside to ice. But they would be tired now, and inattentive, their eyes gritty as they neared the end of their watch.

He was anything but tired. He felt like a coiled snake ready to strike, and this enforced stillness, this tense waiting, was agony.

He dropped his gaze to the base of the city's fortifications and tried to make out the river that flowed along Winchester's eastern border. Their scouts had reported that the Itchen was running fast and high, and today the river was going to be their first challenge. They would have to cross it before they could attempt to scale that damned wall. A few miles upstream men had been working through the night to dam the Itchen's flow. They could not stop it completely, but Athelstan hoped that they could block some of its force long enough for several score of men to ford it despite the burden of their weapons and ladders, and despite the deadly rain that the Danes would be flinging on them from above.

He turned to glance back toward the eastern horizon, but there was no sign yet of the rising sun, and the dawn chorus had not yet begun. The only sounds in the gloom were the creak of leather and occasional whickers from the horses.

In front of him, some way down the hill, he could see the vague shapes of men kneeling on the dew wet grass. They would be praying now, watching the sky for the first hint of day, and pissing themselves in fear. When it grew light enough the guards above that gatehouse would see them—could not possibly miss them, they were so close, and well within range of any archers stationed on the walls. But that was what Athelstan wanted. It was all part of his mad plan.

"We shall be fodder for their bowmen," Athelstan had warned them, "a feint to draw the defenders to us on the eastern wall just before the fyrd attacks their western gate."

Edmund hoped to God that the plan worked and that Ulfkytel's men and Æthelmær's fyrd would make it swiftly through the western gate and into the city because if they did not, by midday most of the men poised now on this hill would be dead.

None of them had much liked their odds of surviving this assault, but no one had questioned Athelstan's commands. The mutilation of the hostages at Sandwich had enraged everyone, and now the men were thirstier than ever for Danish blood. When Athelstan had forbidden the taking of prisoners, insisting that every Danish shipman still in England must die, his men had cheered.

Edmund glanced at his brother again, and in the greying light he could see the hint of a smile on that determined face, as if he welcomed what lay ahead—as if he embraced the possibility of death in the hours to come.

He shook his head. Athelstan had been in a fey mood ever since word had come that the king had returned to England. His brother had laughed when that news reached them, had called for mead to celebrate their father's resurrection, and downed cup after cup until he collapsed, senseless. Since then he had been a man driven. He had somehow found the delicate balance of savagery and cunning that he needed to plan and lead successful assaults, and their army had wrested burh after burh from Danish garrisons. The men loved him, but they were wary of him, too, because he was reckless and far too eager to take risks.

While he admired Athelstan's fierce determination, Edmund sometimes wondered if his real brother had been spirited away and a viking changeling left in his place. With each battle Athelstan became more heedless, and this attack on Winchester was the most foolhardy of all. If his brother's risky scheme to get an army inside the western gate didn't work, then they were all dead men.

He leaned toward his brother and whispered, "Do you think Morcar convinced the Danes that he is still their ally?" There were many things that could go wrong with this plan, but that the Danes in the city knew of Morcar's defection and should prevent him from opening the western gate from the inside was the most likely.

"Morcar seemed confident enough," Athelstan murmured, "and last autumn he was well known to the garrison here as one of Swein's war leaders. If he fails to persuade the Danes that he is still Cnut's man, when the sun rises we might see his body hanging from those walls. It was a risk that Morcar was willing to take."

Edmund grunted. "And if Morcar or one of his men has somehow let slip that there is an army waiting outside the western gate?" He paused, and Athelstan turned to him with the chilling smile that Edmund had seen so often of late.

"That is a risk that I am willing to take."

Edmund shifted in his saddle as he thought again about the risks his brother was now willing to take. Their father may have returned to England, but he would find that his eldest son had at last become the man that the king had feared for so long. There was bound to be trouble between them, far worse than in the past, especially if today ended with Athelstan in control of the royal city and prepared to challenge their father for the kingdom.

He clenched his teeth. One problem at a time. First, they must take this city.

Drawing in a long breath he caught the smell of wet grass, damp wool, and horseflesh, and at that moment he heard the first bird call in the June sky. The darkness had bled to grey, and as he surveyed the city below, where the white towers of two great minsters were now visible beyond the shuttered eastern gate, horns winded an alarm from the city ramparts.

Edmund waited for a signal from his brother. Athelstan, though, remained still as stone.

"Take a good, long look at us, you bastards," Athelstan murmured. "Get your men on to the eastern walls and do not look behind you."

Still Athelstan waited, and his army waited with him—a silent menace that did not move. Edmund could see men on the walls staring out at them, others peering down at the river. The dam, then, must have worked. But how long would it hold?

More men appeared on the wall, and then more. How many Danes, he wondered, were still inside that city? And how long was his brother going to wait before he ordered his bowmen to loose?

Edmund glanced behind him again and blinked at the brightness of the glow in the eastern sky. Beside him Athelstan stood in his stirrups and shouted a command.

A storm of arrows sailed toward the city from further along the hill's crest, and the men on the slope below began to run toward the river. Athelstan kneed his horse forward; Edmund followed with the other mounted warriors, targets for the arrows that answered their own. He raised his shield over his head and felt the thump as an arrow struck. And then another, and more, as volleys rose and fell.

He focused his gaze upon the Itchen, ignoring everything except the arrows that rained down, battering his shield and somehow, miraculously, missing his horse. The hail of arrows ceased abruptly as their own bowmen sent flight after flight toward the city and the Danes were forced to duck beneath their own shields. And then they were nearing the river, riding down the high bank and into the water.

They had done this once as boys, a handful of æthelings damming the river with their horses on a summer afternoon and watching as the water spread into a pool. But there had been no murderous Danes on the ramparts raining spears down on them that day; only townsmen whose outraged shouts had sent them, howling with laughter, back up the bank.

Now he urged his horse into the water and was nearly unseated by the river's surging force. He clenched his knees tighter against his mount, gritting his teeth against the bitter cold and cursing as a spear slammed into his raised shield.

He was not the only one cursing. All around him men roared defiance, and the clamor of their shouts combined with the thunderous noise of the river made his ears ring. A horseman beside him took a spear in the face and fell, screaming, into the water. Horses thrashed wildly despite their riders' efforts to hold them still as they struggled against the Itchen's still powerful onslaught.

Arrows continued to fly from the hill behind them and, at last hazarding a glance to his left from beneath his shield, Edmund saw that most of their men had made it through the churning, waist-high water. He shouted to Athelstan who slung his shield across his back and leaped from his horse to one of the ladders now hugging the stones and began to climb. Dozens of men surged to the ladders now, and Edmund sprang from his horse to join them.

He climbed, cursing as the ladder trembled and swayed beneath his weight while the shield slung over his arm offered little protection from the hail of missiles falling all around him. After an interminable age he reached the top rung to see an ax blade arcing toward his head. Rearing backward, he nearly lost his footing, but before the Dane could swing at him again he shifted his shield to his hand and slammed its edge into bared teeth. Heaving himself up the final rung he made it at last over the wall, and then it was all grunt work—slashing, thrusting, kicking—pitching men over the edge of the parapet as he and a band of Hampshire men made their grim way along the fighting platform amid the crush of men and weapons.

He could not say how much time passed as they fought there along the top of the wall, but it seemed an eternity. At one point he heard a distant horn but had no way of knowing if it was Æthelmær and the fyrd advancing from the western gate or more Danes who seemed to drive at them like an endless tide. He was stalking a warrior in a corselet and helm, a tall man who glared at him and used spear and shield to keep him at bay when the man suddenly screamed and fell face down at his feet with a knife in his back. And then there were only English warriors in front of him and behind him.

It was quieter now, and Edmund felt as if he had just come out of a daze. He saluted the man who had killed the big Dane, then bent over, hands on his knees, trying to catch his breath and looking about him to get his bearings. He had worked his way toward the north side of the wall, but he had not made it very far. He was only a stone's throw from the guard tower near where he had first climbed the wall. In the streets below men were still fighting, and flying above them he saw Ulfkytel's banner.

So, the fyrd had made it inside. And it was not just the fyrd men who were covered in Danish blood. There were others down there as well, men who wore no mail and carried only a club or a hammer—anything they could use as a weapon. The men of Winchester, it seemed, had joined in the battle to take back their city.

He grinned as he spotted one damned fool wielding a shovel, and not doing too badly with it, either. Then his attention was caught by a knot of warriors huddled together on the ramparts beyond the tower, swords at the ready, clearly protecting a fallen comrade. One of them was Godwin, and seeing him there, Edmund's gut clenched with fear.

He forgot about the fighting below, and weaving through the press of men trying to get down to the streets so they could slaughter more Danes, he ran to see who was lying at Godwin's feet.

Chapter Twenty-Six

June 1014
Wherwell Abbey, Hampshire

Athelstan's feet were planted in the center of a wide circle of stones that erupted from the ground like monstrous deformed fingers. A woman stood before him, her face and figure swathed in billowing black shawls that writhed like snakes, and as she beckoned to him with a skeletal hand her voice vibrated through his blood.

Whoso would hold the scepter of England must first hold the hand of England's queen.

The shawls slipped away, and it was Emma smiling at him, holding out a hand that he tried to grasp but could not touch as the voice surged through him again.

The sons of Æthelred shall walk a bitter road, all but one.

Then the nightmare drifted away and he was fully awake, the despair that lingered from his dream overwhelmed by the terrible pain in his chest. The cushions at his back that kept him upright were meant to aid his breathing, yet each indrawn gasp wracked him with agony.

"You said that his wound would heal!" Edmund's voice, coming from somewhere behind him, was little more than a hoarse whisper.

"My lord," came the leech's reedy reply, "the wound is healing."

"Healing!" Edmund's low growl was laced with fury. "*Christ*, man! Look at him! He worsens by the hour!"

"It is the damage inside, lord, that is sapping his strength. The blade went deep, and if it scored the lung—"

"Do not tell me what caused the wound, you fool! Tell me when it will heal."

"Forgive me, my lord, but I do not know."

Athelstan dragged his eyes open and found his sister Mathilda at his bedside. Her eyes met his, and he read compassion and grief in them. There would be no healing. She knew it, just as he did.

She took his hand, and he clung to her with what little strength was left him. Other than the pain and the struggle for each shallow breath, she had become the one constant in his world. Every time he woke, she was there, like an angel come to minister to him.

He had known her but little before this; her life had been circumscribed by convent walls from an early age, and she had never ventured to her father's court. Only fourteen winters old, she looked and acted far older. She had done what she could during these wretched days to distract him from his pain, telling him stories about her life in the abbey—a life that seemed to content her.

It comforted him that he would spend his last hours on earth in her care.

He dredged up a smile for her, but it was his brother that he must speak with now. There was so much that he wanted to ask Edmund, and there were things that he needed to tell him, if he could only remember all of them. *Jesu*, it was a grinding effort to speak, and each shallow breath began and ended in pain.

"Edmund." It was the merest whisper, but it sufficed.

Mathilda slipped away and instantly his brother was there. Edmund seemed larger than he remembered, as solid as a church tower and surging with life. He thanked God for that, because soon it would be Edmund's task to shoulder the burdens that he could no longer carry.

"The king—" he began.

"The king is at London," Edmund said quickly. "The city has submitted to him, although I am told that the fighting was fierce."

"So, he did it," Athelstan rasped. His father had subdued the north, and now that he controlled London, the kingdom was his again.

"It was not the king who took London," Edmund said scornfully. "His viking allies pulled down part of the bridge so that their ships could get past it and attack from the river where the city's wall offers little defense. That brought an end to the fighting."

Imagining such a feat, Athelstan barked a weak laugh, immediately regretting it as the fit of coughing that followed made him clutch his chest in agony.

"Do not speak any more!" Edmund's voice was harsh with some emotion. Anger, most likely, Athelstan thought, or dread of what they were both about to face.

"I must," he breathed, gripping Edmund's hand to reassure him. His brother needed to be strong, but just now he looked like a man about to leap off a cliff, and terrified by the prospect below him. "The will."

"It has been copied and will be delivered to the king," Edmund's voice broke. He seemed to be having as much difficulty breathing as Athelstan himself. "He sent word that he would honor whatever bequests you wish to—" His voice broke again, and he swiped at his eyes with the back of his hand. "But Athelstan—"

Athelstan had never seen his brother weep, and Edmund's tears moved him. He wished that he could comfort him, tell him that the pain had become more than he could bear and that he welcomed an end to it. But he did not have the necessary breath, and there were other, more important things that must be said. He grasped Edmund's arm, clutching at him to emphasize what few words he had left to give him.

"The will shields all of you," he rasped, "but you must placate the king." He stopped, struggling to catch a sip of air. "He has won a victory, and for a time he will be merciful. Use the time well."

He closed his eyes, gasping raggedly, consumed by the need to breathe. When he opened them again Godwin, not Edmund, sat beside him, and the candles had been lit. He could see Mathilda asleep on a chair in the corner, her head resting against the wall.

He'd been wandering in nightmare again, among the stones, with the prophecies ringing in his ears.

"Edmund," he whispered. There was something he must tell his brother. About the scepter and the queen's hand. About the bitter road.

In a moment, Mathilda was at his side.

"I sent Edmund to get some rest," she said. "Shall I fetch him?"

He nodded. When she was gone he looked at Godwin, grateful to find someone there that he could entrust with a task that he could not give to Edmund.

"Do me one last service?" he whispered.

"Anything, my lord."

Athelstan slipped the ring from his smallest finger and put it in Godwin's hand. "Take it to Normandy, to the queen. She will understand."

He closed his eyes again. *Jesu,* he was weary. He would rest now. He had done all that his strength allowed. Whatever else remained must be left to God.

Chapter Twenty-Seven

"Athelstan opposes me even from the grave." With an oath, Æthelred flung his son's will across the table toward Eadric and began to pace, wincing at the pain in his leg but too angry to remain still.

Little more than an hour ago he had stood between the ealdorman and young Edward in the royal chamber above the Old Minster's high altar watching the throng that had gathered in the nave to pay tribute to Athelstan. Some of the mourners had reached beyond the barrier of tall brass candlesticks to lay a hand upon the smooth wood of the coffin and bid his faithless son a last farewell. Edmund and Edwig, standing near the bier, had shed tears for their dead brother and, fool that he was, he had pitied them.

They had come to him earlier to beg his forgiveness, pleading that their only offense, and Athelstan's, had been to disobey his command to go into exile with him. There had been no attempt at rebellion, they insisted, no plot to take his throne, no consorting with his enemies. He had listened to their excuses, and he had granted his forgiveness.

And then, when the mourning service was ended, he had read the damned will.

Even in death, Athelstan had betrayed him, and the sweet taste of triumph that had accompanied his return to Winchester was now bitter as gall.

He glared at Eadric and demanded, "Do you see what he has done?"

Eadric looked up, meeting his gaze, one eyebrow raised in surprise.

"He has included the names of men who are..." Eadric paused, as if searching for an appropriate word.

"Traitors!" Æthelred supplied. "Ulfkytel, Siferth, Morcar. They were all there at the funeral. Traitors, every one." He jabbed a finger at the parchment on the table. "Athelstan thought to protect them by naming them in his will. He has even bequeathed to Godwin Wulfnothson the estate I seized from his treasonous father." He scowled, remembering the crowd in the minster, the many hands that had touched that coffin. "I did not see Godwin at the church today. Likely he is already on his way to Compton to claim his lands."

"I have made inquiries about Godwin, my lord. No one seems to know where he has gone. Only that he is on some mission for Athelstan."

Æthelred grunted. He had no interest in the whereabouts of God-damned Godwin. The man had only supported Athelstan because, like all the others, he hoped for some personal gain. In return they had been granted what little his dead son could give them.

His own retainers were just the same. Loyalty was a commodity to be bought and sold; anyone who thought differently was a fool.

"Lord king," Eadric said slowly, his eyes on the will, "Athelstan has bequeathed the Sword of Offa to Edmund." He looked up, brows furrowed in conjecture. "Surely that is in the king's gift, to go from your hand to your designated heir. It should have been returned to you. Can you not simply take it from him?"

"I cannot," he growled. "The will has already been attested by four witnesses, including the Bishop of Winchester and Edmund himself. It will be read aloud today at the witan session, and if I make any changes they will be challenged. My hands are tied." He grimaced. "I did not foresee that even on his deathbed Athelstan would find a way to undermine me."

With Offa's Sword in his possession, Edmund could present himself as heir to the throne and defy him just as Athelstan had. *Jesu!* He had lost one ambitious son only to have another take his place.

"But my lord, this document honors men who submitted willingly to Swein, men who betrayed your trust!" Eadric protested. "You cannot let that stand!"

"Nor do I intend to! Morcar and Siferth conspired with Swein even before he sailed from Denmark, I am certain of it. They are Elgiva's kin, and the roots of their treachery, I'll wager, go back to her father and brothers. But I cannot prove it, and if I deprive them of lands and titles without proof of their treason it will only lead to further unrest. I shall tax the bastards heavily, though, as punishment for submitting to Swein without making even a pretense of resistance. I may not be able to destroy them, but I want them crippled."

"And yet, lord king, the nobles who turned against you may do so again."

Æthelred limped slowly back to his chair, tallying a list of those he suspected might once more rebel. Siferth, Morcar, Ulfkytel. Even Uhtred could not be absolved of all blame. Thurbrand was another. He had led the Danish garrison in London, but had fled before the city was re-taken. Where was he, now?

"You are right, of course," he said slowly. "I am still faced with a nest of traitors in the north."

Æthelred rubbed his chin, his thoughts drifting to Cnut and what he might be plotting. Thorkell would have him believe that Cnut would soon return at the head of yet another viking army, but he could not credit that. Swein's son had been driven ignominiously from England. He had lost a vast number of ships and men, and his reputation in the northern lands would be that of a rash youth who had attempted to claim a kingdom and had failed. Cnut would need to make a name for himself now with smaller victories in the Norse lands or the Baltic before he could convince men to follow him west again. It might take him years.

No, he need not fear Cnut. It was Edmund and the conspirators within his own kingdom that threatened him now. While they lived, and while Edmund lusted for his throne, he could not be safe. Vengeance, though, must wait until his kingdom was more settled.

"I shall take my time to plan my revenge," he said slowly. "God has favored me these past months, so who knows? He may strike down my enemies with His own hand and thus save me the trouble."

"If He does not, my lord, put the matter into my hands," Eadric suggested. "I shall see to it that your vengeance against Cnut's allies is carried out, in the end."

Æthelred regarded his son-in-law silently. His chief councilor was no different from any other grasping nobleman. His only rivals for power in Mercia were Siferth and Morcar, and Eadric had much to gain by disposing of them.

Still, in this instance, as in most others, he and Eadric were in accord.

He nodded. "So be it. In the meantime, we must keep a close watch, I think, on Edmund."

July 1014
Fécamp, Normandy

It was mid-morning, and Emma had slipped away from the ducal palace with only Wymarc for company and two hearthmen for protection. She was hoping to escape for a time the worries that consumed her, but as she strolled in sunshine beside the Narrow Sea, its surface so calm that it looked like glass, her mind was clouded with troubles that gave her no respite.

Æthelred was in London now, but there had been no news from England for more than a week, and no word at all of Athelstan. She hoped to learn, soon, of some amicable agreement struck between Æthelred and his sons, but a fear nagged at the back of her mind that neither side would see reason. Even the intervention of Archbishop Wulfstan might not be enough to prevent the king from committing some rash act of vengeance against the æthelings.

As if that were not worry enough, today she had been presented with a dilemma that she had not anticipated. It was why she had asked Wymarc to walk with her today. She needed advice.

"My mother and Judith met with me this morning," she began, "to discuss my plans for returning to England." Sighing, she continued, "They are urging me to allow Goda to remain here."

Wymarc gave a little gasp and stared at her in surprise. Then she was quiet for a time, and Emma, too, was silent, patiently waiting for Wymarc's counsel.

"They are, of course, concerned for the child's safety," Wymarc said slowly. "And perhaps, Emma, they are right to worry. England will be unsettled now for a time, and it will do no harm for Goda to remain here until next summer. By then, England will—"

"No," Emma interrupted her gently, touching her arm. "They wish her to remain in Normandy as part of my brother's family. Richard has proposed that my lands in the Cotentin be granted to Goda to be her dowry when she marries, and he would have me relinquish all control over decisions made regarding the child. She would no longer be my daughter, but Richard's ward."

Wymarc was silent again. Emma became aware of the hissing of the waves and the cries of the seabirds that wheeled above, their mournful notes a perfect accompaniment to her own bleak thoughts.

"What of Judith?" Wymarc asked. "Has she agreed to this?"

"It was Judith who first proposed the idea. Goda is like a daughter to her, and I cannot deny the bond between them. I have seen it." And often, in the darkness before dawn, she had wept bitter tears over it. She halted and looked out to sea, to where England was merely a dark line on the horizon. "Judith, my mother, Richard, even my brother the archbishop all seem to be in agreement about this." She grimaced. "They are formidable adversaries."

"But the king!" Wymarc protested. "Surely he would not agree to renounce all claim to his daughter!"

Emma shook her head.

"He has done so already. It was part of the pact that he made with Richard before he sailed back to England. I am only consulted because my mother insisted that I must agree to it."

But it was her mother who had raised the strongest arguments for Goda to remain in Normandy, Emma thought, recalling Gunnora's words.

If you take the child back to England, Emma, you will wrench her from the only family that she can remember. To what end? Æthelred has shown no interest in the child except as a bit of chattel that he can trade to his benefit. He will do that soon, you may be sure, and you will be powerless to stop him. Is that what you want for Goda?

It was not what she wanted, but she had not yet found the strength of will that she would need to give her daughter away forever.

She and Wymarc began to retrace their steps, and looking ahead she saw a man striding purposefully toward them. He was still some distance away, but she could see that he wore a heavy traveling cloak. Her heart gave a little leap, for surely this was someone bringing news from England. As he drew closer, though, and she recognized who it was, she was filled with misgiving and her steps faltered.

"It is Godwin," she said to Wymarc. "I will speak with him alone."

Wymarc and the two hearthmen left her, and Emma waited for Godwin to approach. He dropped to one knee, bending his head before her, and she stiffened, rigid with foreboding.

"Rise," she said, and when he stood and faced her she saw tears in his eyes.

He held out his hand, and in his palm was a golden ring.

"Athelstan bid me give you this, my lady."

She had to force her mouth shut against the anguished cry that rose in her throat. Silently, with a trembling hand, she took the ring and placed it in her own palm, recalling the moment that she had slipped it upon Athelstan's finger and he had promised that he would wear it always.

Clutching the ring, she pressed her hand to her breast, and for a time she could not find the voice to speak.

At last she whispered, "How did it happen?"

She listened, dry-eyed, as he told her of the sword stroke that had felled Athelstan on the walls of Winchester, and of the relentless illness that neither the efforts of the leeches nor the care of the nuns had been able to vanquish.

"Edmund was with him at the end," Godwin said gently, "and his sister Mathilda never left his side. He lacked for nothing, my lady."

Nothing but breath, she thought, and life, and the future that should have been his.

Long after she had sent Godwin to the palace to impart the terrible news to Athelstan's sisters, she walked along the beach, burdened with her grief. At last, amid boulders that lay scattered at the foot of the high chalk cliffs, she sank to the pebble-strewn shore. There, hidden from the sight of all but God, she wept for Athelstan, for the youth who had been her friend, and the man who had been her only love. When she had no more tears to shed, she sat, listless, staring into the distance. The sun still hung in the sky above the Narrow Sea, but it seemed to her that the land beyond—the shadow that was England—must now, for her, be forever shrouded in darkness and sorrow, and she had no wish to ever go back.

A.D. 1014 This year, on the eve of St. Michael's day, came the great sea-flood, which spread wide over this land, and ran so far up as it never did before, overwhelming many towns, and an innumerable multitude of people.

The Anglo-Saxon Chronicle

Chapter Twenty-Eight

October 1014
Fécamp, Normandy

News of Æthelred's return to power drew his daughters Edyth and Wulfa back across the Narrow Sea to a kingdom where order had at last been restored. Emma, though, made no move to follow. Nothing awaited her in England now but her memories of Athelstan, memories that would haunt her both waking and sleeping. She would look for him, she knew, in every royal hall, searching for those startlingly blue eyes, that shock of bright hair. She would listen for the sound of his voice offering counsel or arguing with his brothers or the king. She would never find him, never hear him, and she could not bear to face the emptiness that came with the loss of him.

She ignored her mother's admonitions that she was neglecting her lands and her people; she burned her brother's sharply worded letters of censure; she paid no heed to the speculative glances of Godwin and Abbot Ælfsy who remained in Normandy with her small household. Even the gentle prodding of Wymarc and Father Martin did not move her. She surrendered to her grief as if to a lover, knowing that in doing so she was committing a grave sin, yet unable to do anything else.

And so things continued, until word filtered into Fécamp of the calamity that had struck on an afternoon in late September along England's southern coast. Merchants arrived with stories of harbors that had been devastated by a great wave; of ships that had been swept inland and left, battered and broken, far from the sea. They claimed that they had seen countless bodies of men, women and children lying like bundles of rags on the beaches or floating off shore.

Over the course of many days, more news of the devastation trickled in, and Emma greeted each new messenger with dread. Even the larger towns on the English coast had been savaged by the sea, she was told, while numerous small villages had been entirely swept away. Hantone and Stanpit were gone, and no one left behind to even tally the dead. Moulham and Whitecliff, Hoburn and Pagham—all had been destroyed by a tide that many believed had been directed by the hand of a wrathful God.

In the third week of October a letter arrived from the abbess of Nunnaminster, and Emma's hands trembled as she opened it, for she knew that it must contain yet more terrible news. The priory at Bexhill, she read, had been washed away, and of the twenty sisters living there, only one had survived to carry the news to the mother convent at Winchester. The letter ended with a plea that made Emma weep with remorse and shame.

In times of peril, it is not the king to whom our people look for compassion, for succor, and for intercession with an angry God. It is the queen. Sweet lady, why have you abandoned us?

Her heart now twice broken, Emma was at last forced to act. She had been selfish in giving in to despair, and she could do so no longer. She must shoulder the burden of queenship again, and bear her burden of grief in silence.

Three days after receiving the abbess's letter she held her daughter in her arms for what, she feared, might be the last time. Then, with Alfred and his nurse, with Wymarc, Father Martin, Abbot Ælfsy, Godwin and all the members of her household, Emma boarded a ship and set out for England.

October 1014
Redmere, Holderness, Northumbria

Elgiva paced the floor of her hall, irritated and impatient. Sihtric stood nervously just inside the door, and she could feel him watching her, troubled.

"My lady, I would be happy to find Arnor for you and drag him here by his nose," Sihtric offered.

Her hearth man's suggestion made her smile despite her annoyance. Sihtric was brawny enough that he could probably do it, too. He was a valuable tool, loyal and obedient, not to Cnut like the rest of the men, but to her. As her reeve he had kept this manor and its people in good order while she had been with Cnut at his Gainsborough camp, else she might have returned here to find only barren fields and an empty buttery.

"He will come," she assured Sihtric, more confidently than she felt.

That bastard Arnor was taking his time responding to her summons, no doubt to make the point that he was Cnut's man, and not hers to command. But she needed his help with the plan that she had already set in motion. It would be no easy task to persuade him to aid her, but she had her arguments ready. And because it was Arnor—a brute who argued with fists, not words—she was going to have to keep her temper in check.

When Arnor sauntered in at last he greeted her with a curt nod. No doubt he believed that he had far better things to do than attend Cnut's wife, but for now she would have to put up with him, so she swallowed her ire.

"I want you to prepare your ship, Arnor," she said, "to return to Denmark. I presume that ten days is enough time for you to undertake whatever is necessary to make your vessel and your crew ready."

He raised an insolent eyebrow and one side of his mouth slid up into his usual hateful sneer.

"My orders, lady," he said slowly, "were to deliver you to Holderness and bide here until a message arrived from—"

"I know what your orders were," she snapped. She began to pace again, and now she allowed some of her worry to show. It was real enough. "It has been six months, though, since you were given those orders, and there has been no further word." No word from anyone— not Cnut, nor Eirik, nor Alric. Even Thurbrand's ugly face would have been a welcome sight if he brought news with him. News had filtered north before summer's end that Æthelred was once again England's king, and that Cnut's fleet was gone, although no one could say where. Other than that, she knew nothing.

"You have done as you were commanded," she continued, "No one could fault you. But what if a message was sent and by some mishap it never reached us?" There might be other reasons, too, for Cnut's silence. He might be wounded; he might even be dead. But to give voice to those possibilities only made their likelihood more real, and she did not wish Arnor to see the full extent of her fear. "How much longer can we afford to wait here?"

He shrugged. "Cnut will find a way to send for you," he said. Then, his tone careless, "If he wants you."

She heard the barb in his words, the implication that her husband might be done with her. That was, indeed, one of the possibilities she had considered. Her marriage to Cnut had brought him allies, but now that her kinsmen had all deserted him, what further use had he for his English wife?

If Cnut was alive, though, he would want his son.

"I will not cower here like a wounded doe any longer," she said. "Æthelred will send men to kill Cnut's children if he discovers that they are here. They must go where their father can protect them. This child," she placed her hand on her rounded belly and saw, with satisfaction, his gaze drawn there, "must be born in Denmark. But if we wait much longer, the winter gales will trap us in England for another season. I dare not take that risk."

He tugged thoughtfully at his beard, his eyes still on her swollen belly, and some of her tension drained away. He was a stubborn ox, but even he must recognize the truth in her words. She waited in silence and, finally, he nodded.

"Aye, then," he said slowly, "I will take you and the children."

"And some of my household," she said. "Twenty folk in all."

"No!" he barked. "Ten only. I'll not leave any of my men behind to make room for your English folk."

"Very well," she agreed. "Ten." At least she would not arrive in Roskilde without any attendants at all. "But there must be one other. My husband wishes King Swein's body returned to Denmark for burial there. He made me swear that if anything should prevent him from doing that, I would see to it. And so I will, with your help."

Cnut had never asked her any such thing. But if he was dead, his elder brother would not be pleased to see her arrive at his court with Cnut's children in tow—children who would have claims upon his hospitality and perhaps his throne. Swein's body, though, would be welcomed with honor, and that should guarantee her a place at the Danish court, whether Cnut was alive or not.

Arnor crossed his arms over his chest and gave her his familiar, disdainful scowl.

"And how do you propose that we retrieve the body? We would need an army to fight our way into Jorvik, and even if we did that, we do not know where Swein is buried. None of my crew was there when—"

"I was there," she snapped. "I know where the grave is. And we will need no army to enter Jorvik." He was looking at her now as if she were moon mad. But she had thought this through, and she knew that it could be done. Her way. "Arnor, this is not something to be undertaken by force of arms. My father was once the ealdorman of Northumbria, and his memory is revered in Jorvik. I shall be a grieving daughter, mourning both a father and a father-in-law. I will take six of my English hearth men; no Danes." And she would take silver; a very great deal of silver, for she would have to bribe anyone who might have the authority to stop her. "You need only have the ship ready to depart when we return."

"And if you fail?" Arnor asked.

"I will not fail," she said. "Sihtric has already been to Jorvik and—"

"And if you fail?" he repeated, louder this time.

"If I fail," she sighed, exasperated, "you will take my children to Denmark and report to Cnut that his wife and unborn son are lost." She pressed her hand against her belly again, and now she smiled. "Tyra foretold that Cnut would have two sons. His second son is here, beneath my heart. If I succeed—and I will succeed, Arnor—this child will be born in Denmark, and you will have had the honor of escorting us there."

Cnut's unborn child was her guarantee that Arnor would wait the full ten days she needed to accomplish her task, and not simply sail off and leave her stranded.

He was silent for a time, rubbing a finger thoughtfully across his lower lip. He was weighing not just her words, she suspected, but Tyra's power to foretell the future. She waited, hiding her anxiety and impatience behind a serene expression. Arnor could prevent her from going to Jorvik. He could destroy all her careful preparations—the elaborately carved coffin, the elegant palls that would cover it, the silver that Sihtric had already placed in grasping English hands—merely by saying no. Finally, after an agonizing delay, he gave her a curt nod.

"Ten days," he grunted, "and tomorrow will be day one." Then he turned on his heel and was gone.

She sent Sihtric away as well, to make the final preparations for the journey to Jorvik. Then she sank into a chair, exhausted.

Would ten days be enough time? She believed so. She had calculated that it would take six days to make the journey to Jorvik and back, and she had added another four in case there were delays because of foul weather or mishaps. Beyond that, she could only hope that Swein's gods, whoever they were, would look favorably on her efforts to return him to his homeland.

Ten days later, the gods had given their answer. Elgiva returned to Redmere just before sundown, riding beside Sihtric at the head of her small company. Some little way behind her, the ox-drawn wagon that carried Swein's remains rattled noisily as it turned into the rutted track that led to her manor gate.

The little group traveled as fast as the burdened wain would allow, although Elgiva could not refrain from glancing back occasionally and shouting at the driver to hurry. Her venture in Jorvik had been successful, but it had not been without complications. There had not been the secrecy that she had hoped for, so she could not be certain that they had not been followed. And the journey had taken far longer than she had anticipated.

Once more, under her breath, she cursed the archbishop whose unexpected arrival in Jorvik eight days earlier had nearly ruined everything. The silver that Sihtric had showered upon the gate wards to smooth her passage through the city to the ealdorman's hall had been useless, for once Wulfstan was in residence, it was his permission that had to be obtained. For three days she had been forced to shelter outside the city walls not knowing when—or if—the archbishop would allow her to conduct her gruesome business. And always, at the back of her mind, was the fear that she might not make it back in time, and that Arnor would sail without her.

She had made use of the delay by gathering what news she could of events in the south that would be of interest to Cnut—of Æthelred's triumphant return to London, of Athelstan's death, of a flood that had devastated much of the southern coast. She had heard, too, of Cnut's harsh treatment of his hostages before he sailed from Sandwich. That last had explained the cold looks she met when the archbishop finally gave her permission to enter Jorvik. No one had accosted her or her hearth men, but she could not be certain that some fool might not, even now, be trailing behind them, waiting for an opportunity to avenge the outrage committed at Sandwich. She had no wish to lose her nose or an ear.

One more night in England, she told herself, and then she would be gone.

She could not see the palisade yet, but she was on familiar ground now, so when Sihtric suddenly raised his hand and cried "Stop", she reined in her mount and turned to him with impatience.

"Why?" she demanded.

"Something is wrong," he murmured. "Do you not smell it?"

And then she did—an acrid stench that was not the comforting aroma of cooking fires but the stale odor of an ash pit, of a great burning.

Suddenly afraid, she urged her horse to a canter despite Sihtric's warning cry. Once inside Redmere's gate, the smell was overwhelming, and in front of her she could see its source. The hall, the brew house, the sleeping quarters, and the workshops were masses of charred, broken timbers. She looked around in horror, but she could see no one, hear no one in the ruins all about her.

She slid from her saddle, took but a few steps away from her mount and collapsed to her knees.

Her children. She had left her children here.

She clutched her middle, keening and rocking, and only dimly aware of Sihtric suddenly at her side. She gasped, trying to catch her breath between sobs while the stench of ashes clawed at her throat.

Through her tears she saw someone moving on the far side of the yard and a moment later, as a gang of men appeared there, running through the orchard with swords drawn, Sihtric dragged her to her feet.

"It's Arnor!" Sihtric hissed into her ear.

She wiped her streaming eyes, peering at the Danes who were racing toward her like a black wave. Had Arnor done this then? Did he hate her so much?

Beside her, Sihtric shouted, "Shields!" But she knew that the men clustering around her could not possibly protect her from the Danes' oncoming rush. She braced herself for the lethal blow that must come.

Arnor, though, halted suddenly and, sheathing his sword, he raised empty hands. His men followed his lead, and her knees nearly gave way again, this time with relief.

"We took you for Uhtred's men!" Arnor shouted. He spread his arms, encompassing the destruction all around. "This is their work! Do not be afraid for your bairns, though! They are safe!"

If it had been anyone but Arnor telling her this, she would have kissed him.

"Where are they?"

"On the beach now, awaiting your return." He scowled. "If I had not promised you ten days, lady, I would have had them halfway to Denmark by now."

The wagon had entered the gate while he was talking, and she heard the driver mutter a curse.

"I warned you that there would be trouble sooner or later," she said to Arnor. "How can you be certain that Uhtred was responsible for this? Was he here?"

"Not that I saw," he grunted, "but men were wearing his badge. They burned Thurbrand's hall at Aldbrough first, but one of his people managed to get away and warned us they were coming. The ships were already loaded, and we hid in the woods, so when the bastards got here all they found was a deserted steading."

"And Thurbrand's people?" she asked as she followed Arnor to the palisade's smaller, rear gate that faced the cliffs and the sea.

"Some dozen or so did not make it out of the hall in time. Those still alive have taken shelter at his hall at Ringbrough. His sons escaped harm, but his lady wife died in the blaze."

Elgiva halted and drew a shocked breath. Her mouth went dry, and she was unable to swallow.

Catla did not deserve such a wretched end. She had been a good wife to Thurbrand, though he had treated her little better than a slave. Even so, if Thurbrand still lived, he might one day make Uhtred pay dearly for the burning of his manor and the death of his wife.

Arnor led her down the path to the beach where campfires burned beside a string of tents clustered against the foot of the cliffs. She found Thyri and Swein asleep in one of them, curled together like puppies. Satisfied that they were safe, she ate the food that was handed her, but when she crawled into the tent to lie beside her children, she slept little.

The next morning she stood on the deck of Arnor's vessel as it rose and fell over heaving waves. The bones of King Swein lay in the hold beneath her feet, and her children and servants huddled together in the tent that had been rigged mid-ship. Eastward the sun rose above an empty, beckoning sea, but Elgiva's eyes were fixed westward—on the high cliffs that slowly shrank as England grew more distant.

One day, she vowed, she would come back. Cnut had to be alive, somewhere, across this bitter sea. He must be! She would find him, and when she did, she would remind him that he had an English wife and English children, and that despite all that had happened, he still had a claim to the English throne.

Chapter Twenty-Nine

25 December 1014
Kingston, Surrey

Edmund stood with Siferth and Morcar on the high platform that lined three sides of Kingston's great hall. The railing in front of him was garlanded with fragrant boughs of pine and holly, and the rafters above strung with colorful banners that flaunted the emblems of Æthelred and his ealdormen.

The king, Edmund thought, was making a point by observing his first Christmas since his return from exile here, at Kingston, where the mighty kings of Wessex had, for generations, celebrated their coronations. The hall itself was a reminder that Æthelred was England's rightful, anointed ruler. His father, he suspected, was hoping that tonight's feast would erase the memory of last December's disasters and the bitter winter days that he and his court had been forced to spend in that dank, windswept hall on Wight Isle.

The noble assembly gathered below, noisily awaiting their sovereign's arrival, suddenly stilled, and then began to cheer. Edmund looked toward the screens passage where the royal company, led by England's two archbishops, was now entering the hall. The king was the central figure in the stately procession, his every step dogged by the limp that he tried and failed to disguise. A heavy golden crown rested upon his thinning, white hair, and the face beneath was creased with age. He wore a saffron colored tunic trimmed in wide bands of gold, and his scarlet cloak of fine wool was lined with ermine and gathered at the shoulder with a ruby-studded clasp—Norman gifts, Edmund had learned. And further proof, if any was needed, of Duke Richard's determination to see Emma's son named heir to the English throne.

The queen walked several paces behind the king, and Edmund followed her progress with narrowed eyes as she took her place on the dais. She wore a gown of deepest grey, so dark that it was nearly black, with bands of silver edging its draping sleeves. Silver thread glistened, too, in the folds of the silken black headrail that covered her bright hair.

She looked, he thought, like the queen of the night.

Siferth, beside him, whispered, "The lady is slender as a wraith in that dark gown."

"She is no wraith," Edmund muttered as the tall, slim figure below lifted her eyes and seemed to spear him with her stern gaze. "She is a Norman. Make no mistake, there is steel beneath all that silk."

Morcar grunted agreement. "Is that why her son is the only ætheling on the dais, my lord?" he asked. "Has the queen turned your father completely against you and Edwig?"

"With Eadric's help, I suspect," Edmund replied. "My brother and I are as much out of the king's favor, my lords, as you are." He gave Morcar a rueful smile. "But as my father looks for guidance to men whom I neither like nor trust," he gestured toward Eadric and Thorkell seated at the high table, "I am content for now to watch from the shadows."

He suspected that by absenting himself from court these past months he had given his father more reason to mistrust him, and had provided Emma with numerous opportunities to promote her son. Still, it had been time well spent—procuring the support of lords who, while they had dutifully bent the knee again to his father, still resented and even hated the king.

Now he listened closely as his father addressed the gathering, recounting with relish the battle for London that had led to England's victory over the Danes. When Æthelred ended his tale the crowd roared their approval, and the king raised his arms as if to embrace them all.

"Our enemies beyond the sea," his father cried, "have been defeated utterly, and we need no longer fear them! I know this to be true, for the Almighty has granted me signs of His favor. England is now at peace and will remain so, for God Himself is our protector!"

Edmund stiffened and uttered a quiet curse. At his side, Siferth whispered, his tone incredulous, "Your father cannot truly believe that the Danes are defeated!"

"Oh, but he does," Edmund replied. "He has ever been blind to the truth, even when it is staring him in the face. Get word to the others," he said urgently. "We will meet in my quarters late tonight, when the king and his court have gone to their beds."

He waited for a time, watching Siferth and Morcar move among the tables below to deliver his summons to the select few who listened and nodded. Satisfied, he left the great hall, stepping into the frigid night and making his way to his quarters in the village. He ordered his servants to bring flagons of wine and mead, and as they did his bidding, he sat alone on one of the benches, staring into the fire. He thought about his father's heedless and unrealistic promises, and in light of them, what he would have to do in the weeks and months to come.

Some hours later the men had responded to his summons, and they stood or sat in groups of twos and threes, murmuring together and casting occasional anxious glances toward him. After what the king had said tonight, Edmund thought, they had reason enough to be anxious. Then, sweeping his gaze around the chamber as he prepared to address them, he frowned.

"Where is Godwin?" he asked Morcar.

"I do not know, my lord," Morcar replied. "I gave him your message."

"He left the feast before I did," Ulfkytel said. "He should have been here by now."

"Perhaps, my lord," Siferth's quiet voice was at his ear, "it is better that Godwin is not with us. How certain are you of his loyalty? He is in the queen's confidence now. Whatever you say in his presence will reach her ear, and then perhaps the king's. Are you willing to risk that?"

"As Godwin is not here just now," Edmund replied dryly, "there is little risk of that tonight."

Nevertheless, Godwin's absence worried him. He did not wish to believe that one of his closest companions was a spy for the queen. He surveyed the faces around him, of men he trusted with his life. The fate of England might now be in their hands. It was time to begin.

"My lords," he addressed them, "I have summoned you here to discuss the threat that we still face from the Danes."

"What threat?" Edwig shouted, slurring his words and favoring the company with a drunken grin.

Edmund glared at him. Since Athelstan's death his brother had lapsed into old habits and was rarely sober.

"Did you not hear what the king said tonight?" Edwig continued, his tone mocking and shrill. "The Danes are gone for good and will never return. He knows this because God sent him a sign!"

"God sent him no sign!" Siferth scoffed. "The king has lost his wits."

"The king," Edmund said sternly, "is afraid to face the truth! Every man here knows that the Danes will return. If Cnut does not come himself, then it will be another like him, someone just as ravenous for English blood and English silver. But when it happens, I promise you that I will not sit in London watching while the king wrings his hands and begs God for deliverance. If my father will not defend the kingdom, then I will. War is surely coming, my lords, and we must prepare for it."

He heard mutters of agreement as he glanced around the circle. Most of these men had kin who had been murdered or mauled at the hands of Swein and his son, and their hunger for vengeance had not yet been slaked. Only Æthelmaer, the greybeard among them, looked uncertain.

"Æthelmaer!" Edmund called to him. "What troubles you?"

The old man gazed up at him, thoughtful, his lips pursed. He said, "My lord, I do not understand why your father is so certain that the Danes no longer pose a threat. Could it be," he paused, took a breath, "could it be that your father knows something that we do not? Could the Norman duke have provided information that has persuaded the king that—"

"No, my lord, the Norman duke did not." The voice that rang through the chamber was as unwelcome as it was unexpected and, muttering a curse, Edmund turned to confront the speaker.

Emma stood in the doorway with Godwin at her side.

"My brother," Emma continued, "believes that Cnut will return to England very soon." Her green eyes fastened upon Edmund's. "As do I."

Emma was neither surprised nor offended when Edmund greeted her with a quiet curse. She had expected it. His enmity toward her was long-standing, despite Athelstan's efforts to dispel it. And although

Godwin had tried to dissuade her from coming here tonight, insisting that he should speak to Edmund on her behalf, she had refused. How could Godwin succeed where Athelstan for so many years had failed?

No. This was her battle, and she must win it. She would speak her mind, and Edmund would have to listen whether he liked it or not.

"I am not the enemy, Edmund, that you have always believed me to be," she said. "Your brother Athelstan knew that, and he trusted my counsel." The stab of pain that lanced through her as she said his name nearly undid her, and she paused to draw a breath before she could continue. "Now that he is gone, I would have us speak openly to one another."

It was something they had never done, although Edmund's distrust of her had been apparent for years in every glance and every coldly uttered greeting. They had enemies in common, though, and she must find a way to make Edmund her ally, not her adversary.

"I am listening," he replied. But his voice was cold, and he folded his arms across his chest as if to place a physical barrier between them.

For a long moment she hesitated while she felt every man in the chamber regarding her—with suspicion, no doubt. But if her sons were to have any future in England, she must find a way to gain the trust of these men.

"I believe we are all agreed," she began, "that the Danes will soon return. I think we can also agree that the king has shown tonight that he has neither the will nor the foresight to contend with the threat that will soon be upon us. Despite his recent victories, Æthelred is aging and his energy fading. I see him when others do not, and I know that even with the help of men like Thorkell he will be hard pressed to repel another Danish invasion. It is you, Edmund, who must do that." She locked eyes with him. "It is what Athelstan wanted and why he passed the Sword of Offa into your keeping."

Edmund raised a skeptical brow.

"What are you suggesting, my lady? That I usurp my father's throne?"

No!" she said. "I did not come here to goad you into treachery against the king. You are bound to him by blood and by oaths, and you must honor that. But I acknowledge here, in the presence of these men who support you, that your claim to the throne outweighs that of my sons. And that as your father's heir, you must act to defend the kingdom if the king does not. Or if, for any reason, he cannot." She drew a long breath. "I fear that such a time may soon be upon us."

There were whispers among the men. They had all seen her son on the dais tonight in a place of honor near the king. They must all believe that she had encouraged that gesture of royal favor toward Edward. But these men did not know her, and they could not read the fear for her children that she lived with day and night in this viper's nest of a court.

Edmund's dark eyes scoured her face. "Why would you acknowledge my claim before that of your son?"

She met his gaze, and held it.

"Because I wish to see both my sons grow to manhood, and if Cnut captures the throne, the lives of all the king's sons will be forfeit! England must have a warrior as its king, Edmund. It must be you."

For a time he made no answer, and her confidence that she could persuade him to trust her had begun to waver when the silence was broken at last by a voice that was slurred with drink.

"She's lying, Edmund. It's a trap. She will betray us to the king and see us all killed just to put her brat on the throne."

She looked past Edmund to Edwig's sneering, wine-flushed face and said, "There are traps being laid, Edwig, but not by me."

Edmund's eyes narrowed. "Meaning?" he asked.

"Eadric saw you standing with Siferth and Morcar in the hall tonight, and he has been whispering poison against you in the king's ear."

"Eadric is a coward and a snake," Siferth growled. "Let him whisper all he wants. I do not fear him."

"Snakes can be deadly, Siferth," she said, "and the king listens to this one. Edmund," she said, gazing unblinking into his eyes, "you have to find a way to gain the confidence and the support of the king even if you must charm that snake Eadric to do it. Convince your father that the Danes will return and persuade him that he must be ready to oppose them! I will support you in every way that I can, but I beg you, do not prepare in secret for the war that is coming. He will discover it, misjudge your purpose, and find some way to undermine you. Even this gathering tonight will raise his suspicions should he hear of it, and we all know that Eadric trades in secrets and lies. No one here is safe from his treachery."

The whispering around them began again, but Emma kept her eyes fixed upon Edmund. His face was still dark with distrust as he studied her face, and because she could think of no further arguments to persuade him that she was not his enemy, she merely reached out to touch his arm.

"Have a care, my lord," she said.

That night she lay awake for many long, uneasy hours, not at all certain that she had succeeded in dispelling Edmund's enmity toward her. He had said little, and he had ever been one to keep his thoughts hidden. At the very least, though, she told herself, she had given him something to think about, and had delivered a warning about Eadric that she hoped every man in that chamber would heed.

Part Three

The Unravelling

Chapter Thirty

March 1015
Roskilde, Denmark

"Where," Elgiva whispered, "do you suppose your father has disappeared to today?"

The babe in her arms, but three months old, gazed solemnly up at her as if he knew a thousand secrets. His only response, though, was to pat her breast as he continued to suck her dry.

It was mid-morning, and on the other side of the large chamber young Swein and Thyri were playing contentedly, watched over by Tyra, so all was quiet. Elgiva nestled into her cluster of cushions and sighed. She would not be alone like this for long. Cnut's kinswomen would be back soon, and then she would be in the midst of a whirlwind. Although even then, she thought, she would still be alone.

She was not welcome here. None of them wanted her here—not even Cnut.

What a fool she had been to come! Even on that first day when her ship had landed he had bid her only the briefest of welcomes before closeting himself with his brother and Arnor and a handful of men. Their claims on him, then and now, were far stronger, it appeared, than hers. He had not visited her bed that first night nor any night since. And whenever she had caught him looking at her as her body thickened with his child, she had seen no desire in his eyes.

It had been Alric who had sought her out that first day, who had listened to her news of England and had told her in turn of the terrible battle they had fought at Gainsborough and of the fleet's frenzied departure amid a hail of spears and arrows. Even now it was Alric's wolfish smile that could make her forget, for a little while, Cnut's indifference.

Looking down at her suckling babe with his thick mane of curly black hair that was so like her own and so unlike his father's, she wondered again where Cnut had gone. It had been snowing since daybreak so he could not be too far away. Although, she reminded herself, she could not be absolutely certain of that. The last time he'd gone missing he'd sailed to the Baltic, abandoning her without a word to the tender mercies of his elder brother's pale-haired young queen. That lady had treated her with all the warmth of an ice maiden, and it was worse when Cnut returned, for he had not come alone. He'd brought his younger sister and his wretched mother—the wife that Swein had repudiated decades before. His elder half-sister Gytha had arrived from Norway soon after, and now there were three of them—Cnut's tall, flame-haired, female kin who looked down their long noses at her as if she was no better than dirt beneath their feet.

She could not bear them. She could not bear this Danish court. Most of all, she could not bear this royal chamber where she was the unwanted companion of Harald's Danish queen.

She wished that she had never left England.

Just as her babe's eyes drifted closed, the chamber door flew open and, wakened, the child began to wail. A rush of frigid air sent the hearth flames at Elgiva's feet into a momentary uproar as the small army of women filled the chamber, thrusting fur cloaks and woolen scarves into the hands of household slaves.

Queen Sigrid, Elgiva noticed, was not with them. Likely she had remained in the church to pray that her womb would soon quicken, although her prayers would do her little good. She had been wed a full year now, and if Harald had not yet filled her belly with a child, he likely never would.

As she attempted to hush her squalling son, Elgiva suddenly found Cnut's younger sister beside her, peering down at the child in her arms. Estrith, at seventeen, could have been Cnut's twin. Her face, while not beautiful, was boldly arresting, and her thick, rust-colored hair, so like Cnut's, hung over her shoulder in a long braid.

"Your babe looks nothing like my brother," Estrith proclaimed decisively. "Are you certain he is not a changeling?"

Elgiva stiffened. She had worried that her son's dark locks amid a crowd of red-haired Danish royals might lead to idle speculation among the servants. Yet here it was, emerging from the mouth of Cnut's sister.

"He is no changeling," she snapped. "What are you suggesting?"

Estrith blinked at her.

"I am suggesting nothing, Elgiva. It was but a jest. Forgive me if I—"

"The child is Cnut's!" She could not keep her voice from trembling with outrage. "How dare you—"

"Peace!" Cnut's witch of a mother pinned her with a cold stare. "You are too quick to find offense, Elgiva, where none was intended. It only serves to raise suspicion that you have something to hide. I trust that is not so."

Elgiva opened her mouth to protest, but realized it would be pointless. Gunnhild would not listen to her. She had already forgotten her, and was calling for bread and cheese so Cnut's sisters could break their fast.

Feeling impotent and still angry, Elgiva stood up and paced the floor, her babe heavy on her shoulder as she listened idly to the talk that swirled about her like a windstorm. Estrith could speak of nothing but her betrothal to Jarl Ulf—an alliance that, Elgiva knew, had been foisted upon the reluctant jarl, although no one dared breathe that to the besotted Estrith. Gunnhild worried aloud that Sigrid might never give King Harald a son, which was probably, Elgiva thought, the only thing on which she and Cnut's mother would ever agree.

But when Gytha spoke of a war council, Elgiva halted in her tracks and stared at Jarl Eirik's wife.

"What war council?" she asked.

Gytha looked at her, one eyebrow raised as if surprised that she should have the audacity to even speak to her.

"The one to be held at Aalborg next month," Gytha replied. "Harald has summoned the jarls."

"Did Cnut not tell you?" Estrith asked, her grey eyes wide with surprise. "He is going to press them for help in his campaign against your English king."

Elgiva felt a sudden surge of anger. No, Cnut had not told her, and he should have. If the jarls were gathering to discuss Cnut's next campaign against the English, then surely she should be there.

"Who else will go to this meeting, besides the jarls?" she asked.

"Everyone," Gytha said, so sweetly that Elgiva knew that a barb must surely follow. "Queen Sigrid certainly will go, and we shall all attend her. Well," Gytha smiled coldly, "not you, of course."

Elgiva's answering smile was just as cold. "I am Cnut's wife," she reminded Gytha. "If Harald's wife is to go, then I must go as well."

Gunnhild barked a laugh. "Don't be foolish girl! Sigrid is the queen of Denmark, while you are merely Cnut's English concubine. And now that your English kin are powerless, you are of no use to him except as a brood mare." Her eyes flashed with malice. "Possibly not even that. So while Queen Sigrid has a role to play at the gathering, you most assuredly, do not."

And you, Elgiva thought, are a bitter old woman whose husband sent you back to your brother because he could no longer bear the sight of you. Or perhaps it was your waspish tongue that so repelled him.

She kept her thoughts to herself, though, for as she peered down at her now sleeping son the words of a long-ago prophecy suddenly floated into her mind.

Your children will be kings.

Kings of England, she asked herself, or of Denmark? Or perhaps, she thought, glancing from one of her sons to the other, of both kingdoms.

"When Cnut has conquered England," she said to Gunnhild, "I shall be the English queen at his side and the mother of the heir to his throne. And," she said slowly, "if Queen Sigrid remains barren, I expect that I shall be the mother of the heir to Harald's throne as well." She offered Gunnhild a thin smile. "So it would seem, my lady, that I have reason enough to attend this gathering of jarls."

Gunnhild merely glowered at her, and Elgiva, satisfied that her tormentors had been silenced for now at least, placed her milk-drugged, slumbering little son in his cradle.

She would have to confront Cnut about that council, though, and insist that he take her with him. She was tired of being treated as an outcast, and it was time that she put a stop to it.

Cnut faced his brother-in-law across one of the long tables in the king's hall, deserted tonight but for the two of them. Eirik's bald pate gleamed in the light of two flaming torches bracketed on the walls, and the brown eyes in his seamed, grey-bearded face regarded Cnut narrowly over the rim of his ale cup as he took a long swallow.

Cnut gazed back at Eirik, unflinching. He had outlined his plan for retaking the English throne, and now he had to persuade Eirik to join him in his quest. If he agreed, others would follow, along with their men. And he needed those men.

"At the Aalborg gathering," Cnut said, breaking the heavy silence between them, "I will ask the jarls to pledge their ships and their men to me." He grimaced. "I am aware, however, that my reputation has been tarnished. Men see me as merely the younger son of a great warrior, handed a kingdom that I let slip away. Few will be eager to follow me unless I can satisfy them that I will succeed at this next endeavor. If you support me, others will follow your lead."

Eirik grunted. "Men will follow you only if you promise them wealth; and they will stay with you only if you make good on that promise the moment that you land on English soil."

"Agreed," Cnut said, leaning forward across the table. "That is why I intend to strike this time where the wealth is—in Wessex. The southern shires are vulnerable now, because the great flood last year destroyed many of the coastal fortifications. With any luck we can drive deep into England before their king even learns that we are there."

Eirik pursed his lips but made no immediate reply. Cnut swallowed a mouthful of ale and the moments passed, but his sister's husband continued to gaze thoughtfully into his cup as he swirled his ale.

Finally Eirik said, "That might succeed, Cnut, if, as you say, luck is with you." He lifted his eyes from his ale cup to meet Cnut's gaze. "Trusting to luck, though, will hardly convince the warlords to join you."

Cnut set his own cup on the table. There was more that Eirik had not yet heard, and now was the time to tell it.

"I have ships already," he said, and his words seemed to ring in the empty hall. "Forty ships of my own, thirty that my brother has promised and," he paused to give his next words emphasis, "another thirty from my uncle."

Eirik's brows shot up.

"Your uncle! I wondered why you lingered so long in the Baltic last summer. So," he said, drawing the word out like a sigh, "Poland's ruler wishes to see his sister's son on the throne of England."

"Boleslaw is currently at peace with his neighbors and has been looking for a way to keep his jomsvikings busy elsewhere. I offered to assist him with that. They will be repairing their vessels at Wolin and gathering supplies through the coming months, and we should see them here by summer's end."

"One hundred ships," Eirik breathed. He shook his head, bewildered. "In the name of all the gods, how many more do you need?"

"The same again, if I can get them," and when Cnut saw Eirik staring at him with open-mouthed astonishment he continued, "I lost England because my English allies deserted me and I did not have enough men to hold the kingdom. That will not happen again."

Now Eirik looked doubtful once more. "Ten thousand is a great many mouths to feed."

"We sail only after the harvests are in—here and in England," Cnut replied. "If luck is with us, by winter our battles will be done." He reached across the table and grasped Eirik's arm. "Join me, and I will reward you with lands and wealth beyond your dreams."

Slowly, Eirik nodded and his mouth widened into a grin as he grasped Cnut's hand with a grip as strong as a vise.

"I am with you," he said, and when he raised his cup, Cnut joined him in a salute.

"I will speak for you at Aalborg," Eirik continued when they had drained their cups, "and I will bring you twenty ships." His gaze suddenly slid past Cnut. "Your woman, I think, wants a word."

Cnut turned to see Elgiva, wrapped in a brown cloak, watching him from the doorway with an expression as dark as a storm cloud. She had been unhappy during her stay here at his brother's court; but she had been unhappy, too, at Gainsborough and at Holderness. He had begun to wonder if there was any place at all where she would be content.

"We shall speak more later," he said, and nodding to Eirik, he stood to greet his wife.

"Elgiva," Cnut said as Eirik slipped past her and out the door. "What is it?"

"I wish to know, my lord," she said, "why your mother and sisters were told of a war council at Aalborg, while I was not."

She was glaring at him, outrage burning in her dark eyes, and he braced himself for the quarrel that was coming. She was like a tossed coin, he thought, that flashed light and dark as it spun, but almost always landed bright side down.

"I saw no reason to speak of it to you," he said, "as you will not be attending."

"And why is that, my lord?" she demanded. "Harald's wife will go, and your sisters. Even your mother is to go! Why would you keep me away? It is my future that you will be planning, not theirs!"

"We will be planning a war against the English, Elgiva," he said patiently, "against your people. The men there will see you as the enemy, and I cannot—"

She raised her fists and would have struck him had he not snatched her wrists and held her fast.

"Do not call me your enemy!" she cried. "Not after all that I have done for you!"

"Listen to me!" he snarled while she struggled against him. "I have not forgotten what you have done for me, but you cannot help me with this! When I was seeking support from the English, I needed you at my side. They knew you as Ealdorman Ælfhelm's daughter, and that helped me gain their trust. But at Aalborg I must reach out to Danish jarls! I need men like my brother and Eirik with me; not an English woman whose kin have deserted me."

Her eyes blazed as he said those last words. He had added fuel to her anger, but it was the truth and she would have to accept it.

"And so you shut me out," she spat at him, "as if I were no more to you than some trinket you toss into a corner when you have grown weary of it."

She stopped struggling, and he released her, watching as she chafed her wrists.

He huffed a sigh. "I shut you out, Elgiva, because here in Denmark you are a hindrance, not a help. I know that you dislike this place. You have made no secret of it. But I will not put my venture at risk because you are discontented. You will not go to Aalborg, but will remain here with your servants and children." She began to protest but he continued, "Thurbrand and Alric will stay behind as well! You must understand that I cannot afford to have any English among my retinue!"

She glared at him, but the fight had gone out of her and she merely spun on her heel and stalked out of the hall. She was still furious, he knew, and he knew from experience that nothing he could say would appease her.

Watching her as she disappeared into the night, he realized that he no longer cared enough even to try.

Chapter Thirty-One

July 1015
Islip, Oxfordshire

On a clear, midsummer morning, so early that the sun had barely scraped itself above the horizon, Emma walked through the grounds of her Islip estate with Abbess Ælfwynn, continuing a conversation they had begun at the king's great council at Oxford the week before. As they strolled past the bountiful kitchen garden and through the orchard fragrant with blossoms, Emma was painfully aware of the stark contrast between the plenty around them and the specter of famine that so absorbed them.

There had been ominous reports from all along the southern coast of fields made barren by the previous autumn's devastating flood, and no one could predict when the poisoned earth might recover. So while the king's greatest concern at the recent council had been to raise the coin he needed to pay his viking army, hers had been to find ways to alleviate the misery of those who had managed to survive the winter but had been left with nothing except their lives. Abbess Ælfwynn was her staunchest ally in this matter, and so, as they walked, they weighed difficulties and sought solutions.

Upon cresting a low hill Emma noticed in the distance that a group of a dozen or so armored men were riding hard along the Oxford road. Beside her, the abbess raised her hand to block the sun and asked, "Who is it? I cannot make out the banner."

"They are royal hearth guards," Emma replied, and as the company thundered into her manor yard and all of them quickly dismounted, a finger of foreboding crept up her spine. "Something is wrong."

She was already striding toward the newcomers when she saw them force their way into her hall. Foreboding turning to fury, she gathered up her skirts and began to run. She had covered only half the distance when, pausing to catch her breath she saw the guards reappear with Siferth's wife in their midst and her own people swarming behind them, shouting protests. Aldyth, struggling and weeping, was forced onto a horse with one of the guards.

Emma began to run again, but she was still too far away to stop the king's men from wheeling their mounts round and surging out of the yard, taking Aldyth with them. One rider, though, remained behind, his horse's bridle held firmly by two of her Norman guards despite his efforts to break away. When more of her men joined the fray, Emma, almost upon them now, saw him reach for his sword.

"Hold!" she shouted, and the rider, seeing her at last, snatched his hand from his sword hilt as if it had burned him.

"Give the queen the writ!" he roared as, breathless, she joined the group surrounding him.

Instantly Father Martin was at her side with a parchment bearing the king's seal. She read it swiftly—a few stark lines that ordered the seizure of Siferth's wife.

Heartsick—frightened for Aldyth—she demanded, "What is the lady's crime? Where are you taking her?"

"I am on the king's business, my lady. I can say no more than that." He glared at the men who still clung to his bridle and snarled, "Release me, or the king will know of it."

Angry and frustrated, aware that only the king could solve this riddle, Emma commanded, "Let him go."

As he rode away, she turned to her distraught household. Wulfa, white-faced, stood clutching her babe in her arms; Wymarc was on her knees consoling a wailing Alfred; Father Martin had his arm around the shoulders of the panting abbess; servants and hearth men whispered together, their faces bewildered or frightened.

Emma pointed to two of her hearth guards and said, "Quickly! Get to your horses and follow them. I want to know where those men are taking Lady Aldyth, but make certain that they do not see you. The rest of you will accompany me to the king at Oxford. We leave within the hour."

Soon after, she was again in the door yard, giving her steward instructions as she prepared to ride to the city. A cry from the gate ward, though, alerted her that more riders were approaching.

Not king's men this time, she saw, recognizing Ulfkytel and Godwin riding through the gate with six men following behind. They dismounted swiftly, and Ulfkytel and Godwin hastened forward, their faces grim. Anticipating more trouble, she braced herself for it.

"My lady," Ulfkytel said, "we are come with grievous news for Siferth's wife."

Emma felt her heart plummet. "The king's men took her away not an hour ago. I do not yet know where. Tell me what has happened."

Ulfkytel and Godwin exchanged a look.

"Siferth and his brother Morcar are dead," Ulfkytel said, "slaughtered by Eadric on the orders of the king."

"Dear God," Emma whispered.

"They were the first to support Swein's bid for the throne, my lady," Godwin said. "The king is exacting his vengeance."

Emma nodded. She understood now why Aldyth had been spirited away. As Siferth's widow she inherited his lands in the Five Boroughs, and any noble who took her to wife could claim her properties, demand the fealty of the men there, and wield power in the north. That was something the king would want to prevent.

"My lord," she said to Ulfkytel, "you are not safe here. You must take your wife and your child to Thetford. They are within. Go to them. Quickly now."

If this was Æthelred exacting vengeance then Ulfkytel might well be the next to die. His people, though, would protect their lord and his family, and it would take an army to pierce the East Anglian defenses.

She turned to her steward. "See that they have spare horses and provisions for the journey." Beckoning to Godwin she said, "See to your men, my lord, then come inside. I would hear more of events at Oxford."

Soon she was seated in the great hall with Father Martin, Wymarc, and Abbess Ælfwynn, listening as Godwin recounted the story that had spread through Oxford that morning like wildfire—how the brothers Siferth and Morcar had accepted an invitation the night before to dine with Eadric, and had been set upon by the ealdorman's retainers.

"Oxford was in an uproar when we left," Godwin said, "and the king's hearth guards were everywhere."

Sweet Virgin. She hoped that Edward had not been caught up in this.

"Is my son still in the city?" she asked.

"No. He set out for Winchester three days ago with Bishop Ælfsige. Edwig went with them."

"And Edmund?" she asked anxiously. "Where is he?" Siferth and Morcar had been his friends and supporters. Edmund would not let this act of vengeance go unanswered.

"He left for London yesterday. I have sent men after him with the news. I think Eadric purposely waited until Edmund was gone before he acted, for fear of what the ætheling might do."

And what would Edmund do, Emma wondered, when he learned what had happened? Might he, in turn, murder Eadric? Might he even attack the king at Oxford?

Beside her, the abbess stirred. "My lady, I am concerned for Lady Aldyth."

It was the gentlest of reproofs, reminding her of a queen's duty. Aldyth had been under her protection when she was seized and was still her responsibility. Emma drew a long breath, thinking how frightened Aldyth must be, not knowing where she was being taken, or why. Perhaps not even aware of her husband's cruel fate.

"The king will confine her somewhere," she said thoughtfully, "and it will be nowhere near her lands or her people. My men have orders to follow her captors and report back to me, and as soon as I discover where she has been taken, I will do what I can for her."

It would be little enough, she feared, for Aldyth was the king's captive. Still, she could send her furnishings and clothing, and assign servants to care for her—and protect her, if need be.

Later, when Wulfa and Ulfkytel had departed for Thetford, Godwin lingered behind to await news of the whereabouts of Siferth's widow. When her household was no longer frantic with activity, Emma summoned him to her.

"When you learn where Aldyth has been taken," she said to him, "what will you do?"

But he shook his head and, gazing intently at her, said, "I will not be the one to act, my lady. It will be Edmund."

His words chilled her, for that was what she feared more than anything else—that Edmund would make some move against the king or against Eadric and in doing so, would tear the kingdom apart.

She closed her eyes, weary and frightened. The king had sworn to the lords of England that he would refrain from vengeance, that he would deal equably with his people and follow the rule of law. Yet in ordering the slaughter of two of his nobles he had broken that pledge. It seemed to her that in this bitter time, there was no rule of law in England, that vengeance alone ruled. One act of outrage led to another, as unstoppable as boulders tumbling down a hill.

Determined to at least try to prevent that, she looked again at Godwin.

"You must persuade Edmund that he cannot retaliate against Eadric or the king. If he does, the king will condemn him and it will lead to war between father and son."

"I will tell him, my lady," Godwin replied. Then he blew out a heavy breath. "But do you believe that he will listen?"

No. She did not. And because he would not, all of England was likely to suffer, and her own sons might well be at risk amid the chaos that would ensue.

Chapter Thirty-Two

August 1015
Malmesbury, Wiltshire

"Tell me that you will do as I ask."

It was a command, not a request; and Edmund saw the abbot, whose youthful looks belied his heavy responsibilities, flinch as if he'd been struck.

Abbot Wulfsine bent his dark, tonsured head over his folded hands, apparently consulting heaven for guidance, and Edmund forced himself to be patient. A great deal depended on what the abbot said next.

It was well after midnight as they stood together in the near darkness of the chapter house of Malmesbury's great abbey. Situated within the ramparts of an ancient fortress, this was not only a place of prayer and learning, it was also a formidable prison. Edmund wondered if it had been Eadric or the king who had decided to immure Siferth's widow here for safekeeping.

For weeks now she had been confined within these high stone walls and, according to his spies, watched over by some fifty monks and a handful of royal guards who were in turn watched over by several steely-eyed servants of the queen. Tonight, though, his own retainers far outnumbered all of them, and he had met with little resistance as he demanded admittance to speak with his old friend, the abbot.

After what seemed to Edmund an interminable time, Abbot Wulfsine cleared his throat.

"Your arguments are persuasive, Edmund, and I am willing to do as you have asked. But if the lady is unwilling, what then?"

"Would you have me take her unwed?" Edmund demanded harshly. "For I shall take her, abbot. Do not doubt that for a moment."

"What I would have you do, my lord, is take the time to win her consent!"

Edmund scowled at him. "Time, abbot, is the one thing that I do not have."

"So you will force her? Against her will?"

"If it comes to that. Yes."

"Then no! I will not agree, unless you swear to me that she will come to no harm at your hands!"

"*Christ!* You have known me since we were lads! Do you think so little of me that you need ask that?"

Wulfsine huffed an agitated sigh. "I think, Edmund, that you are a desperate and angry man just now. So, yes, I ask it."

For answer, Edmund brushed past his friend and stalked to the Bible that lay open on a stand at the far end of the chamber. He slammed his hand, palm down, upon the book.

"I swear that I will not harm the lady, and that I will protect her from anyone who might seek to physically constrain her." He glared at Wulfsine. "Will that suffice?"

He saw the abbot's doubtful nod, and then slid his gaze to the doorway. Siferth's widow stood there, ushered here straight from her bed, apparently. She wore no headrail, and her dark hair hung in a plait that fell over her shoulder. Her feet were bare beneath the hem of her night shift and the grey woolen cloak that she had thrown over it. The serving women on either side of her each held a candle, and in the flickering light Edmund tried to read the expressions that flashed across Aldyth's face as she recognized him. Fear and resignation, he thought. But mostly fear.

She was a tall woman, and handsome, with large brown eyes and a wide mouth that was just now clamped shut, as if she were clenching her teeth in anger. Perhaps she was. He did not blame her. It should never have come to this.

"Leave us, please, if you would, abbot," he said.

The abbot hesitated, casting a worried glance at him before going to Aldyth's side. She stood immobile, twisting her hands and trembling as he whispered something to her—assurances, perhaps, that all would be well.

But it would be many long months, Edmund suspected, before all could be well again.

Wulfsine gently escorted Aldyth into the center of the chamber and, with another warning glance at Edmund, he and the others left them alone.

Aldyth's eyes darted around the chamber as if searching for some means of escape. She was like a nervous, high-strung mare that needed a gentle hand, Edmund thought. It was one of her many misfortunes that tonight he had not the time nor the temperament for gentling.

"You need not be afraid," he said roughly. "I mean you no harm."

She glanced up at him, then away, then back again, sweeping her gaze over his chain mail and sword.

"I know why you have come," she said. "You would make yourself lord of all Lindsey and the Five Boroughs." She raised frightened eyes to his. "What will you do after that?"

It dawned on him that she did not fear him, nor did she fear what the next few hours would bring. She was looking much further into the future and was afraid of something far worse. She had already guessed what he intended to do; had already imagined the turmoil that was likely to come of it.

"I will call on the men of the north to accept me as their lord," he said, "and I will call on them to fight."

"And then you will defy your father," she said. "You will break faith with your king, just as Siferth did. And you will die just as he did: murdered, unburied, your body left somewhere to rot, unmarked and unblessed."

Her voice broke on her last words, and although she turned her face away from him, she could not hide the emotions that beset her. He had small comfort to offer her, but he gave her what he had.

"Siferth was buried at Ely, my lady, by my order. I saw him laid in his grave. Morcar lies beside him." He strode toward her as he spoke, until the distance between them was reduced to an arm's length. "And yes, I will defy my father if I must. Someone must defend the kingdom, and I believe that task is mine."

But she was shaking her head at him. "Betrayal is still a sin, my lord," she said huskily, "even if you are on the side of the angels. You will be forced to pay a price in the end for it, and so will I."

"If there is any sin here, it falls upon my head, lady, not on yours."

"That is not true! If I give you my hand then I am complicit in your betrayal." She gave a wild, humorless laugh and wrapped her arms about her middle. "But I have no choice, do I?"

The eyes that fastened on his were pleading, but he could not give her the answer she wanted.

"No," he said, as gently as he knew how. "You have no choice."

The ceremony was held there, in the chapter house. It was brief, performed by the abbot, and witnessed by Godwin, Withar and half a dozen Benedictine brothers. Their union was consummated in the guest chamber where Aldyth had been housed for the past six weeks. That part of it, too, had been brief. Edmund took no pleasure in it nor gave any. But it was accomplished, and in little more than an hour he and his wife, accompanied by eighty of his retainers, left Malmesbury, riding north along the Fosse Way toward Lindsey.

A.D. 1015 Then, before the Nativity of St. Mary went the ætheling into the Five Boroughs and all the people submitted to him. At the same time came Cnut to Sandwich, and went soon all about Kent into Wessex, and then plundered in Dorset, and in Wiltshire, and in Somerset. King Æthelred meanwhile, lay sick at Cosham.

The Anglo-Saxon Chronicle

Chapter Thirty-Three

October 1015
Cosham, Hampshire

Emma set out from London for Cosham on horseback accompanied by four attendants, an armed escort of twenty hearth guards, and a sense of dread that cloaked her like a mantle. For eight days she journeyed south in mild autumn weather, and as the road unspooled before her, she brooded over what might be waiting for her at its end. Cnut's army was ravaging in Dorset, and if the Danes had learned that the king lay helpless and sick in neighboring Hampshire they might have attacked the royal estate where Æthelred had taken refuge. The king might already be dead and she a widow—her world changed so completely that she could not begin to encompass what it would mean.

The daylight hours of her journey were dogged by anxiety as rumors of war pulsed like frantic heartbeats through every town and village that she passed. In the long, empty nights, her worry mushroomed into fear. Her fate, that of her sons, and that of England itself rested upon the faltering life force of an aging king pitted against the fierce ambition of a youthful Danish warlord.

It seemed to her a cruel jest that Æthelred had been betrayed by illness when his response to Cnut's precipitous return had been unusually swift and decisive. He had ordered Eadric to gather the Mercian fyrd and strike the Danes from the north while the king himself prepared to sail with Thorkell's fleet to attack them from the south. He had been deaf, though, to her pleas that he send to Edmund for help.

"I cannot trust him!" Æthelred had said. "His marriage to Siferth's widow was an act of treason, and he is as much my enemy now as this Danish upstart!"

When she had failed to change his mind, she had sent her own message to Edmund, warning him of Cnut's landing in Dorset and urging him to come to his father's aid. It would heal the breach between father and son, she had written, and might well save the kingdom from disaster. Edmund's confirmation that he was leading a force south had arrived just before she learned that the king's sudden illness had forced his fleet to land at Cosham, nowhere near his intended destination. Æthelred's battle strategy lay in ruins, while there had been no word at all from Eadric and his west Mercian fyrd.

She hoped, though, that he and Edmund would join forces and confront the Danes even as she worried that Æthelred was dead, the English defense in disarray, and the kingdom in danger of being overrun by a massive viking army.

Her fears were uppermost in her mind as she arrived at the Cosham estate and was led to the chamber where the king lay. It was an airless, darkened room in which the honeyed scent from a single branch of candles did little to mask the fetid smell of sickness that fouled the air.

The cluster of priests and servants attending the king parted as she approached the great, curtained bed. Æthelred lay on his side with his knees pulled up close to his chest as if to curl himself around some grievous pain. His face beneath the round, black cap that covered his head and hair was the color of wax, and even in his sleep it was creased into a grimace of agony. She pitied him, as she would any creature wracked by torment, and she whispered a silent prayer for mercy.

The king's physician—a monk of middle years, robust, round-faced, and well known to her—greeted her anxiously.

"Do not wake him, my lady, I beg you. Sleep is the only thing that gives him respite from the griping in his stomach."

She nodded, and assured that the king was well attended, beckoned to the physician to follow her into the chamber that had been prepared for her. When the door had shut behind them, she asked anxiously, "Will he live?"

He hesitated, folding his hands, opening his mouth and then closing it again while she waited in an agony of suspense, convinced that his reluctance to speak meant that he was about to give her the worst possible news. Her thoughts flew to her sons in London, in the care of Wymarc and her Norman hearth guards. She had left orders that if the worst happened and Cnut's armies raged across England unopposed, her children were to be spirited across the Narrow Sea.

To what kind of future she could not say, but at least they would be alive.

The physician finally cleared his throat to speak and she dismissed thoughts of that unimaginable future to dwell on the present.

"The king's stomach pain and the bloody flux that accompanies it need not be fatal," he said. "He has brief periods of relief that give me hope that he will recover. However, even during such respites, he is so weak that he is indifferent to everything around him or, as you saw just now, he falls into a restless sleep." He shook his head. "It is his lethargy that concerns me. I do not like it; it is a further sign of the imbalance of his humors."

Not dying, she thought, yet too ill to counter any rumor that his death was imminent.

She queried him about his treatment of the illness and the prospects for the king's eventual return to health, and when he had answered all her questions, he offered some final words of caution.

"While the king is likely to recover from this, its effects will linger for many months. And he is of an age, my lady, when one infirmity is often followed by another that is far more deadly. You must, I fear, prepare yourself for what inevitably lies ahead."

She thanked him, and when he had left her, she sank into a chair, exhausted and uncertain what to do. Æthelred had lived long past the age of his father and grandfather, and no man lives forever. The death of a ruler must always cause some disorder, but it would be disastrous if Æthelred were to die now, while the kingdom was rent with such turmoil.

She glanced up as servants slipped into the room to lay food and drink upon the table at her side, and she was surprised to see Ealdorman Ælfric at the door, his lined face filled with concern. He was an old friend, and pleased as she was to see him, it alarmed her to see him here now. He should have been with Eadric's army, a good many days' march to the west.

"Lord Ælfric," she said, frowning. "I thought you were with Eadric's force in Dorset." She had spoken more sharply than she intended, and regretting it, she said, more gently, "Pray, my lord, sit down. You have news, for me. What is it?"

Ælfric drew a bench toward her and sat, resting his elbows on his knees as he leaned forward, his expression grave.

"I was with Eadric, my lady, but not in Dorset. We were still in Worcestershire when we learned that Edmund was bringing a force south from Lincoln, and Eadric led his army north to confront him."

"What?" Emma straightened and stared at him, horrified at the prospect of English men slaughtering each other. Cnut, it seemed, need only stand aside and watch England destroy itself.

"Eadric swore that if the ætheling was not stopped, he would join Cnut; that Edmund meant to take the throne by force."

"But Edmund was responding to my request that he support Eadric and the king!"

He nodded. "I guessed as much. And that is what I told Eadric. I urged him to meet with Edmund, and when he refused, I held my men back and sent word of what was happening to the archbishop at Worcester. Wulfstan arrived in time to prevent a battle—rode straight on to the field between their lines and threatened hellfire to any man who dared draw his sword or raise a spear."

"Thank God," Emma murmured. But she could see from his grim expression that there was more, and that she was not going to like it. "And?" she asked.

"Wulfstan tried to persuade them to join forces, but there was too little trust between them. Edmund led his men back north, and when we learned that the king was ailing, Eadric sent the fyrds home and came here. I accompanied him, and found the king as you saw him just now—vilely sick and half out of his mind with pain. Eadric wasted no time in concocting a string of lies about Edmund and what had happened. To his credit, Æthelred refused to listen. He said that he was dying and that Eadric must make his peace with the ætheling because Edmund would wear the crown soon enough."

So, Emma thought, now that Æthelred felt death pressing him, it was Edmund whom he would name his heir. Given the menace that was Cnut, that was as it should be.

"Meantime, there is still a Danish army out there somewhere," she mused, "and no English force gathered to stop it. Where is Eadric?"

"Gone, my lady!" Thorkell strode into the chamber, fury radiating from him as he knelt before her. "The bastard fled two days ago and took forty ships with him!"

She stared blankly at him for a moment as she took in his words.

Dear God, she thought. Was there to be no end to this litany of disasters?

"Gone where?" she cried. She looked from Ælfric to Thorkell and read in their faces the same fear that was in her mind. If Eadric believed that his power, position, and wealth would vanish once Edmund took the throne, he would offer his allegiance to the only man who would reward him lavishly for his support and who, with Eadric's help, might well capture the English crown. "Where is Cnut?" she asked urgently. "Do you know? Does Eadric know?"

"Our scouts report that Cnut is leading his army north into Somerset," Thorkell said. "And yes, Eadric knows it."

"Have you alerted Edmund?" she asked.

"We sent men after him," Ælfric said, "but he is likely back in Lincoln by now."

She sat in silence for a time, thinking through all the dangers facing them, and she settled at last on addressing the one that was most dire.

"The longer the king remains here," she said, "the greater the chance that Eadric will lead Cnut and his army to us. The king must be moved to safety, yet his physician claims that he cannot travel until his condition has improved. What is your counsel?"

"It is two days' journey to Winchester, my lady," Ælfric said. "The city's walls are far more easily defended than the palisade that surrounds this estate."

She frowned, considering his suggestion. If they tried to move Æthelred now, it would mean two days of agony, and there was no guarantee that the journey alone would not be the death of him.

She turned to Thorkell.

"What say you, my lord?" she asked.

"At last report, my lady, Cnut's army was somewhere near Glastonbury. It will take a week or more for Eadric to reach their camp, and longer than that for a Danish force, even a small one, to make its way here. I say we give the king ten days to recover then sail back to London."

Emma sat back in her chair, thinking. Winchester was safer than Cosham, but London was the strongest refuge in all of England. Waiting to move the king might be a risk, but it was one that she was willing to take if London lay at the end of it.

"The king will be safest in London through the winter," she said. "And the more distance we put between him and Cnut's army, the better." She nodded to the two men. "I thank you both for your counsel, my lords," she said. "In ten days we shall set out for London. Let us pray that by then the king will be well enough to survive the journey."

October 1015
Near Axbridge, Somerset

Cnut watched in silence as his huscarles escorted the English ealdorman into the great tent that served as his headquarters. Was it an ill wind, he wondered, or an auspicious one that had driven Eadric here? The ealdorman had ridden into the Danish camp with only a few retainers, signaling that he had come in peace. But Cnut already knew a great deal about Eadric, and what he knew made him eye the Mercian with suspicion.

King Æthelred's henchman was black-haired, black-eyed and, he suspected, black-hearted. Rumor had it that Eadric had slain Siferth and Morcar while they were guests in his hall, but that was only his most recent crime. Elgiva had often spoken of how Eadric had arranged a magnificent feast for her father and the next day had murdered him along with a handful of his retainers. That had been years ago, but no doubt there had been other killings since, committed at the behest of the English king.

So why had Æthelred sent Eadric to him today?

He flicked a glance at Alric, who was standing beside the ealdorman, his hand on the hilt of his sword and his body poised to spring should Eadric make any threatening move. There was a long-standing enmity, Cnut knew, between these two men, rooted in that long-ago murder of Elgiva's father. Alric had been Ælfhelm's man then, had barely escaped that slaughter, and would not trust Eadric any farther than his sword could reach.

But Eadric seemed not to notice Alric or his menacing stance. The ealdorman's eyes were fixed upon Cnut's own, meeting scrutiny with scrutiny. One brow was raised—with interest or insolence Cnut could not tell—and his thin-lipped mouth was set in an ingratiating smile. Beneath his traveling cloak he wore a mail burney, although his whip-thin frame suggested a cleric rather than a warrior.

There was, too, Cnut would wager, a shrewd, calculating mind behind that comely face, and possibly some treachery at work. So was the treachery aimed at himself or at the English king?

Were Elgiva here she would no doubt insist that the ealdorman could not be trusted and that he should be granted a slow, painful death. Happily, Elgiva was in Denmark, and in any case, the ealdorman had come under a banner of truce.

He gestured Eadric toward a table where stools had been drawn up, and he beckoned to Alric and Eirik to join them. Whatever this was about, he wanted them to hear it.

"I presume," he said to Eadric, "that you have a matter of some import to discuss with me. A message from your king, perhaps?"

Eadric pursed his lips, glanced down at his folded hands and said, "I am here, my lord, on my own behalf," he looked up with a genial smile, "to propose an alliance between us that I believe will be to your advantage as well as mine."

So it was Æthelred who was to be the victim of Eadric's treachery. And this, Cnut supposed, would be a negotiation, assuming he was willing to consider Eadric as an ally.

Well, he would certainly consider it.

He called for mead, and as the goblets were filled he said, "Before we discuss any alliance, Lord Eadric, tell me what has turned you against your king."

It was one thing to submit to a foreign enemy when one had no recourse. It was another to break faith with a king who had, as he understood it, showered this man above all others with wealth and power.

Eadric did not flinch at the question, but met his gaze steadily.

"King Æthelred was near to death when last I saw him. That was ten days ago. If he is not already dead, he will be soon, and I see no advantage in risking my life for a corpse."

Cnut glanced at Alric, who shook his head. There had been no rumor of the king's death.

"What of the king's eldest son? Surely he will claim the throne. Will you not give him your pledge?"

"I will offer my support, lord, to whoever offers me the greatest reward." Eadric flashed a cold, venal smile at him then said, scowling, "Edmund will offer me nothing. He has ever been my enemy—envious, I suppose, of the favors that the king showered on me." He leaned forward, his hands wrapped around his mead cup, his eyes glittering. "Those favors were well-deserved, my lord; and I would earn favors of you now if you let me. I can bring you forty ships—an army of Northmen eager for silver. They will swell your ranks and assure your victory."

Cnut raised a brow in surprise.

"Thorkell's men?" he asked.

"Some of them were, once. Others arrived in England last year with the Norseman Olaf and chose to linger." Eadric's mouth widened into an arrogant smile. "They are my men now."

"Forty ships," Cnut mused. Two thousand men, perhaps more, who could swing the balance of victory in his favor. The success of his campaign depended not just on skill and luck, but on the number of warriors that he could keep in the field. He would certainly lose some to battle and some to sickness, and it would be difficult, if not impossible, to replace them. Eadric must know this as well; must know the immense value of what he was offering.

"And what favors do you want," he asked slowly, "in return for your ships and your men?"

Eadric lifted his hand to toy with his short, well-shaped beard, no doubt calculating just how much he might be able to get.

"My men will, of course, expect a share of the plunder," Eadric said slowly. "As for myself, I wish to retain the properties that I already hold, as well as my post as ealdorman of Mercia. I would also require," he added, flicking his hand as if recalling some minor detail, "certain other lands in eastern Mercia that are adjacent to my current holdings."

Holdings, Cnut knew, that were already vast. It was not a small request. He considered Eadric, who was eyeing him now with hawk-like attention, waiting for an answer.

The man was King Æthelred's son-in-law and closest advisor. He had, by his own admission, deserted his lord while he lay sick and dying. He appeared to be as craven, black-hearted and untrustworthy as his reputation suggested, and there was not a single thing about the man that he liked. But he could not afford to turn down Eadric's offer. Two thousand men might make the difference between conquest and bitter defeat.

Cnut looked to Eirik, who gave an almost imperceptible nod of assent.

They would bargain, then.

Sometime later, after Eadric had departed, apparently satisfied with their negotiations, Cnut met with his warlords. They went over all that the ealdorman had revealed about English defenses and began laying plans for the campaign ahead. When Cnut eventually dismissed them, Alric lingered behind, clearly with something on his mind.

"You don't like him," Cnut said. "Neither do I."

"His men will be useful, certainly," Alric replied. "But you realize, do you not, that Eadric will turn on you the moment that he sees even some small advantage to himself in doing so?"

"The thought had occurred to me," Cnut said sourly.

"And what about the lands that he wants to claim? They rightly belong to Elgiva. Are you going to strip them from her and turn them over to Eadric?"

Cnut sighed and said, "If he aids me in capturing England's throne, I will have to give him what he has asked for."

"And if he betrays you?" Alric persisted.

"If he betrays me," Cnut assured him, "I shall reward him in an altogether different way."

Chapter Thirty-Four

November 1015 - January 1016
London

I t was early November when Emma rode beside the king through London toward the royal residence. This was the last mile of their journey from Cosham, and she felt as if she were taking part in a funeral procession with a living corpse at its center. The king had survived his illness, but he was pale and gaunt as he sat astride his mount, staring straight ahead and ignoring the citizens who lined the streets under a crisply blue winter sky to gawk at the only monarch that most of them had ever known.

As his physician had warned, Æthelred had not come through his illness unscathed. His vigor never returned, and as winter settled in, the strange, dark moods that had occasionally troubled him in the past—when he would start and stare at some invisible horror—became a frequent occurrence and a worry to both Emma and to the physician who continued to attend him.

The witan met with the king at Christmas, but it was a small, gloomy gathering at which Æthelred was alternately distracted or listless. That left it to Archbishop Wulfstan to preside over meetings that were overshadowed by the grim recounting of Eadric's betrayal, by reports of the continued Danish threat in the west, and by the conspicuous absence of Æthelred's sons. Edmund, it was reported, was still with his bride in the north midlands; Edwig was rumored to be in Bruges, well out of the reach of the king's wrath; and at Emma's insistence, her own sons had been sent to Canterbury with attendants whose orders were to hasten them to Normandy if the Danes should overwhelm the English.

Eager for news of the movements of Cnut's army, she was present at every council session and paid close attention to the reports, official and otherwise, from the magnates and churchmen in attendance. Now more than ever before she was impressed by Archbishop Wulfstan's vast web of informants. He reported that Cnut and Eadric had captured Bath without a battle, and that their combined armies had settled near that city, presumably to wait out the winter there. Edmund, he said, was making preparations for a campaign against them in the spring.

With God's help, Wulfstan assured the assembled company, Edmund would drive their enemies from the land. Emma saw the archbishop glance at the king—hoping, perhaps, for some words of support for his eldest son—but Æthelred did not return his gaze and remained obstinately silent.

Over the next weeks winter storms wracked the kingdom, and in London the citizens rarely ventured far from their hearths. The few travelers who arrived from outside the city brought reports of roads littered with debris, of fords that were impassable, and of rivers treacherous with ice; but they carried no news of either the Danes' activities or of Edmund's efforts to raise an army in the Five Boroughs. Emma complained to the archbishop of feeling deaf and blind to anything that might be happening beyond the city walls, but he assured her that nothing of any moment was likely to occur until winter's end.

On a late January evening when vespers had been sung and when the king had, as was his habit now, retreated betimes to his bed, Emma remained in the royal chapel, kneeling before the altar. In the midst of her solitary prayers she felt a hand upon her shoulder, and looking up she found Wymarc bending over her.

"Edmund is here," Wymarc whispered. "He is waiting for you in your chamber."

A surge of alarm brought Emma quickly to her feet. After so many weeks of silence, Edmund's errand must be urgent indeed to have driven him here in the depths of winter.

"Tell Edyth that her brother has come," she said to Wymarc before hurrying to her quarters.

There she found Edmund still wrapped in a heavy traveling cloak and restlessly pacing the floor. To her surprise, his wife was there as well. Aldyth stood beside the glowing brazier, looking worried as she watched Edmund. When she turned to allow a servant to remove her cloak Emma saw the telltale roundness beneath her breasts that explained the pallid weariness in her face.

Emma strode into the room and took Aldyth's hands. They were cold as ice, and she began to chafe them.

"You should not be traveling in your condition," she scolded.

"I wished to come, my lady," Aldyth said. "I was certain of a welcome, from you at least."

"She is safer here than in the north," Edmund said.

Emma sent him an inquiring glance and said, "You had best tell me what has happened then."

Edmund considered where to begin while Emma led Aldyth to a bench and wrapped a shawl about her shoulders. He studied the two women—the wife that he had come to care for deeply, and the queen that he was schooling himself to trust. He would be putting that trust to the test tonight because he needed Emma to intercede with the king on his behalf.

"The Danish army is on the move, and we are facing a winter campaign," he said. "It is urgent that I speak with the king and convince him to—" He paused as Edyth swept into the chamber.

"My father cannot help you!" she said, her voice strident. She marched up to him, her face flushed with anger. "The king is old and infirm, and he has suffered enough. Why can't you leave him alone?"

"Because while our father lives, Edyth, he has a kingdom to defend. I am doing all that I can, but your husband's treachery has weakened my—"

"You drove my husband to treachery! He would never have joined Cnut if you had trusted him, but you were ever his enemy! You have always opposed him!"

"I oppose him because he is a liar, a thief, and a murderer! And now he is in league with our enemy! While it might have suited my father to favor such a warped and twisted piece of filth, I will not stoop so low. Eadric is desperate to cling to his wealth and power, and because he knows that he will never get it from me he has gone haring off to seek it from Cnut! Now their combined armies have begun burning their way through Gloucestershire and Warwickshire, and I have not the men to stop them! Does that make you proud of your husband?"

His words seemed to flay his sister. Her face crumpled with weeping, but he could not pity her. She had shut her eyes to the truth about Eadric for too long. It was time she woke up and saw what a dangerous threat he was to all of them.

At the touch of a hand upon his arm he turned to see Emma beside him, her face grave.

"Why is it that you have no men?" she asked. She, at least, seemed to understand the urgency of the situation. "Have you not called up the levies in Mercia?"

"I have! But Eadric is their ealdorman and they are sworn to him, not to me! I am asking them to take up arms against their rightful lord, and they dare not do it unless the king himself gives that order."

"But you are the king's son!" Emma protested.

"That does not matter; not while the king lives. The thegns do not owe allegiance to me; they owe it to their ealdorman, who is Eadric, or to the king himself. My hands are tied. The only way that I can convince them that I have the king's support is to have him with me on the field and at my side. But the king fears me now as much as he fears Cnut! He thinks that I mean him harm and that I will betray him just as Eadric did." He took Emma's hand. "My lady, I am here to beg you to be my advocate, to persuade the king to see me and help me convince him to ride with me to battle."

She was silent for a long time, searching his face, and as the moments passed he feared that she would refuse him—that she would turn out to be the enemy he had long suspected her to be.

Finally she said, "The king will not be persuaded to see you, Edmund, on my word alone. You are right, he is afraid of you. He is afraid of his own shadow now! We must call the council together, bring in every member still within the city. Archbishop Wulfstan is one of them. Go to him tonight and ask him to summon the witan members to a meeting with the king on the morrow. I will make certain that the king is there."

He was already reaching for his cloak. Edyth, though, planted herself in front of the door, rigid, her arms folded across her body.

"I forbid it!" she cried. "If you send my father into battle you are sending him to his death! He is an old man and he is sick!"

"He is still the king, Edyth," he reminded her, "and only he can decide what he will or will not do. No one else can make that choice for him. Not even you."

He pushed past his still protesting sister and flicked a brief, parting glance at Aldyth. As he dashed from the chamber, his mind was already intent on the arguments he would lay before the archbishop. When he stepped into the freezing night, though, he made first for St. Paul's. Before he did anything else, he would have to go down on his knees before God and beg forgiveness for the single thought that, like a worm, was boring into his mind: that all of England would be far better off if his father was already dead.

January 1016
London

Æthelred sat in his great chair, his head resting against its high back and his body bolstered by cushions that did little to ease his aching limbs. A heavy fog had settled over London this morning, and its damp, chilly breath seeped even through stone walls, so that he was cold despite the fire that burned in the hearth but a few steps away.

He had dismissed the councilors who had spent the last hour pleading with him to go to war. Their arguments, particularly those raised by Edmund and Emma, still echoed in his head. They would have him lead an army against the Danes in mid-winter despite his age and his infirmities.

They did not want a king. They wanted a Savior.

And Edmund likely wanted him dead.

He closed his eyes and considered all the possible, wretched tomorrows that lay before him whether he agreed to their demands or not until, in the silence, someone spoke.

"What is it that you are afraid of, my lord?"

He knew that voice, so he did not bother to open his eyes and confront perhaps the only man in England who was brazen enough to disobey his king by lingering behind when he had been ordered to leave.

Christ! He was too weary to debate this now. He rubbed his aching forehead and wished the man across the sea.

"Your son demands your help," the implacable voice continued, "and you should have agreed to what he asked with alacrity. Why do you hesitate?"

He opened his eyes then and scowled at Archbishop Wulfstan, whose formidable, black-robed frame towered over him. The face above the long white beard was creased with age and the steely eyes regarded him with keen interest. He was like a hawk eyeing its prey. He was here, certainly, to goad him into action.

"My son asks too much of me," Æthelred snarled.

"Ah, I see," Wulfstan said. "He wishes you to fulfill your oath as protector of your people. Yes, it is a great deal to demand of a king, especially one who has always found it a trial to be tutored in kingship by his sons." His voice was laced with mockery. "First by Athelstan and now by Edmund."

"And by my archbishop, as well, it seems," Æthelred muttered. "Is that not why you are here? To berate me for my indecision?"

Wulfstan drew closer to him and, supported by his crozier, bent to pierce him with an expression so fierce that Æthelred wanted to shy away from it, but there was nowhere to go.

"First, I would know why you are so afraid of your son. Because I can see your fear. I can even smell it on you."

"Yes, I am afraid of my son," he said, glowering at the archbishop, "because he covets my throne and because he has men to do his bidding who have no love for me! The men who follow Edmund were once Siferth's men! They welcomed Swein to England and proclaimed him king, and for that crime I harried their lands and slaughtered their kin. How long do you think I would survive in their midst?"

Wulfstan's brows rose in surprise.

"We are speaking of war, my lord. No man rides to battle without acknowledging the possibility that death waits for him there."

"And because of that no man fails to arm himself against it! Tell me, then, how I should arm myself against a knife in the back."

The archbishop straightened, and his stern expression softened.

"Your God must be your armor, my lord. Men fear Him, and fear His wrath. Put your trust in God, and He will protect you just as a king protects his people. You have a duty to your kingdom that you cannot shirk, even for fear of death. No one expects you to stand in a shield wall, but you cannot deny Edmund's demand that you ride at his side and lead the men of London to battle."

Æthelred shifted his gaze, looking past the archbishop into the chamber's darkest corner where, from its depths, his brother's shade glowered back at him. Edward was always near him now, despite his frantic prayers for deliverance from the wraith's malevolence. It was not death that he feared. It was the agony that came before it that terrified him, and the judgment and punishment that must follow.

"God has abandoned me," he murmured.

"It is not God who has abandoned you, lord king, but men—sinful men who did not deserve your trust."

Æthelred groaned and covered his face with his hand.

Eadric. He had known that the man was unscrupulous and deadly—a raptor trained to kill upon command. He had never imagined, though, that his hawk would turn on him and rip out his throat.

Wulfstan's voice continued inexorably. "You thought that you could dice with the devil and win. You have been proved wrong. Now it is Cnut who is playing that devil's game. One day he will come to regret it, but only, my king, if you play your part. Cnut purposes, with Eadric's help, to make himself king of all England. Will you sit back and allow it to happen?"

"I am old, archbishop, and weary," he protested, glaring at Wulfstan. "War is not a game for old men."

"War is not a game at all!" Wulfstan railed at him. "And I did not persuade the magnates of England to beckon you from exile only to have you sit on that throne and wallow in self-pity. Whatever fate awaits you is one that you have shaped with your own hands. If you are a king, then you must act. If you cannot do that, then give your crown to Edmund and take yourself back across the Narrow Sea, because you are of no use to us here!"

For a long moment Æthelred met Wulfstan's fierce gaze with his own, his jaw clenched with helpless outrage. Finally, though, he looked away, not into the corner where Edward's shade hovered, but into a halo of candles whose light was meant to banish the darkness.

If he was not a king, then he was nothing.

So, he must be the king. He would have to agree to what Edmund and Wulfstan demanded. By imagining that he could avoid it he was merely deceiving himself. He would be wary, though, on his guard for treachery every moment of every day and night.

He slumped in his chair and waved a hand at the archbishop.

"I will summon the fyrd of London," he sighed, "and we shall ride north with Edmund to challenge Eadric and Cnut. But I'll not trust to God to protect me from my English enemies! If I feel threatened by those who should be my allies, I shall leave them. I do not choose to be murdered by my own people." He shifted his gaze to the wraith in the chamber's dark corner. "I will not suffer the same fate as my brother."

A.D. 1016 When they were all assembled...it was told the king that those persons would betray him who ought to assist him; then forsook he the army, and returned again to London. Then rode Edmund the ætheling to Earl Uhtred in Northumbria...They went into Staffordshire and to Shrewsbury and to Chester; and they plundered on their parts, and Cnut on his. He went into Northamptonshire along the fens...thence into Northumbria toward York. When Uhtred understood this he hastened northward, and submitted for need, and all the Northumbrians with him.

The Anglo-Saxon Chronicle

Chapter Thirty-Five

March 1016
Wiheal, Northumbria

Cnut squinted up at a pale sky, sensing that it was near midday although the sun was hidden behind a veil of cloud. He rode south with Eadric and Eirik at the head of a force of sixty warriors over grassland already furrowed by the passage of horses and men. Their camp lay behind them on the western outskirts of Jorvik, and their destination—the manor hall at Wiheal—lay some way ahead. As his company covered ground at an easy pace Cnut thought with some misgiving about what would take place there.

Uhtred, apparently, was prepared to submit to him, with all the appropriate oaths and the accompanying surrender of hostages. His capitulation had come as no surprise. Uhtred and his Northumbrians could not reach their safe havens of Jorvik and Bamburgh unless they punched their way through the much larger Danish force that lay directly in their path, so Uhtred had been forced to submit. He'd had no other choice.

But when his own army marched south toward Wessex again in the days ahead, Cnut thought uneasily, the only thing to prevent Uhtred from once more throwing his support to the English was the oath of submission that he would give today. And there was no guarantee that Uhtred could be trusted to keep such a pledge. After all, Uhtred's hall was where Swein had met his death. Had that been chance, or had Uhtred been behind it? All these months later, Cnut still could not say. Yet he needed an ally in the north strong enough to fend off the Scots while he went south to deal with Edmund and the English. Uhtred might be that ally, but trusting him would be a risk—one that he was not yet certain he would be wise to take.

A shadow on the horizon resolved itself into a single horseman, and he recognized one of the men that he had sent ahead to see that preparations for the coming parley were in place.

"Uhtred has arrived at Wiheal, lord, with forty of his retainers," his scout reported as he reined in his mount. "Thurbrand and his men are—"

"Thurbrand? He is at Wiheal?" He didn't like the sound of that. Thurbrand had a score to settle with Uhtred. If those two met....

"Yes, lord. He camped nearby last night, and when we—"

Cnut did not wait to hear the rest. He spurred his horse to a gallop, cursing Thurbrand, cursing himself, and only vaguely aware of his retainers thundering behind him. When he rode through Wiheal's manor gate, he knew that he was too late. Knots of men, their mail tunics streaked with gore, were pawing through weapons stacked in piles around the yard.

He dismounted and stalked toward the hall where his own banner, not Thurbrand's, hung prominently from a staff near the door. Uhtred would have recognized that banner; would have surrendered his arms, confident of the guarantee of safe passage he had been given.

He would have walked into a trap.

Cnut grabbed the banner, hurled it to the ground, and ducked inside the dim hall. Lengths of thick cloth had been strung between the supporting pillars on both sides of the large chamber to form separate, smaller alcoves where armed men could be concealed as they waited for the signal to strike.

For Uhtred and his men, there would have been no escape.

The place stank of carnage, and bodies littered the floor. Thurbrand stood in the middle of the hall, a seax in his hand and the blood-soaked body of his enemy at his feet. In half a dozen strides Cnut reached him and backhanded him across the face.

"Do you have any idea what you have done?"

Thurbrand raised a hand to wipe blood from his lip and muttered, "I have done you a favor, lord." He tossed his seax carelessly to the floor. "I have rid you of an enemy."

Cnut hit him again, harder still, and this time the big man staggered from the blow.

"You have robbed me of an ally, you bastard!"

He could hear his own men entering the hall now, muttering in surprise as they saw the bodies.

"Get Thurbrand's men back in here," he shouted to them, "to clean up this carnage and bury the dead. Thurbrand is to dig Uhtred's grave with his own hands. When it's done, bring him to my camp. In chains."

He stalked from the hall, too angry to say anything more. Until he had his rage under control he dared not attempt to reckon with the lord of Holderness.

Cnut waited two days before he summoned Eirik and Eadric to his tent and had Thurbrand brought in. But when he saw the big Northumbrian thrust to his knees in front of him, hands chained behind his back, Cnut had to struggle to master his anger.

"Give me one good reason," he snarled, "why I should let you live!"

Thurbrand glowered up at him. "I saved you the trouble of killing Uhtred yourself."

Cnut's response was a savage blow that Thurbrand, trussed as he was, could not evade.

"I did not want Uhtred dead!" he shouted. "I granted him safe passage! That slaughter at Wiheal proclaims me a liar who cannot be trusted to keep his word!"

But Thurbrand, blood flowing from his lip and his nose, appeared unrepentant. "Uhtred would have betrayed you, Cnut," he roared, "no matter how many oaths he swore! He deserved to die! Have you forgotten that your father was murdered in his hall? That his men burned my wife alive? Their blood cried out for vengeance and I acted for both of them!"

Cnut would have struck him again, but Eirik gave a shout and grabbed his arm.

"Thurbrand has the right of it!" Eirik hissed at him. "As long as Uhtred lived, he would have been a threat to you in the north."

"He would have turned against you, my lord, sooner or later," Eadric agreed. "His ties to the old king and his son were too strong."

Cnut slanted a glance at Eadric whose ties to Æthelred were just as strong as Uhtred's had been. Both men had been granted vast lands by the English king; both men had wed one of Æthelred's daughters. Whatever was true of Uhtred was just as true of Eadric.

He did not say what he was thinking, but he drew in a long breath to calm his rage. He folded his arms and studied Thurbrand, weighing his crime and considering what penalty to impose. Thurbrand had avenged his wife's death, which was his right; but he had acted in defiance of orders, and that could not go unpunished.

"You are missing the point, all of you," he said. "Even if Uhtred's death benefits me, Thurbrand acted without my consent." He pointed at the man kneeling before him. "I told you to stay away from Wiheal because I knew that Uhtred was your enemy. I wanted you nowhere near him! You knew it, yet you chose to defy me. Eirik!" he said, his eyes still on Thurbrand. "How would you punish a man who deliberately disobeyed your orders?"

Eirik did not answer immediately, and Cnut roared, "How?"

"I would execute him."

He had known the answer before asking the question, and Thurbrand had known it, too. Still, Cnut was silent for a time, counting his own heartbeats, and letting Thurbrand sweat.

"I ought to take your head," he said at last, "and mount it atop the gates of Jorvik. I might do that yet." He scowled at the man before him. "But not today." Thurbrand had been a loyal ally for years, and that loyalty could not be ignored. "Go back to your lair in Holderness, Thurbrand, whatever is left of it. But you will have to make your way there without coin, horses, provisions, or companions. And understand that from this day forward, you are lord of nothing."

When Thurbrand had been hauled out of the tent Cnut considered the two men before him. Eadric was watching him with hungry, glittering eyes, thinking, no doubt, that Northumbria still needed a strong leader to control it. Eadric was about to be disappointed.

"Eirik," Cnut said. "You will be my jarl in Northumbria. I will leave enough men with you to fortify Jorvik and hold the north against either the English or the Scots, whoever comes calling. They will test you, so be on your guard. You, Eadric, will accompany me south along with the bulk of the army, and we will take to the ships. Æthelred, I'm told, is in London, and Edmund appears to be headed that way. If we can trap them both inside the walls and lay siege to the city, this campaign might soon be over." He frowned at Eadric. "The old king, it seems, is taking an almighty long time to die."

Eadric shrugged. "Even so, he must be gravely ill. I assure you that he is no threat."

Cnut grunted. Even a king about to meet his God must be deemed a threat if he was still able to call men to arms. Eadric was a fool to think otherwise.

"If you are wrong, Eadric," he said, "we may find two armies waiting to fall on us in the south, one led by the king and the other by his son. I do not like our odds if that should happen, so let us hope that you are right."

Chapter Thirty-Six

April 1016
London

The royal bedchamber was silent but for the sibilant prayers of Æthelred's archbishops and the intermittent rasp of the king's labored breathing. Emma gazed down at the shrunken frame outlined beneath the blankets, and with his every exhalation her own breath caught as she waited for the next rattling gasp.

The stench of illness in the room was not quite masked by the honeyed scent from the branches of candles placed around the bed, but the light they gave off was enough to banish any hint of shadows. She had ordered candles to be burned in this chamber day and night, for she knew better than anyone that Æthelred feared the dark.

Let him have the light, she thought, until the final darkness engulfs him.

He would die in his bed as he had wished, rather than struck down by the hand of a vengeful enemy; but Death itself had been a cruel and merciless foe. Æthelred had been subject to days of torment, his effort to draw air into his failing lungs a wide-eyed, panicked struggle. It had been terrible to watch and no doubt far worse to endure. Now, though, he seemed to have fallen into something that was deeper than sleep. Each gasping breath was shallower than the one before it, and his hollow cheeks and the grey hue of his skin told her that the end was near. She and the others gathered here were witnessing the final, losing battle in Æthelred's desperate struggle to stay alive.

Emma considered the three royal offspring keeping watch with her over the king's prone body. Edmund, standing at the foot of the bed, was still disheveled from four days of hard riding in response to her urgent summons. His expression was set in a grimace, bearing no sign of sorrow or even compassion as he stared at the waxen face on the pillow. He had not hastened here to reconcile with a dying father, but to claim a dead king's throne.

Edyth knelt with closed eyes, praying, her head bent over her clasped hands, her face a solemn mask that disguised whatever she was feeling. Next to her, Edward rocked back and forth, scowling, his arms folded across his chest as if to contain his boiling resentment. He had long nurtured a desperate expectation that he would be granted the crown when Æthelred died, but Edward was a mere eleven winters old, and England was at war. It needed a warrior king to defend it, and Edmund's arrival this morning with a small army had dashed her son's futile hope.

She had done what she could to prepare her son for his father's passing and also for what Edmund—King Edmund—would expect of him in the days to come. But Edward's bitterness and disappointment were there on his face for all the world to see. There would be trouble between the brothers, she feared, in the days ahead.

Once Edmund took the throne, Edward's fate, all their fates, would be in his hands. And as she studied Edmund's stern expression, all the questions that had been spooling through her mind for months surfaced again, and her folded hands tightened with anxiety. Could she persuade him to allow her to remain at court as dowager queen, or would he force her to retire to a convent, the fate of so many widowed queens before her? What would happen to her sons? Might Edmund send them across the Narrow Sea to her brother, and her with them? Richard, she did not doubt, would swiftly arrange a second marriage for her; one that would be to his advantage and without any regard for her wishes.

As she pondered such dismal prospects, the king opened his eyes, and his face convulsed with terror as he gazed at some vision that only he could see. She gently touched his shoulder but, as so often in the past, it did not ease him. How many times had she seen him stare like this in horror at empty space? What did he see that so frightened him, even now, at the end of his days?

His mouth formed voiceless words, and he lifted a clawlike hand as if to push something away—a futile effort. Almost immediately his hand fell to the bed, and his ragged breathing halted. It did not begin again.

Two days later Emma walked, straight-backed and dry-eyed, behind Æthelred's coffin as it was carried from the palace to the minster of St. Paul's. Four royal children—Edmund, Edyth, Edward, and Alfred—trailed in her footsteps. A vast crowd lined the streets to pay silent homage to the dead king, most of them having known no other ruler. It had been thirty-seven years, Emma reflected, since Æthelred had been crowned following the murder of his half-brother, King Edward. Then, swiftly, she pushed the thought of murdered royal half-brothers from her mind lest the very thought summon a similar disaster.

Inside the great stone church, amid billows of fragrant incense and the mournful chanting of the office of the dead, Æthelred's soul was committed to God. Emma, relieved that the long death watch was over, could not grieve for the husband and king who had inspired neither her love nor her respect. He had suffered from a darkness of soul that seemed to consume him, and she could only pray that in death he had found release from the shadows that had both tormented and goaded him.

On the following day, the same throng of prelates and nobles who had gathered to mourn the old king met again to acclaim Edmund his successor and, as Emma had foreseen, not a single voice was raised against him. Edmund's wife, Aldyth, in seclusion as she awaited the birth of her child, did not witness the coronation that swiftly followed. Emma, though, stood with Alfred's hand clutched in hers as Archbishop Lyfing anointed the new king. Placing the crown upon Edmund's bowed head the archbishop prayed, in a voice that carried throughout the great church, "May God make you victorious and a conqueror over your enemies! May he grant you peace in your days."

The congregation erupted in wild cheers, but Emma felt her throat constrict with fear for Edmund. His enemies—England's enemies—would soon learn that Æthelred was dead. They would count that a victory, and they would redouble their efforts against the English. She did not think it likely that Edmund or his people would see peace any time soon. Nor did the young king seem to harbor any illusions about what lay ahead. Beneath the old king's scarlet, ermine-lined cloak Edmund wore a burney of gleaming chain mail. Unlike his father, Edmund would be a warrior king. Standing erect before the altar, and looking out at the nobles who were preparing to kneel before him and offer oaths of loyalty, his expression was one of fierce determination. He knew what challenges lay before him, and he was not afraid. Emma, watching, recalled another oath-taking a dozen years before this. She had been heavily pregnant with Edward, and Æthelred had ordered his thegns to swear allegiance to her unborn child. His action that day had set his elder sons against her child, torn his kingdom and his family apart, and ensured that her son would be raised with false assurances that one day he would rule England. Today, though, Edward would be among the first to bend the knee to his half-brother, the king.

Her son made his pledge with a ringing, confident voice, but Emma saw the thunderous expression on his face, and surely Edmund saw it, too. She did not doubt that the new king must count his half-brother as one of the enemies that he must overcome, and her heart quailed at what that might portend.

The long line of nobles who bent the knee to their new sovereign had come from every town and estate within a day's ride of London. Thorkell the Dane, Emma noted, was not among them. She had seen nothing of him since Edmund had arrived in the city. Where was he? His absence gnawed at her, another worry among the many that beset her.

Finally, when the day had drawn to a close and she had retired to her chamber, she received a summons to wait upon the newly crowned king. Once again, she donned the sober robes of a widowed queen and, anxious about what role, if any, she was to play at Edmund's court, she followed the torch bearer toward the king's apartments.

The door was shut and flanked by two hearth guards, but as Emma approached, Edyth emerged from the chamber, stony-faced, her lips set in a thin, angry line.

Alarmed, Emma stopped her. "What has happened?"

"I am ordered to leave the city," Edyth said, her hoarse whisper strident with rage. "My brother, it seems, means to rule both his kingdom and his family with an iron fist."

She wrenched her arm from Emma's grasp and stalked away. Watching her go, Emma felt her pulse quicken. If Edmund treated his sister so harshly, what lay in store for his half-brothers or for a stepmother that he had mistrusted for more than a decade? Preparing herself for evil tidings, she strode into the king's chamber.

Edmund stood alone in the center of the room. Behind him the door to an adjoining chamber stood ajar. If she chose to look there, she would see the bed where she had sometimes slept beside the king; where Æthelred had taken his final breath. Purposely she kept her eyes averted from it. It was not Æthelred, though, who filled her thoughts at this moment. It was Athelstan. He should have been the young king facing her here tonight—would have been if God had not been so cruel. And as she reached for him in memory, she could hear his voice from long ago, telling her what she must do.

Far better to look toward the future, Emma, whatever it may bring, than to dwell on the unhappy past that you cannot change.

Bearing his words in mind, she made her obeisance to Edmund, and as she studied him, waiting for him to speak, she steeled herself to confront whatever fate he'd set for her.

He had traded the armor and ceremonial coronation cloak for a tunic of black wool, trimmed and belted with silver. The rough beard that was the badge of every warrior on campaign had been scraped away that morning for the coronation, and now a dark shadow marked the end of a long and trying day. Her stepson looked older than his twenty-seven winters—a change that seemed to have taken place overnight.

He glanced at her, then escorted her to where two chairs faced each other at the far end of the chamber.

"Sit."

The curt command added to her unease, but she obeyed. When she looked up at him she found that his grim expression had softened somewhat, although not enough to ease her apprehension even a little.

"I am sorry," he said. "I have had disastrous news from the north and there is no gentle way to break it to you." He sat down heavily and drew a long breath. "Uhtred is dead, and a great many of his thegns with him—slain on the orders of Cnut."

Stricken, Emma's thoughts flew north, to Uhtred's wife.

"Dear God," she whispered. "What of your sister Ælfa? Is she safe?"

"It was Ælfa who sent me the news. She and her daughter have taken refuge in the fortress at Bamburgh. She has asked that Edyth be allowed to join her in Northumbria, and I have agreed to it. Edyth and her daughter will travel with Archbishop Wulfstan's retinue when he returns to Jorvik. It will be a difficult journey, but I doubt they will be in much danger from the Danes. After all," he said bitterly, "Edyth's husband is Cnut's ally."

Edyth, though, did not wish to go. Even with her father dead and her husband branded a traitor, Edmund's sister was eager to remain close to the seat of power. For now, that was London. No wonder she was angry at being sent away.

"Where is Eadric?" Emma asked. "Do you know?"

"Not for a certainty," Edmund replied, massaging his forehead.

It was a gesture that reminded her of his father, but there was little else about Edmund that was reminiscent of the old king. Edmund was taller and broader, and he was the only English royal who was dark instead of Saxon fair. She did not yet know if he was as ruthless as Æthelred, but she suspected that if he was not so now, he must become so before long. Kings, her brother had once warned her, must be ruthless to survive. She hoped that Edmund would not be as heartless as Æthelred—would not govern, as Edyth had claimed, with an iron fist.

"I believe," Edmund continued, "that Eadric is with the Danish fleet, which is now somewhere off the Wessex coast. Cnut has to keep moving in order to feed his army. It is impossible to know where he will go, and I cannot remain here to wait for news of him."

She was not surprised that he intended to leave the city. Edmund would not cower inside London's walls as his father had.

"Where will you go?" she asked.

"Into the west, to Berkshire, Wiltshire, and beyond," he said, "to persuade the nobles of the western shires to give me their support now that my father is gone. Archbishop Lyfing will ride with me to add his voice to mine. I need all of Wessex behind me, not just London. I have to raise a force large enough to challenge Cnut's army." His expression grew thoughtful and his gaze drifted away from her face. "It sickens me to say it," he murmured, "but Uhtred's murder may be to my advantage. It will help me convince the western lords that Cnut cannot be trusted to keep any promises he may have made to them when they submitted to him last fall. Arguments and threats may not be enough, though. I may have to use force, and I do not know how long it is likely to take."

"Or what Cnut will do in the meantime," she murmured, and in her mind she saw again the tall warrior with watchful black eyes and a penetrating gaze approaching her across the deck of the *Wind Rider*. She tried to imagine where she would go if she were at the head of a fleet in search of food. The bay at Sandwich seemed the most likely haven, or the Thames estuary. Or...She felt cold suddenly, in spite of her heavy gown. She said, "He will strike here. Edmund! He will attack London!"

"We cannot be certain of that, but yes, he may. Uhtred's death has given him Northumbria, and Eadric has handed him much of Mercia; he must take Wessex next, and London is the key to it."

If he was attempting to reassure her, he was failing dismally.

"But if you are not here to lead the defense—"

"London has never fallen," he said, "not while there has been a king within its walls. As I have said, I must go west, but I need a royal presence to hold the city against the Danes. Edyth will journey north, not just because Ælfa has asked for her, but because Eadric has ever had too strong a hold over her, and I cannot trust her." He drew a breath. "My wife will remain here, of course, but she is in childbed and even if she were not, the Londoners do not know and trust Aldyth." He leaned toward her, resting his elbows on his knees and folding his hands beneath his chin. "But they trust you. That is why, my lady, you must make a decision." His eyes pinned hers. "If you wish to leave the city— to leave England even and take your sons with you—I will not stop you. But I would ask you to remain in London and hold the city for me." He paused, drawing a long breath. "I intend to drive Cnut out or destroy him, but if I fail and England falls to the Danes, the lives of your sons will be at risk. So think very carefully before you give me your answer."

She met Edmund's steady gaze, but her thoughts were on her sons. Three years before, when London had been threatened, she had pleaded with the king to send her children away. But she had known then where the threat was. Today she knew only that there was a Danish fleet somewhere between here and the safety of Normandy's ports, and that her children's lives would be forfeit if they fell into Danish hands.

What was the greater risk—to remain in London or to attempt to flee to Rouen?

And, in the end, where would be the greater reward? In Normandy her sons would have to look to their uncle for support that he might not be willing to give. In England, they were the brothers of the king.

She had once feared that Edmund was her sons' greatest enemy. Now she saw him as their only hope and hers as well. But she needed some assurance that when this was over, he would provide for them.

"When you have defeated Cnut," she said, "what will happen to my sons?"

Edmund sat back in his chair, and folding his arms he raised one speculative brow. But surely, she thought, he must have known that she would ask for some pledge of future reward.

"They will have places at court, and properties to maintain their status," he said, "but only if I am convinced of their loyalty to me."

Loyalty, she thought, was the one thing his father could never depend upon. Yet it was what a king had to demand, or coerce, from those he ruled, especially his kin. Alfred was only four winters old and still too young to be aware of any of this; but she would have to make certain that Edward understood what he owed his new king.

She said, "Then I will do all that you ask of me; and I will instruct my sons to do so, as well. But I am no shield maiden, Edmund. I cannot lead men into battle."

"That is not what I am asking. Godwin will head the garrison here, and he is an able commander. But you are no stranger to the needs of a city under siege. You have tended the wounded. You have managed supplies when the city was under attack and you have counseled the city leaders in meeting the needs of those seeking refuge here. You can be a symbol of English defiance that people can look to for hope. That is what I need from you."

This time she did not hesitate.

"You shall have it, lord king."

He gave a brusque nod and stood up. "I shall meet with the witan tomorrow; as dowager queen you have a place in that assembly. I will expect you and Edward to attend. In two days' time I shall ride west with my hearth men. London will be in your hands."

She was, she realized, being dismissed. But as she, too, rose to her feet she remembered the long line of men who had sworn fealty to him today, and the one man who had not been there.

"Will Thorkell and his men go west with you, or remain here to guard the river?"

"Neither. I know that you trust him, Emma, but I do not. Now that my father is dead, I am concerned that Thorkell will do just as Eadric did and offer Cnut his ships and—"

"Cnut and Thorkell are enemies!" she protested. "If they should meet, they will try to kill each other!"

"Then I hope that they do meet! The fewer Danes left alive in England the better!" He strode to a table that was littered with scrolls and wax tablets. "Thorkell has been banished," he said over his shoulder. "He sailed this morning, and all his men with him."

Stunned, she could only stare at his back in silence for a few thudding heartbeats. But the deed was done, and she could do nothing to change it.

She lay awake long into the night, recalling events that had taken place, years before, inside the walls of All Hallows Church. Thorkell had pledged himself to her protection and to the protection of her children. Now Edmund had sent him away. He had deprived her, and London, of a fierce warlord and an ally who would have helped safeguard the city; in Thorkell's absence, the risk that she was taking by remaining in London might prove even greater than she had feared.

Chapter Thirty-Seven

May 1016
Isle of Sheppey, Kent

Cnut's camp on the Isle of Sheppey bordered the River Swale, and although the nearby inhabitants had fled when the Danish fleet made landfall, the shepherds had not been able to save their flocks from the ravenous viking army. As Cnut strode purposefully through the encampment past cook fires where mutton was roasting on makeshift spits, he reflected that tonight, at least, his men would sleep with their bellies full.

One of his huscarles, approaching from the river, fell in beside him and announced, "A longship has entered the Swale, my lord. Arnor's, by the look of it, back from his mission to Roskilde."

Cnut frowned. "Only one ship?" he asked.

"Only one, my lord. She's riding low in the water, though; full of supplies, I'll wager."

Already tense and distracted, and now disappointed as well, Cnut merely grunted. Supplies were welcome, but what he needed, and what his urgent message to his brother had asked for, was more men. He'd left a good-sized force with Eirik at Jorvik to quell any trouble in the north. But now that Æthelred was dead, London was vulnerable, and he would need all the men that he could get if he was to take the city.

"Send Arnor to me as soon as he lands," he ordered, and turned his mind to the more immediate problem that was waiting for him in his quarters.

He nodded to the guard posted at his tent and ducked inside. Thorkell, hands bound and mouth gagged, knelt on the ground between two guards.

The big Dane had been his prisoner for three days while he tried to make up his mind what to do with him. Now they would talk—negotiate, he hoped—although this meeting could just as easily turn ugly. Thorkell had been his father's ally and his own; had taught him, even more than Swein had, the warriors' way. But that was long in the past. There was bad blood between them now and broken trust that needed mending, if that was at all possible.

"Get him to his feet," he ordered.

His huscarles obeyed, and Cnut took a long look at his old ally. Thorkell had changed only a little in the five years since last they met. The long tail of hair that swung from the back of his shaved scalp was now streaked with grey. His silver arm rings had been replaced with gold, and there was a large, golden cross hanging from a chain around his neck—marks of favor, Cnut supposed, from the English king. But Thorkell's face was still swarthy, and the ugly scar on one cheek just as livid. He'd suffered some blows when his ship was boarded, and one of his eyes was swollen shut. The other fixed balefully on him.

The big man looked hale enough, though, despite his fifty-odd winters—and angrier than a wounded boar.

"Put him there," Cnut said, gesturing toward one of the chests scattered about the tent. "Remove the gag and free his hands. Then wait outside."

"Lord?" one of the guards asked, and both of them looked at him, hesitating.

"There is no danger," he assured them, although he was far from certain of that. "We are old friends," he said wryly, "Thorkell and I."

His men were right to question his wisdom in releasing the big man's bonds. Thorkell had sworn to murder him, and even unarmed Thorkell was dangerous. He needed nothing but his hands to kill.

It was a risk he had to take, though, if he wished to gain Thorkell's trust.

When it was just the two of them, he watched warily for some threatening move. But Thorkell merely glared evilly at him with his one good eye and snarled, "It's taken you long enough to decide to treat with me."

Cnut smiled as he reached for a flagon that stood on a nearby coffer.

"You were spitting fire when they brought you in," he said. "I thought it wise to wait until you were in a better temper."

He filled two cups with ale and offered one to Thorkell, taking care to keep himself out of the man's lethal reach.

"I thought you wanted me dead," Thorkell growled. "I wasn't going to make it easy for you." He accepted the cup and sniffed it suspiciously.

"It's not poisoned," Cnut said, and took a long swallow from his own cup. "As I recall," he added, wiping his mouth with the back of his hand, "you were the one who swore vengeance, not me." He studied Thorkell's angry, resentful face. There was a wound festering between them, and before they could come to any kind of understanding, it had to be lanced. "You seemed to think that I ordered the murder of your brother. I didn't."

Thorkell's mouth twisted into a sneer.

"You would say that, whether it was true or not." He lifted his cup to his lips, his black gaze still fixed on Cnut as he drank.

Cnut had no way of proving the truth of his claim; it had all happened years ago. The mysterious death of Thorkell's brother had led to this pointless enmity between them; it had driven Thorkell into the arms of the English and had delayed Swein's conquest of England, and now his own, by years.

In all the time that they had been enemies, though, there had been no opportunity to meet with his old ally to try to convince him that he had played no part in Hemming's death. Now that the English had cast Thorkell out, the opportunity was here. The man was his prisoner and had to listen to him—which was not the same thing as believing him.

Nevertheless, Cnut searched his mind for some way to cross the vast divide of mistrust that lay between them. He had nothing to offer, it seemed, except the simple truth.

Slowly, emphatically, he said, "I had nothing to do with Hemming's death. I was sworn to him as I was sworn to you. And like you, Thorkell, I am a man who honors my pledges."

Thorkell remained stubbornly silent, his glowering expression unchanged. The wound, it seemed, needed further probing.

"Why would I want to kill your brother?" Cnut persisted. "I had nothing to avenge and I gained neither honor, nor advantage, nor profit from his death." He looked into his cup, then squinted at Thorkell.

"You profited, though. You confiscated all the English geld that should have been shared among the three of us, and you have been eating out of Æthelred's hand ever since." He gestured with his cup to the golden rings on Thorkell's thick, bare arms. "You do not look any the worse for it."

Thorkell's lip curled in disgust.

"Do you really think that I would kill my own brother? For gold?"

"No. I do not. Nor do I think that you would have bent the knee to the English king unless you believed, however mistakenly," he insisted, "that I had betrayed you by ordering Hemming's murder." Cnut slammed down his cup and, disregarding the danger, went up to Thorkell and grasped the cross hanging at the big man's breast. "I swear, by the Christian God and by whatever pagan deities you still honor, that your brother's death was none of my doing. Nor do I know who it was that killed him."

He thrust the cross back at Thorkell. It was all of it true. There were some, like his shipmaster Arnor, who had pointed the finger for Hemming's death at Alric; but those rumors had faded long ago, and Alric had demonstrated his worth and his loyalty many times over.

No. He did not know how Hemming had died. And if Alric had had a hand in it, he did not want to know.

Thorkell made no reply, and for a few moments they glared at each other while the silence between them lengthened. Cnut waited, tense, but patient. He could guess what was in Thorkell's mind. His paymaster, Æthelred, was dead, and the son who had taken the old king's place on the throne had dismissed Thorkell, his ships, and the warriors in them. Maybe this King Edmund could no longer pay them; maybe he did not trust them; maybe he was simply a fool. But Thorkell's shipmen were hungry for battle and for silver, and they knew that Cnut needed men. Thorkell knew it, too, and the canny old warlord was certainly no fool.

Was that enough to persuade him to abandon his quest for vengeance? By God, he hoped so. If it wasn't, he did not relish the choice that he would have to make. Release Thorkell, and he would be watching his back for the rest of his life; kill Thorkell, and he would have to kill all of Thorkell's shipmen, too. And Thorkell, damn him, knew it as well as he did.

At last Thorkell drew in a heavy breath and, slowly releasing it, he stared into his empty cup. He said, "My brother was weak, heedless of everything except his lust for drink and women and silver. He was a man who was not easy to like or to trust, and I'll not deny that he had enemies. More than a few." He looked up, his face working with some emotion. "So," he paused for emphasis, "I am willing to accept your oath that you did not kill Hemming, Cnut. Even so, there is another matter that lies uneasy between us."

Cnut raised a brow. "Go on."

"For three years now I have served the English," Thorkell said heavily. "I fought at Æthelred's side when he drove you from Gainsborough." Cnut felt Thorkell's one good eye bore through him like steel. "If you are not going to kill me for that, then tell me why not, and what it is that you want."

It was the opening that Cnut had been waiting for, and he felt his tension ease. He reached for the jug and refilled both their cups.

"I am told," he said, "that Æthelred's son has banished you from England—that you owe him no allegiance. Is that the way of it?"

Thorkell, in the act of raising his cup to his lips, hesitated for an instant. Then he tossed back a mouthful of ale before he replied.

"It is." His voice was firm, but he did not meet Cnut's gaze.

He was hiding something, Cnut thought, uneasy again. What was he missing here?

Suspicious now, he ventured, "Then there is nothing, I take it, to prevent you from supporting my claim to England's throne? For you must know that is what I want—not just your men, but your mind. You know the English and how to outwit them."

Thorkell pursed his mouth, and there was a calculating glint in his one good eye.

"In return for what?"

"Plunder for your men," Cnut offered. "Lands and titles for you. Once I have conquered this kingdom, I will need capable men to help me rule it."

Thorkell grunted. "It will take more than wits, Cnut, to conquer England. You may think that you have brought these people to their knees, but I warn you, this war has only just begun. The Londoners will oppose you, just as they did your father. King Edmund will defy you, and because he is nothing like the old king, the English will rally behind him."

Cnut said drily, "They have not rallied behind him as yet. Eirik holds Northumbria, and Eadric has handed me Mercia. The men of the west have—"

"None of that matters, now that Æthelred is dead," Thorkell said. "Edmund wears the crown, and he is the warrior that his father never was. That changes everything. Wessex will resist you, and the Northerners will soon be having second thoughts. As for Eadric, he's a lying bastard. His allegiance will shift depending on which way the wind blows."

Cnut eyed him narrowly.

"Are you saying that you will not join me?"

"I am saying that you will face challenges far greater than you suppose. If I am to pledge myself to you, then the reward must be more than the mere promise of titles and lands."

"And that would be—what?" Cnut kept his voice casual to hide his unease. How much silver was Thorkell going to demand?

The old warlord looked into his cup, then, smiling, lifted his eyes to Cnut's. "I want Æthelred's widow. And I want her sons. For safekeeping."

Cnut stared at him, trying to work out the meaning behind the words. For safekeeping? To hold them for ransom, more likely. The widowed Emma and her sons would fetch a vast price from the Norman duke who would likely pay any amount to reclaim his royal kin.

"And you would keep them safe—how?" he ventured. "By turning them over to Duke Richard in return for their weight in gold? You have a high opinion of your worth, Thorkell," he scoffed. "Why should I hand them to you when I could offer them to Richard myself?"

Thorkell shrugged. "Give me your oath that you *will* deliver them to Richard, and I will be content with that."

Cnut continued to gaze at the big man. There was something here that he did not yet understand, but Thorkell's expression was as impenetrable as stone.

"Why?" he asked. "What concern are they of yours?"

Thorkell did not answer at once, and Cnut wondered if he was weighing how much he wished to reveal.

Finally, Thorkell said, "It is not Edmund who holds my pledge. It is the queen. I swore that I would protect that lady and her children." He raised his cup in a salute. "As you have said, I am a man who honors my oaths."

Cnut exhaled a long breath. So that was what Thorkell had been hiding—a vow that he had made to the English queen. Considering his own dealings with the lady, it did not surprise him that she had been able to wring such an oath from a Danish warlord.

"So it is not their ransom payment that you are bargaining for," he said, turning the idea over in his mind, "but their very lives." He frowned, examining the possible consequences if he should agree to what Thorkell asked. "Her children are Æthelred's sons—"

"And they are too young to be a threat to you unless you harm them in some way. Do that," Thorkell's tone was ominous, "and you would be condemned in every church throughout the kingdom. The English would hate you even more than they do now, and you would make a dangerous enemy of the Norman duke."

It was a shrewd assessment, Cnut thought. It was not in his best interests to harm the children of the queen. In any case it was Æthelred's eldest son, this warrior king, who was the real threat. War, though, was a dangerous business, especially for those too young to defend themselves.

"I am preparing to lay siege to London," he said. "You know what happens when food grows scarce. People sicken and die—children sooner than anyone else. If the sons of the queen are in that city, I cannot guarantee their survival or their safety. Neither can you."

Thorkell nodded, his fingers stroking his beard. "But let us suppose," he said slowly, "that they should, by chance, fall into our hands. What then?"

Cnut fixed him with a hard look. Thorkell never left anything to chance.

"You mean," he said, "if you should contrive to get hold of them." And suddenly everything fell into place, and he understood the game that Thorkell had been playing since he sailed from London. "You cunning bastard! You purposely set your ships on a course that would get you captured and hauled before me so that you could bargain for the queen and her sons!"

Thorkell shrugged. "I might have planned it differently had I known you would keep me chained up for three stinking days." He peered at Cnut over his raised cup. "I will not abandon the queen, Cnut. If you want my ships and my men, you must grant what I ask."

Cnut was silent, thinking it over, remembering the slender girl with bright hair and flashing eyes who had once felled him with a stone; the formidable woman who had bargained with him for the lives of her people and for a ship filled with treasure. England's widowed queen was a force to be reckoned with, and far too valuable to entrust to anyone else.

"If the children should fall into our hands," he said slowly, "they will be given into your care. I swear that I will not harm them, nor do I wish to have their deaths upon my soul. But I shall be the one to determine where they live and how they live. That is the best that I can offer you."

Thorkell gazed at him for a spell, and Cnut could see him weighing the offer, considering whether it was enough to redeem the pledge he had made to the queen. At last Thorkell gave a brief nod.

"Agreed," Thorkell said. "What about the lady?"

"The lady shall be my concern alone." He met Thorkell's doubtful gaze with his own cold stare, and when Thorkell did not reply he continued, "Like every other woman in the kingdom, Æthelred's widow will be a prize of war, although a very great prize. Once I have taken London, I will need every advantage in order to secure my claim to the crown; she may have a part to play."

Thorkell grunted what Cnut hoped was acquiescence.

"And how will you take London?" Thorkell asked. "You spoke of a siege, but you cannot surround the city unless you get your ships past the bridge. Will you do as Olaf did, and pull it down?"

"I am not that reckless," Cnut began, but he was interrupted when Arnor stepped into the tent.

"My lord," Arnor called.

Here at last was news from Denmark that he was eager to hear. Cnut set down his ale cup and in a few strides he was beside Arnor.

"Will my brother send more ships?" he inquired softly.

"No, my lord," Arnor whispered. "King Harald regrets that even if he had ships, he cannot spare the men to crew them. He says that you must make do with the force that you already have."

Cnut muttered a quiet curse, although the answer did not surprise him. It meant, though, that Thorkell's four hundred jomsvikings had just become even more valuable to him than before.

"Tell your men to get some rest," he ordered Arnor. "Tomorrow we strike camp and sail toward London."

Swiftly he returned to Thorkell, and sitting opposite him he said, "So, my lord, I would have your answer. Will you join me in my bid for the English throne?"

Thorkell downed the last of his ale and held his cup out for more.

"I will," he said gravely. "Now, tell me how you will force London to submit."

Cnut refilled both their cups and, with more than a little relief, saluted his new ally.

"With shovels, my friend," he said, and smiled. "We are going to dig our way around London."

Chapter Thirty-Eight

June - August 1016
London

*I*t took the Danes three weeks to shape the noose that they would use to strangle London. Emma marked their progress every evening at nightfall from atop the city walls or from one of the towers that rose beside each of the city gates. She saw them drag their vessels through the canal that they had cut around the southern end of the bridge; she watched as they landed on the Thames' northern shore and began once more to dig.

The Londoners did what they could to stop them. Archers manned the walls day and night targeting anyone who stepped outside the canopy of shields that protected that vast labor force—some of them Danes, but many of them English captives forced to sling shovels full of mud. The defenders' efforts, though, merely delayed the inevitable.

"One has to admire Cnut's determination," Godwin grimly observed to Emma one evening. They were standing inside one of the Ludgate's towers, and they could easily survey the ditch and the lengthening, defensive mound of dirt in front of it.

"He is more than determined," Emma murmured, forced to admit to a grudging admiration for Swein's son even as she hated and feared him. "He is clever and he is bold. Let us pray that, for us, it does not prove a deadly combination."

When the Danes completed their trench, it surrounded the entire city. All the landward approaches to London were sealed while on the broad breast of the Thames the only things that moved were the dragon ships of the enemy. Nothing could get in or out of the city—not people, not food, not goods, not even rumor.

In mid-June, forty of those enemy ships sailed west, toward Berkshire. Emma wondered anxiously if Cnut had discovered where Edmund had gone and had resolved to capture or kill him. As no English scouts could get inside the city, though, she had no way of discerning Cnut's purpose or of tracking the movement of his ships. The lack of any news drove her to near distraction.

The Danes, meanwhile, used their ditch to scuttle like rats around London's wall, unseen and unchecked, so that the city garrison never knew where to look for the next assault.

And the assaults came almost daily.

Attackers and defenders alike died, and London was given no respite. Yet despite their travail, the Londoners' dogged resistance remained strong. Thrice the Danes sent messengers offering to lift the siege in return for London's surrender. Thrice Godwin waited the full three days they were given to consider the offers before he rejected them, roundly cursing at the Danes while his garrison jeered from where they watched atop the walls.

Emma met with Godwin daily to assess conditions in the city, and he was often accompanied by Edward and Robert when they weren't at their lessons or at arms practice. Her son and his companion were not yet twelve, too young to be posted upon the walls. But at Emma's suggestion they spent many hours shadowing Godwin, so that they knew as much about London's defenses as she did—perhaps more.

As the weeks passed, as the number of dead and wounded grew, and as supplies of grain dwindled Emma became more and more anxious. How long, she wondered, did they have until they would be forced to accept the Danish demand for the city's surrender?

One evening in early July when the long summer twilight was fading into darkness, the longships that had sailed west three weeks earlier returned. Emma was in the queen's apartments with Aldyth when a messenger brought the news. Aldyth's infant son, barely two months old, lay sleeping in his mother's arms, and Alfred sat on the floor at Emma's feet, absorbed by a growing tower of wooden blocks. The women of the household were busy with their weaving or their sewing, and when the messenger reported the return of the ships the women exchanged anxious glances.

They are afraid of what this means, Emma thought. If the Danes have won some victory in the west, it will shatter any hope that the siege might soon be lifted. And hope is all that we have.

Alfred abandoned his blocks to climb into her lap, and as she brushed her fingers through her son's bright hair, she offered Aldyth a reassuring smile.

"Tomorrow, perhaps, there will be some sign of the king," she said.

Aldyth pressed her mouth into a thin line, and the eyes that met Emma's were dark with despair. "You say that every night, my lady," she whispered. "But how much longer can London continue to resist?"

Emma clasped Alfred close while she gazed solemnly at the infant in Aldyth's arms. If London should fall into Danish hands, every royal son would be slaughtered. She lifted her eyes to meet Aldyth's, and aware of the others who listened she said, "You know the answer to that already. We shall hold out until Edmund comes. However long it takes."

Later that night when she met with Godwin, she hoped he might have learned something about the return of the longships, but his first words surprised her.

"The Danes have requested another parley, my lady," he said urgently, "midday tomorrow, outside the Aldersgate at St. Botolph's Church."

"It has been only three days since we refused their last offer." Emma observed. "I wonder what they are up to."

"If the Danes are so eager to meet with us again, they will either tell us something that we are not going to like, or they will have devised some trick to persuade us to open our gates."

She nodded. "Then we must listen carefully to what they have to say, and accept nothing as fact that cannot be proved. This surely has to do with the return of those dragon ships." She could see from the set of Godwin's mouth that he thought so, too, and that he was worried—even more so than usual. "I will attend this parley," she said decisively. "The bishop should be there, too, and some of the city magnates. You decide who." She frowned. "It seems to me unwise, though, to venture outside the walls to meet with them. Is the Danish messenger awaiting your reply?"

"He waits at the Ludgate."

"Tell him that we agree to the parley, but not in the church. My council will gather inside the Aldersgate tower and listen to what the

Danes have to say from there. We shall let our enemies stand outside the city gate and endure the midsummer sun."

Godwin nodded and asked, "Do you want Edward there?"

She hesitated. Edward was convinced that her friendship with Thorkell the Dane was the root cause of this war and held it against her. If she were forced to negotiate with the Danish leaders—placate them perhaps—her son would misinterpret anything she said.

And there was an even stronger argument for keeping Edward away from the parley.

"I'll not parade Æthelred's son before our enemies. He would be too tempting a target."

When she was alone, Emma paced the floor, her mind in turmoil. She tried to face the worst that might happen—that King Edmund was dead or captured and that the battle for England was lost. She could not bring herself to believe it, though. She could not accept that God would so forsake the English.

The next day, when the summer sun was at its highest point in the sky, Emma stood with her advisors in one of the twin towers of the Aldersgate. She peered down at the six mail-clad horsemen ranged below and recognized Eadric at their head. He was squinting up at the tower and the walls, obviously uneasy.

He must fear some treachery, she thought; no doubt because he would not be above treachery himself.

Looking past him she found Thorkell, and her heart gave a lurch of dismay.

For three years she had trusted Thorkell; had defended him to any who doubted his loyalty to the king; had feared for his life if he should fall into Cnut's hands. Now, the man who had once sworn that he would protect her children from harm had thrown in his lot with the Danes.

What had Cnut said or done, she wondered, to appease Thorkell and win his trust again?

Swiftly, though, she pushed that question from her mind. The trouble at hand was enough for now. She searched the faces below again, this time for one man in particular. She did not find him.

"Cnut is not with them," she whispered to Godwin, who was to speak for the Londoners.

Apparently it was Eadric who was to treat with Cnut's English foes today. And that was a clever move, Emma thought, because Eadric was a master of persuasion. He could make even the most blatant lie sound like truth sprung from the mouth of God.

"Where is Cnut?" Godwin called out to the clutch of riders below. "Must we always speak with men who are mere underlings?"

Eadric shrugged. "You have yourself to blame for that, Lord Godwin. Your demand that we attend you in the open while you cower within your stone tower struck me as, forgive me, somewhat suspicious. I urged my lord to remain in our camp lest your bowmen on the walls prove ignorant of the customs of parley and loose their shafts at us. The bearer of bad news is never welcome."

"We are well aware of the customs of parley," Godwin called down to him, "although it seems that Cnut does not always honor them. We have heard how Uhtred was butchered at Wiheal," he sneered, then he asked abruptly, "What is your news?"

Eadric's gaze encompassed everyone looking down at him from the tower. "There has been a battle at Sherston, in Wiltshire," he called. "Edmund's force was soundly beaten, and whatever hope you may have that your king will relieve this city, you must abandon it."

Cruel tidings, Emma thought, if Eadric spoke the truth. She flicked a glance at Thorkell, looking for confirmation. His eyes met hers, and his expression was solemn, like a man burdened with a task he did not relish.

It was just one battle, she told herself. They could not abandon hope because of a single engagement! Nevertheless, she held her breath and her heartbeat quickened as Eadric spoke again.

"I urge you, my lords, not to prolong the misery of your people, for it will avail you nothing! There is no king in England now but Cnut, for Edmund, son of Æthelred, is dead!"

Even as the terrible words sounded in her ears, Emma saw Thorkell's head jerk toward Eadric, his expression one of shock, quickly followed by fury.

Eadric, she realized, was lying! Thorkell could not have made it any plainer if he'd shouted it. Whatever had happened at Sherston, Edmund was alive. She was as sure of it as she was of her own existence.

There were moans of despair from the men around her, though, telling her that she was alone in her conviction. Even Godwin had swallowed the lie, for all the blood had drained from his face and he appeared incapable of speech.

Trembling with anger she stepped forward a pace to command Eadric's attention.

"What proof can you give us, Lord Eadric," she called to him, "that what you say is true?"

He acknowledged her with a slow nod. "My lady," he said. He heaved a sigh like a man struggling to control his grief. "I have no proof, other than what I witnessed with my own eyes. I give you my oath as an ealdorman of England that I saw King Edmund fall and that I saw him carried from the field when the English fled."

Emma slid a glance at Thorkell. He was still glaring at Eadric, his mouth set in a grimace of disgust.

Another lie, then. Would the men around her see it? Would they recognize this as nothing more than a ploy to convince them to surrender the city?

No, they would not. They would be remembering that Eadric was Edmund's brother-in-law, and that he had long been the trusted councilor of King Æthelred. He appeared to them to be as grief-stricken by Edmund's death as they were, and he had gilded his lie with an oath. Why should they doubt him?

She bit her lip, restraining the rage that was boiling inside her because now was not the time to challenge him. She must wait until all the council was together; until Eadric could not dispute her with more lies.

Now Godwin stirred, and when he spoke his voice was as cold and brittle as ice.

"You have brought us grievous news, my lord. You will forgive us if we do not thank you for it."

"I take no pleasure in delivering such evil tidings." Eadric's false compassion made Emma grind her teeth, but she kept silent. "Cnut," he went on, "has charged me with relaying an offer to the people of London, and in particular to you, my lady."

Emma raised a brow at this. Any offer from Cnut would be more to his benefit than hers, and she raised a hand to quell the anxious muttering of her advisors.

"And what would that offer be, Lord Eadric?" she called.

"In return for London's surrender, Cnut guarantees that Æthelred's sons by Queen Emma will be safely escorted to their uncle in

Normandy, and that as long as some other minor conditions are met, no one in the city will be harmed."

Emma's breath caught in her throat. Freedom for her sons! He was dangling before her the one boon she could not possibly refuse. She could feel the men in the tower stirring uneasily, feel their eyes on her as they waited for her response. She wondered what they feared most—that she would reject the offer, or that she would snatch at it.

"Your offer is generous, my lord," she called to Eadric. She would play the game, for a little while. "But I cannot agree to it unless I know what conditions the city must meet."

"Of course!" Eadric called. "We shall require hostages, as well as some token tribute from the city—payment for our trouble and for the loss of so many valiant warriors. My royal lord Cnut, though, wishes to assure the people of London that he holds them in high—"

"How much tribute?" she demanded.

Irritation flashed across Eadric's face at the interruption, but he dispelled it quickly. "Fifteen thousand pounds, my lady."

She heard more whispering around her as the Londoners reacted to this. It was an outrageous sum that would beggar the city if they agreed to it.

"And if we should reject this offer?"

"Then the siege will continue," Eadric said, his voice stern and no longer with any hint of compassion. "Do not expect mercy for any of your people when we breach your walls which, I promise you, we shall do soon enough. With the return of our ships we have near a thousand more men to aid us in that effort."

He gazed up at her with such calm certitude that she was filled with sudden misgiving. What if she was mistaken and everything that he said was true? She was bargaining for the lives of her children, for the city itself and the lives of all the people in it—thousands of them! If she were wrong, men would die on the walls; women and children would die of hunger or disease—all for nothing.

She could not make this decision alone. She needed time and counsel.

"You have given us much to consider, Lord Eadric," she said, "and there are men within the city who must be consulted, as I am sure you know. You will have our answer in three days."

"Alas, my lady," Eadric said, "I fear that King Cnut is impatient. He wants an answer today. You may have three hours to make your decision."

She had hoped to procure a few days of truce, respite from the Danes' assaults upon the city; but it was clear that was not to be. This abrupt refusal to give them more time, though, hinted at an urgency that banished all her doubts. Cnut was not impatient. He was afraid.

"In that case, my lord, we shall detain you no longer," she said. "Our answer is no. I suggest you return to your camp before our bowmen on the walls forget that you have been granted safe passage." Swiftly she turned to the men around her, and heedless of their shocked faces she ordered, "To the great hall. Now."

She watched them file toward the door, throwing anxious, doubtful glances at her even as they obeyed her command. Then she turned to Godwin who was staring at her like one turned to stone.

"Why did you refuse him out of hand?" he demanded.

"Because Eadric lied," she hissed. She described what she had observed and concluded, "You know better than anyone, Godwin, what a monster Eadric is. His lies sent your father to exile and death. He is lying now, I know it; and to place our trust in him would be the greatest folly."

As she spoke, she was relieved to see the despair in his eyes gradually replaced by hope. But she was keenly aware, as he must be, that she had just taken a terrible risk.

In the great hall they found some thirty or so men—prelates, merchants, and thegns—gathered to hear the outcome of the parley. Aldyth was seated among them, and the face she turned toward Emma was pale as bleached linen. She was frightened, Emma suspected, not just for Edmund, but for her son. Emma went to her and whispered, "All will be well."

Placing her hand on Aldyth's shoulder to brace them both she studied the faces of the Londoners on the benches. Some of them trusted her; some of them disliked her. But she was the face of royalty in London for now, and they had to listen to her.

"My lords!" She waited for the murmur of voices to still. "Eadric the traitor wishes to persuade us to surrender the city. To convince us to do so, he would have us believe that Edmund and Cnut fought a battle at Sherston and that King Edmund died there."

She waited as shouts of dismay, protest, and grief filled the hall. Concerned for Aldyth more than anyone, Emma squeezed her shoulder in a silent gesture of reassurance as Godwin slammed his hand upon the table and shouted, "Be quiet, damn you!"

When their voices trailed into silence, Emma told them of Eadric's offer and the conditions linked to it. At first, they merely stared at her, too stunned by the amount of tribute that the Danes were demanding, she guessed, even to give voice to questions.

But the questions would come, and before they could she continued, "We were given little time to consider these terms and so, for good or ill, my lords, I have refused to surrender the city. I do not believe that our king is dead."

In the silence of the great hall her words echoed back to her, as if to mock her.

Our king is dead.

She drew a breath and continued, "I know Eadric well. He is a foul murderer and a liar who betrayed his king and every solemn oath he swore before God. Are we to believe the word of such a man? Are we to believe his new master, Cnut, who promises mercy if we submit to him? He promised mercy to Uhtred, and when Uhtred surrendered he was slain with all his retainers." She paused, studying the faces of the men, allowing them to digest her words. "My lords, these are men we cannot trust. They wish to cozen us, to frighten us with lies, to weaken our will to resist."

Beside her, Godwin pressed both his hands flat on the table and leaned forward to speak.

"Eadric's refusal to give us even a few days to consider the Danish demand tells us that they want a swift end to this siege—an end that will see them inside these city walls. Eadric knows something that we do not; and what he knows, I think, is that our king has raised an army as he promised. If a battle was fought at Sherston it was the English who won it, not the Danes. I stand with the queen. The king is alive and we must hold out until he returns. Be assured though," he warned, "that the Danes will redouble their assaults upon our walls. We will be sorely tested, my lords, and we must stand firm."

"And if Eadric is not lying?" someone asked. "What if there is no relief coming?"

"That is the question that Eadric wants you to ask!" Emma cried. "He seeks to undermine our courage with uncertainty. Eadric is lying. Wipe all doubt of that from your minds. The Danish offer has been refused, and we must continue to resist. Edmund is alive! He will come to our aid. I know it and you must believe it. Have faith!" she cried. "And fight!" She drew a long breath. "And pray, my lords. Above all, we must pray."

The Danes attacked the next day at first light, and the citizens fought them with renewed resolve. London did not fall, and in the days that followed its people never wavered in their defense of the city. Those who could not fight prayed, with Emma often in their midst. Each evening at twilight she visited the tower above the Ludgate to speak with the keen-eyed guards on watch and to search, as they did, for some sign of an army approaching from the west. Invariably she returned to her chamber disappointed and more worried than she had been the evening before.

The siege was in its sixth week when, on a morning shrouded in thick fog, the winding of war horns raked the city as they had so many times before. This time though, it was not the English who raised the alarm, but the Danes. Church bells began to ring one by one all across London, adding their voices to the clamor.

Emma ran from her quarters into the yard and stopped, listening. Archers stationed atop the northern wall that enclosed both the palace and the city had begun to shout and point. And above the sounds of horns and bells and shouting she could hear the clash of steel on steel. Pushing her way through the crowd of frightened household folk, she hastened to the Crepelgate tower, dashed inside, and ran up the narrow, winding stairway to the lookout that gave her a view of the moorland on London's northern border.

Out beyond the great ditch that skirted the outer wall, the blanket of fog swirled and churned with the movements of armed men who struggled against each other in the growing light. For a time she could only discern what seemed to be a maelstrom of men and steel and mist until Edmund's red banner with its golden dragon appeared through the ribbons of fog. She recognized the king at the center of a line of men as it moved slowly forward, driving the Danish line back toward the wall.

Moments later Aldyth was beside her, and Emma reached for her hand as they looked down on the battle that had erupted below them.

"Thank God," Aldyth whispered, her eyes filled with tears. "He is alive!"

Now Emma could see more English warriors emerging from the distant forest that in this light was no more than a dark smudge against the sky. Edmund's army must have spent the night in silence beneath the trees, and they had come to the city's aid—not from the west as had been expected, but from the north.

Before long, the fighting moved further south on both sides of the city, and an unstoppable tide of fierce English warriors forced the Danes to their ships. By mid-morning Cnut's fleet was fleeing into the west, and London's gates were flung wide. Edmund rode into the city at the head of his army on a wave of excitement and fierce joy. When at last he entered the royal precincts and dismounted before the great hall, Emma watched through tears of relief as England's warrior king gathered his wife and new son into his arms.

She did not see the king again until much later that night when she was summoned, along with Godwin and a small council of advisors, to report to him on affairs within the city. Edmund in turn recounted how the men of Wessex had renounced their earlier allegiance to Cnut and proved it by battling against the Danes at Sherston.

"We fought them until it grew too dark to see," he said, "and we would have challenged them again the next day, but the bastards fled to their ships in the night. They left their dead for us to bury along with our own, and by our count there were as many Danish corpses as English." He gazed, frowning, into the middle distance. "If we are ever going to see an end to this," he murmured, "it is Cnut who must die. Strike off the head of the snake and it will not grow another. Without their leader our enemies would scatter like chaff before the wind."

He sat back in his chair and his face was so grey with weariness that Emma's heart ached for him.

"Cnut is sailing west," Edmund continued, "and if he is not stopped his army will ravage Wessex again. I will give my army a day to rest, and then we shall go after him."

Emma wanted to protest that a day was not long enough. Edmund was tired. Surely his men were tired, and many were wounded. They needed time to recover. But he had not asked for counsel, and there was a determined set to his jaw that she had seen often enough on his father's face. Edmund's mind was made up, and any argument would be futile.

His final words before he dismissed them were a warning.

"Cnut wants London," he said. "You have done well to keep him at bay, but do not cease your vigilance. If I do not find and kill that devil, you had best be ready because, I promise you, he will be back."

Heeding his words, in the days that followed Emma worked with Godwin to prepare the city for what she hoped would never happen—the renewal of the siege. She ordered that all food rents from shires bordering the northern bank of the Thames be delivered to London immediately, well in advance of the usual Quarter Day surrender at Michaelmas. London citizens who were too injured or too sick to fight were sent to villages outside the walls, and Godwin gathered men from nearby towns and estates to replace them.

Throughout the summer, though, the Danish army ravaged throughout England. In London, Emma met with messengers who brought news of slaying and burning, first to the south of the Thames in Surrey and Kent, then to the north, where Cnut's army raided deep into Mercia. Always, the messengers assured her, the Danes were shadowed by Edmund as he wielded Offa's Sword at the head of his armies. Yet although the English and the Danes clashed again and again, Edmund could not claim an absolute victory that would drive his enemy from Britain.

A.D. 1016 Then assembled King Edmund all the English nation, and the enemy fled before him into the Isle of Sheppey; and the king slew as many of them as he could overtake... Ealdorman Eadric then returned to the king again at Aylesford; than which no measure could be more ill-advised than this, his acceptance back. The enemy, meanwhile, returned into Essex and advanced into Mercia, destroying all that he overtook.

The Anglo-Saxon Chronicle

Chapter Thirty-Nine

September 1016
London

Emma witnessed with misgiving Edmund's return to London with Eadric in his retinue, and that same night she approached the king to voice a protest against such a dangerous alliance. When she entered the chamber Godwin was already there, heatedly insisting that Eadric was a traitor who should be imprisoned rather than welcomed again to the king's council. Edmund paced the room restlessly, listening to Godwin's arguments with far more patience than she had ever seen his father exhibit. But when Edmund finally raised a hand to stop Godwin's long list of Eadric's offenses, his face was flushed with anger.

"I accepted Eadric's submission because I had no choice! He brought two thousand men with him from Cnut's force that Cnut could not replace! It crippled the Danes, and soon after they crossed the Swale to Sheppey, they boarded their ships! I thought Cnut was beaten and would sail for Denmark! I never expected him to land in Essex and start harrying again!"

"And who prevented you from crossing to Sheppey and attacking Cnut's crippled army?" Godwin persisted. "Who convinced you that Cnut was beaten? Was it Eadric?"

Edmund turned away, sweeping a hand in silent frustration. He made no answer, but his silence was answer enough.

"So you listened to Eadric's counsel," Godwin persisted, "and it proved as false as the man himself! Yet even so you continue to trust him!"

"Do not upbraid me for following his counsel, Godwin, when you were not there to offer counsel of your own!" Edmund cried. "I made the decision to allow the Danes to escape. The fault was mine, and I must live with it."

"Lord king," Emma said quickly, before Godwin could remind Edmund that all of England must live with that unfortunate decision, "there is a graver issue here than false counsel. Eadric betrayed your father. Now he has betrayed Cnut. What is to prevent him from turning against you if it suits him to do so?"

"I know what Eadric is, my lady," Edmund snapped. "But I must work with the tools that God has given me, even those that are hopelessly flawed. If I am to hold this kingdom I need warriors, and as long as vast numbers of Mercians continue to follow Eadric as their lord and war leader, I need him."

Edmund was as furious as Emma had ever seen him, but she suspected that his anger was directed mostly at himself. It seemed to her that his alliance with a man he so despised, however necessary he might still believe it to be, ate at him like a canker.

Several days later she was at the council session when Edmund announced that the Danes were marching along the River Stour toward Cambridge.

"No doubt Cnut believes that I will do as my father so often did," Edmund told his ministers, "offer him tribute and a winter truce. But Cnut is wrong. I have already chased the bastard across Wessex and bested his army four times on the slaughter fields. I will not rest until I drive him out of England or die in the attempt."

The men gathered in the great hall pounded their fists upon the table in agreement—all but Eadric. Emma happened to glance at him just then, and saw him eyeing the men around him with a sour expression. When he noticed her watching him, he met her gaze with a lifted brow and saluted her with his ale cup before taking a drink.

She did not trust him. When the great battle that Edmund envisioned began, which side would Eadric be on?

Eadric left the next day with his retainers to summon the Mercians to the muster that would soon take place at Hertford. Uneasy, frightened of she knew not what, she went again to Edmund to urge him to be wary of Eadric.

Edmund, too, would soon be leaving for the muster, and his chamber was in disarray as his servants hurriedly packed coffers in preparation for his departure. The king stood at a table littered with maps, and although he listened to her fears, they did not seem to trouble him overmuch.

"I despise Eadric," he told her, "but I do not fear him. He has given me his oath because he believes I will triumph over Cnut. He will support me as long as I am winning, and I assure you, I intend to continue winning. Nevertheless, I thank you for the warning." Then he pulled in a long breath and speared her with a hard look. "While you are here, there is another matter I must discuss with you. It's to do with Edward."

She had seen her son that morning, standing with Godwin and Robert as they watched Eadric and his retainers ride out of the palace gates. Her heart gave a little lurch of alarm as she thought of a reason why Edmund might wish to speak to her about her son.

"Edward is not of an age yet to go to war, my lord," she said, "if that is what you would ask me."

"He is nearly twelve winters old, Emma," Edmund said. "That is old enough. And I am not asking you." She gazed into his eyes and read the silent challenge in them. She might be Edward's mother, but Edmund was his king. "Your son," Edmund said, "has asked to attend me. I have granted his request."

She recalled how Edward had once resented Edmund, had been unable to hide his outrage that his elder half-brother was granted the crown in his stead. Edmund's success against the Danes, though, had transformed him into a hero in her son's eyes. Much as she approved of that change, she had no wish to send Edward into battle, even at the king's side. Edmund, though, was giving her no choice.

"Edward is an ætheling," he reminded her as if, for a single moment, she could ever forget it. "He must learn the art of war. Even if he never takes the throne, he must be able to command men in order to support me. I will not allow him to stand in the shield wall, but he will ride with my army and learn how to plan and conduct a battle."

She was silent for a time, not trusting herself to speak. Edmund was right, and whatever Edward's future might hold, she could not prevent this.

"Under whose banner will he ride?" she asked at last. "Godwin's?"

"No. Godwin is to remain in London, and the two of you will continue to hold the city in my name. I will assign Edward and Robert to Ælfric's host; Withar will ride with them and keep a close eye on the lads." His expression softened. "Emma," he said more gently, "you can trust me to see that Edward will come to no harm. I give you my word."

She thanked him, knowing that he meant to reassure her. But they were both aware that it was an empty promise. No man or boy or even a king could truly be kept safe from harm in the midst of a battle.

Several days later, just after dawn, she stood with Wymarc and Aldyth in front of the great hall as King Edmund and his retinue prepared to depart for Hertford. Private farewells had already been shared, and Emma suspected that the parting between Edmund and Aldyth had been a painful one, for it was obvious to all the women in the household that the king's wife was again with child.

The column began to move, and King Edmund, riding at its head, drew close to where they stood. Emma saw him fix his gaze upon his wife and place his hand over his heart; Aldyth mirrored his gesture. It was not the first time that Emma had witnessed such silent communion between the rough warrior king and the woman who had been forced against her will to marry him; yet Emma still regarded the tenderness that had blossomed between them with a kind of aching wonder. Her own efforts, long ago, to forge such a bond with her royal husband had failed utterly. Æthelred had given her neither affection nor even respect. It was Athelstan who had offered her the love and tenderness that she craved, and she had come to believe that such a deep emotional bond could not exist within the bounds of royal marriage.

Yet somehow, miraculously it seemed to her, Edmund and Aldyth had found it.

She searched for Edward amid the men thronging past and found him at last, clad in shining mail, a sword belted at his side. Wymarc's son rode beside him, bearing Edward's banner, and Robert's face was lit with pride as he looked up at his mother. The expression on Edward's face, though, was one of sober determination and, when he glanced up at her, of triumph. He had achieved his purpose. He was riding to rid England of the Danes he so hated, and she had not been able to prevent it.

Her heart clenched with anxiety for him as she whispered, "Go with God."

And now, she thought as the last of Edmund's company rode through the gates, the waiting begins again.

Chapter Forty

October 1016
London

As winter drew near the citizens of London began to prepare
for the lean months that lay ahead. But along with the sacks
of grain and the barrels of salted meat that they carted into
the city's warehouses from Middlesex farms they brought grisly tales of
Danish atrocities in Essex. Cnut's army still ravaged there—burning
crops, plundering towns and villages, and slaughtering any who opposed
it, while King Edmund's vast army stalked their Danish foe. Soon, it was
said, there must be a reckoning, but as the mild autumn weather turned
cold and wet, and there was no word of a battle, the atmosphere in
London grew heavy with tension and dread.

On an afternoon darkened by thick clouds and a misting rain, an
armed and battered rider appeared at the Aldersgate. His mount was
lathered from hard riding, and when the horse stumbled to its knees, he
abandoned it and continued on foot, at a run, to the palace.

Inside the great hall the royal household had gathered for the
evening meal. Emma, seated at table beside Aldyth, stiffened as a
servant hurriedly approached Godwin; and when Godwin stood up and
shot her a meaningful glance before striding from the hall, she
whispered to Aldyth, "We are needed."

She called to Wymarc and led both women to the king's
apartments, aware that, behind them, the hall had gone silent.

She found Godwin and two hearth guards standing over a man who
had collapsed to a stool and was gasping for breath. He had come from
battle, that much was certain. She could see rents in his chain mail, and
the trembling hands folded around the cup he held were torn and

bloody. One finger was bent at such an awkward angle that she was certain it must be broken. Then he lifted his head, and beneath the bruised cheekbones and the blackened and bloodshot eyes, she recognized Withar.

She reached for Wymarc's hand. Edward and Robert had been in Withar's care. Why were they not here with him? Where was Edmund? If there had been a battle, where had it been fought? And when? Had the Danes been defeated? And where in the name of God were the boys that Withar had been ordered to keep safe?

She wanted all of the questions clamoring in her mind answered at once, but the man had not yet found the breath to speak. Torn between impatience and dread, she reminded herself that it was Godwin's role as garrison commander to ask for answers, not hers. She would have to wait.

Withar drank thirstily, dragged in a breath, and drank again. Finally he dropped his hands to his sides and the cup slipped from his fingers and clattered to the floor. Still panting, he looked at Godwin, and Emma read grief on his face, and outrage. He was striving not to cry.

She felt her heart shudder to a stop.

"Well?" Godwin snapped.

Withar pulled in a long, quavering breath, grimaced, and began, "We met the Danes at Assandun Hill. Two days ago." His voice was little more than a croak, and he cleared his throat and tried again. "The battle lasted most of a day. At sundown they were nearly beaten. But Eadric! That bastard!" he cried, his voice breaking. "He fled. Took all his men with him! They opened a gap in our flank and the Danes tore into it. We could not stop them!" He shifted his gaze from Godwin's face, and his eyes grew unfocused. He was staring, Emma thought, into his memories of havoc. "It was a slaughter," he breathed. "*Christ*, Godwin! It was a slaughter."

Emma's throat constricted with despair as Godwin seized Withar's shoulders and shook him so hard she heard his teeth rattle.

"What of the king?" Godwin shouted. "Withar! Is Edmund alive?"

"Alive," Withar gasped, his senses returning. "Wounded."

Before Godwin could speak again Aldyth's voice, sharp as a blade, sliced through the chamber. "How badly is Edmund hurt?"

Emma slipped her arm about Aldyth's waist, and she could feel Edmund's wife brace herself, placing a hand against her belly as if to shield the child growing within from his answer.

"My lady, I do not know. He was hurt in the shoulder, but we had no time to tend to anyone, not even the king. We were running for our lives and he—"

"Where is Edmund now?" Godwin demanded.

Withar had control of himself now and, straightening, he said, "He is riding west. Making for Gloucester."

"Gloucester?" Godwin sounded incredulous. "Why Gloucester? Why not here?"

"Because the Danes are pursuing him, and he dare not lead them here for fear they will lay siege to the city again! If London falls, we are lost."

Emma imagined a wounded stag leading its pursuers away from its forest den, away from its mate and its young. Would Cnut take the bait and follow Edmund? And if he did not, could London withstand a winter-long siege?

She heard Godwin murmur, "I fear that we are already lost," and she flinched at the bleak misery in his voice.

"No!" Withar protested. "Edmund will raise another army in the west. This is not over!" Withar's faced creased into uncertainty, though, despite his bold words. "He will need leaders," he breathed, shaking his head. "We have lost so many. Ulfkytel is dead. Godwin of Lindsey. Ealdorman Ælfric. Too many to name. *Christ!*"

Emma closed her eyes. Edmund had said that her son would ride with Ealdorman Ælfric. And Ælfric was dead. The question that had been burning in her mind was on her lips now because she could wait no longer for the answer.

"Withar," she said. "Where is my son?"

He met her gaze then looked away.

"Not dead, my lady." His mouth clamped shut.

She waited for him to say more, but he did not. Surely, though, there was more that he was not telling her.

"If Edward is not dead," she pressed him, "What then? Is he hurt? Sick? Withar, where is my son!"

He did not look at her this time, and she had to strain to hear his mumbled reply.

"Captured. The lad Robert was taken, too. I tried to reach them but I could not fight my way through to them."

Emma felt as if the ground beneath her moved. She swayed; then, supported by the physical presence of the women on either side of her, she steadied herself. This was not a mortal blow. But it was bad enough. Edward was alive. How long, though, would he remain so in the enemy's hands?

Some hours later Emma summoned Withar and spoke with him again, gently coaxing the rest of the story out of him—how King Edmund had been injured when the Danes burst through the gap in the English flank; how Withar had rushed to his aid, abandoning Edward and Robert in Ælfric's care; how he had seen, from across the field, a handful of Danes overwhelm Ælfric's retainers and drag the ealdorman from his horse.

"I saw the lads trying to shield the old man," Withar recounted, "but there was no one to help, and I could not reach them. When last I saw them, they were in Danish hands. Alive, but..." He gazed up at her mournfully. "I failed you, my lady. Forgive me!"

"Nay, Withar." She sighed. "Your first duty was to your king. You are not to blame."

But Eadric, she thought, must one day be made to answer for his treacheries.

That night she repeated Withar's account to Wymarc, trying to find some comfort in what little she knew.

"Edward and Robert were captured, not killed; they must still be alive," Emma reasoned, although a voice inside her mind howled with fear that no son of Æthelred was likely to find mercy at the hands of Cnut.

"They sell children into slavery, the Danes." Wymarc's face was slack with despair and her brown eyes glazed with tears.

In all the years that Emma had known her, Wymarc had ever been able to find hope when all seemed hopeless. But this time, Emma realized, she would have to be the one to find some flicker of light in the darkness.

"They are high-born captives," Emma said. "They have greater value as hostages than as slaves, but only if they remain alive and unharmed." She took Wymarc's hand and squeezed it. "They will be treated well; I am certain of it."

Yet she knew that the Danes did not always treat their captives with honor. At Sandwich they had cruelly mutilated their young hostages; and when Archbishop Ælfheah had refused to pay the ransom they demanded, they had murdered him.

This was not the time, though, to dwell on Danish butchery.

"They will make some demand in exchange for the lives of our sons," she assured Wymarc, despite her own misgivings. "Whatever they demand, we shall pay it."

But what if the price they demanded was more than anyone could pay—not gold or silver, but something far more valuable? A city, perhaps? Would Cnut demand the surrender of London in return for Edward's life? Would Edmund, Emma wondered, pay so heavy a price? Or if it was demanded of her, would she pay it?

Dear God, she prayed, *do not force me to drink from that bitter cup.*

It was late when she and Wymarc at last went to their beds, but when Emma knelt to pray she saw the familiar faces of men who no longer walked this middle earth. She grieved for the men lost at Assandun—for Ealdorman Ælfric and for Ulfkytel—men she had known and trusted. She whispered prayers for their souls then prayed for those that were left behind to mourn them. Her stepdaughters, Wulfa and Ælfa, were both widows now, and she berated God for his cruelty.

Then, in the next breath, she called down His curse upon Eadric, the devil's spawn who had once again betrayed a king and whose actions had led to her son's capture by the Danes.

Her anxiety for Edward made her head throb with pain, and finally she threw on a heavy shawl and, aided by the light of a candle, made her way to the nursery. The wet-nurse slept on a big bed, curled around Aldyth's infant son, heir to Edmund's throne. Across the chamber Alfred lay on his own small cot, and as Emma sat beside him her heart swelled with love. She caressed his fair hair even as her thoughts dwelt on Edward.

Where was he sleeping tonight?

Abandoning all hope of sleep herself, she wrapped her shawl close about her and rested her head beside her son's. She heard a distant bell ring the watches of the night, and she saw the dawn creep slowly into the room, heralded by birdsong. It was not yet full light when a young serving girl slipped into the chamber.

"It is early," Emma whispered to her, lifting her head from Alfred's cot. Her son still slept, swaddled in his blankets. "Is something amiss?"

"My lady, I am come to tell the wet-nurse to ready Lady Aldyth's babe for a journey."

Emma frowned and rubbed her eyes, trying to clear her head of drowsiness and make sense of what the girl was saying.

"Where is Aldyth going?"

"To Gloucester. She is to leave today, so the babe must be—"

But Emma was already on her feet and no longer listening. She found Aldyth in her chamber surrounded by frenzied servants and open coffers.

This, Emma thought, was madness.

"Aldyth, you cannot go to Gloucester," she protested.

Aldyth rounded on her, eyes reddened from weeping, Emma guessed, as much as from sleeplessness.

"I am going to my husband," Aldyth's voice was frantic, pitched high with fear. "I will not stay here to be trapped when the Danes lay siege to the city again." She was trembling and, hoping to calm her, Emma took her by the arm and coaxed her to a bench.

"Leave us," she called to the servants as she sat beside Aldyth. When they were alone, she said gently, "The Danes are following Edmund. If you try to reach him you risk falling into enemy hands before you get anywhere near him. That is the last thing that Edmund wants. Surely you know that."

"I do not know what Edmund wants!" Aldyth wailed. "He sent me no message! My husband has abandoned me!"

"Your husband is a king in a desperate bid to keep his kingdom," Emma said reasonably, although she was not certain that Aldyth was capable of reason just now. "You cannot be his first thought when there is a Danish army at his heels. Aldyth, listen to me! If you try to go to Edmund you will be venturing into danger."

"The danger is here!" Aldyth turned on her with wide, panicked eyes. "Cnut will send his army to surround London again. They will take the city and they will kill my son! I cannot stay here and wait for it to happen!"

She began to cry, and Emma drew her into her arms. This woman had already suffered more adversity, she thought, than any woman should have to face. She had lost two children to pestilence; her husband had been murdered; she had been arrested and imprisoned, then forced to marry a rebellious ætheling. It was no wonder that she feared disaster was about to strike her again. But to flee into Mercia was to run toward danger, not away from it.

"Aldyth," she whispered, "the journey to Gloucester is long and difficult, and filled with peril. You are with child. Do not risk your own life and those of your son and your unborn babe by trying to reach Edmund now. I understand that you are afraid; but if you must leave London, at least go where you will be safe."

"Where? Where can I go that will be safe?"

And Emma already knew what answer to give her. "Go to Winchester," she urged. "It is protected by walls and a garrison, and the journey is an easy one. Godwin will send messengers today to find Edmund, and I will send him word where you have gone."

Aldyth was wringing her hands, clearly tormented by indecision. Emma waited, searching her mind for more arguments should she need them.

"Will you come with me?" Aldyth begged. "My lady, you must not stay here! It is not safe! The Danes want London, and they will come. They will take the city, I know it!"

Emma felt the fine hairs on her arms rise at what sounded like prophecy; but Aldyth could not possibly know what the Danes would do, any more than she could. Nor could she leave, even if she wished it. If there should be news of Edward or a demand made for his ransom, she must be here to respond. And she had promised the king that she would remain in the city.

She took Aldyth's hands. "Godwin and I have been charged with holding London," she said gently, "so I cannot leave. But you can. Take your babe to Winchester, and wait there for word from Edmund."

Aldyth gazed at her, practically writhing in her uncertainty. At last she gave a brief nod and, calling for her servants she announced, "We go to Winchester, not Gloucester. I want to leave within the hour."

Relieved, Emma left her, and as she made her own way back to her apartments, she thought of Alfred asleep on his cot. Should she send her son out of the city with Aldyth?

No. Alfred was not yet five winters old, and to part with him would be more than she could bear. He belonged with her and, in truth, she did not believe that he would be any safer in Winchester than he was in London.

Over the next few days Godwin's scouts in the west confirmed Withar's report that most of the Danish army was pursuing Edmund's depleted force. Meanwhile scouts in the east sent word that a small enemy fleet had sailed from Essex, and the following week that fleet, made up of twenty longships, sailed up the Thames toward London.

Emma watched stoically from the walls as the ships moored near the bridge, and the city closed its gates. It appeared that London would be under siege again, and winter was approaching.

Aldyth, she told herself, had been right to flee.

Chapter Forty-One

October 1016
London

"We may have to give them whatever they demand, my lady," Godwin warned.

Emma bristled at such grim counsel. It was as dismal as these near-deserted London streets, she thought, gazing around her; which did not make his words any less true. Nevertheless, what she would be willing to give the Danes depended on what they wanted.

"I will not surrender the city," she said firmly. "I will not open London's gates to the enemy. Not yet."

She rode between Godwin and Bishop Ælfwig in the early morning chill of late October, escorted by a dozen men from the London garrison. They were passing just now through the ceap that had once been vibrant with crowds, its stalls laden with goods from as far away as Byzantium. Now, though, the stalls and the surrounding streets were all but empty.

"If our gates remain closed for much longer," Godwin said, "London will not be worth the taking. Winter is nearly upon us, and our food stores will not last until spring. By February, our citizens will be starving unless we do something to prevent it."

Or unless Edmund should do something, Emma thought. But what? He had ended last summer's siege with a surprise attack, but it would take a miracle for that to work a second time.

Nevertheless, with every breath she prayed for a miracle.

When they reached the little church of All Hallows, she found no solace within its cold stone walls. The priest, forewarned of the parley, had placed branches of burning candles upon the altar, but their light and their honeyed scent did little to ease her sense of dark foreboding. There was no sign of the Danes who were to meet them, and as they waited, memories of an earlier parley in this same church, years before, assailed her. The images that flooded her mind—of Archbishop Ælfheah's broken body lying on the altar step, of Edward held fast with a knife at his throat, of Athelstan shouting at her that Danes could never be trusted—added to her sense of approaching doom. They sharpened her fear for her son and renewed her despair that Athelstan was gone and that she'd been left to face so many horrors without him.

And now there were countless others dead as well—great men and small, English and Danes, women and children. So much blood spilled that it sickened her to think of it.

Whatever was to happen here today, she wanted the killing to stop.

Dear God, give us an end to this foul war.

As if in answer to her prayer the church door was flung open and several mail-clad men entered. The sound of their footsteps echoed through the nave as they strode toward the altar. That Eadric was one of them did not surprise her. At Assandun he had again proven himself a traitor. Now he was Cnut's man once more. Would he lie, as he had lied to them at the Aldersgate parley when he claimed that King Edmund was dead? Would he bring news of her son? And if he did, would it be the truth?

She did not recognize the men with him. They were clearly of high status, for they wore fur-trimmed cloaks around their wide shoulders, and flaunted gold rings on their arms and around their necks. Their faces—scarred and pitted and weather-worn—contrasted sharply with Eadric's smooth, comely visage; and they appeared older by a good many years.

One of them, a bald, barrel-chested man with a grey beard, wore a cross on a gold chain. The other—tawny-haired, with swirling designs inked in black upon his face and a wooden hammer of Thor at his breast—glanced around the nave with alert, suspicious eyes. When they reached the altar all three bowed a courteous greeting, and then they stepped aside to allow a fourth man, who'd been hidden as he trailed behind them, to come forward.

Instead of mail he wore a chasuble and cope, and in his hand he clutched a sealed scroll. Emma raised her brows in surprise as the bishop of Hereford knelt before her.

"My lord bishop," she said coldly, "the sight of you is always welcome, although on this occasion I must question your choice of companions."

The bishop stood up and, apparently undaunted by her chilly words, he greeted her and the men with her before introducing his companions.

"You will know Lord Eadric of course. This is Jarl Eirik," he said, and the bald man nodded. "This," the bishop gestured to the warrior with the inked face, "is Jarl Halfdan. We are sent here by King Edmund to deliver this document."

Sent by Edmund? she thought, frowning in disbelief. Two Danes and a traitor?

The scroll passed from one bishop to the other. Bishop Ælfwig inspected the seal, broke it, and unrolled the parchment. Emma glanced at the elegant Latin script only long enough to make out *Ego Edmund Rex* at the bottom.

While Bishop Ælfwig silently studied the document in his hands the Hereford bishop said, "What my brother bishop is perusing, my lady, is a copy of the treaty signed at Alney by King Edmund and King Cnut. They are now allies and sworn brothers, and they have confirmed their friendship with pledges and oaths. We come to you today—these men, as you see, unarmed and bearing you no ill will—to negotiate London's submission as defined within this document."

Emma studied the familiar, cunning lines of Eadric's face, then looked to Eirik and Halfdan. Almost as if Athelstan stood at her side, she heard his voice at her ear.

All Danes are liars; you cannot trust them.

Beside her, Bishop Ælfwig's hands holding the document were trembling. "According to this," he said, "Edmund and Cnut have divided England between them. Wessex is to be ruled by King Edmund. Mercia and Northumbria have been ceded to Cnut, and London, too, goes to the Dane." Stricken, his eyes met Emma's. "King Edmund has abandoned us to our enemies." The parchment slipped from the bishop's suddenly nerveless fingers and would have fallen to the floor had Godwin not snatched it.

For a long moment there was only silence in the church. Emma stared at the scroll that Godwin was reading now, willing it to be a forgery. But the royal seal that dangled from the lower edge of the parchment was as familiar to her as her own. Nor did she believe that the bishop of Hereford would take part in such a ruse. For once, Eadric was telling the truth. The king had kept for himself the wealthiest shires, those south of the Thames. But all the north, including London, belonged to Cnut.

Their king had indeed abandoned them.

Eadric said amiably, "You must not judge Edmund too harshly, lord bishop. Because of his loss at Assandun, he was negotiating from weakness. Cnut insisted that he would have the city, and although Edmund argued against it, the few lords who remained with him refused to go to arms again over the matter. They valued their lives, it seems, more than they valued London. You must accept that Cnut is your king now, and when the greater part of his fleet arrives here, which will be soon, your city will be expected to welcome it peacefully."

"And if we do not?" Godwin demanded defiantly. "We still have a garrison within the city, and we can use it to defend London against the Danes."

"To what end?" Eadric asked. "This treaty delivers the city to Cnut. Edmund has given hostages from every shire in Wessex as pledges of his good faith." His dark eyes flicked to Emma. "Your son, my lady, is one of them."

She gazed at him steadily, but her heart beat hard and fast at this reminder of Edward's peril.

"If London balks," Eadric's oily voice continued, "if its citizens refuse to abide by the terms of the agreement, the hostages will die. Is that what you want?" His kept his eyes locked on hers. "Surely not! Surely you would wish your gates opened and your markets busy again. Your new king, Cnut, has no wish to see your city suffer any longer. In truth, he intends to winter in London with his fleet." He paused and frowned slightly. "There are, of course, certain obligations that will be required of you."

Emma swallowed hard, then found her voice. "And they are?" she demanded.

"Your garrison will surrender its weapons. Today. In addition, by day's end you will deliver twenty hostages into our hands, to be held as pledges until the city has paid a tribute of eleven thousand pounds."

"It will take us years to pay such a sum!" Godwin exclaimed.

"Not quite so long, I think," Eadric replied. "This is a wealthy city, which is why Cnut wants it. You should be grateful that he demands so little of you. You may, of course, choose the hostages that you will surrender, all but one—the captain of the London garrison is to be the first." He smiled coldly at Godwin. "That is you, I believe."

But Emma was imagining what London would be like under Danish control.

"We have heard what viking armies do when they capture a city," she said, only barely controlling her anger and revulsion. "Our garrison will not lay down its weapons without some guarantee that our women will not be raped and the city plundered." It was probably a hopeless defiance, but it was worth trying.

"We are your guarantee, my lady." It was Jarl Eirik who spoke. "We have been ordered to maintain peace inside the city until King Cnut himself arrives to take control. You have the king's oath on it, and I have given him my oath that I will see it done."

He used the English tongue, and she realized that these were men who must have been raiding in England for so many years that, like Thorkell, they had acquired the language. Now they would use it to rule Cnut's new kingdom. She doubted that it would improve the lot of the English.

"When we open our gates," she said coldly, "the Londoners must be free to leave the city, to cross the Thames into Wessex if they so wish." There would be some who would not be easily reconciled to their new Danish overlords. She was one of them.

"Not everyone will be allowed to do so, I fear." This time it was Halfdan who answered her. "You, my lady, and you, lord bishop, must remain inside the palace until the king gives you leave to depart. There are men outside now, waiting to escort you there."

"So we are to be prisoners," Emma said, her voice flat. It was the one thing she had heard today that did not surprise her.

"You are to be guests of my lord the king."

She knew the truth of it, though. They would be hostages, like Edward and Godwin and all the others. And they were powerless to prevent it because King Edmund had agreed to it. His treaty had robbed them even of the means to negotiate their own surrender. Her stomach clenched with fear when she thought about her sons and the fate that might await them as prisoners of the Danes.

If she had gone to Winchester with Aldyth, she and Alfred would be safe in Wessex now. Instead, because she had been unwise and had trusted in God and in Edmund, both her sons would now be in Danish hands.

She had begged God for an end to the war, and he had answered her prayer.

He had given England a bitter defeat.

October - November 1016
Roskilde, Denmark

When word of Cnut's great victory at Assandun reached the king's long hall at Roskilde, a roar like thunder went up from the crowd that was gathered below the dais. Elgiva, pinned at the queen's table between Cnut's mother and his sister Estrith, listened breathlessly to the account of the battle.

So he has done it, she thought. At last.

But as Cnut's messenger regaled Harald's court with his description of how the English had fled the slaughter field at a place called Assandun, Elgiva felt a growing resentment. She should have been there when Cnut thrashed the English. She had begged him to take her with him, had twined her arms around his neck and clung to him, confident that he would not leave her behind. He had refused her, though, and so coldly that it still chilled her to think of it.

"You will remain at my brother's court, Elgiva," he had said, clasping her wrists and thrusting her away from him. "When I want you, I shall send for you."

He had not sent for her, though. Even when Arnor had arrived in the spring with news that Æthelred was dead, there had been no summons from Cnut. Desperate, she had gone to Arnor with gold in hand, insisting that he take her with him when he returned to Cnut's camp.

"Cnut needs warriors," Arnor had sneered, laughing, "not his concubine."

"I am Cnut's wife," she had corrected him. Reminding herself that he was a shipmaster, and that she needed a ship, she had resisted the urge to slap him for his insolence.

"His wife?" he had smirked. "Nay, my lady, I remember a handfasting, but I do not remember any English priest. I wonder, do you think that Cnut will want his concubine in his bed once he is a king and can have any woman in his new realm? Even a queen?" His grin had made his face even uglier. "Likely he'll plunder Æthelred's widow just the way he's been plundering England. I'll wager she would find him a welcome change from that withered stick she married." He bent toward her, and she recoiled from his foul breath. "She'll spread her legs for Cnut soon enough. Take my advice, lady. You will not wish to be there to see it."

She had slapped him then, but his foul words and derisive laughter had stung. Once Cnut attained the English throne, would he forget all that she had done for him?

She had brought him allies. She had borne his sons. She had been endlessly patient when he abandoned her again and again to do his father's bidding, or to raise his armies, or to fight his wars. She had told herself that her reward would come when Cnut was king. Now that the crown was within his grasp, did he think to leave her to rot here in Denmark while he took Æthelred's widow to his bed?

When last she had seen Emma, standing on the broad deck of a merchant ship and drab as a rag in her grey cloak, she had looked nothing like a queen. Her green eyes, though, had flashed bright enough, and they had held Cnut's intent gaze while she beguiled him into allowing her to sail across the Narrow Sea with a ship full of treasure.

She hated that memory, and she felt her face flame as she thought of Emma in Cnut's bed, of Emma persuading him to make her his queen.

That must not happen, she told herself. She could not allow it.

She became aware again of her surroundings and of the excitement in the hall—the talk of Cnut's great victory and the treaty that had divided England between the English and the Danes—and she made up her mind. Already men were boasting that they would join Cnut—to snatch what plunder they could, like carrion crows feeding off the corpse of England. Surely one of them would agree to take her across the sea.

She found the man she was looking for next morning when Estrith's husband Ulf announced that he would sail for London within the week, taking his bride and some few of her companions with him. After some sweet-tongued persuasion, Estrith agreed to include Elgiva and her son among her attendants.

Their vessel, one of six, slipped from its mooring on a chill morning at the dawn of November beneath a wide, blue sky. A bitter wind bellied the sail, but Elgiva, wrapped in an ermine cloak, did not feel its bite. She welcomed the strong breeze, for she was eager to be in England, and the sooner the ship carried her there, the better.

Her son Swein, one hand clinging to her cloak and the other clasping Tyra's fingers, stared at the shore. Elgiva, too, looked toward the grassy bank where her daughter and younger son stood on either side of their grandmother. The children would be safe enough with Gunnhild at Harald's court, she told herself, and she needed only one son to make her point with Cnut.

Smiling, she gazed down at Swein and ran her fingers through his coppery curls. He would serve to remind her husband of his obligations to her. At five winters old Swein was the very image of his father, and clear proof of her status as the high-born English wife of the man who now ruled half of England and must one day claim it all.

Part Four

Royal Hostage

Chapter Forty-Two

November 1016
London

When Elgiva's ship docked at Thames side she was disappointed to discover that Cnut was not within the city. As she was escorted to the palace, though, along with Estrith and her attendants, she learned that in Cnut's absence Alric was in command of the London garrison, and her disappointment winked out.

She was eager to see her old lover again. He might prove quite useful, especially since he held such an important post. He had Cnut's trust, to be sure, but he had ever been willing to do her bidding—for a price.

Once inside the palace gates she glanced toward the queen's apartments. They were still occupied, she was told, by Emma and her youngest son under the watchful eyes of Cnut's most trusted huscarles.

Elgiva bit her lip. She would dearly love to know why Emma was still in London, and why she had not yet been ransomed to her Norman kin. She and her brat must be worth a small fortune.

She suddenly recalled all too clearly what that swine Arnor had said—that Cnut could take even an English queen to his bed—and she breathed a quiet curse. She would have to find Alric and discover from him where Cnut was and what exactly he was planning to do with Æthelred's widow.

It was not until well past midday that she was able to slip from the guest lodgings to go in search of Alric and whatever answers he could give her. She paused on the threshold before continuing into the bright sunlight, uncertain where to look first. The yard was busy with huscarles, grooms, shipmen, and servants. An elderly cleric emerged from the queen's quarters, leaning heavily on a staff as he shuffled toward the chapel, and she recognized Emma's Norman priest.

So, she thought, Father Martin was allowed to wait upon his Norman mistress. There must be others here as well who answered to Æthelred's widow.

She would have to be wary of Emma's spies.

A moment later Alric appeared on the steps of the great hall, and she felt her heart skip a beat. He glanced up and, seeing her, he smiled. As he made his way to her she studied him, wondering if the many hardships that he had faced in Cnut's war against Edmund had changed him. He looked much the same, though. If anything, he seemed to have thrived, for his bold swagger struck her as even bolder than she remembered. The belt of his tunic boasted a magnificent golden buckle, and his dark green mantle was trimmed with fur. A skittering breeze lifted its hem to make it snap and swirl behind him as he bowed to her in greeting.

She glanced around. There were a great many curious eyes fixed upon them, and she felt exposed and vulnerable.

"Where can we talk?" she asked Alric.

He took her arm and led her across the yard and through a narrow passage between the chapel and the hall to one of the stone towers that would take them up to the wall walk. They ducked inside, and as they made their way up stairs that curved around a central stone pillar she asked the question that was foremost on her mind.

"When will Cnut arrive in the city?"

"He is making his way here now," Alric told her, "but slowly."

"Why slowly?" she asked. "And why are you not with him?"

Abruptly he stopped and turned to face her. In the narrow stairwell they were pressed close together, and Alric's familiar, wicked smile made her breath catch in her throat. Despite the damp chill that seeped from the stones behind her, she felt a sudden rush of warmth.

They had shared a passion once that had raged like wildfire between them, but it had been long smothered by time and distance. Now, though, Alric's gaze seared her, and she realized that it would take very little to fan that spark of desire into a flame again.

"Cnut sent me here to command the London garrison," he whispered against her ear. "It will be some weeks, my lady, until your husband enters the city. Until then, everyone in this royal burh answers to me." His lips brushed her temple. "Even you."

She shivered beneath that gentle grazing of his lips against her skin, and when he lifted her palm and kissed it, tendrils of pleasure unfurled inside her. In another time and place she would have responded eagerly to these bewitching sensations, would have melted against him and raised her mouth to his. She dared not do that now, though. Not here. She was too close to achieving all that she had so long desired, and she would not jeopardize it by succumbing to the temptation that was Alric. There were too many prying eyes and loose tongues at a royal court to take such a risk. He knew it as well as she did.

"Have a care," she whispered, placing a finger against his mouth. "I am the wife of a king now."

"Ah, but Cnut has not yet knelt to receive a crown," he said.

He slipped his hands around her waist, but with a small sigh of regret she pressed her palms against his chest to keep him a little apart from her.

"Even so," she whispered urgently, "he will be crowned. And I must be the good wife at the king's side."

With a disappointed sigh he eased himself away from her.

"Cnut will be crowned," he agreed, "but it will not be as we had hoped. He will be only the king in the north, not the ruler of all England."

Apparently resigned to the distance she wished to enforce between them he smiled regretfully and started up the stairs again, drawing her with him. She pondered his words, though, as she stepped into the sunlight that bathed the wall walk.

On the parapet, perhaps ten paces away, she saw Cnut's white banner with its image of a black raven fluttering in the light breeze. It was one of dozens that flew above the walls, marking the city as his. Ten paces beyond it, a Danish warrior in chain mail stood watch, alert to any threat from beyond the wall. He did not so much as glance at them. They were, essentially, alone.

She gazed into the distance where, under a cloudless sky the barren moor stretched northward toward a small village; beyond that the southern skirt of a forest climbed into low hills. She was far more aware of Alric, though, and of his hand grazing hers in the folds of her skirt, than of the stretch of Mercia that sprawled before her.

Ruthlessly, she forced her thoughts back to Cnut, and to Alric's earlier words. Although her husband's raven banners flew from London's walls and he claimed all the land north of the Thames, Alric had the right of it—Edmund still ruled in the prosperous south. Apparently, her cow-eyed cousin Aldyth had borne him a son, and already there was another babe ripening in her belly.

It would not do. Cnut must take up arms again and rid himself of Edmund and his whelps. And he must do it soon.

"Why has my husband not yet come to London to claim his crown?" she asked, her eyes fixed on the distant northern horizon.

"Because this peace that has been brokered is a fragile thing," Alric replied, "and Cnut is no fool. He is inspecting each of the largest burhs in Mercia and demanding immediate oaths of allegiance from the local magnates and all their retainers. He wants no uprisings in the north come spring."

Elgiva huffed a sigh. "He was ever one to set a great store by oaths. I have never understood why. They are easily given and just as easily broken."

"He has Archbishop Wulfstan with him," Alric observed dryly. "No doubt that will add some ecclesiastical weight to the oath-taking."

That gave her pause. Wulfstan would attempt to school Cnut in the responsibilities of kingship. Would that include legitimizing her sons by having Cnut's handfast union with her blessed by the church? Or would he encourage Cnut to set her aside and marry elsewhere? Kings had done it before. Even Cnut's father had set aside Cnut's mother in order to strengthen his claim on Sweden by wedding its dowager queen.

Arnor's taunting words nagged at her now like a persistent pain.

Do you think that Cnut will want you when he can have a queen?

She bit her lip, worrying about what Cnut might be hearing, what he might be thinking. He had once said that she would be the English face of Danish rule in England, but that had been years ago and now she did not know his mind.

She looked up at Alric and asked, "What can you tell me about Æthelred's widow?"

He pursed his lips, and when he frowned, she knew that she was not going to like his answer.

"Cnut has ordered that the lady be given all the respect due a dowager queen. She is, of course, closely guarded; but she is allowed visitors and is frequently attended by nobles and clergymen. Even I am summoned to meet with her on occasion, when she wishes to discuss some problem within the city that someone has brought to her attention." He tugged thoughtfully at his beard and his frown deepened. "She may appear to be a prisoner, my lady, but she has spies everywhere. She also has a great deal of movable wealth in her chambers that we have been forbidden to touch, and as you know, wealth can purchase powerful friends. You should be wary of her."

She looked again toward the distant horizon. "She should be in Normandy, not here in London," she said through clenched teeth. Then she asked the question that so frightened her. "Does Cnut think to wed her? Will he set me aside and make that Norman witch his queen?"

Alric did not answer her immediately, and she hardly dared breathe as she awaited his reply.

"I have not heard him speak of it," Alric said at last, "but he would be foolish not to consider it. Marriage to Edmund's stepmother would be a political move that would give Cnut supremacy over him."

"Pah!" Elgiva cried. "If Cnut goes to war again in the spring and conquers Wessex, there will be only one king in England. Supremacy will not matter."

But if Emma were no longer in England, Cnut would not be able to even consider such a marriage.

She stood in silence for a time as the ghost of an idea began to shimmer in her mind. She peered up at Alric, frowning as she sorted through her thoughts.

"You told me," she said, "that you are in charge of everyone in the palace. Does that include the huscarles who guard the queen?"

He was eying her intently, one brow lifted with obvious interest.

"It does," he said.

She smiled, and taking his hand she held it up to admire the ruby ring on his smallest finger. It glinted bright as blood in the sunlight. She had given it to him years before as payment for dispatching that Danish brute, Hemming. Now he could render her another service; one for which she would be even more grateful.

She told him what she wanted done, and before he escorted her back to her quarters, they had agreed upon how to put her plan into motion.

In the weeks that followed, she courted the men of Cnut's fleet who were already in the city. She persuaded Ulf to hold lavish feasts in the king's great hall, and night after night, gowned in furs and silks and bedecked with gold, she bore the welcome cup to the guests assembled there. She moved among the Danes and the Norse, the Frisians and the Swedes, learning their names and making it clear that as the wife of their king and the mother of his sons, she could be a powerful friend or a formidable enemy.

By the time Alric alerted her that Cnut would return to London in the first week of December, Elgiva's plan for the king's formal entrance into the city was in place. The night before he was to enter the city, Cnut's jarls would meet him at one of the royal estates beyond the walls to feast with him and to escort him into London the next morning. And while their backs were turned, Æthelred's widow and her sons would be secretly spirited out of England.

Chapter Forty-Three

December 1016
London

Elgiva stood just inside the screens passage of the royal great hall, rocking nervously on her heels. She had readied herself for battle today by donning a fine gown of crimson wool beneath a pale grey cloak, and on her plaited dark hair she wore a slender circlet of bright silver. In front of her, a small army of servants was draping and gilding the vast chamber for tomorrow's royal welcome feast, but she was only dimly aware of them. Instead, her mind was on the one man who was about to ruin all her carefully laid plans.

Thorkell should have already left the city with the other Danish jarls. They were to spend the night in Cnut's company, then escort their king into the city in the morning. But Thorkell appeared to be in no hurry to join them. He was lingering somewhere within the walls, near the river she'd been told, and it was already past midday.

She wondered nervously if the big Dane suspected something. She imagined him prowling the hythes, sniffing the air like a hound, alert to anything that struck him as unusual, and she cursed him under her breath. If Thorkell did not leave the city soon, all her efforts would be for naught.

Hearing footsteps approaching from behind her she turned and saw Alric.

"Well?" she asked.

"Thorkell is making for the Ludgate now," he told her, "along with most of the men who have been guarding Edward. My men have replaced them, and they will see that the ætheling is on the ship before the tide turns. Where is Alfred?"

"In the garden with all of the queen's attendants." Elgiva drew a long, relieved breath. "Now that her cubs are in our hands, I will treat with the lioness."

Alric laid a hand upon her arm.

"Remember, she must go willingly. Our orders from Cnut are to give her all courtesy. Some of my men may balk if she resists and we have to use force."

"She will not resist," Elgiva said confidently. "She knows that her sons are in danger while they remain in London, and she will be eager to get them out of the city. See that the horses are ready, and tell your men to wait for my summons. This will not take long."

She watched him stride toward the guard house, and then she made for the queen's apartments. The Danes posted there knew her well, and as they stepped quickly aside to let her pass, she acknowledged their admiring glances with a smile. One of them threw open the door of the chamber that had once, for a brief time, been hers. Inside, she paused for a moment, recalling Tyra's warning that she might never return here. Tyra had been wrong. She was here now, and she meant to stay. This chamber, she thought as she glanced around, would soon be hers again.

It was far more lavishly furnished than when she had sheltered here three winters ago. Every wall was covered with linen hangings intricately embroidered with scenes from the gospels or with brilliantly colored showers of blossoms and vines. There were embroidered cushions on the benches that lined the walls, and in the center of the chamber a glowing brazier sent up waves of warmth.

She would make some changes when she reclaimed this chamber, she supposed, but not many. It was comfortable enough to suit her, for now.

The room's single occupant, wraithlike in a gown that looked like it had been spun from shadows, sat at an embroidery frame set against one wall. Greenish light from two glazed windows cascaded over slender hands that rose and fell as they made the pale linen on the frame bloom with color. Elgiva crossed to her and, her arms folded beneath her cloak, she gazed sternly down at Emma and waited to be acknowledged.

Emma, her eyes still fixed on her task, observed, "You appear to have gone to some trouble, Elgiva, to ensure that my son and the few attendants left me should be elsewhere just now. I must presume that you have something to say to me that you wish no one else to hear. I am listening."

For a long moment Elgiva continued to regard her old enemy in brooding silence. Emma was far too arrogant, she decided. She still thought herself a queen, and that was Cnut's fault. He had foolishly made her imprisonment much too pleasant, and it was long past time to do something about it.

She said, "I wish to talk to you about your sons, Emma. I have seen Edward." And she watched with satisfaction as Emma put aside her needle, dropped her hands into her lap and turned to face her.

"You saw him—where?" Emma asked icily, her green eyes appraising Elgiva as if trying to determine the truth of her claim.

"Thorkell has been keeping him under guard at the æthelings' haga, and I had a brief conversation with him there." The boy had been as haughty as his mother, filled with spite against Cnut, and convinced that God would one day set him upon England's throne. He struck her as a stupid, foolish youth, as pathetic in his useless defiance as his father had been. "Wymarc's son was with him." She had almost forgotten that Wymarc had a child, a lad of little consequence, merely the by-blow of one of Emma's Norman followers who had died at Danish hands even before his son took his first breath.

Emma searched her face, and apparently deciding to believe her said, "I have been told that my son is being well cared for. I hope it is true."

Elgiva bit her lower lip. So, Emma must have spies even among Thorkell's men. What else had they told her?

She said, "He is treated well enough, but that is not likely to continue once Cnut arrives in the city. It was unwise of you to remain in London with your sons after the old king died. You should have returned to Normandy where your children would have been safe."

Abruptly, Emma stood up and strode to the brazier.

"What is past cannot be mended, Elgiva," she said, warming her hands over the glowing coals, "and I will not defend my decisions to you or to anyone."

As Elgiva studied the tall, slim, black-gowned figure, she realized how very thin Emma was. That was the result, she supposed, of living in a city under siege. She'd heard that many of the old and the very young had died. They would still be alive if their precious queen and her counselors had had the wit to surrender the city when they were given the chance.

"I do not care to know what was in your mind then, Emma. But you must realize that my husband perceives all of Æthelred's sons as dangerous. They incite rebellion by their very existence," she warned. "I know Cnut. He will not suffer your sons to live."

Emma turned to face her, chin raised. Still arrogant.

"If he murders them, he will earn the enmity of Edmund and of my brother in Normandy. Will he risk that?"

Elgiva shook her head slowly. "You know as well as I do that a king has many ways to deal with those he deems threats. Æthelred sometimes blinded them, or have you forgotten? He blinded my brothers, and left them to die in agony. It would have been more merciful to kill them outright."

Emma lifted folded hands and rested her chin upon them, her eyes shut. Against what? Elgiva wondered. Memory? Truth? Despair?

"I have not forgotten the fate of your brothers, Elgiva." Emma's eyes flicked open, and they were as cold and piercing as a shaft of ice. "Nor have I forgotten the hostages that Cnut mutilated at Sandwich."

"I think we both know that men are cruel," Elgiva observed. "Kings, Emma, are cruelest of all."

"Which is why the women close to them must strive to temper that cruelty, if they can," Emma hissed. "My sons are innocent children."

Elgiva huffed a sigh. "Edward was captured on a battlefield. He is no child. Do not imagine that you can soften my husband's heart by begging him to be merciful! He owed you a life once, perhaps, but that debt was paid. Now he owes you nothing. You, your sons, and all that you possess are spoils of war. Cnut will dispose of your children as he sees fit, and likely he has already promised you to one of his warlords. Perhaps that would suit you, but it will not save your sons."

Emma's eyes flashed, but Elgiva read fear in them as well as fury.

Good, she thought. I want you afraid.

"Why are you here, Elgiva?" It was the voice of a still proud queen—cold, hard, and needle sharp. "You have been in the city for weeks, and have never approached me. Why now?"

Elgiva considered the woman facing her—taller than she was and pale haired where she was dark. Nevertheless, she thought, we are alike in some ways. We do not break, but nor do we bend easily.

"I am here," she said, "because it is not too late to save your sons."

And there was that appraising glance again.

"How?" Emma asked.

"I have arranged for a ship," Elgiva said. "It will carry all of you to Normandy." The ever faithful Sihtric had followed her instructions with his usual alacrity and without question. Alric had arranged the rest. "The journey will be difficult, I fear. This late in the year the seas are rarely calm, but I have seen to it that you will be in good hands."

Emma gazed at her with lips pressed tight together. There was no relief in her face; only suspicion.

"*You* have seen to it?" Emma asked. "Why? When last we met, you were urging Cnut to stop me from fleeing to Normandy. What has changed?"

"It was the treasure on your ship that I wanted," Elgiva said with a shrug, "not you. And now you are wasting time," she said to forestall any more questions. "The ship is waiting, and there are men outside who will escort you and your younger son to the hythe. Edward is there already. You must be quick."

Emma's eyes widened with shock.

"Now?"

"Cnut returns to London on the morrow and then it will be too late, so it must be now. Take only as much as you and your attendants can carry." This time, Emma would not be leaving England with a shipload of royal treasure.

But Emma made no move to do as she was bid. "Why send us to Normandy?" she demanded. "Wessex lies just across the river. My sons will be safe there. We need only cross the bridge."

Elgiva gave a sharp, quick burst of laughter. "So you can throw your support behind Edmund in the war that is surely coming? I am not such a fool! No! You are to cross the Narrow Sea." She strode to the door. "The shipmen have been promised that Duke Richard will reward them for the return of his sister and her sons. See that he does it." She flung open the door and called, "Guards!"

Half a dozen of Alric's men herded Emma's attendants and her youngest son inside, and Elgiva listened with approval as Emma gave her people swift instructions. But in the frenzied chaos that followed, Emma's face was drawn with worry, and in her eyes Elgiva could read speculation and doubt.

Emma was too cunning not to be suspicious, Elgiva thought. But once she was on the ship, her fate would be sealed. Eventually she would discover that the ship was bound for Sweden, not Normandy, but by then it would be too late.

The winter sun was already low in the sky when Emma and her attendants mounted their horses for the short journey through the narrow streets to the river. Elgiva watched from the steps of the great hall, and Estrith came out to join her.

"Where are they going?" Estrith asked. "Did my brother order this?"

No, Elgiva thought smugly. I did. "Your brother hopes to curry favor with the Norman duke," she lied, "by sending Emma and her sons to him."

And when the ship dropped anchor at last in Sweden, Sihtric knew what message to deliver to King Olof.

The children must not live.

She watched as Alfred was lifted up to perch in front of his mother, and as Emma threw her cloak back to wrap her arms about him, Elgiva saw that the queen had made no effort to disguise her rank. Emma had donned gold and jewels that gleamed at her breast and all along her arms.

She was so very prudent, Elgiva thought. She had been told to take only what she could carry, so she had gilded herself with wealth. Likely each of her attendants was just as richly bedecked as she was. Yet even a queen's ransom would do her little good where she was going.

Alric had mounted his horse now, but as Elgiva watched him turn in his saddle to assure himself that the company was ready to move she heard a low rumble coming from outside the palace walls. It grew steadily louder, and a shout went up from the guard atop the gatehouse. Moments later a cluster of horsemen poured into the yard behind a white banner bearing a black raven, and seeing that banner, Elgiva felt her heart plummet.

Emma, already mounted with Alfred in front of her, watched in despair as Cnut led half a dozen armed riders through the palace gates. Until this moment, her sons' chances for freedom had been slim. Now they had vanished completely.

She had not believed Elgiva's claim that they would be sent to Normandy. More likely their ship would make for Denmark where they would be quietly disposed of. She had been hoping to thwart that scheme though—had brought gold enough to bribe the ship's crew to drop anchor near the Thames' southern shore tonight so that she and her sons could make their way to Edmund.

It might have worked.

It could not work now.

Cnut reined his horse to a halt, and quickly taking in the scene before him he shouted a string of commands. Suddenly the yard was full of movement and clamor, and as the newcomers dismounted Emma saw open space in front of her. The possibility of escape—of wild flight through the streets of London and over the bridge to Wessex—flashed into her mind. Before she could act, though, her reins were snatched from her hands and Alfred dragged from her arms. Amid shouts and the winding of horns that announced the arrival of yet more armed horsemen she, too, was forced to dismount, and she gathered a frightened and sobbing Alfred into her embrace.

Swallowing her fear and frustration, she soothed her son with whispered words and kisses. As she held him close, she searched the faces of Cnut's men. She saw Thorkell among them and, to her astonishment, Godwin. She had believed him imprisoned, although she had not been able to discover where. What was he doing here among Cnut's house guards? She could not puzzle it out, and a moment later her view was blocked by a trio of Danes. She screamed a protest as one of them snatched Alfred from her and carried him away while the others led her firmly in the opposite direction.

Frightened for her son, she glanced back over her shoulder and saw him thrust into Wymarc's arms. Then the maelstrom of restless horses and shouting men was behind her as her captors led her around the corner of the great hall. They marched her down its length and ushered her at last into the royal chapel, abandoning her there without a word.

The heavy wooden door slammed shut, and she was alone in the gloom and the sullen, brooding silence of the little church.

Chapter Forty-Four

December 1016
London

Emma pushed at the chapel door but it was barred from the outside. She was imprisoned here, at least for now.

Above her, shafts of late afternoon light lanced through the high windows, alternating with gloom that made the familiar faces of the saints painted on the walls seem vaguely sinister instead of comforting. The chill that seeped from the broad stones of the floor made her shiver despite her heavy cloak. Trembling with fear as much as cold, she approached the altar. A chair for the king's use sat there, but she was too distraught to sit. Thinking to find some solace in prayer, she fixed her eyes on the altar's silver cross, but a string of urgent questions crowded into her mind instead.

What had brought Cnut to London, unannounced and unexpected? Why was Godwin with him? Had any part of Elgiva's plan succeeded? If it had, Edward might be on a ship making for—where?

She drew in a quavering breath. Amid the chaos in the yard she had seen Thorkell wheel his horse around and spur it back through the gates. He would ensure that his prisoner was still secure. Edward would never make it out of the city.

Whatever had happened, whatever was about to happen, her sons' lives were in Cnut's hands and, as Elgiva had warned, he would show them no mercy.

Would he kill them, or imprison them, or simply mutilate them?

She looked at her be-ringed fingers, at the gold that covered her arms and hung in long, glittering chains around her neck. Could she purchase safety for her sons? Would she even be given the opportunity to speak with Cnut and attempt to strike a bargain?

And then another question wormed its way into her mind. Why was she here alone, separated from her household and from Alfred?

Elgiva had hinted that she had been promised to one of Cnut's warlords. She shuddered, imagining herself compelled to submit, even within these chapel walls, to some outrage that would consummate a forced marriage. It was all too possible. The Danes had committed far more barbarous acts.

There were too many unanswerable questions, and as she considered them her anxiety grew. Assaulted by dread and cold, she paced the width of the nave to keep warm. She tried again to pray, marking the passage of time by the sound of St. Paul's distant bells that pealed one hour and then another. At long last the creak of a door hinge alerted her that her solitary vigil was over, and she turned to face whatever hammer blow would fall next.

Cnut was striding purposefully toward her, his figure now shadowed, now bright as he moved in and out of bands of light and dark. He seemed even taller than she remembered; more threatening. This was the warrior who had won the great battle at Assandun and who wore a longsword at his side, even here in the house of God. He was richly attired—his scabbard chased with silver, his forearms gleaming with golden rings, and the wolf pelt around his shoulders clasped paw to snout with a massive brooch of gold and amber.

She owed him an obeisance, for he had made himself king in the north. But hidden behind that golden title was the cruel warlord who had once ordered the mutilation of a hundred young hostages and had spent nearly two years savaging England and its people.

She would not bend the knee to such a man.

More outraged now than frightened, she searched that lean face for some hint of what was in the mind behind it. He was angry, certainly. His jaw with its reddish beard was fixed and his mouth set in a grim line as he halted in front of her.

She wondered if she was to bear the brunt of his displeasure however little she deserved it. She remembered all too well his warning when last they had met.

Take care that you do not fall into my hands again.

And now, here she was, at his mercy. But he was not a man known for mercy, and her concern was not for herself, but for her children.

He offered her a courteous bow, but she ignored it.

"Where are my sons?" she demanded in Danish, her strident voice echoing through the little church.

His response was to drag the king's chair to where she stood.

"Sit down," he ordered. English words from the mouth of a Dane; meant to impress upon her, she supposed, his supremacy over half of England.

But he had not answered her question. She asked it again, in English this time.

"Where are my sons?" She clung to the hope that he would not harm them; that despite what Elgiva believed, Cnut would be reluctant to destroy his newly won peace with Edmund by committing some heinous crime against the half-brothers of the Wessex king.

"Your sons," he said, "are at the æthelings' haga."

Her heart gave a sudden lurch. When last she had seen Alfred, he had been safe in Wymarc's arms. No longer.

"Both of them?"

"Yes."

For several heartbeats she could not move, imagining a terrified Alfred convulsed in tears as he was dragged away from Wymarc. It was an unnecessary cruelty, and she had not been there to stop it.

In front of her, Cnut gestured to the chair. "Sit down."

This time she obeyed him, for her knees were weak with despair. Cnut towered over her, feet apart, one hand resting on the pommel of his sword. The sight of that sword kindled her anger again, and she set her mouth in a determined line. Throwing back her shoulders and stiffening her spine she lifted her eyes to his, not as a supplicant, but as an adversary. A cornered adversary, to be sure, but she would not grovel before him.

"My sons belong in Wessex," she told him. "They are the brothers of King Edmund! Whatever ransom you would demand for them, ask it and Edmund will pay. But if you harm them, he will not rest until they have been avenged. The peace that you forged at Alney will be worthless, and the realm that you divided between you will be thrust once more into chaos."

He gazed at her gravely, silent for a time, while she prayed that her words might speak to his reason if not his compassion.

"My lady," he said, "Edmund, king of Wessex, died at Bath three days ago."

He had spoken softly, yet the words seemed to ring in the air like a thunderclap. Reeling from the shock of it, she could only stare at him.

"No," she breathed, although Cnut's eyes as he held hers were so hard and unflinching that she could not doubt the truth of what he said.

As shock speared through her, she dropped her head into her hands. She recalled Edmund as she had last seen him—clad in shining mail, his hand at his breast, his eyes fixed upon the face of his wife. He had looked invincible. Ironside, they had called him. England's warrior king.

But Edmund had lost his war, and now his life.

She felt her eyes well with tears, but she blinked them away. She would not weep, she told herself. Grief must wait.

She glared up at Cnut, hating him because he was alive and Edmund was not. She knew him to be fierce and cunning; knew he would balk at nothing in his quest to rule all of England; that he would sacrifice anyone to get what he wanted.

Her throat aching with anguish she forced herself to speak despite the grinding pain of her grief.

"Must all of Æthelred's sons die, my lord, so that you can sit upon the English throne?"

Cnut looked into the cold, glittering eyes of Æthelred's widow and knew for a certainty that she believed him responsible for Edmund's death. That she hated him for that and for a great many other things as well, he did not doubt. English blood had been shed in his name—a vast tide of it spilled in the savagery of a war that had won him a kingdom. Now he must craft a peace—one that would continue through his lifetime and beyond.

That endeavor must begin here. Now. With this dowager queen.

"I swear to you, my lady," he said solemnly, "that I had no hand in Edmund's death. His passing was God's will, not mine. But now the throne of an undivided England is mine to claim, and I assure you, I shall take it."

She had folded her hands in front of her and he could see their telltale mottling of white and red that betrayed tension and anger. Her face, though, had become a mask, cold and starkly beautiful. He could not tell if she believed him.

She said, her voice rough with rage, "Edmund leaves an infant son and three brothers, all of whom have claims on Wessex that are far stronger than yours. You cannot take the English throne without shedding their blood!"

He regarded her thoughtfully, taking her measure as he weighed his response. She was perched on the edge of a simple wooden chair, yet she held herself as rigid and commanding as if she were seated on a gilded throne. Even in the dim light she glittered with jewels, her arms covered with golden rings like some shield maiden sprung from an ancient saga. He dared not underestimate her, for she was more than that. She was a crowned and anointed queen, steeped in the politics of power.

She was also his enemy, until he could persuade her to become his ally.

"At Alney," he said, "Edmund and I became sworn brothers. He named me his heir, as I named him mine, our oaths pledged in front of witnesses. According to that agreement, Wessex now is mine. That is the claim that I shall lay before the great lords of all England."

She lifted a single brow. He had surprised her.

"You will summon the witan?" she asked.

"At Christmas. Here in London."

Her gaze slipped past him, as if she could see into the future. "And no one on that council will dare to oppose you," she said coldly, "because you will flood the city with your warriors," she turned stony eyes on him, "who will be armed to the teeth."

"If you were in my place," he challenged her, "what would you do?" He already knew how she would answer. This queen of England was sprung from viking stock. She understood as well as he did how useful the threat of force could be. It was in her blood.

She looked away from him, hesitating; but the answer came at last, on a whispered sigh. "I would do the same." She turned to him again, clearly frightened now. "What will you do to my sons?"

It was the obvious question, and he was ready for it.

"They will not be harmed. I give you my oath on that. But Edmund's close kin cannot remain in England."

"So it is to be exile, after all," she said bleakly. "As Elgiva planned all along."

"It will be nothing like what Elgiva planned!" he replied sharply. "She would have sent you on a voyage that you were not meant to survive." He had prised the details of that venture out of Sihtric; his lady wife, it seemed, had much to answer for.

The queen appeared unsurprised by his revelation. "I did not believe that Elgiva would spare my sons, despite her comforting lies," she murmured. Then she glared at him. "What comforting lies will you give me?"

How long, he wondered, would it take him to win her trust? Months? Years?

"No lies, my lady, only truth." he said. He hoped that some of it, at least, would comfort her. "Some weeks ago, as soon as the Alney Treaty was signed, I sent envoys to your brother. At my request, Richard has agreed to foster your sons in Normandy." Recalling the conditions that the duke required, he added, "For a price; which I will gladly pay."

She was staring at him, wide-eyed, incredulous. For the moment, it seemed, speechless.

"Richard has demanded," he continued, "that your sons travel with whatever attendants and possessions you deem necessary, and with a shipmaster of your choosing. They will take gold enough to pay for their support while they are young." He hesitated. He had not wanted to broach this subject today, but he had come too far now to turn back. "I will send with them, as well, gold enough to pay the bride price that your brother has demanded for your hand."

She sat frozen for a long moment, then stood up and paced away from him. When she turned to face him again, her eyes bright with outrage, he was suddenly a youth again, confronting a bold young queen who brandished a knife in his face and ordered him to let her go. He had not released her then, and he was not about to do so now.

"You have been cheated!" She hurled the words at him. "I am a queen of England, and my hand belongs to me, not to my brother. I will not give it to one who already has a wife and sons."

He had anticipated just such a response. Eventually, though, she must bow to the inevitable. She had no other choice.

"Archbishop Wulfstan has assured me," he said, using a measured tone that he hoped might placate her somewhat, "that I would not be the first king of England to set aside the wife of a union that was not blessed by the church."

She folded her arms and raised her chin, eyes blazing. She was clearly not placated. Thank God she did not have a knife.

"You, my lord, are not yet a king of England. You merely stand with your foot on its throat and your hands bathed in its people's blood."

"Yet I shall wear the crown of England, my lady, I promise you. And I shall have England's queen to wife." Because he needed a queen—this queen. And if she ever stopped despising him, she would make a valuable ally.

"So I am to be forced into this marriage," she said. "You would make me bend to your will; make me watch as your sons are awarded the titles and properties that rightly belong to mine."

"Your sons will have their lives," he reminded her. "That is my pledge to you. And in return you will, I trust, give me more sons. A fair enough bargain, I think."

"Fair!" she cried. "I am a prisoner in my own city! My sons are your captives! My king lies dead and still unmourned! Yet you dare speak to me of marriage and what you believe is fair?"

He had no answer for that. She spoke the truth. He had dared, and far too soon. She was looking at him with hatred and despair, and they were barriers that he could not hope to surmount. At least, not today.

Frustrated, and angry with himself for his ill-timed offensive, he called for his guards.

"They will escort you back to your chambers," he said.

She made no reply, but merely glared at him, defiant and outraged, before she turned and stalked away.

When the door shut behind her he paced the empty church for a time, thinking back to his conversations with Archbishop Wulfstan about marriage to Æthelred's widow. Wulfstan had been dubious at first. Widowed English queens, it seemed, belonged in convents. It was only reluctantly that the archbishop had agreed to give his blessing to their union, and only if Æthelred's widow was willing.

Emma, though, was not willing. Not yet. She was like London itself, fiercely refusing to submit until persuaded that no other path was open.

And even then, unless he found a way to change her mind, she would come to him only grudgingly.

But he did not want a bitter, grudging bride. He wanted a woman who would be his partner and his queen; who would advise him; who would help him bind England's wounds. He had won a kingdom. Now, in order to forge a peace, he must win a queen—even woo her, he supposed.

And before he could do that, he had to confront his wife.

Elgiva woke to the sound of men's voices. The trolls who had deposited her here—to keep her safe, they said—must still be standing guard in the passageway. They had ignored her repeated questions and demands for release, and the last thing she remembered was snatching off her silver circlet and throwing herself on the bed, weeping with fury and frustration.

She sat up, still dazed with sleep, and looked blearily about the chamber. Someone had been here while she slept. A fire burned in the brazier, candles had been lit, and there was food on a table near the door. She eyed the bread and cheese, but her stomach was too knotted with anxiety even to touch it, and she was almost dizzy with questions.

How long had she been here, and why was she still alone? She had shared this chamber with Estrith and her household. Why were they not here? Where was her son?

She thought back to Cnut's arrival amid the shouting and chaos in the palace yard. Something momentous must have occurred to bring him so unexpectedly to London, something that had nothing to do with her plan to rid England of Emma and her brats. He couldn't possibly have discovered that, so it must have been something else. But what?

The voices outside her door ceased, and now she heard the notes of a distant bell. She counted each stroke, but as the tolling continued, she realized that it was not marking the hours. It was a death knell.

A chill coursed through her, and she had a sudden, vivid memory of Cnut on the night that his father had died. He had been angry and defiant because the death of a king meant danger. Today, when he had charged through those palace gates, he had been just as angry; just as defiant.

Because of the death of a king?

We are to keep you safe, the trolls had said to her.

She hardly dared to believe the possibility that glittered in her mind, bright as a silver penny. Edmund must be dead! Unlikely as it was, she could think of no other explanation.

Who, then, would claim the throne of Wessex? Edmund's only son was a mere babe; his brother Edwig had fled across the sea even before the old king died; and his half-brothers were Cnut's captives.

She felt a sudden thrill of expectation and excitement. More than a year ago, when she had bid Cnut farewell in Denmark, he had been a landless warlord leading an invasion fleet into possible oblivion. Now, if Edmund was indeed dead, Cnut was not merely the ruler of half a kingdom; he was poised to become king of all England!

She rose quickly from the bed. Despite whatever danger he might be expecting, Cnut would need his English wife at his side. He would send for her soon to join him. She was certain of it.

She poured water into a bowl and scrubbed her face. Loosening her long plait of dark hair and cursing Tyra all the while for not being here to help her, she dragged a comb through the thick curls until they cascaded down her back. The scarlet gown that she was wearing would do, but she rooted through her casket of jewelry and slipped several gold chains over her head so that they fell in loops to her waist. She barely had time to place the silver circlet on her head again before one of the trolls thrust open the door and announced that Cnut wished to see her. Throwing her ermine-lined cloak about her shoulders, she stepped out of the chamber and into her future as Cnut's queen.

She could still hear the bell tolling as she was ushered into the room that she had ordered prepared for Cnut as King in the North. In the flickering candlelight the sails of a great fleet painted on one long wall seemed to billow above a churning sea. On the opposite wall a battle raged around Cnut's white banner with its shrieking black raven. Below that painted banner, seated on the throne-like wooden chair that had been carved at her bidding, was her husband. His neck and wrists were ringed in gold, and the fingers that tapped restlessly against the arms of his chair glittered with gems. No crown graced his long, rust-colored hair, yet he looked very much a king—and his expression was forbidding.

Disconcerted by his unexpected grimness, she halted before him and made a deep obeisance. Hearing his murmured "Rise," she straightened and accepted the cup of honey wine offered by a servant who bowed to Cnut, then left them alone. She took a large gulp of the sweet liquid, grateful for its fierce warmth because she was beginning to understand that something was very wrong. She hoped there was more wine.

"My lord," she began, "what has hap—"

"Sit down, Elgiva."

She glanced at the chair placed in front of him and, more than a little uneasy now, she lowered herself into it. When she looked up, she found that he was watching her, stone-faced.

What had made him so angry? Had she been wrong about Edmund? Had some other catastrophe occurred—something she could not even imagine? She felt her blood throbbing in her temple as she waited for him to speak.

"What has happened," Cnut said succinctly, "is that three days ago, King Edmund of Wessex died."

She had been right, then! Yet Cnut was in a temper about it, rather than rejoicing at their good fortune. She would not ask him how Edmund had met his end, lest it provoke him further. All that mattered was that there was no one in England now to stand between Cnut and the English throne except a handful of children who were easily disposed of. Emma's brats would be gone already if Cnut had not arrived in London so unexpectedly and thwarted her plan.

"Then you are now the king of all England, my lord, and I congratulate you!" She raised her cup to him in a salute. "The feast planned for the morrow will be an even greater celebration than I anticipated."

"There will be no feast, Elgiva. The citizens who fought and bled and starved for Edmund will be mourning his death for days, and I shall respect their grief because if I do not, there will be rioting in the streets. As I mean to be king of Englishmen and Danes alike, I will not begin by kindling more hatred between them." He speared her with a hard look. "You and I, though, have other matters to discuss."

"You are angry," she said. "I cannot think why." But his ominous words filled her with unease.

"I ordered you to remain in Roskilde!" he said. "Why did you disobey me?"

She took another swallow of the mead, searching for an answer that would appease him. The truth—that she had left Roskilde because she feared he would never summon her to London—would hardly suffice.

"I merely anticipated your wishes," she lied. "When I learned of your victory at Assandun I was certain that you would send for me." She looked into his eyes and said fervently, "I came for your sake, my lord. Everything I have ever done since you took me to wife has been for your sake."

"Has it?" He searched her face, as if he would peel away skin and bone to read what was in her mind. "And your scheme to send Queen Emma and her children to die in Sweden? Was that for my sake as well?"

So, Sihtric must have told him everything. Not even Alric knew of the message that was to be delivered to the Swedish king. In any case, it did not matter that Cnut had discovered it. The æthelings had to be disposed of somehow, and her plan was as good as any. It could still work.

"Of course it was for your sake," she said evenly. "You would be rid of Æthelred's spawn without bloodying your own hands. It is the perfect solution and you—"

"Murdering young children does not strike me as a perfect solution to anything!"

She gaped at him. He must be mad, she thought. In this case it was the only solution!

"As long as Emma's children live they pose a threat to mine!" she told him, because apparently he needed telling. "I was attempting to protect our sons! I was trying to do what you should already have—"

"You acted without my knowledge or permission! You used my men to help you, and for that they will be punished. They are still alive only because they were obeying your orders."

She continued to stare at him, stunned that he would actually punish men who were acting in his interests. Had her plan succeeded, he would never even have known who they were. Emma and her sons would have simply disappeared into the night. Cnut might have been angry that he had lost his hostages, but she would have appeased him eventually.

"What will you do to Alric?" she breathed.

Cnut's eyes narrowed, and she wished that she had held her tongue.

"I begin to think, Elgiva, that Alric has always been your man, and never mine."

Her mouth went dry. Did he suspect that Alric had been her lover? That she had conspired with him to kill Thorkell's brute of a brother? But even if he did, he could not be certain.

She met his gaze, defiant. "I am your wife! Surely it makes no difference which of us Alric answers to."

"Not any more, no," he said. "Alric no longer matters, and that is not why I summoned you." He drew a long breath and said coldly, "You should have remained in Denmark."

A tremor knifed through her and she could not keep her hands from trembling.

"I do not belong in Denmark!" she cried. "I am your English wife, and I belong here at your side! My sons are your heirs!"

But he was shaking his head. "Our alliance, Elgiva, no longer serves me." He raised a speculative brow. "I'll wager that you have known that for some time, just as I have."

"What I know is that our alliance served you well enough during all the years that I aided your efforts to conquer England! It served you when I had to endure Thurbrand and his insufferable scorn! It served you when I bore your children! Do not think that you can put me aside now, after all this time! You promised me a kingdom!"

"A promise that I fear I cannot keep," he said. "You will be provided for, of course, but you cannot remain at my court. Not even for another day."

She stared at him for several heartbeats as Arnor's jeering voice echoed in her mind.

Why should Cnut want you, when he can have a queen?

She could guess now what he had been doing while she had been locked in her chamber. He had gone to Emma, drawn to her like a moth to a flame.

She hoped that they both burned.

"How long have you been coveting Æthelred's queen?" she hissed. "When did she first beguile you? Was it on the ship, when she cozened you out of that royal treasure? Or was it when she was your captive all those years ago? Or, were you *her* captive? Forgive me," she sneered, "I misremember."

Her mocking words, though, did not appear to move him. It was as though there was an invisible wall between them and that nothing she said could get through it.

"You will leave for Northumbria on the morrow," he said. "Tyra will accompany you, and Arnor will see you safely to my sister at the jarl's hall in Jorvik."

He spoke impassively, as if he had not just condemned her to a kind of hell, living under the thumb of a woman who despised her.

"Gytha will be my jailer, you mean!" she cried. How Gytha would enjoy that!

"When matters in the realm are more settled," he continued, "and if you prove yourself deserving of my trust, I shall grant you properties that once belonged to your father. You are to remain in the north, though. You will not be welcome at my court."

The full force of the calamity that she was facing suddenly overwhelmed her. It was as if the ground she stood upon, once so solid, had given way. He would banish her—from London, from the court, from everything that she desired.

All men are cruel, she reminded herself, and kings cruelest of all.

"Did Emma demand that I be banished?" No doubt she would think it a fitting revenge.

"Archbishop Wulfstan demanded it."

So they were all in league against her—the archbishop, Cnut, and that Norman witch. It was a battle, she realized, that she could not win. She was going to have to negotiate for whatever she could salvage from the ruins.

She rose to her feet with all the dignity she could muster, clutching her wine cup with both hands to mask their trembling. "If I am to go to Northumbria," she said, "I want my children to accompany me, as you will have no use for them."

"We are not bargaining here, Elgiva," he said. "Swein will go to East Anglia to be fostered with Thorkell. Harald and my daughter will remain in Roskilde at my brother's court, at least for now."

She glared at him, almost overcome with rage. In taking her children, he was leaving her with nothing! She wanted to spit at him just as she had on the day that she had been forced to wed him, when she had believed him merely the vile son of a Danish viking.

Now he was to be the king of England, and she was to be a nithing.

But a thought began to niggle at the back of her mind, reminding her that now was not forever; urging her to be as gracious in defeat as her rage would allow.

Honey, she told herself, not vinegar.

"As you will, my lord," she said, and with a massive effort she softened her expression into the appearance of acquiescence. She drained her cup, and although she wanted to throw it at his head, she merely tossed it to the floor where it landed with a satisfying clatter. She made an obeisance to the king who was still her husband, whatever he might tell himself, and stalked from the chamber.

As she was escorted back across the yard she thought about the prophecy that her old nurse had repeated to her so often—that she would be queen and that her sons would be kings. She still believed it. One day—and she was determined that it would be soon—her properties and wealth would be restored to her. In Northumbria, far from the eyes of Cnut's court, she could once more forge alliances that would be useful, should the marriage that Emma had so cunningly arranged prove unsuccessful.

With luck, Emma might never bear Cnut a son. She might even die trying.

Elgiva smiled to herself.

One could only hope.

Chapter Forty-Five

December 1016
London

Emma stood with Edward in the hall of the æthelings' haga. It was just after sunrise on a raw December morning, and they were alone except for the six armed Danes who stood watch near the door. Cnut's men accompanied her everywhere now, constant reminders that she was a prisoner.

Aware that the Danes could hear her every word, she spoke to her son in the Norman tongue that would likely be the only language he would hear in his new home.

"When you arrive at my brother's court, Edward, send me word that you are safe." She grasped his shoulders and would have embraced him if his fierce expression and rigid stance had not warned her against it.

He was furious, she knew, that he was being exiled. He blamed her for it, as he blamed her, it seemed, for everything. But she could do nothing to prevent the journey that lay ahead of him. Cnut had decreed that her sons be gone by Christmas, and that was now only days away. Their departure could be delayed no longer, and although this morning the weather was fair, she took little comfort in that. No one could say what rough sailing the three ships might encounter before they reached safe haven.

Alfred had already departed for his waiting ship. She had been able to hold him for only a little while before she'd had to surrender him to his nurse. She had promised him that all would be well and had urged him to be brave. But her unshed tears were still knotted in her throat, and now she must bid Edward farewell—this man child who at twelve winters old did not wish to leave England, yet was impatient to be away—from her, at least.

The expression on his face was stony, and he would not meet her gaze, looking anywhere but at her. This parting might be their last, though, for many years; perhaps forever. She could not let him go without once more trying to bridge the divide that had yawned between them for so long.

"Edward, listen to me," she said. "I am not abandoning you, you must believe that. If I could keep you here with me, I would. But I cannot, and England is too dangerous for you now. In Normandy you will be safe."

He looked at her then. She had expected to see anger, grief, even despair in his face. Instead she saw rage and loathing, and she felt her heart shatter.

"Is it true, Mother," he asked, his youthful voice still reedy, "that Cnut visits your bed every night? The shipmen say that you rut with him like a whore and that he has already planted a babe in your belly."

She stared at him, outraged by the vileness of the lies, and stunned that he would repeat them to her. Dear God! What other ugly tales had he heard while he was a hostage of the Danes?

She felt heated blood rise to her face, and it was only with a very great effort of will that she managed to contain her fury.

"No, Edward," she said coldly. "None of that is true."

"Then why do you stay here with him?" He was still contemptuous, still coldly accusing. "Why do you not go with us to Normandy? You could have fled when my father died, yet you did not. I think you hoped even then that Cnut would defeat Edmund and make you his queen. I think you wanted Edmund to die!"

Every word was like a stone hurled against her heart. Did he even know what he was saying? Or did he just wish so badly to hurt her that he would spew at her anything that was cruel?

Desperate to make him listen she gripped his shoulders more tightly and shook him.

"You know that is false!" she hissed. "You cannot believe that I wanted Edmund to—"

"Everyone knows that you are to be Cnut's queen!" He cried, wresting himself from her grasp, his voice breaking, his face blotchy and contorted with anger. "Do not lie to me!"

She gaped at him, despairing. How was she to get through to him? How was she to explain the complications of conquest? There was so little time! Even now she could see Brihtwold and one of Cnut's hearthmen in the doorway, come to fetch him.

She said fiercely, "I have not agreed to that marriage, Edward! You must believe that!"

"But you will! You have long been a friend to the Danes! Even when the archbishop lay murdered at your feet all those years ago, you defended them! You even made Thorkell your ally!" He was shouting at her, buffeting her with bitterness that he'd been hoarding for years. "Now you will become the queen of that Danish usurper—receive a crown from his hands that should have been mine to give, not his! But you never wanted to see me on my father's throne, did you? You always stood in my way, always opposed me! With this marriage you will place the kingship of England forever out of my reach, and never, never will I forget that or forgive it!"

He turned his back on her then, his shoulders erect as he strode toward his waiting escort.

I am giving you a future, she wanted to tell him. *In Normandy you will at least be alive!*

But Edward was already gone.

She stood still, trembling, her eyes misted with unshed tears as she listened numbly to Brihtwold's assurances that he would deliver her sons safely to Rouen. Somehow, she found the words to thank him.

When the shipmaster had taken his leave of her she sank to a bench, still shaking with anger and grief and loss.

Edward was still too green and inexperienced to understand the realities of war and conquest. But she understood them, as did Richard and Cnut, and even Godwin who, it seemed, had bent the knee to Cnut the moment he had been told of Edmund's death. Like them, she knew that an uncertain future sprawled ahead of her like a vast game board. A single move mattered little if, in the end, one could win the game.

It was true that she would marry Cnut, because it was the only move left to her for now; but it was merely one move in a very long game. There would be many more to come. What Edward did not comprehend was that marriage to Cnut kept her in the game. It meant that she had not lost.

And because she had not lost, then neither had her sons.

Part Five

The Queen's Hand

A.D. 1017 This year King Cnut took to the whole government of England, and divided it into four parts: Wessex for himself, East Anglia for Thorkell, Mercia for Eadric, Northumbria for Eirik.

The Anglo-Saxon Chronicle

Chapter Forty-Six

January - April 1017
London

E mma was not surprised when the witan granted the kingship of England to Cnut. It happened in London at the Christmas Council, and because the city was surrounded by Cnut's armies not a single minister was either brave or foolish enough to raise an objection. Nor was she surprised when the canny Archbishop of Jorvik had regretfully refused to crown and bless the new king. That office, Wulfstan explained, belonged to the Canterbury archbishop, and as he was in Rome, Cnut would have to wait until the archbishop's return for his formal coronation.

He would also have to wait for his queen, Wulfstan had informed him. For, despite what Cnut and the Norman duke had agreed between them, Lady Emma, Dowager Queen of England, must first give her consent before any marriage could take place,

And Emma, still a royal hostage in the palace at London, refused to consent until Cnut agreed to the one condition she demanded of him.

"I want your pledge that only the sons I bear you will have a claim to your throne," she said when Cnut met with her and made his formal proposal of marriage, complete with documents granting her properties and income.

Cnut slowly shook his head. "I will not disinherit my sons," he said, his tone steely. "Their mother is gone. That should be enough."

"It is not enough, my lord! In marrying you I shall be disinheriting my sons by Æthelred." Her children were safe at her brother's court now, but they faced a life of exile. She could aid them only from a distance and only if she wielded authority and wealth, not just as Cnut's queen but, far more importantly, as the mother of Cnut's heir. That was where a queen's real power lay. "You once spoke to me of a fair bargain," she reminded him. "If I am to be your queen, then where children are concerned, the scale must be balanced from the start. Both pans must be empty."

She expected him to argue, or at the very least to make a counter offer—one that she intended to refuse, hoping that through sheer obstinacy she would get what she wanted. He did neither. He merely regarded her for a long moment before making a curt bow, turning on his heel and leaving her chamber. He left London as well, and because she could not discover where he had gone or when he meant to return, she worried that she might have made a grave miscalculation.

Two weeks later though, on a snowy night in mid-January, Emma was seated with Godwin in a quiet corner of the great hall, a tafl board between them when, to her relief, Cnut entered the vast chamber with a clutch of retainers and called for food and drink. He strolled through the hall greeting the men seated at the trestle tables, and eventually he approached Emma and Godwin. Folding his arms, his face unreadable, he stood beside them to watch their play. Emma greeted him with cold civility then did her best to ignore him; but when she took Godwin's king to win the game and he bowed to her in gracious defeat, Cnut took his place. The tokens were re-positioned on the board, Cnut nodded to her, and Emma made the first move.

For a time they played in silence, until she reached to capture one of his tokens and Cnut snatched her hand and held it. Running his finger along the scar that marred her palm he asked, "How did you come by this?"

His finger's grazing touch sent a shiver racing through her, and she was so astonished by the sensation that for a moment she could not speak. Slipping her trembling hand from his grasp she gathered her somewhat scattered wits and recounted the events that had taken place at All Hallows four years before: how she had grasped the blade of a sword to keep both Thorkell and her son alive; how Thorkell had pledged to keep her children safe; how he had broken that pledge when he had allied with Cnut.

"You wrong Thorkell, my lady," Cnut said gruffly. "He refused my offer of an alliance unless I guaranteed the safety of your sons. They were never in danger from Thorkell." His dark eyes seemed to gleam in the firelight as they held hers. "Or from me."

It was a revelation, and the first move in another kind of game that continued for some weeks as they spent long winter evenings facing each other across the tafl board. He questioned her about the workings of the court and the functions of the men of power. She answered him as best she could, while she probed his mind in her turn, trying to measure his understanding of the duties and obligations of a king toward his people.

"You will find it a difficult task, my lord," she warned him one evening, "to earn the love of the English people. There has been too much enmity, too much English blood spilled in your name."

"Can any king be loved by his people?" he asked her. "Feared, assuredly, and respected perhaps, but seldom, I think, loved." He sighed. "The best that I can hope for from the English, I expect, is eventual acceptance, and then only if I can rule wisely."

"Yet you cannot hope to be accepted by everyone," she observed. "There are too many factions in England. Not just English and Danes, but Mercians and Northumbrians, East Anglians and men of Wessex, nobles and churchmen. No king, no matter how wise, could appease them all."

"Which is why a king must have knowledgeable counselors," he said. "I have conquered England; now I must learn how best to govern it. To succeed at that," he raised an eyebrow pointedly, "I will look to my queen for counsel."

She stared at him in surprise, for that was something that Æthelred had never asked—not of her.

"And will you follow your queen's counsel?" she challenged him.

"I will listen. And I will weigh it as I weigh the advice of all my counselors."

She could not help but recall, though, the cruelties committed during his war against the English, and the recollection so angered her that she forgot to be prudent.

"I hope, lord king," she said sharply, "that you will choose your advisors wisely. Who was it, pray, that counseled you to murder Ealdorman Uhtred at Wiheal after you promised him safe conduct? Who advised you to mutilate your English hostages at Sandwich?"

Her questions struck too close to the bone. Slowly Cnut rose to his feet, his face working as he sought to control whatever emotions assailed him. She expected him to order her from the hall without deigning to give her any answers. She was wrong.

"Uhtred's death was planned and executed without my knowledge." He spoke softly, but she could hear the suppressed fury beneath his quiet words. "It was an act of personal vengeance, and the man responsible was punished. As for the hostages, their kin broke the solemn oaths they had made to my father the king. Such a betrayal is an offense punishable by death, my lady, in England just as in Denmark and Normandy. By allowing the hostages to live I showed more mercy than others would have granted them."

He stalked from the hall then, his expression thunderous. Some of his retainers, seeing it, stared at her with undisguised disapproval. She did not care. She had forced him to defend his past actions, and she was not sorry. Even kings should be accountable to someone.

She suddenly recalled, though, Elgiva's taunting words to her, that kings were the cruelest of men, and her own reply that their queens must try to temper that cruelty.

She had had little success at tempering Æthelred's violent deeds, though. Would she fare any better if she should wed this Danish viking?

Yet by slow degrees, over many winter nights and amid far-ranging conversations, she came to know something of Cnut's mind and—to her astonishment—she came to respect him, even if she did not always agree with him. There were times, when Cnut was away from London—for England was flooded with armies answering to half a dozen different warlords that he had to reward, or charm, or threaten into obedience—when she found that she missed their far-ranging conversations and their often exhilarating and sometimes maddening arguments. To her surprise and annoyance, she found that she began to miss the man himself.

During his absences he sent her lavish gifts—rings and jewels; relics in gold-encrusted reliquaries; an illustrated gospel book; a spirited horse with a finely tooled leather saddle. It was a traditional form of royal wooing, but it did not move Emma. She adamantly refused his repeated offers of marriage, just as he adamantly refused to agree to the single condition that she demanded.

But each gift that he sent her; each request for her counsel on some matter of policy; each whispered word or gentle touch that made her tremble and aroused a yearning in her mind and body to which she dared not succumb—seemed to her a kind of seduction. And as the weeks passed, she began to fear that he would win in the end; that he would eventually break her will to resist him. Even if she did not agree to the marriage, he could force her. The archbishop would surely denounce him for it, but he could not prevent it, and Cnut knew that.

Winter's end brought rain that turned the streets into rivers and violent winds that lashed the Thames into a frenzy of waves. In the king's hall on a blustery April night Emma once again faced Cnut across the tafl board. He had just made a cunning move that she had not anticipated and did not like. She would lose if she did not find a way to oppose it.

She took a sip of wine as she pondered the game board in front of her, and glancing at him over the rim of her cup, found that he was watching her, his mouth curved in a confident half-smile. Caught by the intensity of his gaze she returned it for several long, thudding heartbeats. Even after so many weeks, she was unable to fathom what was going on behind those dark eyes and, frustrated, she dropped her gaze back to the board.

Reaching for one of her ivory game pieces, she placed it so that it menaced his king. Then, while he considered his next move, she fixed her eyes again on that lean, comely face. She was finding it increasingly difficult to ignore the sensations he aroused in her with just a glance, a soft word, or an inadvertent touch. He had kindled something that she had believed she would never feel again.

"My lady," Cnut said gently, his eyes lifted to hers, "You cannot win."

Startled, she looked to the board and saw that the only move left to her would cost her the game. He was right; she could not win. But was it the game on the board between them that he meant, or the far greater contest that they had been waging these past months? She would have to concede the first, but she was not yet ready to grant him victory in the second. There was yet one more move open to her in that game and, as it happened, tonight she was prepared to make it.

"As you say, my lord," she observed. "It appears that I must retreat for now and hope for better fortune at our next encounter. May I have your permission to withdraw?"

She made her obeisance, but before returning to her chamber she looked for the bishop who that morning had brought her alarming news and had asked her for advice. She had given him her counsel, and now he eyed her inquiringly from across the hall. She nodded to him, and he nodded back.

Message sent and received. The bishop would know what to do next, and she left it in his capable hands.

Cnut watched as the queen, trailed by her attendants and the huscarles assigned to guard her, navigated her way through clusters of men and women toward the wide doorway of the great hall.

"The lady does not like to lose." Thorkell eased himself into the chair that Emma had vacated, and Halfdan pulled up a stool beside him.

"No more do I," Cnut murmured, his eyes still fixed upon the retreating queen.

"Then you will be well matched when you take her to wife," Thorkell said. "Which will be when?"

Cnut lost sight of Emma and turned to Thorkell, newly arrived in London from East Anglia. The big Dane considered himself still oath-bound to the queen, and Cnut knew that his question was not an idle one.

"We have yet to reach an agreement," he confessed, and frowned. He would have to press the queen on that again soon. He had had reports of late that warned of unrest in Mercia, and Eadric, it appeared, was at the root of it. Should he be forced to lead an army against the ealdorman, he wanted his business with the queen settled first.

"Why not just bed her and worry about agreements later?" Halfdan asked. "My men believe that you've already taken her countless times. True or not, it is common talk in the alehouses."

Cnut took a long pull from his ale cup, thinking. He had been inclined more than once to do what Halfdan was suggesting. He wanted Emma to wife. He wanted her in his bed, not sitting near him, just out of his reach. But he could not compel her—into his bed or into marriage. To do that would be a misstep, and one he might never be able to correct.

"If I force her," he explained, "I risk turning not only the queen, but Archbishop Wulfstan and most of the churchmen in England against me. I cannot do it. I need their support."

"Then give the queen what she is asking for and take what you want," Halfdan urged.

Cnut scowled at him. "How do you know what I want?"

"Anyone with eyes can see that by the way you look at her, my lord," Thorkell said. "What does *she* want?"

"My pledge that only a son that she bears me will inherit England's throne; that my sons by Elgiva be set aside along with their mother."

Halfdan shrugged. "One son is much like another."

Thorkell, though, was shaking his head. "Deprive young Swein of his right to a crown and it will lead to bad blood between you and the boy. Swein will not thank you for agreeing to it."

No, Swein would not thank him, and such a pledge might raise doubts about whether Swein and Harald were even his sons.

"How is Swein faring?" he asked Thorkell.

"Well enough," Thorkell replied. "He makes no complaints; he has tutors, and my men are training him in arms. He has grown fond of my lady wife, and Wulfa treats him the same as her own lad. She is a king's daughter. She knows what is required of her."

Cnut nodded, satisfied. He had been unwilling at first to allow Thorkell's marriage to Ulfkytel's widow, but in the end he had deemed it necessary. The alliance would aid Thorkell in controlling East Anglia. In any case, the lady seemed to have become reconciled to it, and he was content to have Swein fostered in the household of a Danish warlord and a daughter of the old king.

The thought of Æthelred's daughter, though, raised another question in his mind.

"What of Edmund's wife and son?" he asked.

"Two sons now," Thorkell replied. "The child was born ten days ago on my estate near Ipswich. There is a ship waiting to deliver the children and their mother to your uncle in the Baltic when the weather allows."

"Say nothing to anyone else about that," Cnut warned him. "My uncle will see that Edmund's sons are sent to some distant haven, but I want no one in England to know where they have gone."

He was about to ask Thorkell about the temper of his East Anglian subjects when he saw Godwin leading two men purposefully toward him through the groups clustered in the hall. One of them was the familiar figure of the bishop of London. Short, thin, and with a head as bald as an egg, Ælfwig looked almost childlike beside the robust bulk of his companion, Bishop Eadnoth of Crediton. He wondered what had brought Eadnoth all the way from his see in Devon in such foul weather when the next council was still weeks away.

When greetings had been dispensed with and the bishops were seated he turned to Eadnoth.

"What news from the west, lord bishop?"

Eadnoth's bushy grey brows bent together over the bridge of his nose.

"Ill news, I fear, lord king," he said. "The ætheling Edwig has returned to England."

Ill news, indeed, Cnut thought. He had rid himself of Emma's sons and had arranged for the disappearance of Edmund's. Now, it seemed, he must deal with yet another claimant to the throne.

"Where is he?"

"He landed first in Exeter," the bishop replied, "and rode north with a group of West Saxon lords whose sons were mutilated at Sandwich and who bear you ill will, lord king. I have learned since that they have been seen in Worcester." He grimaced. "I fear that the ætheling may be making his way to Lord Eadric."

And Eadric, his spies had reported, had been holding secret meetings with powerful west Mercians.

He considered Bishop Eadnoth in silence for a time, his mind busy with speculation. Finally he said, "I am grateful for this news, bishop. There are, I am certain, a great many men in England who would have kept it to themselves." Men who would watch and wait; who would act only when they were certain which way the wind blew.

"I gave you my solemn oath at the Christmas witan," Eadnoth replied, "I cannot break that pledge; nor would I do so even if it did not cost me my immortal soul." He set down his cup and placed his palms upon his knees, leaning forward, intent. "Edwig's appearance in England now can only lead to more conflict, and the English are desperately weary of war. They have suffered its ravages for too long, and I will not stand by and watch it all begin again; especially if it benefits a man who would, I believe, be a stain upon the throne. We need a just king in England. Edwig is not that man." He eased back in his chair and folded his arms. "I pray daily, my lord, that you will be."

Cnut met the bishop's steady, challenging gaze for several heartbeats. Then he nodded slowly. "That is my prayer, as well, bishop." Frowning, he considered the matter of Edwig and he said to Godwin, "You were once a companion to Æthelred's sons. What can you tell me about this ætheling?"

Godwin grimaced. "Edwig is a weak man, and easily led. He would not return to England unless he was certain to find support. If he is making for Mercia, then we must assume that Eadric has offered that support in return for Edwig's favor once he captures the throne. Lord Eadric covets the vast power that he had when Æthelred was alive. You have not given it to him, and I suspect that he is hoping that Edwig will. And we all know that treachery is second nature to Eadric."

Halfdan set his cup down with a thump. "There are still a great many Danish warriors in England," he growled. "This ætheling would be a fool to attempt to bring an army against us."

"Edwig *is* a fool." Godwin said. "And Eadric can supply him with a Mercian army."

"Should Edwig raise his banner," Bishop Eadnoth said, "there are powerful men who will support him, men who believe, lord king, that you mean to deprive them of their lands and their authority in favor of your Danish followers. If you move quickly, you can prevent a rebellion. But I urge you to offer the English magnates some assurance that you are no longer their enemy."

Cnut grazed his chin thoughtfully with the back of his hand. "And how, bishop, would you suggest that I do that?"

Eadnoth did not hesitate. "Make the queen your ally in this," he urged. "She is your link to the old ruling dynasty. She can be your peaceweaver, if you let her."

Cnut considered the bishop's counsel. He would be happy to have the queen act as his peaceweaver, but it would mean surrendering to the condition she had set upon their marriage.

He was silent for a time, sifting through possible actions and their consequences, weighing all that he knew and all that he guessed.

"I have had reports from Mercia," he said slowly, "that Eadric is gathering men. Their numbers are few as yet, but I expect that with Edwig's arrival that will change. Eadric himself has recently left Shrewsbury, and appears to be making for London, although with no show of force. Not yet. Presumably he is meeting with supporters as he makes his way here for the Easter witan." He paused, taking in the faces around him. "His arrival in London would give me an opportunity to put a stop to whatever he is planning. I would hear your counsel. Godwin?"

"I think that you should kill the lying snake the moment he sets foot in the city," Godwin said. "Make him an example of what happens to a faithless thegn."

The bishop of London stirred uneasily and said, "Lord king, I would advise you to be more circumspect than that."

"Why?" Halfdan grunted. "Any man who plots against his king deserves death."

"That is true, lord," the bishop replied. "But all of England will be watching to see if King Cnut will fulfill the promise he gave at Christmas that he would be a just ruler. To slay a man as Godwin suggests, even one as deserving of punishment as Eadric, would be perceived as a willful abuse of power, not justice."

Bishop Eadnoth leaned forward and said urgently, "Send men to Shrewsbury, my lord, to find Edwig and his followers. Have them brought here. Question them, and pronounce judgment based on the law."

"Before the whole council?" Cnut ventured.

The bishop's shrewd brown eyes held his for a heartbeat. "Before the whole world, lord king."

That, Cnut thought, was wise counsel. In Normandy and Denmark, in Paris and Rome and every other place where the news of events in England would spread, he must be seen as a Christian king who ruled wisely and justly. And as Eadnoth proposed, he must have the queen at his side. He had always known that. She must be his peaceweaver, the bridge between himself and the magnates of England.

He looked around him at the men and women in the hall—a handful of priests and abbots, his own jarls and many English thegns, a few wealthy London merchants and their wives, his sister Estrith and her attendants. And he made up his mind.

They would be the witnesses he needed. He was weary of playing games with his beautiful, captive queen.

He shouted for his servants and gave a string of orders. He had to act swiftly, before Edwig's arrival in England brought an overwhelming tide of support that would sweep him from his throne.

An hour later Cnut stood beside Godwin just inside the entrance to the royal chapel. They were flanked by the two bishops who now wore ornately embroidered chasubles and, Cnut noted, uneasy expressions. He was not surprised. They would have to answer to Archbishop Wulfstan if this turned out badly.

At the far end of the nave the altar blazed with candles, and near it six monks stood chanting a Latin psalm. Cnut could barely hear them over the thrumming voices of the assembled crowd that had been herded here through the rain from the great hall.

He glanced toward an alcove where three monks held the ecclesiastical trappings that would be necessary for what was about to take place. Satisfied, he cast an inquiring glance at the bishop of London. The bishop nodded and, assured that the preparations for the ceremony were complete and adequate, however hastily they had been arranged, Cnut said to Godwin, "Fetch the queen."

Chapter Forty-Seven

April 1017
London

Emma, cocooned in her thick, hooded cloak of white fur, followed Godwin through the palace yard, their way lit by torchbearers who guided them around muddy pools of rainwater.

It was late, long past vespers, and the night was dark. The wind had died to a whisper, but a light rain still fell in a gentle mist that coated her hands and face. Wymarc walked at her side, and a string of attendants trailed behind. Armed guards accompanied them, marking Emma as Cnut's royal hostage.

Despite the late hour she had been summoned to the king. Godwin had not explained the purpose of this summons, but she hoped that Cnut was about to agree to the condition she had set upon their marriage. Bishop Eadnoth could be very persuasive.

When they passed the great hall she slowed her pace, surprised and alarmed that it was not to be their destination. She grew even more apprehensive when Godwin continued toward the royal chapel. Ahead of her, the church doors had been flung wide and she could see Cnut flanked by the bishops in their ecclesiastical robes.

This was another move, then, in the game that she and Cnut had been waging all winter. But it was not, she feared, the move she wanted him to make. As she drew nearer the chapel she heard voices spilling out of it like rushing water—the sound of a restless, expectant crowd.

Wymarc touched her arm. "I think you are about to be wed, Emma, whether you agree to it or not."

"So it seems,"she murmured, her heart racing. Cnut must have persuaded, or bribed, or somehow coerced the bishops to perform the ceremony even without her consent. It would be a forced marriage after all. She could not stop it.

She reached the doorway and halted abruptly as the din of voices faded into the plaintive notes of a psalm that was suddenly quelled. Cnut was eyeing her with the same watchful expression he wore when he made a clever move at tafl that he knew would give him the game, and behind him a vast sea of faces was turned toward her. As she made her obeisance before the king his words from earlier that evening echoed in her mind.

You cannot win.

She straightened, and as Cnut drew close to her she tensed, meeting his eyes with a stern, inquiring gaze.

"Lord king?" she asked.

But Cnut was beckoning to a monk who bore a silver reliquary and who, approaching the king, dropped to his knees. Cnut faced the altar and the now silent crowd, and placed his hand on the reliquary.

"I give my solemn pledge," he proclaimed, "before God and before these witnesses that only a son born to me by the Lady Emma, daughter of the duke of Normandy and dowager queen of all England, shall inherit this kingdom upon my death. So help me God." He said it again, this time in Danish.

As Emma listened she felt a surge of triumph. She had won.

Immediately, though, Cnut was whispering in her ear.

"In return for this pledge, I require your hand in marriage. Tonight."

He fixed her with a look that was as severe as it was impatient. It unnerved her, making her catch her breath with misgiving. Was he already planning some act of retribution against her because she had forced him to act against his sons' interests?

If so, there was nothing she could do about it. He had met her demand, and now she must pay the price. That was the bargain. She had no choice.

She drew a long, tremulous breath, as if she were about to plunge into deep water.

And she gave him her hand.

The ceremony was lengthy, the exchange of vows taking place during a holy mass followed by numerous benedictions. It was near midnight when Cnut led her back through the cheering throng in the nave, and she was once more the wife of a king of England. They walked slowly, pressed by the crowd on all sides, and Cnut placed his arm around her waist to better guide her. She wondered if he could feel her trembling.

When they reached the church door he halted, and keeping her close beside him he turned to address the crowd.

"The feasting," he announced, "must wait for another time, for we are bound by the Lenten fast. And tonight there is another more important matter that demands my attention."His words were met with rude shouts and laughter that accompanied them through the mizzling rain to the royal apartments where Cnut ushered her into the king's chamber. There, in the light of a dozen oil lamps that glowed from niches on the walls, they were greeted by a swarm of attendants. Cnut's sister Estrith was there and, to Emma's relief, Wymarc.

The women led her to the inner room where she had so often been summoned to lie with Æthelred, and the moment that she entered that chamber, a thousand bitter memories assailed her. She stood wooden with recollection and foreboding while she was stripped of cloak and headrail, of heavy gown and shoes and stockings.

Wymarc seemed to sense her apprehension for she whispered, "It will not be the same, Emma. This king is not a stranger."

Emma cast her a grateful smile, but Wymarc had not seen the harsh expression on Cnut's face just after he had made his pledge to her in the church. She had seen it, though, and Elgiva's bitter words, unbidden and unwelcome, once more slipped into her mind.

Men are cruel, and kings are cruelest of all.

What did Elgiva know of Cnut that she had yet to discover?

When she had been stripped of everything but a smoc of the finest embroidered linen, her attendants would have led her to the bed, but she refused. She would not play the part of a submissive, virginal bride and cower beneath the blankets to wait for her lord. She would meet Cnut as a queen should meet a king—boldly, face to face.

She did not have long to wait. Cnut soon appeared, framed in the doorway, and so tall that he had to bend slightly to enter. He wore a long, pale tunic of light wool, and in the lamplight his coppery hair and beard were flecked with gold.

"Leave us," he said.

The chamber emptied quickly, although Wymarc lingered near the door to offer a reassuring smile that Emma answered with the briefest of nods. Then Wymarc, too, was gone, and she was alone with the man who was now her husband and her king. In the church she had suspected that he was angry, resentful that he had been forced to pledge the oath she had demanded of him.

Was that the way of it?

She stared at him, barely able to breathe as she waited for some word or gesture from him. The tense silence between them lengthened, though, and she was assailed by vivid memories of her first wedding night—of Æthelred crudely ordering her to remove her shift and raking her with suspicious, scornful eyes as she stood before him, naked and vulnerable. He had used her body for his pleasure, with no concern at all for the frightened girl who was no more to him than chattel that he had purchased at the price of a crown. She had hated everything that he had said and done to her that night.

Before she had left Normandy to wed that king, her mother had counseled her to use her youth and beauty to gain her husband's favor. She had failed at that, with Æthelred. He had desired her body, but had granted her little in return. Their marriage had continued as it had begun—a bitter brew of suspicion, anger, resentment, and pain.

Now she had another chance to please a king and to win his trust. But she was no longer young, and although Cnut had wooed her with gifts and subtle words meant to placate and reassure, she could not be certain that he truly desired her, body and mind, or if, like her first marriage, this was to be a strictly political alliance—cold and manipulative and empty.

Cnut was only a few steps away from her now, and as she searched his face, full of doubts, he slowly covered the distance between them. Gently grasping her shoulders he bent to kiss her, tenderly at first, and then deeply, and more insistent until she slipped her arms about his waist and opened her mouth to his. She was still lost in the sensation of his mouth and body pressed to hers when he drew a little away from her, and for the first time since she had been delivered to him in the chapel, he smiled.

"I have wanted to do that," he said, "since the day that I first saw you, and you brandished a knife at me."

His words took her back there again, to the forest of Devonshire when her eyes had been locked with those of a youth who showed no fear at the sight of the blade in her hand.

"Surely not," she whispered, searching his face just as she had that day. "You were a mere lad then."

"I was old enough to understand that you were a treasure that had been squandered on an unworthy king."

He folded her in his arms and pressed his mouth to hers again—another long, lingering kiss that made her knees so weak she had no choice but to cling to him. Then, with infinite care he untied the laces at her throat, and whatever she may have read in his face at the chapel, it could not have been resentment, for he was regarding her now with tenderness. With slow, steady hands he freed her from her shift, then lifted her in his arms and carried her to the bed. Swiftly discarding his tunic, he lay beside her and they faced each other in the lamplight, body to body, skin to skin.

She soon realized that however impulsive and hurried the wedding, their coupling was to be a far more languid affair of mutual exploration and discovery—of pleasure given and received. They played a different game altogether now, one that demanded cooperation and generosity. The wily, ruthless conqueror of England was, she found, a courteous lover. That was her last thought before the touch of his hands and his mouth drove all thoughts from her mind.

She fell asleep with his seed inside her and his body molded to hers, and she woke still spooned in his embrace—his hand cupping her breast and his bearded chin grazing her shoulder. Beneath a shard of morning light that slanted in past the shutters, she turned in his arms to face him, and the game began again. When they were sated with each other she lay with her head against his breast listening to the throbbing of his heart that seemed an echo of hers. And in the silence, all the thoughts and fears that had fled her mind in the night returned.

She had cast the die and won the throw. Now, though, she would have to admit to the part she had played in last night's events. There would be a reckoning, and she suspected it was coming when she felt him draw breath to speak.

"I learned last night that the ætheling Edwig is in Mercia."

She made no reply, and after a few moments he sat up and peered at her with narrowed eyes. "You knew that already," he said, and it was an accusation. "Bishop Eadnoth spoke to you first when he should have come directly to me."

She reached up to touch his face. This man was a ruthless warrior, his hands stained with blood. He was also her king and her lord, and if she would be his queen, she must dare to trust him with the truth.

"The bearer of bad news, my lord," she whispered, "risks the anger of the king. The bishop did not know how you would respond to what he would tell you. He came to me for counsel, and I told him that he need not fear your wrath."

He arched a brow and grasped the hand that cupped his face.

"And did you ask the good bishop to urge me to make my hostage queen my ally and peaceweaver?"

She swallowed the knot of foreboding that his words raised in her throat, but again she told him the truth.

"I saw an opportunity and I took it," she confessed. "Does that surprise you?"

To her astonishment he barked a laugh. "No. It would surprise me far more if you had not." He lay back down again and pulled her into his arms. "I am content to have the matter of the marriage settled, Emma, especially now that I must deal with a possible rebellion in Mercia."

She heard the anxiety in his voice, and she felt as if she had been rudely wakened from a dream. The future—Cnut's very hold on the throne—was uncertain; made even more so with Edwig's return to England. She had no doubt that Æthelred's son would challenge Cnut for the crown. There would be more English blood spilled, and now that she was irrevocably bound to Cnut as his queen, that blood would be on her soul as well as his.

"What will you do about Edwig?" she asked.

"I have already ordered men to Mercia to bring the ætheling and his conspirators here to London. They will be tried at the Easter court. The punishment for rebellion is death, and it must be delivered swiftly and publicly. To make a point."

She closed her eyes, thinking back to when she had last spoken to Edwig. It had been that Christmas at Kingston, when she had approached Edmund to offer him her support. Edwig had been flushed with wine that night, his mouth set in a sneer. He had ever been cruel and callous, as drunk as often as he was sober, and nearly incapable of self-control. He was no saint.

But the blood of kings ran in his veins. He was her son by marriage, and she owed him whatever protection she could give. She lay very still, uncertain if she should say what was in her mind. Yet if she did not say it now, there might never be another chance.

"Lord king, I would ask a boon," she said, "a morgengifu." By tradition, it might be an estate or a payment in gold or silver. Had any bride ever before asked for a life? "Let Edwig live," she whispered. "Banish him, certainly, but I beg you, do not kill him."

She was half afraid that her request would arouse his suspicion and raise a barrier between them that she would not be able to breach. She could almost feel Æthelred's brooding presence hovering nearby, leering at them.

For a time Cnut said nothing, and she held her breath as she waited for his reply.

At last he said, "Edwig is a threat to me. You know that. Why should I let him live?"

It was not assent, but it was not a refusal, either.

Emboldened she said, "Because like you, he is the son of a king. Because he has given you no oath and therefore he has not betrayed you." She drew a long breath and offered the final, most important reason. "Because I am your queen and your ally in all that you do, and I would not have my stepson's blood upon my hands."

Cnut, though, made no reply.

Chapter Forty-Eight

Easter Monday, April 1017
London

Easter Sunday had been chill and rainy, but Easter Monday dawned fair and warm, and when the witan met, the shutters of the great hall had been flung wide to let in the midday sun. A gentle breeze wafted through the vast chamber so that the brightly colored banners hanging from the roof beams fluttered and danced.

The hall's festive air, though, was belied by the stern faces of the numerous, watchful, mail-clad warriors posted along the walls, and by the wary looks given them by the men on the benches. Emma, seated on the dais with the king and Archbishop Wulfstan, was one of the few who knew what was to take place here today, and she thought that it would have been more fitting had the chamber been draped in black.

Unknown to the men gathered here, an ealdorman was to be accused of plotting Cnut's overthrow. The conspirators who had been captured at Eadric's estate in Shropshire had been brought to London in secret to face the king's justice today—all except Edwig.

"The ætheling slipped away from his captors," Cnut had told her, "no doubt with help from men whose names we do not yet know. If he has any wits at all he has already taken ship to Ireland or the Low Countries. Anywhere that isn't here. I will declare him outlaw to ensure that he flees our realm, but if he should ever return," he warned, "it will mean his death."

She hoped, for Edwig's sake, that he was, indeed, gone. As for Eadric—she glanced down to where the ealdorman was seated on the front bench almost at her feet, his mouth fixed in a fawning smile that made her skin crawl—he could have no inkling of the calamity that was about to engulf him.

The other councilors—bishops, abbots, ealdormen, and king's thegns—wore expressions of doubt or even fear. She did not blame them, surrounded as they were by armed huscarles. Cnut's shield-men attended him everywhere now, and the king himself wore a sword at all times. Such was the burden of a warrior king who ruled by conquest and faced a brewing rebellion.

The Danes seated among the council members were also unarmed and because of it, clearly uncomfortable amid their English neighbors. They were warriors who had followed Cnut to England and had been rewarded with lands that had once belonged to English thegns—something, Emma had warned Cnut, that did not sit well with the English. It was why Cnut wanted her here today, believing that her presence on the dais beside him would go some way toward reassuring the English magnates that their status, their traditions and customs would be honored, even in the court of the Danish king. The tension simmering in the hall between Englishmen and Danes, though, was so thick that she could taste it, acrid at the back of her throat. She doubted that her presence made any difference.

When Archbishop Wulfstan rose slowly to his feet to begin the session, Emma stood with the rest of the gathering as he led them in prayer. After the last Amen rang through the hall, the prisoners were led in and forced to stand, shackled and filthy, in full view of the crowd. They were the well-known sons of great lords and at their appearance the murmuring in the hall grew loud before it dropped precipitately into stunned silence when Cnut began an account of what had taken place in Shropshire.

Emma saw Eadric stir, as if to stand; and for an instant she thought he would try to bolt. But she was not the only one watching him. At the end of his bench a huscarle stood, hand on his sword hilt and eyes fixed hawk-like on the ealdorman. Seeing him, Eadric shrank back to his seat.

When Cnut finished speaking, he took it in turns with Archbishop Wulfstan to question the prisoners. Emma could tell from the hopeless expressions on their faces that they expected neither forgiveness nor mercy. Their responses were unrepentant and surly, and she pitied them, but she could do nothing to save them. They had sworn to accept Cnut as king, then plotted against him. Their lives were forfeit. To a man, though, they damned Eadric as having conceived a scheme to murder Cnut and place the ætheling Edwig on the throne.

When their testimony was finished, Cnut consulted with the archbishop before proclaiming the men guilty and ordering their executions on the morrow. As they were led away, he turned to where Eadric sat, ashen-faced.

"Lord Eadric," Cnut said, his voice steely, "the testimony of these traitors condemns you as their leader. What say you?"

Almost before Cnut finished speaking, Eadric surged to his feet, angry and defiant.

"Lord king, I have no knowledge of these men or of any plot to overthrow you. They must have hoped that their punishment would be less severe if they found someone else to blame for their crimes!" He turned to sweep his gaze around the hall and address the entire council. "They could have chosen to accuse any one of you, so no man here should be quick to judge me. I swear that I am innocent!"

"Are you telling us, my lord," the archbishop asked, "that you were not aware that the ætheling Edwig had returned to England? Or that he was meeting with these men at your own estate? That beggars belief!"

Eadric spread his hands wide, the very image, Emma thought, of an innocent man confounded by false accusations.

"My lord, it is impossible for me to be aware of all that takes place on my many properties, scattered as they are across Mercia! When these men were apprehended, I was not with them! How, then, can I be considered their leader? Lord king," his voice slipped into the honeyed tone that Emma had often heard him use with Æthelred, "it may be that these traitors were paid to implicate me in their crimes. I do not wonder at it. There are those, even in this hall, who are envious of the favor you have shown me and who would see me destroyed because of the love I bear you."

It was a skillful performance, Emma thought. So skillful that she feared the king might actually believe it.

She flicked her gaze from Eadric to Cnut. The two men had been sometime allies in Cnut's campaign to capture the English throne. They had fought side by side, and she had been told that, often, strong bonds of trust were forged between men who faced death together on the field of battle. Eadric, no fool, must be relying on that. Would Cnut, like Æthelred and Edmund before him, succumb to his falsehoods?

There was silence for several heartbeats, and in those brief moments of quiet she recalled the many times that Eadric had twisted the truth or committed some heinous act that had suited his own selfish ends. He had counseled Æthelred with lies, turning him against anyone—even his sons—who threatened Eadric's hold on power. He had been Æthelred's willing henchman, a callous murderer who had served his king through cruelty and dishonor, and whose treachery and greed had sown discord throughout the kingdom. At Assandun he had betrayed Edmund, and she had no doubt that now he was guilty of plotting against Cnut. He deserved the same punishment as the men that he had led into treason.

"Lord Eadric!" she called to him. "The prisoners who were condemned here today had already been shriven of their sins before they faced this assembly. It is inconceivable that they would then blacken their souls with falsehoods, knowing they must soon meet their God and His judgment. You, though, have ever trafficked in malice and deceit. Time and again you poisoned King Æthelred's mind with your lies—against his sons, against his ealdormen, against his counselors, against anyone who stood in the way of your ambitious drive for power." She turned to Cnut. "My lord, I beg you, do not allow this creature to escape the king's justice and the punishment he so richly deserves."

"Lord king," Eadric said swiftly, "even before Æthelred died, the Lady Emma begged me to place her son Edward upon the throne, and—"

"Another lie!" Emma cried, but Eadric's oily voice did not falter.

"—because I refused her and threw my support to you instead, she despises me and would see me dead. My king, do not forget all that I have done for you! When you brought your fleet to England, I was the first to bend the knee to you. At Assandun, when Edmund's army threatened to overwhelm you, I withdrew my host from the field and thus guaranteed your victory. It is because of me that you are seated on the throne of England today, and as your true and loyal servant I beg you, do not listen to slanders brought against me, even those mouthed by your queen."

Emma struggled to master her frustration and anger at how skillfully he blended lies with truth to defend himself. That she despised him and wished him dead was indeed true; and no one could deny that his treacherous actions had aided Cnut's war in England. Yet she had never asked him to promote her son as Æthelred's heir, although Eadric had schemed for years to do just that. Now he stood there, arms spread wide, gazing innocently up at the king.

Sweet Virgin! She had already called him a liar three times over. What more could she do?

Beside her, Cnut stood up, and she suspected that, like her, no one in the chamber was breathing as they waited for him to speak.

"Lord Eadric," Cnut said, "you have my thanks for reminding me of all that you have done."

Emma's heart sank. Eadric's twisted words had had their desired effect. She closed her eyes and saw the faces of men who had died at Eadric's hands—crimes for which he would go unpunished.

"By your own admission," Cnut continued, "you broke your oath to a sick and desperate Æthelred in his hour of need even though he had showered you with honors and privileges. At Assandun you again broke your oath to your sovereign lord when you deserted Edmund in the midst of battle." Eadric began to sputter a protest, but Cnut paid him no heed. "Why should I think that you would remain loyal to me when you have betrayed two kings before me? Why should I accept your word over that of my queen who has long known you and whose counsel I trust above all others? The answer is simple. I do not believe you, nor will I forgive treachery and faithlessness."

Several guards now surrounded Eadric, and he shouted curses as they took hold of him.

"I hereby condemn you to death for your treasonous deeds," Cnut proclaimed, ignoring the ealdorman's cries that had become pleas for mercy, "the sentence to be carried out immediately."

Eadric continued to protest as the huscarles wrestled him toward the door, and now every man in the chamber was on his feet. Emma, standing beside Cnut as turmoil unfolded below her, prayed that the English would not riot at the doom pronounced upon the man who had been Æthelred's most powerful ealdorman. If they did, some of them would surely die. But although she saw horror on the faces of many of them, and some cried out in alarm, no one made a move to aid the ealdorman.

Cnut, though, showed his witan no mercy.

"Every man here is to bear witness to Eadric's execution," he commanded, "and learn how I shall reward faithlessness."

In response to his command, the huscarles began herding the stunned nobles from the hall. Cnut and the archbishop left the dais, but Emma made no move to follow them.

There was a very fine line it seemed to her, between desiring justice and desiring vengeance. She was afraid that today, in her heart, she had crossed that line; and although both justice and vengeance would be dispensed out in that yard, she did not wish to see it.

She left the hall and, walking swiftly to skirt the clamoring crowd, she entered the chapel. In that quiet gloom she prayed for the men who had been condemned to die. She prayed for England and for the king. She prayed for forgiveness and she begged God for wisdom.

After some time she heard footsteps approaching, and then Cnut knelt beside her. Neither one spoke, but Emma thought that, in this solemn silence where God could sometimes be found, they might be praying for the same things.

When at length the king stood up, she took the hand he offered to help her to her feet.

"What happened here today," he said slowly, "will not end the unrest in England. Weeks and months of turmoil lie ahead of us—discontent that it will be my duty to quell. You must be prepared for it, because I cannot go about it gently. I will strive to be just, Emma, but I will rarely be merciful. I cannot afford that. Not yet."

She looked into the face of this man who had made himself a king and she recalled what her brother had told her in Rouen—that the foundation of kingship was fear, not mercy.

"You would have your people fear you," she said.

"They must fear my punishment, yes, as they would fear God's," he replied. "If I am to keep chaos at bay, I must be a stern lord, and a fierce one. But I must also have a good angel at my side who will not be afraid to counsel patience and forbearance when it is needed. That must be your task." He gazed at her intently, frowning and, she thought, uncertain. "I warn you," he said, "it will be no easy task. There will be times when you will find it difficult to make me listen."

Nevertheless, she thought, she would have the ear of the king. And she would not be the only one. There would be the archbishops and bishops as well, and she would see to it that there were other godly men around Cnut who would offer him their wisdom.

"I will give you my counsel gladly, my lord," she said. "You have my hand upon it. And my heart."

It was what she had always believed to be a queen's most important duty although until now she had seldom been called upon to perform it.

"You have another task, as well," he said, and he brushed a kiss against her forehead. "Do not forget that you must give me a son."

She had not forgotten. Not for a moment. There would be a child, she was certain. Whether it would be a son was up to God.

Chapter Forty-Nine

July 1017
Winchester

"Not too tight," Emma said.

The agile fingers that were twisting strands of her hair paused briefly, then continued their task.

Emma sighed. She would likely have an aching head by day's end no matter how loosely her hair was plaited. There would be a vast crowd of people at the coronation and at the feast that followed—Danes and Englishmen as well as emissaries from Normandy and the Low Countries. She would have to speak in four different tongues, and the strain of that alone would make her head pound.

She was glad that Cnut had postponed this ceremony until his jarls had settled the unrest that had begun with Edwig's arrival in England and had finally been quelled some weeks after Eadric's execution. Now, for the first time in decades, England was at peace. Fields had been planted and the harvest would go into the mouths of English families instead of the maws of ravaging armies. Throughout the kingdom there was hopefulness that had been missing for many years. She was grateful for it. She expected that all of England must be.

The fingers finished their plaiting, and the creamy headrail was pinned into place. Only later, after Cnut had been crowned and anointed, would she bow her head to receive, for the second time, the slender, golden crown of the queen of England.

She stood up and turned to face the cluster of attendants behind her, but it was Wymarc whose eyes she sought.

"Am I suitable?" she asked.

The fine silk gown she wore, presented to her by Cnut's sisters, was the color of marigolds, its sleeves and hem embroidered in a sinuous design of blue and green. The strands of elegant pearls that hung in loops to her waist had come from Normandy—gifts from her mother. On her left hand she wore the wide, golden band that Cnut had placed there on the night they had wed, and on her right hand the ring engraved with a looping design that Athelstan had worn for so brief a time, and that she would wear in his memory even to her grave.

"You are more than suitable, Emma," Wymarc said with a soft smile. "You are all that a queen should be."

When a servant appeared to announce that the king was waiting at the Old Minster, Emma sent her attendants ahead of her and she followed them, unescorted, down the stairs and into the palace yard. She was not alone, though, she told herself. She carried in her heart the memories of those she had known here, and loved, and lost. Her children—wards of her brother now and sundered from her by the Narrow Sea. Ealdorman Ælfric and Archbishop Ælfheah, who had offered her friendship, comfort, and advice. Edmund, who had finally given her his trust, but had lost his kingdom and his life.

Athelstan, whom she had loved and who should have been a king.

What counsel would he give her, now that she was to be the queen of a Dane who had won the English throne by conquest?

A memory surfaced from years before, and it was as if Athelstan stood beside her, whispering in her ear to offer her a way forward, out of the past.

Do whatever you must to live and to thrive! Do not look back!

That was what she had to do—let go of the past and look to the future.

She placed her hand beneath her breast where the future lay—the child that she would give Cnut. She would love it just as she loved her other children, distant now and safely at her brother's court, but in her heart still. A mother's heart, she had learned long ago, could contain a multitude.

The wide portal of the minster rose ahead of her, and she could see Cnut waiting there, tall and broad-shouldered, with the stature and bearing of a king. He exuded the quiet confidence of one who knew that, by the grace of God, he held a kingdom in his hands. In a little while Archbishop Lyfing would crown him, gird him with the sword of Offa, and admonish him to defend his realm with the aid of Christ.

And, she thought, with the aid of his councilors and his queen.

She greeted him with the solemnity due the occasion, and taking her place beside him she peered into the church. The interior was ablaze with light from hundreds of tongues of flame. They glowed on tall branches of candles that formed an aisle down the length of the nave. They winked like stars on gilded circles that hung from on high. They burned on all the side altars and flickered in lamps along the walls so that every shadow was banished.

She turned to Cnut, and he smiled as he took her hand and brought it to his lips. Then, together, hand in hand, they stepped into the light.

Author's Note

Emma of Normandy was a significant figure in the politics of 11th century England for fifty years, yet she remains relatively unknown today. Perhaps that is due to the thousand years that separate us from her, but there are two other factors that I suspect are just as likely: that women and their actions, even those of queens, were rarely mentioned in contemporary chronicles; and that it has been a long-held, although incorrect, belief that English history began only with the Norman Conquest of 1066. That event, I might add, would never have taken place had it not been for Emma, her children, her familial and political connections, and her marriages.

Emma's marriages, in particular, were what compelled me to write about her. I wanted to explore her relationships with her two royal husbands. What had she experienced during her first marriage when England was under attack by fierce Danish armies? Even more intriguing, what negotiations took place in 1016 that led to Emma's marriage to Cnut, her first husband's mortal enemy? Although the history of that period provides us with only the tiniest clues, this novel is the result of my research and, inevitably, my own theories about how events in England, Denmark and Normandy in those crucial years between 1012 and 1017 may have had an impact not only on Queen Emma, but on other women who lived through the Danish conquest of England.

Beginning with the murder of Archbishop Ælfheah and ending with the coronation of Emma and Cnut, the events that I portray in this book are factual, but Emma's role in them is my own invention. Although we know that she was there and must have played some part in all that occurred, we simply cannot be certain about what that was.

Accounts of Emma's relationship with King Æthelred come from the 12th century chronicler William of Malmesbury, who claimed in *The History of the English Kings* that Æthelred was offensive to his wife and that he slept with other women. I have followed William's lead as I imagined the conflicted interactions between the king and queen. It was William, too, who wrote that Æthelred was haunted by the shade of his murdered half-brother, Edward the Martyr; because of that, Edward's ghost is a silent but threatening presence in all my novels.

Cnut, the conqueror of England in 1016, married Emma some time before August of 1017, but the specifics leading up to that marriage are still matters of conjecture among scholars. Was Emma in England or in Normandy in late 1016 and early 1017? What negotiations took place between the widowed queen and her Danish suitor or, perhaps, between her suitor and Emma's brother in Normandy? Exactly when and where did the marriage and Emma's second coronation take place?

The histories of the time give us conflicting accounts. German chronicler Thietmar von Merseburg, writing in 1018, tells a dramatic tale that has Emma, desperate after enduring six months of siege in London, making a devil's bargain with Cnut. In return for her release from the city she agrees to turn over 15,000 pounds of silver, 300 hostages, and 24,000 coats of mail—astoundingly high numbers that bring Thietmar's entire story into question. In addition she agrees to hand over her sons, Athelstan and Edmund, to Cnut to be executed. The sons manage to escape, but when they return to try to rescue their mother, Athelstan is killed.

Given that Athelstan died two years before this event was supposed to have taken place and given the extravagant sums of tribute paid, this tale appears to be made up of garbled rumors that reached Thietmar in Germany some months after Cnut's conquest. In addition, it beggars belief that Emma's sons or stepsons would be so forgiving of a mother's betrayal that they would try to rescue her after their own escape. Such logic made no difference, I imagine, to anyone eager for a juicy story about a powerful and ambitious queen. It may have been because of Thietmar's tale that Emma would be portrayed by later historians as so cold-hearted that she was willing to sacrifice her children's lives for her own selfish desires—never mind that Emma's children were, in fact, alive and well in Normandy.

The Norman chronicler William of Jumieges, writing in the 1050s, has a different story to tell. He claims that a few days after King Æthelred died, Cnut removed the queen from the besieged city of London and married her, paying her weight in gold and silver to the army in London that had been holding her. There is no mention of King Edmund in this very brief account, and the twelve months that we know passed between Æthelred's death and Emma's marriage to Cnut are reduced to a few days. Again, there are pieces of a story here, but far too few details to inspire much confidence in their accuracy.

Emma's version of events as presented in the *Encomium Emmae Reginae*, penned under her direction by a Flemish monk sometime around 1041, has Cnut searching the world over for the perfect bride, finding her in Normandy, and wooing her with gifts and pleas. Emma, aware that Cnut has children by another woman, finally agrees to the marriage after she extracts from him a promise that only a son that she bears him will inherit his English throne. In opposition to this romantic narrative, the *Anglo-Saxon Chronicle* entry for the year 1017 states baldly that Cnut ordered Emma to be "fetched" so that he could marry her. Where she was "fetched" from is a matter of conjecture, and modern scholars have suggested Normandy, Winchester, and Exeter as well as London.

I have opted for a London captivity for Emma per William of Jumieges and the German Thietmar. I have included, per Emma's *Encomium*, Cnut's wooing, his royal gifts, and the oath that the queen demanded. I have organized events in a way that I believe fits the history, patchy as it is, and makes for good drama. Because I write fiction and not history, I do not claim that things happened exactly in this way, only that they could have. If I have erred somewhat on the side of romance, I am merely following Emma's lead. The *Encomium* claimed that the couple took a vast delight in each other, and there is no question that Emma played a powerful role as queen, counselor and perhaps regent during Cnut's reign.

One of the most difficult tasks I faced in writing this novel was to turn Cnut, England's fierce viking conqueror, into the romantic hero of my story. It helped that Cnut's reputation as a sound, shrewd—although sometimes ruthless—king has weathered the centuries. One ruthless act assigned to him by historians has to do with the murder of Uhtred. While Uhtred's longtime rival for power in Northumbria, Thurbrand, did the actual killing, historians believe it was done with Cnut's approval. But although Cnut benefitted from that murder, there is no proof that he ordered it, so I have absolved him.

In recounting Cnut's handling of the infant sons of Edmund Ironside I have strayed somewhat from the historical record. By the twelfth century William of Malmesbury reported that Cnut dispatched the boys to the Swedish king to be put to death, but that the king took pity on them and instead sent them to Hungary. However, the earliest version of their story, appearing in the *Anglo-Saxon Chronicle* entry for the year 1057 says nothing about Sweden, only that Cnut sent the infants "to be betrayed" in Hungary. Because Cnut's uncle ruled the Polish territory that the boys might have had to journey through, I've given Cnut the benefit of the doubt. He sends them to his Uncle Boleslav with instructions not to kill them, but to send them far from England to be raised in a foreign land and out of his hair.

Emma's relationship with Athelstan as I have portrayed it in my novels has no basis in the recorded histories of the time. Athelstan is not mentioned in any of the English chronicles, so we know nothing about his character or his personal life except that he died unwed and without issue. Were it not for his will, which survives, and for the appearance of his name on charters, we would not even know of his existence. But he was Æthelred's eldest son, and far closer in age to Emma than his father was. Because royal marriages in medieval times were political alliances, and because human emotions and passions existed even in the eleventh century, I chose to have these two characters drawn to each other, adding yet more emotional conflict to a tale of war and political strife.

The antipathy I have invented between Emma and her son Edward is based on later events. When Edward finally became king of England in 1043 at age thirty-eight, he complained that his mother had done less for him than he wished, both before he was king and after. My own thinking is that his childish bitterness went all the way back to when a disappointed, jealous, adolescent Edward was outraged by his mother's marriage in 1017 to a strapping Danish viking who had captured the throne that Edward believed should have been his. Edward never got over it.

The early career of Elgiva (Ælfgifu of Northampton) is shadowy. We know only that she was Ealdorman Ælfhelm's daughter and that at some time during the Danish conquest of England she became Cnut's concubine. Modern scholars suggest that their alliance began in 1013 when Cnut was known to be in England. I have placed it much earlier, in 1006 when historically Elgiva's father was involved in something so heinous that Æthelred had him murdered and his sons blinded. We do not know what Ælfhelm's crime was, but the secret alliance with the Danish royal family that I've invented would certainly have outraged the king and resulted in such vengeance. Elgiva was indeed the sole surviving member of her influential and wealthy family, and because the few sources that mention her portray her as a powerful and ruthless Anglo-Saxon noblewoman, I have given her a pivotal role in the Danish plot to conquer England.

There is no suggestion in any of the chronicles that Elgiva had a daughter. However, buried near the altar of Holy Trinity Church in Bosham, Sussex, is a nameless girl reputed to be a child of Cnut's who drowned in the year 1020 at the age of eight. If this is true, she would have been born in 1012, five years before Cnut's marriage to Emma; so I have made Elgiva her mother.

Another difficult task, one that every writer of historical fiction who bases a novel on the lives of real people must face, is when to end the story. Emma of Normandy would be Cnut's queen until his death in 1035. She would bear him a son, Harthacnut, who would one day rule Denmark and England, and a daughter, Gunhild, who would marry the son of the Holy Roman Emperor. The years between Cnut's death and Emma's passing in 1052, though, would be fraught with uncertainty, political upheaval, a mother's grief and, for a time, exile. Emma would outlive all of her children except her daughter Countess Godgifu of Boulogne and her son King Edward the Confessor. I have chosen, though, to end this novel in 1017, the year that Emma stepped into her role as Cnut's queen and peaceweaver, the role in which she would have the most power, wealth and prestige as wife and advisor to the king, as the mother of his heir, and as a patron of the church in England and Normandy.

Long live the queen.

About the Author

Patricia Bracewell taught literature and composition before embarking upon her writing career. A lifelong fascination with British history and a chance, on-line reference to an unfamiliar English queen led to years of research, a summer history course at Downing College, Cambridge, and the penning of *Shadow on the Crown* and *The Price of Blood*, the first two books in her trilogy about the 11th century queen of England, Emma of Normandy. Patricia conducted research for the final book of her trilogy, *The Steel Beneath the Silk*, as writer-in-residence at Gladstone's Library in Wales. She lives with her husband in Northern California. Visit her website at http://www.patriciabracewell.com

Acknowledgments

This novel has been six years in the making, and there are a great many people who I must recognize for cheering me on and aiding me in countless ways. First and foremost, my husband Lloyd, for his love and support throughout this three-book endeavor. He never once balked as we journeyed together to England, Denmark and France, exploring cities with ancient roots, pressing our noses against museum cases of 11th century artifacts, climbing into abbey and castle ruins, or slogging up muddy trails, over hillocks, and across boggy fields. Without his unflagging encouragement this trilogy could never have been written.

I am indebted to Linda Cardillo, Vana Nespor and the entire team at Bellastoria Press for welcoming me to their stable of authors and working so diligently with me in all the many aspects of producing this final novel of my trilogy. Thank you once again to Matt Brown for his wonderful maps of England and London, and for his immediate responses to my endless requests for changes. And to Duchess Arianwen ferch Morgan of the Society for Creative Anachronism a very special thank you for allowing me to use her image on the cover of this book.

Thanks are due as well to those who alternately listened to my ideas, answered questions and offered sage advice: my critique partners Gillian Bagwell and Christine Mann who spent years reading and re-reading this manuscript; David Levin, pathologist with Washington Hospital in Fremont, California for his observations concerning sword and arrow wounds; Professor Andrew Pfrenger of Kent State University who lent a willing ear as I pestered him about Edward the Confessor over drinks at the International Congress on Medieval Studies at Kalamazoo; Cindie Lovelace for the set of rune stones that helped me add some detail to a tense scene; and Anne and Scott Smith for their compassion, counsel and generosity when a publishing setback had me reeling on their doorstep.

Thank you to Stella Duffy, Louisa Yates, Warden Peter Francis and the board and staff of Gladstone's Library in Hawarden, Wales for granting me the post of Writer-in-Residence in 2014. In Gladstone's history stacks I found the solution to the riddle of where Swein Forkbeard was shipwrecked in 1012 (Pembrokeshire!) and from that seed grew the earliest chapters of this novel.

I'm grateful to David McDermott, Lecturer at Winchester University, for his interest in my work when we met at the 2016 Cnut Conference in London, and especially for his in-depth answers to my numerous questions over the past four years about Edmund Ironside's 1016 campaign against Cnut. I wish I could have included half a dozen thrilling scenes depicting what we discussed about Edmund's movements, but my focus had to be on Emma.

My research for this novel included maps, chronicles, and far too many articles in scholarly journals to mention here. However, the most prominent and well-thumbed books on my research shelves include Pauline Stafford's *Queen Emma and Queen Edith: Queenship and Women's Power in Eleventh-Century England;* the *Encomium Emmae Reginae,* edited by Alistair Campbell, introduction by Simon Keynes; *Æthelred II* by Ryan Lavelle; *Æthelred the Unready* by Ann Williams; *Æthelred the Unready* by Levi Roach; *Cnut* by M.K.Lawson; *Cnut the Great* by Timothy Bolton; *The Reign of Cnut, King of England, Denmark and Norway* edited by Alexander R. Rumble; *The Death of Anglo-Saxon England* by N. J. Higham; *Swein Forkbeard's Invasions and the Danish Conquest of England, 991-1017* by Ian Howard; *Bloodfeud: Murder and Revenge in Anglo-Saxon England* by Richard Fletcher; and *The Godwins* by Frank Barlow.

Finally, thank you to my many readers who discovered *Shadow on the Crown* and hungered for more, and who endured so many years of waiting to discover how my story about Queen Emma would end. You have been the wind beneath my wings.

CPSIA information can be obtained
at www.ICGtesting.com
Printed in the USA
BVHW071214100222
628585BV00001B/98